MW01232939

Amish Girls
S E R I E S

~ VOLUME 2 ~

J. E. B. Spredemann

Blessed Publishing

Published in California by Blessed Publishing.

http.//amishbooks.wix.com/jebspredemann

Cover design by J.E.B. Spredemann.

BOOKS BY J.E.B. SPREDEMANN
(*J. Spredemann)

AMISH GIRLS SERIES
Joanna's Struggle
Danika's Journey
Chloe's Revelation
Susanna's Surprise
Annie's Decision
Abigail's Triumph
Brooke's Quest
Leah's Legacy
Learning to Love – Saul's Story* (Sequel to
Chloe's Revelation – adult novella)

AMISH SECRETS SERIES*
An Unforgivable Secret*
A Secret Encounter*
A Secret of the Heart*

New! NOVELETTES*
Amish Fairly Tales:
Cindy's Story*

COMING SOON!
A Christmas of Mercy (An Amish Girls Holiday)
Rosabelle's Story (Amish Fairly Tales – Novelette 2)*

UNOFFICIAL GLOSSARY OF PENNSYLVANIA DUTCH WORDS

Ach – Oh
Aldi – Girlfriend
Ausbund – Amish hymn book
Bloobier – Blueberry
Boppli – Baby
Bopplin – Babies
Bruder – Brother
Dat, Daed – Dad
Dawdi – Grandfather
Denki – Thanks
Der Herr - The Lord
Dochder – Daughter
Dokter – Doctor
Dummkopp – Dummy
Englischer – A non-Amish person
Ferhoodled – Mixed up, Crazy
Fraa – Woman, Wife
Gott – God
Gut – Good
Gross Dawdi – Great Grandfather
Haus – House
Hullo – Hello
Jah – Yes

Kapp – Prayer Covering

Kinner – *Children*

Kumm – Come

Lieb – Love

Liede – Song

Mamm – Mom

Mammi – Grandmother

Mein Liewe – My Dear

Mudder – Mother

Nee – No

Ordnung – Rules of the Amish Community

Rumspringa – Running around years

Schweschder – Sister

Vadder – Father

Vorsinger – Song Leader

Wunderbaar – Wonderful

AUTHORS' NOTE

It should be noted that the Amish people and their communities differ one from another. There are, in fact, no two Amish communities exactly alike. It is this premise on which this book is written. We have taken cautious steps to assure the authenticity of Amish practices and customs. Both Old Order Amish and New Order Amish are portrayed in this work of fiction and may be inconsistent with some Amish communities.

We, as *Englischers*, can learn a lot from the Plain People and their simple way of life. Their hard work, close-knit family life, and concern for others are to be applauded. As the Lord wills, may this special culture continue to be respected and remain so for many centuries to come, and may the light of God's salvation reach their hearts.

Amish Girls Series - Book 5

Annie's
Decision

J.E.B. Spredemann

Annie's Decision

J.E.B. Spredemann

Amish Girls Series - Book 5

To our family...

You are our inspiration.

CHARACTERS IN ANNIE'S DECISION

The Yoder Family

Jacob – deacon, father

Sarah – mother

Eli & Danika (King) – son & wife, protagonist of Danika's Journey

Annie – protagonist

The Hostettler Family

Judah – father, bishop of Paradise

Lydia – mother

Nathan – oldest brother

Levi – older brother, protagonist of Chloe's Revelation

Joshua – Susie's older brother

Susanna – protagonist of Susanna's Surprise

Maryanna – Susie's twin sister

Paul, Elizabeth, Ella, Micah, and Yonnie – other siblings

The Fisher family

Gideon – father

Esther – mother

Isaac & Rachel – oldest son & wife

Grace – oldest daughter

Joanna – protagonist of Joanna's Struggle, youngest daughter

Jonathan – youngest son, instigator of mischief

The King Family

Philip – father
Naomi – mother
Danika – daughter, protagonist of Danika's Journey
Katie – daughter
P.J. – son

The Lapp family

Sadie – oldest daughter
Andrew – oldest son

Others

Matthew Riehl – friend of Jonathan Fisher and Joshua Hostettler
Chloe Esh – protagonist of Chloe's Revelation, Levi's aldi
Laura and Mr. Scott – Joanna's employers
Caleb Scott – nephew of Joanna's employers
Amanda Johnson – Englisch girl

CHAPTER 1
Pen Pals

"A man that hath friends must shew himself friendly..." Proverbs 18:24

"*M*amm, *Mamm*; look here!" Annie Yoder said with excitement in her voice. "This ad says, '*Wanted: Amish Pen Pals. Preferably girls ages 12-16*'. The address is right here."

Sarah Yoder glanced up at her daughter. "I'm not sure your *daed* will want you communicating with an *Englischer*." Annie hung her head and Sarah sensed her disappointment. "I'll tell you what. Bring it up to your *daed* after dinner tonight. He's sure to be in a *gut* mood, especially when I tell him the news."

"What news, *Mamm*?" Annie wondered.

"Well, it looks like you're going to have to wait until after dinner too." Sarah smiled.

"Mm...this sure is delicious pie," Jacob Yoder said to his wife after dinner.

"Don't tell me; I had nothing to do with it. Annie baked it all by herself," Sarah told her husband, as she served several slices to the remainder of the children who sat around the table.

"Annie, you did a wonderful *gut* job on this pie," her father complimented.

"*Denki, Dat.* Strawberry rhubarb pie is your favorite, *ain't?*" Annie said.

"*Jah, for sure and for certain.*" Her father smiled.

"I have some news," Sarah Yoder nearly whispered, to see if anyone was listening. Everyone turned their eyes in her direction.

Jacob Yoder raised his eyebrows as though asking a question. "Well, out with it."

Sarah looked at the bright faces around the table and smiled. "We're gettin' another *grossboppli.*"

"Really?" squealed Faith, the youngest girl in the family.

"Who, *Mamm*? Is it Hannah?" Annie wondered if her eighteen-year-old sister who had recently married could be expecting.

"*Nee,*" Sarah said.

"*Ach,*" exclaimed Samuel, Annie's older brother. "'Tis Eli!"

Mamm smiled in affirmation. "That's right, Danika and Eli will be havin' their first *boppli* this winter."

Smiles lit up the table like a bolt of lightning brightening an ominous sky. The children each made their guess as to whether they would have a boy or a girl.

Annie seized her golden opportunity to approach her father. "*Dat*, would you mind if I got an *Englisch* pen pal?" she asked with pleading eyes.

"I'm not sure that would be such a *gut* idea, *dochder*," her father said apologetically.

Annie knew it wouldn't benefit her to argue with her father, so she simply lowered her head and sighed. She so hoped to be able to communicate with someone from the outside world – a world she knew very little about. What would an *Englisch* girl her age be like? Did she have the same thoughts and feelings as her? Unfortunately, she would never know.

"Jacob," Sarah spoke up. "Do you think that maybe Annie could have a pen pal on a trial basis? If you're concerned, we could always read the letters ourselves."

Jacob raised his eyebrows again then scratched his beard. He paused a moment. "Well, since you put it that way, I guess I'd be willing to let her try it out."

"Really, *Dat*?" Annie said with joyfulness, almost unable to believe it.

"*Jah*." Jacob smiled at his daughter, glad to see her brighten.

Annie jumped from her seat and threw her arms around her father first, and then her mother. "*Denki!*" she said, as she ran upstairs to pen her first letter to an *Englischer*. Sarah and Jacob looked at each other and smiled.

Jonathan Fisher could barely contain his excitement. *My first car! I can't believe I'm driving a real* Englisch *car. And it's all mine. I wonder how fast it'll go,* he thought as he cruised down the road toward Paradise, Pennsylvania. Doubt flooded his mind; how would his parents' react to his new set of wheels? Would they let him keep it at the house? After all, he was in *Rumspringa.* He knew of other Amish parents who let their sons park their vehicles back behind the barn. *Surely, Dat and Mamm won't mind. Will they?*

Jonathan pulled his blue 1968 Chevy Camaro up beside the house. He stepped out of his car, wearing his new *Englischer* clothes; blue jeans, a t-shirt, and a baseball cap over his new short hair style. He looked at his car again, admiring it, and then headed toward the back porch. He was almost to the door when his father came walking out of the barn.

His father put his hand up over his eyes to shield the sun. "Who's there?" Gideon Fisher asked, not recognizing his son from the back.

Jonathan turned around and his father's jaw dropped. "*Sohn,* is that you?"

"*Jah, Dat.* It is." Jonathan swallowed hard, his confidence quickly dwindling.

"*Ach, was iss das, sohn*?" Gideon asked in a disappointed tone, gesturing to the vehicle.

"It's my car," Jonathan simply stated, briefly removing his sunglasses.

Gideon sighed. "I thought we'd worked all of the foolishness out of you. Now, you look like an *Englischer.* What is the meaning of this?" He shook his head in disappointment.

"*Dat,* I'm in my *Rumspringa,*" Jonathan reminded his father.

Just then, his mother and sister came out the back door. "*Ach,* Jonathan? *Was in der welt?*" his mother, Esther, asked in disbelief. She frowned at her husband.

"Go back inside," Gideon told his wife and their daughter, Joanna. "Jonathan and I need to have a talk." The women briskly turned around and headed back into the house.

Gideon turned to his son. "Jonathan, *Rumspringa* or not, you know I cannot accept this behavior. You may not keep the car on my property. If you choose to keep it elsewhere, that will be up to you. I will pray that *Der Herr* will give you some wisdom."

"But *Dat,*" Jonathan protested. "There are other Amish folk who let their *kinner* keep their cars parked on their property."

"We are not other folk. I intend to keep the rules of the *Ordnung.* If you insist on wearing *Englisch* clothing, you are not welcome under my roof. Do you understand?"

"*Jah, Dat. Ich verstehe,*" Jonathan said angrily and glared into his father's eyes. He stomped to his car and took off in hurry, spewing dust in every direction. Why did *Dat* have to follow the Old Ways so closely?

Heaviness settled in Gideon's heart. After all these years, he still had a hard time relating to his youngest son. He walked back into his shop and closed the door. He fell to his knees and offered up a prayer. "Dear *Gott*, please help Jonathan to choose the right path. Put good influences in his life to steer him in the right direction. I cannot change his heart, only you can do that, and that is what I'm asking. Amen."

CHAPTER 2
The Letter

"Hear counsel, and receive instruction, that thou may be wise in thy latter end." Proverbs 19:20

Annie had checked the mailbox every day for the past week anticipating a letter from her new pen pal. Perhaps today would be the day her first letter would arrive. As she walked out to the mailbox once again, Annie couldn't help but hope it had come. She slowly pulled the door to the wooden box open, closing her eyes. She put her hand in and felt the contents before opening her eyes again. She grasped a small envelope. As she opened her eyes, her lips curved up in a smiled. It was finally here!

Annie glanced at the name in the upper left-hand corner. Amanda Johnson. She quickly slipped her index finger under the flap and pulled out the contents. Looking it over, she noticed it was two pages long, and smiled. The beautiful stationary had a Bible verse embossed in the top center of the paper with hearts on each side, *Trust in the Lord with all thine heart. Proverbs 3:5.* Suddenly, a small photograph slipped out from between the papers and into her hand. She heard her brother calling her and quickly shoved the small photo into her apron pocket. Photos were considered graven images by the Amish and were forbidden by the *Ordnung.* She quickly made her way back to the house to find some privacy in her own room.

Still perturbed from the conversation with his father, Jonathan pulled his car into the small parking lot behind Philip King's herb shop. He walked into the small health food store and noticed Philip was helping a couple of customers. He looked around the store at the many natural remedies that lined the shelves, lost in his own thoughts. He almost didn't hear when Philip spoke.

"May I help you?" the deep voice came from behind him.

Jonathan turned around to face Philip. "'Tis me, Jonathan, Joanna's *bruder.*" Jonathan mentioned his older sister because she had worked for Philip and his wife Naomi delivering honey for several years.

Philip surveyed Jonathan and smiled, offering a hand shake. "Jonathan; *gut* to see you." By the frown on his face, Philip perceived Jonathan's frustration. "Did you need help with something?"

"Um...well." Jonathan nervously shifted his feet, and then figured he might as well just come out with it. "I need a favor, Philip."

Philip raised his eyebrows. "Oh?"

"You see, I bought a car and *Dat* is pretty upset with me right now," he attempted to explain. "Will you come outside with me, Philip?" Philip glanced around the empty shop, nodded, and followed Jonathan to the parking lot. Jonathan walked over and stood near his car.

Philip's eyes lit up and he whistled. "It's a beauty! I like the silver racing stripes."

Jonathan smiled, a little relieved. "You like it? I was hoping you'd let me keep it here for a while."

Philip looked at Jonathan with concern. "I guess I can let you keep it here for a little bit, but if I get any complaints from your father or Bishop Hostettler, you're going to have to move it."

"Don't worry, Philip. I won't let you get into any hot water over this. Any problems and she's gone." Jonathan smiled.

"Jonathan, would you like to join me in the herb shop for a glass of fresh juice? It's on me," Philip offered.

"*Jah. Denki*, Philip." Jonathan followed Philip back into the herb shop.

"Carrot or apple?" Philip asked.

"How about a combination of the two?" Jonathan inquired.

"One carrot-apple juice coming up." Philip took some fresh carrots and apples out of the gas-operated refrigerator behind the long counter. He slowly pushed them through the juicer until he made a full glass. He strained the orange liquid and handed it to his young friend.

"Mm...the carrots are sweet today," Jonathan commented. "'Tis *gut*."

Philip chuckled. "Well maybe you should stop by more often and join me for a drink."

"*Jah*, I think I'd like that."

"Did you know that I once owned a car, too?" Philip asked. "It wasn't as nice as yours, though."

"Really?" Jonathan raised his eyebrows.

"*Jah*, there was a while there when I was seriously contemplating becoming an *Englischer* for *gut*. But the Lord brought me back to the church, as I'm sure He will you, too. Just remember, Jonathan; the choices you make now will affect you for the rest of your life."

Jonathan sat on his stool at the juice bar pondering Philip's words of wisdom. *The choices you make now will affect you for the rest of your life.* Now, *that* was something to consider.

After dropping off the other piece of mail on the kitchen table, Annie made a bee line for the stairs. Once in her room, she closed the door and sat on her bed. She quickly pulled out the picture to take a better look at it. So this is what her new friend looked like. Annie's countenance glowed as she stared at the photo in her hands. *Ach, she's so pretty. I love her curly red hair. Too bad I don't have a picture to send to her.*

Annie finally set the picture down and unfolded the letter. She silently read the words from her new-found friend:

Dear Annie,

I'm so excited that your mom and dad allowed you to write to me. I'm hoping that we'll become good friends and that we'll continue writing each other for many years. I have some exciting news to tell you, but first let me tell you a little bit about myself.

I, too, am 14 years old. I have five siblings – two sisters and three brothers. My mom and dad have been married for sixteen years. My family travels around and we sing in different churches similar to our own. We attend a conservative Baptist church.

Now for the exciting part; my family and I will be visiting a church in Lancaster next Sunday thru Wednesday. Wouldn't it be great if we could meet each other face to face? Then I'd be able to see what you look like and you could hear my family sing. Do you think your parents would let you go?

Please write me back and let me know as soon as you can. I'll be waiting for your letter. In case I don't get your letter in time, I've enclosed the address of the church.

Your Friend,
Amanda

J. E. B. Spredemann

P.S. That's exciting to hear that your brother and his wife are going to have a baby. I love babies!

Annie folded up the letter with an enormous smile. *She'll be here in Lancaster County. I can meet Amanda face to face.* She couldn't suppress her elation and laughed out loud. *Should I ask* Mamm *and* Dat *if I can go? What if they say no? Then my chance to see my friend may be gone forever.* Annie thought for a moment longer, and then decided it would be best to not say anything. She could probably find a ride with someone. *Who do I know that owns a car?*

CHAPTER 3
Good Advice

"Train up a child in the way he should go: and when he is old, he will not depart from it." Proverbs 22:6

nnie's friend Susanna Hostettler knocked on the back door of the Yoders' home. *"Hullo,* Susanna. *Kumm* in. Annie's up in her room," Annie's mother informed her. "You may go on up."

"Denki, Sarah," Susanna replied, then started toward Annie's room after greeting her siblings. She quietly knocked on the bedroom door.

"Ach, Susie!" Annie's face brightened at the sight of her good friend, and they briefly embraced. "I didn't know you were coming by today."

"I wanted to see if you wanted me to pick ya up for the Singin' on Sunday. I'll probably take the pony cart so you can drive it home afterward if you'd like. That is, of course, if you don't have a ride home already. If you do, then I can have my *bruder* take it home. I won't need it so you're welcome to use it," Susie offered.

Annie smiled thinking of Susie with her beau, Jonathan Fisher, riding home from the Singing on Sunday. There was once a time when Annie liked Jonathan, but to her disappointment he'd always been sweet on Susie. In spite of that fact, Annie was truly happy for her friend. She knew that someday God would bring the right boy into her life as well, but she'd just have to be patient for now. Besides, she was in no hurry. "*Jah*, Susie. I'd like to go. I'll bring the pony cart home, too."

"Wonderful *gut*. It will be a lot of fun," Susie said, then changed the subject. "What have you been doin' lately? I didn't see ya at the quiltin' bee last week."

Annie pulled out her letter and handed it to her friend. Susie read the letter with eyes wide open. "So, are ya gonna go see her?"

Annie held her finger to her lips to signal quiet, and then whispered back, "I really want to. I'll have to find a ride, though."

"Sounds like fun, but I could never go. *Dat* would not approve," Susie stated, thinking of her father who was the bishop for their church district.

"Well, I guess we'll see what happens. I'll let ya know," Annie said.

"All right, Annie. Well, I better get back home now. I told *Mamm* that I would help her take the wash down and make supper. See ya on Sunday." Susie left the room and headed home, whistling as she went. Annie knew she was excited about seeing Jonathan at the singing this Sunday.

Gideon Fisher took a walk down to the home of his good friend, Judah Hostettler. The bishop was sitting under an oak tree, sipping on a glass of lemonade, taking a well-earned break. He wiped the sweat off of his brow and noticed Gideon walking his way. He rose up to meet him.

"*Hullo*, Judah." Gideon greeted his friend with a firm handshake.

"What brings you out here today?" While the two friends frequently made social calls, the bishop perceived there was more to this visit.

"Jonathan," he simply stated. "You know he's in *Rumspringa* now."

"What did he do?"

"He brought a car home the other day and he was dressed in *Englisch* clothes. I told him that he couldn't keep the car on my property and that he would not dress like an *Englischer* in my house," Gideon stated adamantly.

"How did he respond to that?" Judah tugged on his ear.

"Well, he took off in his car. He was clearly upset." Gideon sighed. "But he did come back a few hours later, dressed like an Amish boy again."

"May I make a suggestion, Gideon?"

"That's what I was hoping for." He smiled. "You seem to know Jonathan better than I do."

"Don't worry about him so much. He's going to make mistakes. Some folks just gotta try things out for themselves. God says that if we train our children properly that they will come back to Him. Maybe instead of being upset with him, you could pray for him. The things I learned in *Rumspringa* were very beneficial. Pray that God will use this time to teach him some important lessons," Gideon's wise friend counseled.

"I can always count on you for good advice. *Denki,* Judah."

"You know I'm still counting on our two gettin' hitched someday. Let's pray for the Lord's will together," Judah spoke of his daughter Susie and Gideon's Jonathan.

"*Jah.* I'm thankful for your Susanna. Maybe she'll be the one to help bring Jonathan through this. I will pray, for sure and for certain." Gideon left for home, praying as he went. *Surely I can trust God's plan for my son's life.*

CHAPTER 4
Joanna

"A merry heart maketh a cheerful countenance..."
Proverbs 15:13a

Joanna Fisher was busy dusting the living room when her *Englisch* employer informed her that the family was expecting company tomorrow. "I'd like you to make sure that the spare bedroom is in order. You know, dust and vacuum in there," Mrs. Scott advised her.

"Would ya like me to wash up the bedding as well?" Joanna asked.

"No, that won't be necessary. But I would like you to help with the meal tomorrow evening. Do you think your parents will allow you to stay later?"

"*Jah*, I think they'll let me. Would you be able to give me a ride home tomorrow?" Joanna asked, knowing that her parents usually retired early.

"That won't be a problem," Mrs. Scott replied.

"Mr. Scott should be arriving at any time. Thank you so much for helping me with this meal. How do the pies look?" Mrs. Scott asked.

"They look *gut*; should be ready in about thirty minutes." Joanna turned to see who was here when she heard the voices coming in from the front door.

Mr. Scott walked into the kitchen with a young man in his early twenties. Mrs. Scott introduced him as their nephew, Caleb Scott. The young man held out his hand with a broad smile and a twinkle in his eye. "Nice to meet you, Joanna."

Joanna suddenly felt warmth in her cheeks as she shook Caleb's hand. He wore short dark brown hair and the most amazing green eyes she'd ever seen. "*Gut* to meet you, too," she said timidly.

"Joanna, can you stay for dinner?" Mrs. Scott asked. "Or do you need to be home at a certain time?"

"*Nee.* I can stay until you're ready to take me home," Joanna said happily.

"Well, it will probably be a few minutes until dinner is ready. Joanna, will you show Caleb to his room please while I set the table?" Mrs. Scott asked.

"Uh...I can set the table," Joanna offered, feeling uncomfortable about showing Caleb to his room.

"Oh no, that's okay. I can get it. You've done enough already," Laura insisted.

Although Joanna felt awkward, she didn't argue with her employer. She timidly led the way up the stairs to the spare bedroom.

"So, Joanna, how long have you been working for my aunt and uncle?" Caleb asked, attempting to make friendly conversation.

"A few months now; I really enjoy it. Your aunt and uncle are nice folks to work for," Joanna answered.

"I see you've been doing a good job. The house looks great," he complimented.

Joanna didn't know how to respond as it wasn't their way to receive praise. "*Denki,*" she simply said, attempting to remain humble. She stopped at the door to his room, opened it, and gestured inside. "Well, here is your room. I'm going to go see if your aunt needs more help," she said before quickly walking out and scurrying back down the stairs.

Caleb took his suitcase, set it on the bed, and began unpacking. *She seems like a really nice girl. I wonder if she's saved. I'll have to ask her later. Maybe Aunt Laura will let me drive her home tonight.* Caleb's thoughts were interrupted when he heard his aunt calling him for dinner. He hurried downstairs to the dining room.

"Okay, Caleb; you'll sit right here across from Joanna," his aunt informed him. They all sat down around the oak table and Mr. Scott asked his nephew to pray. Each member of the family held out their hands for the one next to them to grasp during the prayer. Since Joanna and Caleb were at the end of the table, they had no choice but to join hands too. Joanna felt a little awkward again, but Caleb grasped her hand with ease. She was definitely not used to this *Englischer* custom which they all seemed to be perfectly comfortable with. When the prayer had ended, Caleb smiled at Joanna and gave her hand a slight squeeze, causing chills to dance up her back.

As they finished up the meal, Caleb complemented his aunt. "Aunt Laura, that dinner was delicious."

"Don't tell me; Joanna prepared it. She's a wonderful cook," Laura informed her nephew with a smile. "Wait till you taste her pie."

"I can't wait. You know I hate to say this, Joanna, but I think you may cook better than my mom," Caleb said, then chuckled. "But just don't let her know I said that." He winked.

Joanna's cheeks immediately turned pink. She was uncomfortable with this much praise and attention. "*Denki*," was all she could manage. *Is it just me, or is it getting hot in here?* "Laura, do you mind if I step outside for some fresh air?" Joanna asked, hoping her employer wouldn't object. She desperately needed it.

"That's fine, but remember that the pies should be cool enough to serve in about ten minutes," she reminded her.

"I think I' ll step outside, too, if you don't mind." Caleb asked Joanna.

Truthfully, Joanna had wanted to be alone for a minute so she could sort through her confusing thoughts. She realized she was more attracted to this *Englischer* than she should be.

She couldn't be rude, though. "That would be fine," she said as she walked out onto the large porch.

"It's a beautiful evening," Caleb commented as he leaned up against the porch rail, looking up at the magnificently decorated night sky.

"*Jah,* it sure is. *Gottes* beauty is all around." She gazed up in awe.

"I was wondering something, Joanna." Caleb asked, "You're Amish, right? What exactly do you believe? I mean about God."

"Well, *I* believe that God sent His son Jesus to die on the cross for our sins; and that three days later, He rose from the dead. All who repent and trust in Him alone for salvation will be saved," Joanna stated confidently.

"Really?" Caleb seemed surprised.

"*Jah,* why do you ask that way?" Joanna wondered aloud.

"I thought the Amish believed in works-based salvation," he stated. "I've heard it called the 'Jesus Plus Plan'."

"Some do, for sure and for certain; but not me and my family," Joanna confirmed. "Many Plain folks teach that we must keep the Old Ways to find salvation."

Caleb appeared to be contemplating something. *Wow! She cooks, she cleans, she's beautiful, and she's saved. What more could a man ask for in a wife?* "Are you married?" Caleb blurted out the words without thinking. He immediately apologized. "Sorry, that didn't come out right." He usually wasn't like this around women, but for some reason this Amish girl had him mesmerized.

Joanna found herself giggling. "'Tis okay; and no, I'm not."

"Do you have a boyfriend or something?" Nothing Caleb said was coming out right and he could kick himself for not keeping his mouth shut.

"*Nee,*" she answered. *Wow, he sure is straight-forward.*

Caleb felt awkward now. He turned away from her to try to hide his embarrassment. *Lord, please help me not to sound like a fool.* Thankfully, their conversation was cut short by his Aunt Laura calling them in for dessert.

After graciously receiving the many compliments on her delicious pie, Joanna glanced at the clock. Fortunately, it was still early so she could stay for a while. Although a bit uncomfortable, she enjoyed the time spent with Caleb. He seemed like a nice young *Englisch* man. Mr. Scott brought out several board games and set them on the small coffee table in the living room. The family all sat around and chatted about menial things. Right away, Joanna eyed the Scrabble game and her face lit up.

"So, what would you like to play?" Laura asked her company, glancing at both Caleb and Joanna.

Caleb reached for the Scrabble game. "Do you like Scrabble?"

"*Jah;* it's my favorite actually." She smiled.

"Scrabble it is, then." Caleb didn't dare let on that Scrabble was his favorite game, too. He'd already made a fool of himself enough tonight. He took out the game board and they each drew seven letter tiles out of the box. "Ladies first."

Joanna was delighted when she saw that her letters formed a word. She quickly placed a B-O-P-P-L-I on the board with a smile. "Let's see, Double Letter Score for the B and Double Word Score makes thirty points!"

Caleb raised his eyebrows and looked at her funny. "Boppli?"

"*Jah; boppli,*" she said confidently.

"I'm sorry, but I don't think that is a word."

"*Jah;* 'tis. *Boppli* is what *Englischers* call a baby," she informed him. "It's Pennsylvania *Dietsch.*"

Caleb chuckled. "Oh, I get it. So we're playing bilingual Scrabble. Two can play at that game," he said slyly. "Let's see if I can beat thirty points. Hmm..." He eyed his tiles looking for something with high point value. He gave a huge grin and took out an E-X-I-C-O-N and added it to her L. "Lexicon. Double Letter Point for the C and Double Word makes...oh, thirty-eight points. Beat that!" he teased.

"What is lexicon? I've never heard it before. Are you sure you're not making it up?" She smiled.

"Aunt Laura, do you have a dictionary around here? Joanna here doesn't believe me, so I need to educate her a little," he teased.

"It's on the brown bookshelf next to the fireplace," his aunt informed him.

"Just kidding, I don't need it," Caleb answered. "A lexicon is basically a dictionary of sorts."

"All right, then. I'll just add this here 'S' to make more than one lexicon." She smiled and stole another good look at his gorgeous green eyes.

"You've got me beat. What is that, like a hundred points or something?" He laughed.

"Well, let me see. It's a Triple Word Point so that would *only* make sixty points." She couldn't help but laugh at her good fortune.

"Ah, you're slaughtering me! How can I top that?" He chuckled, raking a hand through his thick dark hair.

Just in time, Laura entered the room with a large bowl in her hands. "Fresh popcorn, anyone?" she offered.

Joanna had been so into the game, or was it into Caleb, that she didn't even smell the aroma while it had been popping. "*Jah*, I'll take some."

"Me, too," Caleb requested. "We can share a bowl." There he went blabbing again. "That is, if Joanna doesn't mind," he quickly added to save face.

The way Caleb looked at Joanna made her heart do a flip. "'Tis fine."

"Here, throw a piece at me and I'll see if I can catch it." He pointed to his mouth.

"Okay." She tossed a kernel at him and it bounced off his forehead. "Oops!" She cupped her hand over her mouth, trying to conceal a giggle.

He picked it up off of the Scrabble game where it landed and popped it into his mouth with a smile. His face brightened thinking he loved to hear her laugh. "Try again."

She threw another piece and it bounced off his nose. "*Ach,* I'm afraid I'm not very *gut* at this."

"No, no, you're doing fine," he reassured her. "I'm the one not doing a good job at catching it. Here, try throwing it like this." He made a gentle underhand tossing motion.

She followed his advice and the piece of popcorn landed directly in his mouth. "You got it." She clapped her hands.

"Now let me throw one at – I mean to – you." He smiled mischievously.

"Oh, no you don't." She laughed.

"Come on, I promise I'll throw it gently," he pleaded.

"Okay, I guess." She gave a nod signaling she was ready. Caleb gently tossed the popcorn her way and she caught it perfectly, flashing him a beautiful smile.

"See, that wasn't so bad, was it?"

As the night wore on, Joanna completely forgot about the time. She glanced up at the clock and suddenly noticed it was eleven o'clock. "*Ach,* it's late. I should be getting home." She looked up at Mrs. Scott.

"I can drive her home," Caleb eagerly offered, looking at his aunt.

"That would be fine with me. Do you mind if Caleb takes you home, Joanna?" Mrs. Scott asked.

"*Nee*," she said, suddenly shy now. "*Denki* for supper, Laura." Joanna slipped on her shawl which hung on a peg of the hall tree.

"No problem, Joanna. You're welcome anytime," her employer answered back, then tossed something to Caleb. "Here are the keys, Caleb."

Joanna walked out the front door of her employer's home and headed toward the car. Caleb quickly darted ahead to open the passenger side door for her. "*Denki*," she said timidly. Caleb hurried around to his side and slid into the driver's seat.

"So, where do you live?" he asked, slipping the key in and turning over the ignition.

"Not too far. It's about five miles."

Caleb was a little disappointed. He'd hoped it would be a longer drive so they could converse more. "Is there a scenic route?"

"A scenic route?" She laughed. "All of Pennsylvania is scenic; except for maybe the cities."

"I meant a longer way home." There he went speaking his mind again. He hoped he wasn't too obvious.

"Oh; *jah*. Have you ever seen the covered bridge over by Miller's Creek?" she asked, happy to show him around the area she was so familiar with.

"No, this is actually my first time in Pennsylvania. I plan on doing a lot of sight-seeing while I'm here. At least, when I'm not in church," he informed her.

"Oh," she said disappointedly. She was hoping that she'd be able to see him again when she worked for the Scotts. Apparently, he wouldn't be there much at all.

"Hey, I have an idea." He thought for a moment. "Since it's too dark to see anything right now anyway, why don't you show me around another day? Say, tomorrow?" He hoped she'd say yes.

"Well, I'll be workin' for your aunt till two. We can probably go after that," she offered.

"Great. It's a date then!" The words escaped his mouth unintentionally. *I did it again. Why can't I just keep my thoughts inside?* He was so upset with himself. *What's come over me?* He asked himself the question, but he already knew the answer: *it was her.* He smiled to himself and stole a quick glance at her. She was everything he was looking for, but she was Amish. How could he get around that?

"*Jah;* I guess it is," she simply said, without batting an eyelash.

How can I make this work out? I'll be going back home at the end of summer. At least I'm finished with Bible College already. Technically, I don't have *to leave.* But there was the youth conference in California that he planned on attending in the fall. He realized he needed to get on his knees before God and beseech His will. It was clear that he was letting his emotions run away with him. *Is this the one you have for me, God?* He silently prayed.

Joanna noticed that Caleb was unusually quiet. "Is something wrong?" she asked as they drove along.

"No." *Everything is right*, he thought. "Joanna, I had a really fun time tonight." He smiled at her.

"*Jah;* so did I." Her cheeks turned pink again, but fortunately it was too dark for Caleb to notice.

"Would you want to come to church with me next Sunday night for the missions conference?" he asked, hoping she'd give a positive response.

She thought about the Singings that she usually attended on Sunday evening. How different would an *Englisch* church be? "*Jah;* I'd like to go with you," she decided, although she was unsure of what a missions conference was.

"Great! It starts at five because they usually have a dinner first. If that's too early, then we can skip the dinner," he offered.

"I'll have my brother drop me off at your aunt's house at four, then," Joanna stated as they pulled into her father's property. Caleb drove slowly down the tree-lined dirt lane, and then parked just before reaching the front of the house. He quickly got out and opened the door for Joanna again.

As she got out, she noticed how Caleb seemed to study her and did not take his eyes off of her. It stole her breath away. She hoped he wasn't going to kiss her, because she thought she might actually kiss him back. But instead he stood in place. She wondered why he didn't at least reach for her hand or anything, the way Andrew Lapp had when they were courting.

"I guess I'll see you tomorrow," he said with his eyes still transfixed on hers.

She found herself having to look away lest her knees give way. "Tomorrow," she said, as she hurried to the back door and quietly slipped inside. She gave out a deep sigh once she was inside, and placed a hand over her wildly beating heart.

CHAPTER 5
The Singing

"Rejoice, O young man, in thy youth; and let thy heart cheer thee in the days of thy youth, and walk in the ways of thine heart, and in the sight of thine eyes: but know thou, that for all these things God will bring thee into judgment." Ecclesiastes 11:9

Annie quickly dressed for the Singing, and then waited on the porch until Susie would come for her. She saw Susanna coming up the lane with her older brother Joshua. As Joshua's courting buggy pulled up to the house, Annie hopped off the porch swing and headed in their direction. Joshua got down from the buggy and helped her up into the seat.

"*Denki,*" she told Susie's eighteen-year-old brother. Annie would never admit it to anyone, but she secretly had a crush on Susanna's older brother. Of course, he would probably never take notice of her since she was only fourteen. Nevertheless,

Annie enjoyed the Singings and getting together with friends to share food and fun.

They pulled up to the Beilers' barn and walked inside to grab a light snack and a drink. The tables were all set up, but it was still a little early. The girls made their way outside, to where a baseball game was getting started in the Beilers' large field.

"Is Maryanna coming tonight?" Annie asked Susanna about her twin sister, who was raised as an *Englischer*.

"*Ach;* no. I think she said she's going to the movies or something," Susie responded.

Neither Annie nor Susie had ever been to a movie theater, so they didn't really know what it was all about, although they'd heard stories from some the older kids in *Rumspringa*.

An engine roared loudly and they turned to see who was coming. Oftentimes, some of the rowdier boys would bring a car to the singing. It appeared to be an older classic car. All of the boys immediately went over to check it out as it rolled to a stop. The *Englisch*-dressed driver got out and the girls tried to figure out who it was. Susie's jaw dropped when she recognized her beau's handsome face. "Jonathan?" she said in quiet disbelief. The girls made their way over to the shiny blue car.

"How do you like it?" Jonathan smiled at Susie and placed his arm around her shoulder.

Susanna was still in shock. She looked at the car, then looked at Jonathan's clothing and new haircut. "*Ach*, Jonathan. Does your *daed* know?" Susie asked wide-eyed.

"*Jah,* he does." He shrugged nonchalantly. He guided her away from the crowd so they could have more privacy. "I was hopin' to take you for a ride in it after the Singin'." Jonathan flashed her one of his winning smiles.

How could she say no to that? "*Jah,* I guess it would be fun."

"That's my girl," Jonathan said, bringing a smile to Susie's face. "Now, let's go play ball before the Singing starts."

After the Singing, Susie's brother Joshua offered to take Annie home. Of course, Annie understood that he wasn't taking her courting or anything, but just being kind as he always was. Annie happily agreed, although she didn't let her exuberance show.

As they rode along, Joshua attempted to make small talk. Annie wondered why he didn't have a steady girl, seeing he was so nice and all. "*Denki* for taking me home, Joshua."

"Oh, it's no trouble at all," he replied, flicking the reins gently.

"Did you see Jonathan's car?" she asked with her eyes wide.

He chuckled at her expression. "*Jah,* I saw it. It was hard to miss. Pretty nice wheels."

"Have *you* ever owned a car?" Annie knew it was none of her business but she was curious. She couldn't imagine the bishop's son with a vehicle.

"*Nee,* not me; I decided to stay Amish. Never really cared much for things of the world," he stated.

His answer satisfied Annie. "You've already been baptized, *jah*?" Annie tried to recall who had been baptized.

"*Jah,* when I turned sixteen. How about you, Annie? Have you thought much about baptism?" Joshua asked her curiously.

"Well, I'm still only fourteen," she reminded him.

"Oh. For some reason you seem older to me. Maybe it's because you and Susie have always been *gut* friends," Joshua said. His eyes briefly swept over Annie's figure.

Maybe he does want to court me. Annie thought, and then thankfully remembered his question about baptism. "To answer your question, *jah*; I have thought about baptism. It's kinda hard not to, being the deacon's daughter and all."

"*Jah,* I guess *Dat's* being the bishop probably had somethin' to do with my decision, too," he said.

"It wonders me why you didn't take your *aldi* home tonight?" Annie slyly asked, curious what his response would be.

He chuckled again. "I guess that'd be because I don't have one. God hasn't brought along the right one yet."

"Well, I guess that makes sense then." Annie smiled, the moon reflecting off her flaxen hair.

Joshua drove the buggy up to the hitching post on the Yoders' property and hopped down to help Annie out. He thought for a moment and spoke as though he just had an idea. "Hey, Annie; if you're not riding home with anyone next Singing, would you consider going with me again?"

Annie was taken aback. She did not expect this at all. "Um...I don't know, Joshua. You're eighteen and I'm only fourteen."

"I'm not askin' ya to get married yet or nothin'." He laughed, as he walked her to the back porch. "Just to take you home in my buggy. We're friends, aren't we?"

She smiled, attempting to quell the butterflies in her stomach. "Of course we are. Okay, I'll let ya take me home again."

"*Gut.*" He smiled at Annie and held her gaze a moment, then walked back to the buggy with a spring in his step. "*Gut nacht,* Annie."

Annie walked into her house from the back door. *What just happened?* Her excitement quickly turned into disappointment when she suddenly remembered that she had planned to go see her new friend next Sunday. *Oh no! I'll have to let Joshua down. Ach, and I can't tell him where I'm going either. I hope he doesn't think I'm not interested in him.* The last thing she wanted was to miss her chance with handsome Joshua Hostettler. She wondered what she could do. Annie finally decided that writing a letter would probably be her best bet. She'd have Susie deliver it for her.

How am I going to get to the Englisch *church?* Annie wondered, then remembered Jonathan's new car. She smiled. *Of course, Jonathan Fisher will give me a ride.*

"Well, Susie; what do you think?" Jonathan asked, proudly patting the dashboard of his new car.

"'Tis nice Jonathan, but I'm not used to going this fast." Susie gripped the side of the seat tightly for a little extra comfort.

By the grimace on her face, Jonathan speculated that his *aldi* may be a little worried. "I'll slow down some."

Susie let out a puff of air she seemed to be holding in. "*Denki,* Jonathan. Where are we going?"

"'Tis a really special place; you'll see." Jonathan drove as carefully as he could, so as not to frighten Susie. "Hey, I think Joanna's got herself an *Englisch* beau."

"*Ach,* really?" Susie asked in astonishment.

"I think so; saw him drop her off in his car two nights in a row. Did you notice that she wasn't at the Singing tonight?"

"*Nee;* I didn't notice."

"I'm pretty sure she's with him again." He rubbed his chin.

"Your sister, Joanna, with an *Englischer*?" The thought astounded Susie.

"Well, you're with an *Englischer*," he teased.

"*Ach,* Jonathan. You're just as Amish as I am and you know it." She smiled. "Your fast car and *Englisch* clothes don't fool me."

Jonathan smiled. "Susie, you know me so well." He parked at the top of a hill and turned off the headlights. "Well, what do you think?" He gestured out the windshield to the view below.

Susie sat erect to peer out the front window and saw all of the lights from the city below. Her eyes drank in the spectacular view. She gasped. "*Ach*, it's beautiful!"

"I thought you'd like it." He smiled at her, inching closer in the seat.

Susie put her head on his shoulder as they both stared out at the beautiful scene below them. It was perfect.

"Susie," Jonathan said in a serious tone.

Susie sat up and looked at him, wondering what he wanted to say.

"*Ich liebe dich*," he simply stated.

"I love you, too, Jonathan." Susie smiled back, gazing into his eyes. Oh, how handsome he looked with his new *Englisch* haircut.

"Will you take your hair down for me?" he asked timidly, hoping she'd agree.

"*Ach,* Jonathan; you know I can't do that," Susie said regretfully.

Jonathan reached over and gently brought her chin up to gaze into her eyes. "I've already seen it down once before. Have you forgotten? Your *dat* was even there and he didn't say anything against it."

"No, I haven't forgotten. That's when I found out that Mary-anna was still alive. That was such a wonderful-*gut* day." She smiled, remembering that she had just gone to bed when her brother Levi called her down to hear the good news.

"Today is a wonderful-*gut* day, too." He smiled, gently stroking her soft cheek.

"*Jah;* it is." She acquiesced and slowly reached her hand up behind her prayer *kapp* to remove it from her head as uncertainty filled her mind. She knew that what Jonathan had asked was forbidden. Jonathan's hand covered hers as she removed the straight pins and took the white organza covering off. He held it in his hand as she slowly slipped the hair pins out of her bun. Her long brown hair tumbled down her shoulders and back. Jonathan reached up and slowly caressed her soft hair. Her heart beat rapidly as he fervently searched her eyes.

"May I kiss you, Susie?" He didn't wait for a response and slowly moved closer to her, their lips almost touching.

Although desire called to her heart, Susanna reluctantly jumped back. Did she hear horse hooves or was it just her imagination? Jonathan turned his head around to see Susanna's older brother Levi standing at the window. Jonathan quickly rolled the window down.

"Jonathan, what are you doing here?" Levi looked into the car, his eyes adjusting to the dark. His friendly countenance quickly changed. "*Ach,* Susie! What are you doing with your hair down?" he asked angrily, insisting she give him answer.

Susanna remained silent and a guilty look flashed across her face.

A sudden flashback plagued Levi, an unwelcome memory of his beloved Chloe with Saul Brenneman; and he was once again filled with wrath. Levi glanced at Susie, who still said nothing, then back at Jonathan. "Just what were you intending to do with my sister, Jonathan?" he practically shouted.

Jonathan and Susie both looked at each other in embarrassment, wondering what to do. No words could escape their mouths. Susie began trembling and she quickly tried to pin her hair back up in a bun.

"Wait till *Dat* hears about this," Levi threatened angrily.

"*Ach,* Levi. No!" she cried. "Please don't tell *Dat!*"

"Get in my buggy now!" Levi demanded. Susanna looked at Jonathan with apologetic eyes, then quickly opened the door of his car and ran to her brother's buggy. She climbed in next to Chloe Esh, her older brother's fiancée, with her face in her hands.

"I can take her home," Jonathan offered sheepishly.

"I'm sure you can, Jonathan," Levi said sarcastically, aiming a cold glare in his direction.

"That's not what I meant!" Jonathan defended his innocence.

"Wasn't it?" Levi's eyebrows arched. "Stay away from my sister if you know what's best for you," he threatened, then stomped back to his buggy.

Susie glanced up at her beau with tears streaming down her face. "I'm sorry, Jonathan. Goodbye." Why did her words sound so final, as though she'd never see him again?

Jonathan's heart sank as he watched the buggy disappear. He rested his forehead on the steering wheel feeling completely helpless. *I think I've just lost my girl! Please dear God; this can't be happening.*

CHAPTER 6
The Incident

"Wine is a mocker, strong drink is raging: and whosoever is deceived thereby is not wise."
Proverbs 20:1

"Annie," Sarah Yoder called her daughter from the back door. "Will you go over to the Kings' and pick up two jars of honey for me?"

"Sure, *Mamm;* I'll take my scooter." Annie stood from her perched position in the garden and quickly moved to wash the dirt from her hands. Pocketing the money that her mother had given her, Annie rode along on her scooter enjoying the quiet countryside. A rumble behind her indicated an approaching car, so she cautiously pulled off to the side. One glance informed her that the vehicle belonged to Jonathan Fisher. *Just who I wanted to see.* Annie smiled.

Jonathan pulled up beside her. "Hi, Annie."

Annie noticed right away that something was wrong with her friend's beau. "Is everything okay, Jonathan?"

"*Nee.* But it's none of your concern," he retorted.

"I'm sorry, Jonathan. I didn't mean to upset you," Annie said gently.

"*Ach,* sorry Annie. It's not you. I'm the *dummkopp,*" he apologized for his terse remark.

Annie sensed he was a little more at ease now. "May I ask a favor of you, Jonathan?"

Jonathan raised his eyebrows to question her.

"I need a ride somewhere on Sunday night. Could ya take me?" she asked sweetly.

Jonathan had always thought Susie's best friend was nice. "Sure, I'll take ya." He shrugged nonchalantly and offered a slight smile.

"I'll meet ya at the Kings' at six o' clock, *jah?*"

"Okay," Jonathan agreed.

Annie continued on to the Kings' herb shop to pick up the honey for her mother. *It's all set. I'll meet Amanda on Sunday night.* Annie's satisfaction showed through her smile.

Jonathan attempted to see Susie the last two days, but never made it past the door. Her brother Levi greeted him at the door every time, warning him to stay away, lest he tell Bishop Hostettler. Jonathan was not about to give up. He determined to see Susanna whether Levi liked it or not, so he decided to go at night and shine a flashlight on her window.

From her bedroom window, Susie noticed a light outside and moved to peer through the glass. She saw Jonathan and motioned to him that she would be down in a minute. She took a deep breath, hoping Levi was either asleep or not at home. She quickly dressed and pinned up her hair, carefully placing a prayer *kapp* over her head. The *kapp* she'd been wearing the night Levi found her and Jonathan together, had been forgotten in his car. She quietly made her way downstairs and hurried out the back door to meet Jonathan.

As soon as they met each other, they embraced. Susie's eyes filled with tears again. She knew that what she must say was not going to be easy. Jonathan's concerned eyes met hers. "Shh; don't cry, *Liewi*." His gentleness made Susie's task all the more difficult.

"Jonathan, I can't see you anymore," Susie managed to say, as she forced herself from his tender embrace.

"Yes, you can. Levi will get over his anger," he reassured her, gently rubbing her arm.

She stepped back, not to be sidetracked by Jonathan's affections. She had to be strong for both of their sakes. She shook her head. "Jonathan, you don't understand. I don't want to see you anymore."

He searched her eyes, uncertainty filling his features. "You don't mean that."

Susie remained firm. "Yes, I do. I've had time to think over the last couple of days–"

"You're lying to me. I know you don't mean that!" Jonathan said desperately, and lightly grasped her arm.

"I won't be with an *Englischer*. Goodbye, Jonathan." Susie looked into his pained eyes one more time, pulled out of his grasp, then quickly walked back into the house.

Jonathan simply stood there, too dumfounded to move. He stared after her forlornly. *But Susie and I were going to get married. I thought that she loved me too. No, this can't be. God, please, this is too much for me to bear...*

Susanna ran upstairs, not caring who might hear. She threw herself on the bed and sobbed into her pillow.

Susie had to get out of the house. She needed some time alone so she could talk with God. Earlier, she'd spotted Jonathan driving around Paradise with an *Englisch* girl in his car. *How could he get over me so quickly? Maybe he didn't love me after all,* she thought sadly, her heart breaking in two. It was her fault, though; she set him free in hopes that she would one day get him back again. It had been her ultimate sacrifice. *I hope I've done the right thing.*

As she walked past the barn, her brother Levi met her. "Where are you going?" he asked.

"Just for a walk, Levi," she told him, a bit upset with his unwelcome intrusion.

"You're not going to meet *him*, are you?" he asked over-protectively.

Susie gritted her teeth. "*Nee*, I'm not seeing Jonathan anymore," she reassured him with an unsteady voice. She needed to leave before breaking down again.

"*Gut*. It's time you found yourself a respectable Amish boy," he said, seemingly satisfied. "Jonathan's never been anything but trouble."

Susanna knew that wasn't true. Perhaps that's what people on the outside saw because they didn't know him well. But Susie knew Jonathan to be kind, loving, and loyal. She knew he'd do anything for her or any of his friends. "May I go now?" she asked, stomping her foot impatiently.

"*Jah*, you may go," her brother permitted.

Susie knew her brother was just looking out for her best interests, but she was still upset with him. He didn't have any business interfering with her and Jonathan. She took her cares to the Lord in prayer before her emotions got the best of her.

Dear Gott, *please take away my anger for Levi and Jonathan. Help me to be at peace with letting Jonathan go and heal this aching in my heart. Please get a hold of Jonathan's heart and bring him back to the church. Thy will be done,* Gott. *Amen.*

As Susanna neared Miller's Pond, she noticed someone fishing from the dock. The figure stood up and started walking her way, fishing pole in hand. As the person walked toward her, she noticed it was Matthew Riehl. He was someone she once had a crush on and *gut* friend of Jonathan and her brother Joshua.

"Hello, Susie," he said cheerfully, tipping his hat to her. "What brings you out here?"

"*Ach,* just going for a walk," she said, feeling a little lighter since she'd given her burdens to the Lord.

"Remember when you and I went boating out here one time?" he asked smiling.

"*Jah,* I remember," she said. *It was the same day Jonathan gave me my special handkerchief on my thirteenth birthday. And the day I began falling in love with him.* The bittersweet memory made her smile a bit.

Matthew began slowly, "Susie, I know you and Jonathan are –"

"Jonathan and I are not seeing each other anymore," she stated as calmly as she could, hoping her lip didn't tremble.

"You're not?" Matthew seemed clearly surprised. And Susie was equally surprised he didn't already know.

"Oh!" His eyebrows shot up. "Well then, may I take you to dinner on Friday?" *I hope Jonathan won't be upset with me.*

"*Jah,*" Susie agreed. If she was going to move on with her life, she needed to take the first step. Perhaps God had Matthew in mind for her all along. But it still didn't stop the ache in her heart.

Matthew's senses heightened when Susanna met him at the end of her driveway on Friday evening. Not much was said during their time in his buggy, other than chitchat, as they drove to a popular 1950s diner that many of the young people of Paradise frequented.

They pulled up to a hitching post, placed there especially for the diner's Amish customers. Matthew descended the buggy and walked around to help Susie down. He was elated to finally get a chance with Susanna.

Loud rock music suddenly blared from an approaching vehicle. They observed Jonathan's blue Camaro driving up. *Oh no,* Matthew thought, *this isn't going to go over very well.* Jonathan didn't bother parking the vehicle properly, but screeched to a halt, placing the car in park diagonally behind the other vehicles, blocking them in. He stepped out of the car and slammed the door shut.

Susie's heart ached as she glanced at the passenger's side and noticed a different *Englisch* girl than the one she had seen the other day. *How many girls has he met since we broke up?* The girl was holding a brown glass bottle in her hand, surely the devil's brew.

Jonathan, reeking of cigarette smoke and alcohol, staggered up to Matthew. "What are you doing with my girl?" he demanded angrily in his drunken state, throwing a punch at Matthew. Matthew winced and stepped back when Jonathan's fist hit his face. "Some friend you are, Matt," he mumbled.

"*Ach,* Jonathan. You've been drinking," Susanna said worriedly. She knew drinking and driving were not a good combination and feared for his safety. She sent up a quick prayer for her beloved.

"She's not your girl anymore, Jonathan. Leave us alone," Matthew said calmly, rubbing his face. He knew talking to someone intoxicated produced little fruit.

"Oh, she's my girl all right." Jonathan looked at Susie and she noticed his bright sparkling eyes had been replaced with a set of cold dark ones. "Tell him, Susie. Tell Matthew how you took your hair down for me that night in my car."

"*Ach,* Jonathan. Don't say such things." Susie gasped, her eyes filled with tears. Didn't he know what his words were implying? *How can he shame me like this?*

Jonathan reached into his pocket and pulled out the prayer *kapp* Susie had left in his car. It was now wrinkled. "I guess it didn't mean nothin' to ya, huh? I thought you loved me, Susie. But I can see now that I was wrong." He threw the prayer *kapp* at her feet in front of her, then walked angrily back to his car.

"How could you, Jonathan?" Susanna's face fell into her hands and she began sobbing. She'd never been so disheartened in her life. Matthew quickly came to her side and picked up the prayer *kapp.*

Jonathan slammed his door and abruptly took off, peeling out of the parking lot.

Susie was in no mood to eat. "I'm so sorry, Matthew," she cried. "Please take me home."

Matthew opened the buggy door for her and she glanced to the right, noticing Sadie Lapp standing around with some other people. They had obviously seen and heard all that had transpired. Sadie was known for being a gossip and could be downright mean. Wouldn't she love to have something to talk about involving the bishop's daughter. *Surely this will get back to* Dat. *What am I going to do now?* Susanna thought.

CHAPTER 7
Consequences

"For he that soweth to his flesh shall of the flesh reap corruption..." Galatians 6:8a

It was late when Jonathan pulled into his parents' driveway. His music still blaring, he woke up his father who made it outside just in time to see Jonathan crash into the fence. "Jonathan, what are you doing?" Gideon struggled to control his emotions, which were now about to erupt.

As Jonathan staggered out of the car, Gideon could smell the alcohol on him. "Hey, Dad. Hope your day went better than mine," he mumbled unintelligibly.

"You will not come into my house like this. Do you hear me, Jonathan? No drunk is welcome under my roof," his father asserted.

"Yeah, yeah, Gideon. I hear ya, I hear ya," Jonathan replied disrespectfully.

Exasperated, Gideon huffed and turned around to go back into the house. "Please Lord, give this boy some sense," he called out to the sky.

Jonathan stumbled into the barn and collapsed on a bale of hay. A couple of hours later he woke up sweating and shaking. His stomach turned violently inside of him and he stood up and bent over, spewing out all of its contents. Again and again, his stomach contracted, dispelling everything his stomach contained and more. Jonathan had never felt worse in his life and he wished at this moment that he could keel over and die. Finally, the vomiting and dry heaving stopped and he fell over, completely exhausted.

As Gideon pulled open the shop door in the morning, he had to hold back a gag. The entire place reeked of vomit. He looked around and noticed Jonathan lying face-down in a pile of the foul-smelling substance. Gideon quickly walked outside holding his breath, lest he too, retch. He quickly went to the hand-pump and raised the handle up and down until water poured out, splashing it on his face.

Once he regained his composure, he filled up a bucket of water and headed back to the barn. Holding his breath, he walked over to where Jonathan was and dumped its contents over his head.

Jonathan quickly jumped up.

"Better get this place cleaned up quickly," Gideon said, and then headed out of the barn and back into the house.

"Well, Esther. Guess I won't be workin' in the shop today," Gideon informed his wife.

"Breakfast is about ready. Should we call Jonathan inside?" Esther asked, and then nodded to Joanna who was setting the food on the table. Joanna started toward the back door to fetch her brother when Gideon spoke up.

"I don't think Jonathan will want to eat with us this morning. Besides, he's got a lot of work to do right now." Gideon sighed and Joanna sat down at the table with her folks. They all bowed their heads for the silent prayer and Gideon sent up an extra one for his youngest son.

Annie quickly penned a letter to Joshua, and then delivered it in person to Susie. As Susanna came to the door, Annie noticed her friend was distraught over something. Annie went with Susanna up to her room and Susie shared everything with her. "Oh Susie, I'm so sorry." Annie attempted to comfort her friend. "We just gotta keep prayin' for Jonathan; God will bring him back," she said confidently.

"Oh, Annie, I'm so upset with him right now. How could he do that to me? How could he humiliate me in front of all those people? I don't know if I can pray for him," Susie admitted.

"You know that wasn't Jonathan speaking, Susie. It was the alcohol. That's why we're warned so adamantly to stay away from it. It destroys folks' lives," she reminded her friend. "You *must* pray for Jonathan, he desperately needs our prayers right now."

"Okay, Annie. I will try," Susanna said.

"Jonathan still loves you, Susie. You know he does," she reassured her friend. "He just needs help."

Susanna gave her friend a hug, wiping away her tears. "*Denki,* Annie. I needed a friend to talk to."

"You have one in me, anytime," Annie promised. "I gotta go now. Please remember to give that to Joshua as soon as ya see him."

"I will," Susie agreed, pondering why Annie would be giving her older brother a letter.

Jonathan felt much better after he took a bath, which was outside, at his father's insistence. His mother had made him a hot cup of ginger tea and a pot of homemade chicken noodle soup, which helped to settle his stomach. Since his *Englisch* clothes were all filthy and he was under his father's roof, he wore his Plain clothing.

After lunch he drove his Camaro, now with a dent in the front right fender, over to Philip King's. He decided to leave it there until he took Annie Yoder on Sunday night to wherever she wanted to go. Now that he thought about it, he didn't even know where he was taking her. It didn't matter though, he had promised that he would take her somewhere and he would keep his word.

Right now, he needed to get back to the house to repair the fence he ran into with his car. *What a mess I've made of my life. How am I ever gonna get Susie back?* Jonathan thought sorrowfully.

CHAPTER 8
Church

"And if it seem evil unto you to serve the Lord,
choose you this day whom ye will serve..."
Joshua 24:15a

Joanna drove her brother's courting buggy to her employer's residence late Sunday afternoon. Over the last week and a half, she and Caleb had spent many hours together. She had shown him all around Lancaster and they even drove to Hershey and visited the amusement park. Joanna had never had so much fun in her life. Caleb seemed to enjoy her company as much as she did his. She was really looking forward to tonight's missions conference. Caleb spoke about it with such passion and excitement, she was certain she would have a good time.

Caleb met her at the buggy as she drove up and tied the horse to the hitching post. But he didn't help her down from the buggy. Joanna found it slightly odd that he never got too close to her. Aside from holding her hand to pray at a meal, he hadn't touched her once.

"Are you ready to go?" Caleb asked eagerly, after giving Joanna's horse some alfalfa and water.

"*Jah,* I'm ready," Joanna confirmed.

The two of them made their way to the car, and Caleb held the door open for Joanna as usual. As they drove along, Joanna became lost in thought. She studied Caleb out of the corner of her eye. *I don't understand this man. He seems to be interested in me, yet he hasn't held my hand, hugged me, or anything of the sort. Maybe he doesn't feel the same way about me as I do about him.* A seed of doubt invaded Joanna's thoughts. Caleb's odd behavior had her thoroughly befuddled.

"You're awfully quiet tonight." Caleb glanced her way.

"*Ach,* just thinkin' I guess," she answered, staring out the window at the familiar farmland.

"Oh, yeah? About what?"

Do I dare tell him? "About you," she said quietly.

His brow lifted. "Well, I hope it's good." He smiled.

"I'm not sure." She stared down at her hands.

"What do you mean?" He seemed concerned now.

"I don't really know how to say this, Caleb." She took a deep breath hoping she wouldn't sound too forward. "I was just wondering...well, why haven't you held my hand or anything?"

He chuckled. "If you think I'm not interested in you, Joanna Fisher, you're dead wrong. Nothing could be further from the truth. I haven't held your hand because the Bible says it is not good for a man to touch a woman. The young men are supposed to treat the young women as sisters. So, until I'm married I've purposed in my heart not to touch a woman."

"Oh." Joanna was surprised. As far as she knew, she had never heard those verses before.

"You see, if I hold your hand then I might be tempted to kiss you, which, in turn could lead to other things. I'd rather not go down that road and stay pleasing to the Lord," he explained.

"Wow. And Andrew thought that *I* was too conservative because I wouldn't kiss him," she thought aloud.

"Andrew?" He raised his eyebrows, somewhat disturbed.

"*Jah*, he was courting me. I stopped seeing him because he insisted on kissing me. I never let him, though," she said.

Now Caleb seemed to be deep in thought, or was he praying? He didn't speak for several minutes.

"Caleb?" Joanna looked at him quizzically.

"Oh sorry, I didn't mean to zone out on you there," he said. Caleb pulled the car over to the side of the road. Joanna knew he had something important on his heart. He looked at her intently, and took a deep breath before speaking. "Joanna, will you pray about something with me? My parents have been praying for a mate for me since the day I was born. They prayed that I would keep myself pure for my wife and that she would do likewise. I believe that you are the one that God intended for me, but I want to be absolutely sure. There is nothing better for us than God's will, and that's what I want you to pray about with me."

Joanna nodded her head in agreement. She dare not speak lest the tears pricking her eyes fall. She, too, had had similar thoughts about Caleb possibly being a mate for her. She had quickly dismissed her thoughts though, because she thought it absurd since they had only known each other for such a short time. And he was *Englisch.* Now she wondered, was God trying to tell her something?

Caleb turned the engine back on and continued to the church. They both sat quietly praying the rest of the way and wondering what the Lord might have in store for them.

As promised, Jonathan met Annie at the herb shop at six o'clock. "So, where are we going?" Jonathan asked Annie as they got into the car.

She quickly handed him the address. "Lighthouse Bible Baptist Church," she stated with a smile.

"Annie, you want me to take you to an *Englisch* church? What would your *Dat* say?" Jonathan seemed concerned for the deacon's daughter. He knew too well how strict her father was.

"*Ach,* don't worry about me, Jonathan. I can take care of myself," Annie said confidently.

"Whatever you say, Annie," Jonathan said. "Do you think I could stick around for the meeting too?"

"*Jah,* of course." Annie was pleased then suddenly became concerned. She looked at Jonathan's *Englisch* haircut. "Jonathan, you're not thinkin' of becomin' an *Englischer,* are ya?"

"Why not?" he asked flippantly.

"What about you and Susie?" Annie's heart sank.

"She's made it clear that she doesn't want to be with me. She's probably with Matthew Riehl right now," he said sadly. "I don't know how I'm ever going to let her go."

"*Ach,* Jonathan. Susie still loves you. The two of you were meant to be together." Annie attempted to be an encouragement.

"Do ya think so, Annie?" he asked with a flicker of hope in his voice.

"*Jah,* I really do," her response brought a slight smile to his face. "Just pray about it."

The small church building was already packed with people when Annie and Jonathan arrived. Annie looked around for the girl in the picture, and thought she may have spotted her toward the front. "Let's go sit near the front," Annie suggested. She and Jonathan made their way to the third pew from the front. She looked around and noticed that the men and the women sat together. It was quite different from their church where the men and women sat on opposite sides of the room.

"Annie Yoder?" she heard an excited voice call from behind her.

Annie spun around to see the familiar face. "Amanda!" She smiled as she gave her new friend a hug. She turned to Jonathan who had a questioning look on his face. "Amanda Johnson, this is Jonathan Fisher. Jonathan, this is my friend Amanda."

"Nice to meet you, Jonathan," Amanda said.

"*Gut* to meet you, too," he replied somewhat awkwardly.

"Jonathan, Amanda is my *Englisch* pen pal. She and her family are going to be singing tonight," Annie informed him.

"Will you come meet my family?" Amanda asked.

Annie looked at Jonathan to see if he'd mind. "You go ahead," he encouraged. "I'll just hang out here."

Annie and Amanda excitedly made their way over to where the Johnson family sat. Annie thought Amanda's family was very friendly. She was surprised to see that most of the ladies attending the missions conference were dressed modestly in long skirts or dresses, so she didn't feel too out of place. The service appeared to be getting started soon and Amanda informed Annie that she had been asked to play the piano. Annie made her way back to the third row and sat next to Jonathan.

Soon, Annie heard beautiful music coming from the front of the sanctuary and looked up to see her friend behind the piano. Ach, *the piano makes such a lovely sound. I wonder why our Amish church doesn't allow it,* Annie quietly thought to herself. She glanced over at Jonathan and he seemed to be enjoying it as well. *Amanda is so lucky to be able to play an instrument for* der Herr.

As Annie listened to her friend's family sing, her heart filled with joy. The songs were so beautiful and lively. Her favorite was a song called 'What Love'. It was about how a woman in the Bible showed love to Jesus by giving Him the best she had, then the song spoke of the love that God showed to us when He gave the best He had – His son Jesus.

Jonathan was also enthralled by the words of the songs. His favorite was a song called 'In My Father's Eyes'. *God, is it true that in your eyes I have done no wrong? Is it true that to you I am the perfect son, as the song says?* It was very uplifting to Jonathan, because he knew he'd been doing a lot of wrong lately. *I do want to be like the son in my Father's eyes.* He decided he would do all he could to be pleasing to God.

The following message also spoke to Jonathan's heart. *The preacher speaks with such passion and authority. Ach, I wish I brought a Bible so I could follow along,* Jonathan mused.

"As Christians, we should not love the things of the world. Since we belong to Christ, we have a higher calling and need to have a higher standard than the world. Is there somebody here today that's been living a wicked lifestyle and needs to repent?" the preacher asked.

He's talking about me, Jonathan thought.

"Have you ruined relationships with those you love because of selfishness and pride?" Jonathan was certain God was speaking to him through the preacher. "Are you now in the Valley of Decision? One of our young people has written a poem that I'd like to read to you today. Please listen carefully to the words:

The Valley of Decision

The Valley of Decision
What a hard place to be!
The choices made when young
Will shape your destiny

The Valley of Decision
Choosing which life to live
For God or for yourself
To which will you give?

The Valley of Decision
I cry out in frustration
Choices here, choices there
I take in consideration

The Valley of Decision
I go to God in prayer
All my troubles – great and small
The Lord and I both share

The Valley of Decision
I offer to God my prayers
It brings consolation to know
That Someone truly cares

The Valley of Decision
So now what will it be?
I have chosen the ways of God
For He knows what's best for me.

Are you in the Valley of Decision today?" The preacher concluded his message with a prayer.

At the end of the service, Jonathan shot up from his seat and walked down to the altar. He bowed his head and cried silently to the Lord, asking forgiveness for all the wicked things he'd done. He indeed saw that this was his Valley of Decision. Philip King's words of wisdom echoed in his head once again, confirming what the preacher said. *The choices you make now will affect you for the rest of your life.* Jonathan decided then and there it was time he started making some wise choices.

When he finished praying, he felt a hand on his shoulder and noticed a young man beside him. Apparently, he had been praying for him as well. When he lifted his head, the young man introduced himself as Caleb.

Jonathan returned to his seat until the music had stopped and the final prayer was offered. Annie left to go talk to her friend, so Jonathan decided to go find Caleb and thank him. As he came closer to Caleb, he stopped when he noticed a young Amish woman next to him. *Joanna?* Caleb saw Jonathan and strolled up to him, offering his hand.

"Joanna?" Jonathan asked. "What are you doing here?"

"You two know each other?" Caleb asked, eyeing both of them warily. This young man seemed too familiar with Joanna for Caleb's liking. *I hope this isn't that Andrew guy.* He couldn't help the feeling of jealousy, although he knew it was wrong.

"*Jah.*" Joanna laughed. "This is my brother."

Relief flooded Caleb's being and he sent up a prayer of thankfulness.

"So Caleb is the *Englischer* you've been seein'?" Jonathan asked his sister.

"*Ach,* Jonathan. How did ya know?" she asked.

"I live with you, remember?" He smiled.

"Finally, I get to meet someone from your family." Caleb's face brightened. "When can I meet your parents?"

Jonathan peered at Joanna, and Joanna looked at Caleb and sighed. "That might not be such a good idea."

"What? You don't want me to meet your parents?" Caleb asked in disbelief. "I don't understand."

Jonathan spoke up, "Amish folks don't usually take too kindly to *Englischers* coming in to steal their daughters away."

"*Ach,* Jonathan," Joanna chided.

"Is that how your family would perceive me?" Caleb looked to Joanna, who nodded affirmatively. He sighed. "It looks like

I'm going to have to hit my knees more. If it's the Lord's will, He will make a way."

"There is a way," Jonathan informed him. "You could become Amish."

"I could never do that," Caleb said disappointedly.

"Why not?" Jonathan asked, his temper slightly flaring. "You mean you want Joanna to become *Englisch,* but you're not willing to become Amish?"

"No, Jonathan, that's not it." Caleb looked at Joanna. "I couldn't become Amish because I know that's not the Lord's will for me. God's called me to be a missionary."

Annie sat at the piano with Amanda. "Can you teach me to play something?" Annie asked eagerly.

"Sure, what would you like to learn?" Amanda queried.

"How about the song we sang tonight? The slower one from the hymn book."

"Are you talking about 'Our Great Saviour'? Does it go like this?

Jesus, what a friend for sinners. Jesus, lover of my soul'?"

Amanda's beautiful voice filled the air as she sang a little bit of the song for her.

"*Jah,* that's it!" Annie said excitedly.

"That's not the easiest song to start out with when you're just learning, but I guess we can try." She didn't want to discourage her friend. "Do you think you'll be able to come for the rest of the meetings?"

"*Ach*, I don't know. I really want to, but I don't think *Dat* and *Mamm* will let me get away. They don't even know that I'm here right now." She gritted her teeth.

"They don't?" Amanda asked in disbelief.

"If I'd asked them, I'm certain they wouldn't have allowed me to come," Annie stated disappointedly. "You're so lucky, Amanda. You get to hear and sing this beautiful music all the time."

"I have an idea, Annie." Amanda quickly got up from the piano bench and walked to the pew where she had left her purse. She came back and sat down next to Annie and pulled a small box from her bag. "I want you to have this."

"What is it?" Annie wondered.

Amanda opened the box and pulled out a silver rectangular object with square holes on two sides. "It's a harmonica." She put it to her mouth and demonstrated by effortlessly playing 'Our Great Saviour'.

Annie squealed in excitement. "Really, Amanda? I can have this?"

"Yes, it's all yours." Her friend smiled back. "And next time I see you, I want to hear you play something on it. Deal?"

"*Jah;* deal." Annie couldn't hide her humongous smile. "I'm going to try to make it back at least one more time before you leave, Amanda."

"I hope you can. If not, we'll just have to write to each other," Amanda said.

CHAPTER 9
The Rumor

"A talebearer revealeth secrets: but he that is of a faithful spirit concealeth the matter."
Proverbs 11:13

Susie had been in the kitchen helping M*amm* wash dishes when her father called to her. "Susanna, *kumm* outside with me." The tone in her father's voice was distressing.

Susie looked at her mother, who bade her to go. *I wonder what Dat wants.* "*Jah, Dat?*" She swallowed the nervous lump in her throat.

"*Kumm* sit here." Judah patted the chair across from him on the porch, and Susanna sat down. The bishop closed his eyes as though sending up a silent prayer, and took a breath before beginning. "I am concerned. There are rumors going around. It has been said that you have...uh...taken your hair down for a young man. Is this true?" Her father's grave eyes held hers.

Susie started trembling and tears welled up in her eyes. *I can't tell him, he'll be so upset,* she told herself. She sat quietly and did not respond.

"Susanna, I demand an answer from you," the bishop insisted.

"Oh, *Dat!*" Susie cried shamefully.

"Is it true?" he asked in exasperation.

"*Jah,* 'tis." She sobbed.

Judah released bereft sigh and threw his hands up. He rose from his chair and paced the porch, reeling from his daughter's admission. "Do you realize the shame this will cause the family? I am the bishop of this district! How can I get up and speak to the congregation about living righteously when my own daughter is off –"

"*Dat,* please! Jonathan and I didn't do anything wrong," Susie cried.

"So it *was* with Jonathan, huh?" he said shaking his head. "I should have known. I never should have encouraged you and that boy. He's been nothing but trouble from day one. And now after you've already admitted your sin, you expect me to believe that you're both innocent? If I know anything about Jonathan Fisher, it's that things are rarely innocent with him."

Susanna wanted so badly to defend Jonathan, but she was unsure how even *she* felt about him now. He'd been doing so many *dumm* things lately. She thought he cared for her, but now? *What else can I say? It's obvious* Dat *already thinks I'm lying.* She had never heard him use that tone of voice with her. Clearly, she had lost her father's trust.

"I've been a fool to think that you could influence Jonathan for good. It's obvious that he's been influencing you instead," he said to Susie, then looked to the sky. "Dear God, what am I going to do?"

Judah sat back down on the chair and covered his face with his hands, apparently crying.

"I'm sorry, *Dat,*" Susie said through her tears, still trembling.

A moment later, Levi walked up the steps of the porch, stomping his boots, obviously unaware of the exchange taking place. He glanced to his left, before opening the door, and noticed his father and sister sitting on the porch in distress. "*Was iss letz*?" Levi wondered what was wrong.

"Your *schweschder* has brought us shame," Judah stated matter-of-factly. "Certainly you've heard the rumors. Susanna has been behaving inappropriately with Jonathan Fisher...she let her hair down."

"*Dat,* I told you we didn't do any–" Susie pleaded.

"Silence!" her father commanded.

"She's telling the truth, *Daed. All* she did was let her hair down for him; nothing else." Levi now defended his sister.

"How can you be certain of this?" the bishop asked his son. "I've heard otherwise."

"Because I pulled up next to Jonathan's car before they had a chance to...well, you know," Levi said awkwardly. "What you heard was probably just someone's imagination jumping to conclusions. Susanna hasn't seen Jonathan since then; I've made certain of it."

Susanna held her breath, thankful that Levi hadn't been privy to the night Jonathan called her from the window.

"Can it be true?" Judah hoped so.

"*Dat,* Jonathan and I haven't even kissed," Susie said quietly.

"Then I guess *Der Herr* was watching out for you. Surely, it'd been Divine Providence guiding Levi to pull up when he did." Judah sighed in relief, and then turned to look at Susie. "I'm sorry for not trusting you, *Dochder.*"

"'Tis my fault, *Dat.* I never should have let my hair down for him. It was terribly wrong," Susie admitted.

"We all make mistakes," Judah admitted. He'd certainly made his share. "But you need to walk circumspectly where Jonathan is concerned. Sometimes young men tend to want things they shouldn't have until they're married. Do you understand?"

"*Jah, Dat.* But Jonathan and I aren't courting anymore."

Judah caught the sadness in Susanna's voice and patted her hand. "*Der Herr* will guide you and Jonathan. He knows what is best for you. If it is His will, He will pave a path for you and Jonathan. You must trust Him."

Susanna nodded, hoping that God would indeed bring Jonathan back to her. But she knew God's will was best and determined to put her faith in Him.

"*Ach*, what are we going to do about these rumors?" Levi asked.

"Ignore them," Judah stated. "They'll run their course and then everyone will forget about them."

Annie's excitement over meeting her pen pal at church last night had yet to be quelled. *I wish that I could attend every service so I could listen to the beautiful music that they sing.* She knew that wasn't possible, though. Annie felt lucky just to be able to have gone last night. She needed to be sure to thank Jonathan again for taking her. *I have to think of a good reason to tell Dat and Mamm so I can go again. I won't lie to them, though.*

Nevertheless, Annie cherished the harmonica Amanda had given to her. She had to wait until she was certain that there was nobody else around before she could practice with the instrument. It wouldn't do to have somebody overhear her playing. She had attempted practicing the song that Amanda showed her how to play, but it certainly wasn't as easy as Amanda made it look. Still, she had been able to get some of the notes down. Annie decided to go for a walk so she could be alone with her beloved new musical device.

As Annie headed into a wooded area about a mile away from the nearest dwelling, she figured it was safe to take her treasured gift out of its hiding place. She removed the harmonica from her pocket, and admired it once again. She softly blew into the holes searching for the correct notes. *I got it! Maybe I can figure out the next part.* Annie tried several different notes before she found the right ones. She played through the first verse, and messed up only twice. Smiling, Annie played her harmonica over and over, until she decided it was time to head home. She slipped it into her apron pocket, and skipped toward her house.

Upon emerging from the woods, she noticed a courting buggy heading her direction. As the carriage came closer, she noticed the driver as Joshua Hostettler. He glanced up and caught her eye, then quickly pulled over to the side of the lane.

"*Hullo,* Annie," he said with a half-smile. "Can ya go for a ride with me?"

"For a little bit, *jah,*" she agreed.

Joshua stepped down from the buggy to help Annie up. He quickly returned to the driver's seat and set the vehicle in motion, traveling along at a slow pace. "I've been wantin' to ask ya somethin' Annie."

Annie caught a bit of tenseness in his voice and became concerned. "What is it, Joshua?" she wondered.

"Well, you didn't go to the Singin' with me on Sunday." He looked her way and she read the disappointment written on his face.

"*Ach,* didn't Susie give ya my note?" She twisted her hands nervously.

"*Jah*, she did." Joshua took a deep breath. "I went to the Kings' on Sunday to pick somethin' up. I saw you get into Jonathan's car and drive off with him." His lips formed a thin line.

Oh no! Now he thinks that I like Jonathan. What am I going to tell him? Annie was quiet for a moment, pondering what she should say.

"You know, Annie, if you were seein' someone else you could have told me yourself." Joshua continued, "But what I don't understand is why Jonathan Fisher? Don't you know that he's already gotten my sister into enough trouble?" Hurt showed on his handsome face.

Annie's heart sank. She remained quiet, trying to figure out how to answer him. *I have to tell him. I can't let him think that Jonathan and I are sweet on each other.*

"I thought you and Susie were *gut* friends. What kind of friend courts someone else's beau after they've just broken up?"

"Jonathan and I are not courting, Joshua. I needed a ride to Lancaster and I asked him to take me. That's it," she stated, hoping her simple answer would suffice.

"Where did he take you?" Joshua challenged.

"I have a friend who lives far away. She came to Lancaster with her family and asked if I could come and meet her," Annie said, side-stepping the question.

"Oh." Joshua now released a relieved sigh. "So Jonathan's *not* courtin' you?"

"*Ach, nee.*" Annie smiled and shook her head.

"*Gut*. Does that mean I'm still taking you home on Sunday?"

"I hope so." Annie grinned.

"*Wunderbaar.*" Joshua smiled back and placed his hand over hers, staking his claim.

After supper, Jacob Yoder motioned to his daughter. "Annie, let's go into the living room and talk while the others help your *Mamm* redd up." Jacob walked to the living room and sat down on his wooden straight-back chair. Annie sat in a rocking chair nearby.

"What do you want to talk about, *Dat*?" Annie quizzed. She eyed the bookshelf behind her father's chair and wondered whether he'd ever read any of them or not.

"Your friend, Susanna," the deacon stated. His eyes darkened.

"What about Susie?" "Annie began to worry. Had something happened to her best friend?"

"I don't want you to spend time with her anymore," her father said.

"*Ach*, why?" Annie asked, flabbergasted by her father's demands.

"She's been making some unwise choices. I don't want you to be affected by them. And I don't want you to learn her ways."

"But *Dat*, Susie's my best friend," she protested.

"Not anymore," her father stated. "I've made my decision, and that's final."

Annie looked at her father with tears in her eyes, and then ran upstairs to her room.

CHAPTER 10
The Farewell

*"Let everything that hath breath praise the Lord.
Praise ye the Lord." Psalm 150:6*

What is that sound? Annie got up from her bed and went to the window. She peered at the ground below through the glass and saw Jonathan Fisher standing there with small pebbles in his hand. She quickly opened the window. "What is it, Jonathan?" she asked.

"Tonight's the last night of the missions conference. Do you want to go?" he called up quietly.

Annie laughed. "You don't have to whisper, Jonathan. Everyone's gone. *Dat* and *Mamm* went to visit Eli's family. And yes, I'd love to go! I'll be right down." Annie quickly tucked her harmonica into her apron pocket, then took a quick glance at the mirror and pushed a few loose strands of hair behind her ears. She rushed downstairs and decided to write a quick note in case her parents returned.

Annie briskly walked to the crossroad where Jonathan parked his car. She hopped in excitedly and they took off. "I see you brought your *Biewel* this time," Annie commented, looking at the large black book that sat on the console between them.

"*Jah;* I want to follow along when the preacher reads. I brought some paper to take notes, too," Jonathan explained.

"*Ach,* are ya gonna wave it in the air when they sing that song?" she thought about the last time they were in the service and how the people 'waved the answer (the Bible) back to Heaven'.

"I don't know if I'll be comfortable with that. It looked like fun, though. We'll see," Jonathan said, then changed the subject. "Hey Annie, Joshua came and talked to me the other day."

"About what?" She was pretty sure she already knew.

"About you and me." He raised his eyebrows twice in quick succession.

"What did you tell him?" she wondered.

Jonathan tried to think of something good to say. "I told him that I was madly in love with you and that we were planning to leave the Amish and get married." His eyes sparkled.

Annie looked at him with big eyes, her mouth wide open. She knew that Jonathan was mischievous enough to say something like that to Joshua. The only thing she could do was gasp in horror.

Suddenly, Annie heard a chuckle come from behind her. She turned around and saw Joshua sitting there in the back seat with an enormous grin on his face.

Jonathan glanced back at his friend. "Ah, Josh, you should've let me keep her goin' for a while."

"I couldn't help it, I had to laugh!" Joshua said, chuckling again.

"You should have seen the look on her face!" Jonathan exclaimed with a smile.

"You two planned this?" Annie said indignantly. "*Dat* was right; boys are nothin' but trouble."

Jonathan and Joshua smiled at each other and Joshua slapped his friend on the back.

"So Annie, why didn't ya tell me you were goin' to an *Englischer* church?" Joshua asked.

"Well, I thought you might not approve," she said.

"You know, deceit isn't the best way to begin a relationship. Next time, I hope you'll trust me enough to tell me the truth," Joshua said disappointedly.

Annie hung her head. "Sorry Joshua, it's just that you've already been baptized and I thought that if you knew...well. I guess there isn't really a good excuse."

"You're right; there isn't," Joshua stated.

"But you're *here*. I didn't think you'd want to go to an *Englisch* church. You're not in *Rumspringa* anymore." Annie looked at him inquisitively.

"I came because I wanted to be with you," he simply said, then smiled at her with his hazel eyes.

"Ah...you two are so sweet!" Jonathan teased.

Annie and Joshua couldn't help but look at each other and laugh out loud.

"What time did Jonathan say they'd be here?" Caleb asked Joanna as he glanced out the window of his aunt's home.

"By six-fifteen. It's only six right now," she said, glancing at the clock on the wall. "Would ya like a snack?"

"No thanks, babe," Caleb answered without realizing what he'd just said.

"Babe?" Joanna looked at him funny.

"Oh, did I say that out loud? Sorry," Caleb apologized. "For some reason when I'm around you, my thoughts don't want to stay inside my head."

"That's okay, babe," she teased.

"Let's get married," he blurted out.

Joanna raised her eyebrows. "Somethin' else you couldn't keep to yourself?"

"No, I mean it. I want to marry you, Joanna. Will you be my wife?" He wanted so badly to take her hand as she looked into his eyes, but refrained from doing so.

"Yes, I will." Joanna found herself saying. "When?"

"Today would be nice."

"Today?" Joanna asked with eyes wide in disbelief.

"Okay, maybe not today, but soon. Really soon," Caleb requested. "Should I ask your father for your hand?"

"That's not our way."

"You mean it's not the Amish way? That's fine. But shouldn't I at least meet your parents first?"

"It'd probably be better to just wait till afterward."

"After we're married?"

"*Jah*, it'd be best," she confirmed.

"All right, then. I'll talk to the preacher tonight," Caleb said with his face aglow.

Ding dong. The front doorbell rang. Caleb hurried to open the door. "Hello, Jonathan. Oh good, you brought some friends along."

"*Jah*, this is Joshua and Annie," Jonathan introduced.

"Nice to meet you," Caleb said, then looked at his future wife. "You all know Joanna already, right?"

They nodded in agreement. Annie glanced over by the wall and noticed a piano. "*Ach*, a piano." Her eyes lit up.

"Oh yeah, my aunt loves to play. She gives lessons too. Taught me some. I could play something, if you'd like," Caleb offered. "Don't laugh, though," he teased.

"*Jah*, I'd like to hear something." Annie perked up, and then looked to Joshua who seemed a bit uncomfortable.

Caleb sat at the piano and began gently stroking the keys with his fingers. He began with his favorite song, 'Amazing

Grace'. Annie closed her eyes and breathed the music in. Caleb didn't miss a note.

"*Ach,* that was beautiful," Annie exclaimed. "You're so lucky to be able to play like that."

"Well, I don't know how much luck has to do with it. I like to call it a blessing from the Lord," Caleb said. "And, of course, I've been practicing for years."

"*Jah,* music is definitely a blessing," Annie agreed.

Joshua noticed how Annie's face lit up when talking about the music, and he began to worry. If her heart turned to the things of the world, she'd become *Englisch* instead of joining the church. "That's not our way, Annie," he quietly reminded her.

"*Jah,* I know," she spoke in a gentle whisper.

"Joshua, come meet my friend Amanda," Annie said excitedly, as they made their way into the church. He took her hand and they walked down toward the front of the sanctuary.

"Annie, you made it back!" her jovial red-headed friend exclaimed, then gave her a hug. "I was hoping to see you again before we leave tomorrow."

"Amanda, I'd like you to meet Joshua," Annie said with a smile.

Amanda held out her hand. "Nice to meet you, Joshua."

Joshua gripped Annie's hand a little tighter and shook Amanda's with his free hand. "*Gut* to meet ya." He smiled.

Amanda turned to Annie. "So, have you been practicing?"

Annie nodded silently and Joshua gave her a questioning look.

"I'd like hear it. Will you play for me?" Amanda asked excitedly.

"*Jah*," she replied uneasily, knowing what Joshua might think. Annie nervously glanced at Joshua and then took the harmonica from her apron. She brought it to her lips and began playing 'Our Great Saviour'. She played the first verse and chorus, only missing one note.

"That was good. You'll have the whole song down in no time." Amanda smiled. "Come over to the piano and I'll play along with you."

Annie looked over at Joshua with pleading eyes and he gave her the okay. "You two go. I'll just take a seat next to Jonathan," he said, gesturing to the pew beside them.

Annie knew Joshua was disappointed in her, but to his credit, he said nothing and allowed her to go. She tried not to think about it too much and joined her friend at the piano. Amanda began playing first, and then nodded to Annie when to start. Annie thought the two instruments complimented each other well.

Amanda observed that her friend wasn't as excited as she had been earlier. "What's wrong, Annie?"

"Joshua's not too happy with me right now," Annie stated sadly.

"Is he your boyfriend?" Amanda asked.

Annie cheeks reddened. "We're courtin', *jah*," she said. "Our people don't allow musical instruments. They think they're worldly."

"Really?" Amanda seemed slightly shocked. "Have you ever read Psalm 150?"

"*Ach,* I'm not sure," Annie said.

"You should read it. It's about praising the Lord with different musical instruments," Amanda asserted.

Annie looked over at Joshua. "Okay, I will. I better go sit down now before the meeting begins." She made her way back over to where Joshua and Jonathan were and sat down next to Joshua.

"Hey, I kind of like this seating arrangement the *Englischers* have." Joshua smiled at Annie and took her hand, intertwining their fingers. "I get to sit next to my girl." Annie was relieved that Joshua didn't chide her about the music.

When the music began playing, Annie noticed that Amanda wasn't at the piano anymore but sat with her family. She glanced at Joshua when they began singing the hymns and noticed that he seemed to be enjoying himself a little more now. Annie breathed a silent prayer of thanks and sang with all her heart.

The Johnson family sang some different songs than they had on Sunday and Annie enjoyed every one of them. Again, the preaching was dynamic and the Word of God spoke to her heart. Tonight's message was specifically on missions and winning the lost to Christ. "The apathy of most Christians nowadays is appalling. Our apostolic forefathers shared the Gospel at all costs, even giving of their lives for it, and we're afraid to hand somebody a simple gospel tract. There are countless missionaries and Christians around the world who are still facing that persecution today. The least we should be doing is diligently praying for our brothers and sisters in Christ and giving so the Lord's work can continue unhindered." The preacher continued, "We should be doing all we can to pull others from the flames of Hell..."

On the drive home, lively conversation filled the car as each one shared what they received from the message. Annie was happy to see that God had touched Joshua's heart as well. While she was saddened to part ways with Amanda, she took comfort in knowing that they would still be writing to each other.

"The harvest truly is great, but the labourers are few...go ye into all the world and preach the gospel..." The words rang in Joanna's ears and she smiled. *That's exactly what Caleb and I will be doing after we're married!* The confirmation gave her a sudden burst of courage to face her parents.

CHAPTER 11

Disappointment

"Thine own friend...forsake not..." Proverbs 27:10a

CA nnie found containing her enthusiasm difficult when she heard the news from Joanna. Mrs. Scott would need a new housekeeper soon and Joanna had recommended her to take the job. Now all she had to do was convince *Mamm* and *Dat* to let her. *Maybe she'll teach me how to play the piano,* Annie thought with hope. *I'll ask Dat after church on Sunday,* she decided.

"Here it is," Laura Scott said as she took out a large dusty white box from the attic. She smiled at Joanna, "I'm pretty sure this is about your size." She wiped the box down with a wet rag, and then gently opened it to reveal a gorgeous beaded satin wedding gown.

"*Ach,* it's absolutely beautiful!" Joanna said in amazement.

"I know this is fancy compared to what you're used to, but for the *Englisch* this is a pretty simple gown," Laura informed her. "Would you like to try it on?"

"That would be wonderful-*gut*!" Joanna smiled.

"Do you think your family will come to the wedding?"

"Probably not. That's not the Amish way. Maybe my brother Jonathan will. He's still in *Rumspringa*," Joanna said. "He hasn't been baptized into the church yet."

"Oh," Mrs. Scott said with disappointment in her voice. "I bet that groom of yours is trying on his tuxedo right about now."

"Is that why Caleb went into Lancaster with your husband?"

"Well, that and something else that I can't mention." Laura smiled, knowing he had gone to pick out rings.

"This is so exciting. I can't wait till Saturday," Joanna smiled as she slipped into the gown. She glanced into the mirror and gasped. Tears automatically sprang to her eyes. She fingered the beads on the bodice of the gown.

"You are going to make one beautiful bride. Have you thought about how you'd like to do your hair?" Mrs. Scott queried.

"*Nee*. I don't really know what I can do with it," she placed a hand over her brown tresses.

"Well, would you like to wear it up or down?"

"I don't want Caleb to see it down just yet," she said, a pink tinge staining her cheeks. She thought of their wedding night when she would unbind her hair and reveal her glory to her husband. *Ach*, it was coming so soon.

"We could take a few strands down on the sides and curl them. I think that would look nice," Laura offered.

"*Jah*, okay," Joanna agreed.

Laura grasped Joanna's hand and smiled. "Joanna, I want you to know that I'm so thankful Caleb found you. You two will do great things for the Lord, I just know it. And I can assure you that Caleb will be a good husband to you. He's always been kind and caring."

Susie quietly stepped up the porch steps and knocked on the back door of the Yoders' home. She wondered why it had been so long since she'd seen Annie. Annie was in the kitchen, placing the last batch of cookies into the oven. She quickly came to open the door.

"Let's go for a walk, *jah*?" Annie offered, then called back to her mother who was in her room sewing, "*Mamm*, I'll be right back."

"I haven't seen ya in a while, Annie; where have ya been?" her friend wondered.

"*Ach*, Susie. *Dat* doesn't want us to be friends anymore. You know, because of the rumors," Annie said sadly.

Susanna's heart sank. "We can't be friends anymore?" she said as tears formed in her eyes.

"I'm sorry, Susie. I've been wanting to come by and see you so badly. I know you must be needin' someone to talk to, not bein' able to see Jonathan and all."

"*Ach*, Jonathan. How my heart aches for him. What will I do, Annie? Now I've lost my beau and my best friend," she said sadly.

"I guess all we can do is pray," Annie offered. "Have ya seen Maryanna at all lately?"

Susanna thought of her *Englisch* twin. "*Nee*, she and her *Englisch mamm* have been busy with softball games and what not. Even though she lives closer, I still don't get to see her too often." She frowned.

Annie glanced up and saw her father's buggy nearing their lane. "I have to go now, Susie. I'll see ya at Meeting and the hymn sing, *jah?*"

"*Jah*," Susanna agreed, her heart slightly encouraged by that fact.

Annie walked back to the house, saddened for her friend. She couldn't imagine how Susie must be feeling. She had her music and Joshua; maybe even a new job soon. It seemed poor Susanna had nothing.

CHAPTER 12
Proposal

"Teach me to do thy will; for thou art my God..."
Psalm 143:10a

The Fisher family sat in the living room for evening devotions. Joanna expected her father to bring up the subject of baptism sometime soon because he had been hinting at it lately. She silently prayed that God would give her the right words to say to her parents.

"We all know that joining the church is one of the most important decisions a person can make," Gideon began. "It doesn't make sense to put off that decision for no good reason. Joanna, you're twenty years old now and your mother and I are beginning to get concerned. We both made the vow while we were still in our teens and yet you wait."

Joanna looked to her brother Jonathan, who raised his eyebrows. "Well, you might as well tell them," he said to his sister.

"Tell us what?" Joanna's mother Esther asked, looking from Jonathan to Joanna.

"*Mamm, Dat,* I'm not going to remain Amish. I'm marrying an *Englischer,*" Joanna said quietly, realizing she was confirming her parents' greatest fear.

"*Ach,* no. This can't be!" Esther cried.

Gideon was silent, but hung his head in clear disappointment.

"You guys will like Caleb, he's a really nice guy," Jonathan offered.

"*Dat,* please say something." Joanna's lip trembled at the request.

"You will be missed, *dochder,*" he simply said. The somber mood hung over them like a darkened cloud before a summer storm.

Jonathan piped up, "Well, if it makes you feel any better, I'm selling my car and have decided to join the church!" he announced with a smile.

Gideon looked up and gave a slight chuckle. "Jonathan, you never cease to amaze me." This brought a bout of bittersweet laughter to the entire Fisher family as they both mourned and rejoiced simultaneously.

Joanna couldn't be sure, but did she see a flashlight shining on her window? She went to the window and saw Caleb standing below. She smiled down at him and quickly went out to meet him.

She giggled as she walked up to him. "What are you doing?"

"Well, isn't this how an Amish man would propose to his *aldi*?" He smiled.

"You're so sweet, Caleb. Do you want to go inside? I can make us a snack and some coffee," she offered.

"But isn't your family asleep?" he wondered.

"*Jah*, but it's the Amish way. Or we can sit on the porch swing, if you'd rather do that."

"Nah, it's a little cold out. We can go inside," he said.

Joanna quickly put on some coffee and took out some sticky buns. "Let's sit in the living room where it's warmer." She brought two small dessert plates and placed them on the small coffee table her brother had made.

As they sat on the couch, Caleb gazed lovingly into her innocent blue eyes. He stood up for a moment, then placed a knee on the floor in front of her and took her hand in his for the first time. He pulled a small box from his pocket and opened it to reveal a sparkling diamond ring. "I know that I've already asked you before, but I wanted to do it the right way." He sighed and took a deep breath, looking intently into her eyes. "Joanna Fisher, I love you. I can't imagine not spending the rest of my life with you. Will you marry me?"

"*Jah*, Caleb. I'll marry you...tomorrow." She smiled through her tears, as he slipped the ring onto her finger.

CHAPTER 13
The Ceremony

"Hatred stirreth up strifes: but love covereth all sins." Proverbs 10:12

*J*onathan hopped on his horse and rode bareback over to the Hostettler residence. He left the horse near the hitching post and headed to the barn in search of Levi. Levi had been cleaning out some stalls when Jonathan grabbed a pitch fork and began working alongside him. They both worked silently for a few minutes before Levi turned to him. "Did you need something, Jonathan? Or did ya just come to work with me all day?"

A soft answer turneth away wrath. The Bible verse popped into his head. He began as calmly and as humbly as he could, "Levi, I came to apologize."

"Apologize?" Levi's eyebrows shot up.

"*Jah*, for what happened with Susie and...You were right," Jonathan admitted.

"About what?" he asked skeptically.

"Well, I had no business asking Susie to take her hair down. I hope you believe me when I say that I didn't intend to take advantage of her. I know you and Chloe have been courtin' for a while; you must know how it is." Jonathan thought relating to Susanna's brother, man to man, might help his plight.

"I know what it is to want something, but deny yourself the pleasure, yes. You asking Susie to take her hair down is a step, and in my opinion, a *big* step in the wrong direction. And that's the problem. Nobody *intends* for those things to happen, but they do," Levi explained. "It's the natural course of things. We, as men, have a job to protect those we love. Not to expose them and set them up for shame and ridicule, which is exactly what you've done with my *schweschder*."

Jonathan grimaced at hearing the truth of what his inappropriate behavior had caused for his beloved Susie. "That's why I've decided to change my ways. I'm selling my car and I intend on being baptized into the church this fall. I talked to your *daed* about it last night," he shared.

Jonathan's sober demeanor helped Levi determine the sincerity of his words. He then held out his hand to shake Jonathan's. "I'm glad to hear it. Apology accepted." Levi smiled.

"*Denki,* Levi." Jonathan turned to go back to his horse.

"By the way, Jonathan; Susanna's in the house if you'd like say hello," Levi stated.

"*Denki,* Levi." Jonathan left his horse at the hitching post and eagerly made his way to the house whispering a prayer of thanksgiving.

"Levi thought you might be inside," Jonathan said to Susie while she unpinned the laundry from the clothes line.

"Levi told you where I was?"

"*Jah,* I had a talk with him."

"Oh."

"Look Susie, the reason I came by was to let you know that I'm joining the church this fall," Jonathan said.

"*Ach,* really?" Pleasure emanated from Susanna's words. "Well, I hope that's not the *only* reason you came by."

"If you'll have me back, Susie...I'm awful sorry for the pain I've caused ya." Jonathan's sorrowful eyes met hers.

"It wouldn't be so bad if it wasn't for that snippy Sadie Lapp!" Susanna said angrily.

"Susie, don't be bitter at Sadie. I know she's not the easiest person to get along with. But I've heard that hurtful people are usually hurting people. Maybe there's a reason she acts the way she does. She needs our prayers. Besides, it's *my* fault that all of this has happened."

"You didn't spread rumors all over Paradise," Susanna insisted.

"No, but if it weren't for my foolishness, there wouldn't be any rumors to spread. I was wrong," he said sadly. "Please forgive Sadie...and me, too."

She never could resist Jonathan's gorgeous blue eyes. "All right, I will," Susanna agreed.

"Do you think your *vatter* will let you go somewhere with me today?"

"Where?" Susie wondered.

"Joanna's gettin' married today." Jonathan smiled.

"To the *Englischer*?" Surprise brightened Susanna's face.

"*Jah*. Do you think Josh can go, too?" Jonathan knew that Joanna would appreciate the extra guests.

"Well, *Dat's* a lot more likely to let me go with you if Joshua comes, too. Maybe I'll have Joshua ask."

"Okay, can ya meet me at the crossroad near the Yoders' place at one o'clock?" Jonathan asked.

"I'll try my best," Susie said, heading back into the house with a spring in her step and a song in her heart.

"I can't believe your *mamm* let ya come, Annie," Susanna said to her best friend.

"Well, I already finished my chores and *Daed* won't be back home till late tonight because he went to an auction," Annie said, excited to be with her friends.

"I'm glad she let ya come." Joshua turned around in the front seat to wink at Annie.

Susie gasped, and then whispered into Annie's ear. "Is my brother sweet on you?"

Annie smiled at Susanna and nodded.

"Are ya courtin'?" she whispered again.

Annie held her finger to her lips to signal a secret, and then the two girls burst into giggles.

"What are you two laughin' about?" Jonathan asked from the driver's seat.

"Aw, nothin'," Susie answered back.

"You know, Joshua. It seems like these girls are trying to hide something from us," Jonathan said. "What do you think we should do to make them tell what is?" he added, purposely swerving the car back and forth.

"*Ach,* Jonathan Fisher!" Susie exclaimed, slightly exasperated. "If you don't stop that right now–"

"Just kidding, just kidding." Jonathan raised his hands in surrender, quickly placing both hands on the wheel and setting the vehicle to rights. But nobody missed the sparkle of mischief in his eyes.

Laura Scott sat at the piano on the platform of the sanctuary. The notes to 'Here Comes the Bride' drifted through the nearly vacant building as Joanna seemingly floated down the aisle. Caleb stood at the front of the altar dressed in a sharp black tuxedo. He lifted his eyes to behold his bride and was caught breathless at the sight of her in her pure white wedding gown.

Caleb's parents and siblings had flown in from California the previous evening, and now sat on the front row. Caleb's family seemed to adore Joanna as much as he did and fully-approved of his wise choice for a life mate.

Annie and Susanna stood to the left of Joanna as her bridal attendants, and Jonathan and Joshua stood to Caleb's right. Annie's eyes drifted to Joshua who smiled warmly and winked. *Joanna's so lucky! I can't wait till my wedding day.* Annie smiled to herself. *I wonder if I will marry Joshua.* She stole another glance at him, and then attempted to focus her attention on the ceremony.

"Dearly beloved, we are gathered here today to join in holy matrimony Caleb Scott and Joanna Fisher. Marriage is an institution created by God and is not to be entered into lightly..." the preacher continued on.

"Joanna, Caleb has asked to sing a special song for you," the preacher said, then nodded to Caleb. Caleb went and sat at the piano. Joanna seemed surprised at this and Annie and Susie glanced at each other and smiled. This *Englisch* wedding was certainly different than any ceremony they'd ever seen. Annie listened as Caleb's fingers swept over the keys, once again falling in love with the musical instrument.

Caleb sang to the melody of the Bruce Frye song, 'I Do'. *"Do I believe in miracles? I do. The Lord has blessed my life with you. By His grace we've both been saved. This is a union God has made. Do I believe in miracles? I do.*

"Do I love you with all my heart? I do. I never want to be apart from you. And on this day I promise to be faithful and true. Do I love you with all my heart? I do..."

Joanna couldn't help it as tears of joy flowed from her eyes. The beautiful words promised by her beloved groom seemed too good to be true. She felt like most blessed woman that ever lived and she knew she'd cherish this day as long as God gave her breath.

After their vows had been said and the rings were exchanged, the preacher pronounced the couple man and wife. Caleb joyfully took his beautiful bride into his arms and gave her a kiss so sweet neither of them would ever forget.

After the ceremony was complete, they all went to the Scotts' house for a meal. Caleb had announced that he made reservations for their wedding night at a hotel on the beach in Delaware. Joanna and Caleb left happily, and after helping the Scotts clean up, the attendants headed home as well.

"*Ach,* that was so beautiful!" Susie exclaimed on the way home.

"Joanna's so lucky!" Annie said dreamily.

"Looks like you got your work cut for you." Jonathan slapped Joshua's back and laughed.

Joshua ignored the comment. "Hey, I didn't know Caleb could sing."

"Apparently, neither did Joanna." Jonathan chuckled.

"Well, I hope that the man I marry is that thoughtful and romantic," Annie said.

"Like I said, Josh; you got your work cut out for you," Jonathan teased, causing his friend's face to flush.

"Jonathan Fisher, quit teasing my brother," Susie insisted.

"Oh yeah, sometimes I forget that Josh is your brother," Jonathan said, and then grinned. "Hey, if you two get married then we'll all be related."

"Jonathan!" Susanna raised her voice a bit. "First of all, *we're* not even married –"

"Yet," he interrupted.

Susie threw her hands up. "Oh, it's pointless to argue with you."

Jonathan smiled wryly. "I'm glad that you've figured that out already. I can tell our marriage is gonna go along just fine," he teased.

Susanna turned to Annie. "Tell me again why I put up with him."

Annie smiled. "Because you love him?"

"Hey, what's not to love?" Jonathan gazed at Susie in his rear-view mirror and winked. Things were looking up for sure and for certain.

CHAPTER 14
The Decision

"Behold, to obey is better than sacrifice..."
1 Samuel 15:22b

"Annie, we need to talk," Joshua said, his tone serious, as he drove her home from the Singing on Sunday. *Speak the truth in love,* a still small voice reminded him.

"*Jah,* what is it, Joshua?" She wondered.

"About the music."

"Oh," she said disappointedly. She had been secretly hoping this discussion would never come, but she knew it was inevitable. "What about it?"

"I think you already know."

She sat quietly as she contemplated the situation.

"You know the longer you hold onto it, the more difficult it will be to give up," he gently nudged.

"*Jah,* I suppose your right," she agreed quietly.

Joshua thought for a moment. "Do you remember the poem that was read at the church during the first night of the missions conference? The Valley of Decision."

"How do you know about that poem? You didn't go that night," she said.

"No, I didn't; but Jonathan got a copy of the poem and made one for me too," he informed Annie, pulling a piece of paper from his pocket.

"*Jah;* 'twas a *gut* poem."

"Here." Joshua handed a folded piece of paper to Annie. "Will ya think on the words, Annie?" His eyes were pleading.

"*Jah,* I will. But I just want to do *Gott's ville* for my life," she stated self-righteously.

"Do you really, Annie?"

"*Ach,* of course," she said adamantly, frowning at Joshua.

"Well it ain't God's will for you to be playin' that music," he declared.

"How can you say such things, Joshua?"

"Ephesians 6:1 'Children, obey your parents in the Lord: for this is right.' Colossians 3:20 'Children, obey your parents in all things: for this is well pleasing unto the Lord.' " He rattled off the Bible verses, then gently said, "Annie, does your *dat* and *mamm* know about your music? Have they approved it? Would they approve of it?"

"*Nee,*" she said sadly.

"Well, then I would say that *Gott's ville* is clear, ain't so?"

Annie took a deep breath. "*Jah.*"

"I'm not saying it because I don't want ya to be happy, Annie. I'm sayin' it 'cause I don't want ya gettin' hurt," he said
kindly. He took her hand in his and gazed into her eyes, "And I
don't want to lose you to the world. Let's be pleasing to the Lord
together, *jah?*"

Annie smiled at her beau. *"Jah."*

Joanna had never been more nervous to enter her folks' home,
as she was now. With her hand in Caleb's, she took a deep breath
and walked from Caleb's car toward her childhood home. This
had been the place where she was born, and if someone would
have told her just a year ago that she'd marry an *Englischer*
and leave her beloved Amish district, she would have thought
them *ferhoodled.* But *Der Herr* had a way of stirring up the
pot and she took comfort in knowing she was following God's
plan for her life. But, oh how she'd miss her friends and family
in Paradise.

"*Dat, Mamm, das ist mein Mann*, Caleb," Joanna announced as they entered the Fishers' home.

Caleb held out his hand to Joanna's father. "Glad to meet
you, Sir."

"*Gut* to meet ya, *Sohn*," Gideon said as he embraced his new
son-in-law.

Tears formed in Joanna's eyes; she couldn't have hoped
for a better response from her father. His acceptance of Ca-

leb proved to her that God's hand was indeed upon their marriage. She'd been praying for her family to accept Caleb, but she never dreamed it would happen so quickly. She knew many Plain families that wouldn't even allow their loved ones into the house after they left the Amish faith. Fortunately, Joanna had never been baptized into the church, so she wouldn't be shunned.

They all sat around the table talking for nearly an hour. Caleb and Joanna shared their plans of going into the mission field in Central America. Esther and Gideon seemed pleased, and Gideon nodded toward his wife. She arose from her seat and walked to the bedroom then returned with a small rectangular piece of paper in her hand. She handed the check to Gideon, who in turn, gave it to his son-in-law.

"Ten thousand dollars!" Caleb almost fell out of the chair when he read the numbers. "I'm sorry, Sir, but we can't accept this." He handed the check back.

Gideon held up his hands. "Keep it. It is Joanna's dowry." He refused to take the check back.

Caleb looked at his wife. "Praise the Lord! This is great, Joanna. We won't even need to go on deputation."

"Now, you know they're expecting some *grossbopplin* out of that!" Jonathan teased.

"Yes, sir. Grandbabies, coming right up," Caleb answered smiling, putting an arm around his wife. Caleb then became more serious. "Thank you. Thank you, both," he said to his new in-laws with all of the sincerity he could muster.

"*Gern gschehne, sohn*," Gideon answered. "Make sure you come visit."

"We will, for sure and for certain," Caleb promised with a smile.

"*Dat.*" Annie slowly approached her father. "I want to talk to you about something."

"*Jah, Dochder*?" Jacob Yoder queried.

"I have a confession to make. I have been living in disobedience." She sighed. *I hope I don't get the rod.*

"How's that?" her father asked.

"Well, I went to an *Englischer* church last week to meet my pen pal. I really liked the music they sang and played, so she gave me her harmonica so I could practice some songs. I wanted to tell you because God's been convicting me about it. I'm going to send her the harmonica back and tell her that I'm not going to play music anymore," she informed him.

"I'm disappointed in you, Annie," he said sadly.

She hung her head shamefully.

"But I'm also proud of you for coming to tell me about it yourself," her father added.

"*Dat,* I've made a decision. A decision to do what is right and follow *Gott's ville* wherever it leads me," Annie said happily.

Annie Yoder sat on the back porch swing as she read her latest letter from her *Englisch* pen pal.

Dear Annie,

I had such a great time at the missions conference in Lancaster. I'm so glad God gave us an opportunity to meet each other; it will be something I'll never forget.

Don't feel bad about sending back the harmonica and my picture. I wouldn't want you to violate your conscience, especially because of me. You know, I've learned something from you, Annie. You were willing to give up something you love for the sake of doing what's right and I admire you for that. I hope that if I ever have to make the choice that I will follow in my friend's footsteps and do what is right. Remember though, that you will always have music in your heart and that's what matters most to God.

Your Friend,

Amanda

P.S. There's no happier place for God's children than in His will! I hope you'll always remember that.

The End

A SPECIAL THANK YOU

The authors would like to thank Bruce Frye for granting
permission to use his song "I Do". For more
information about his wonderful music,
please see www.brucefrye.org.

We'd also like to thank the Billings family.
"Valley of Decision" poem written and provided
by Emily Spredemann.

Photo of '68 Camaro courtesy of Rich Niewiroski, Jr.

Amish Girls Series - Book 6

Abigail's Triumph

J.E.B. Spredemann

Abigail's Triumph

J.E.B. Spredemann

Amish Girls Series - Book 6

To the Father of the fatherless

"A father to the fatherless...is God in his holy habitation."

CHARACTERS IN ABIGAIL'S TRIUMPH

The Lapp family

Abigail – protagonist, youngest daughter of the Lapp family

Reuben – Abigail's father

Maggie – Abigail's mother

Sadie – Abigail's oldest sister

Andrew – Abigail's oldest brother

Zachariah – Abigail's youngest brother

Caleb, David, and Deborah – Abigail's other siblings

The Fisher family

Gideon – father

Esther – mother

Isaac & Rachel – oldest son & wife

Grace & Adam – oldest daughter & husband

Joanna (Scott) & Caleb – protagonist of Joanna's Struggle, youngest daughter & husband

Jonathan – youngest son

The King Family

Philip – father

Naomi – mother

Katie – daughter
P.J. – son

The Yoder Family

Jacob – deacon, father
Eli & Danika (King) – son & wife, protagonist of Danika's Journey
Annie – daughter, Joshua Hostettler's aldi
Sarah Anne – Eli & Danika's daughter

The Hostettler Family

Judah – father, bishop of Paradise
Nathan – oldest son
Levi & Chloe (Esh) – son & wife, protagonist of Chloe's Revelation
Joshua – son, Annie Yoder's beau
Susanna – protagonist of Susanna's Surprise, Jonathan Fisher's betrothed
Maryanna – Susanna's twin

Others

Daniel Miller – Abigail's best friend
Matthew Riehl – Maryanna's beau
Brandon Love – police officer

CHAPTER 1
Home

"Fear came upon me, and trembling, which made all my bones to shake." Job 4:14

Abigail Lapp's heart pounded as she raced home as quickly as her hundred-pound frame could carry her. She knew she shouldn't have taken an extra five minutes to speak with Daniel Miller, but she felt she should at least explain to him why she couldn't meet him today. Her chores must be done.

She dreaded her fate as she neared the bend in the dirt road that led to her family's small secluded dwelling, and cringed at the sight of her father's buggy near the barn. Was *Dat* home early today? Oh, she hoped it wasn't so.

"Abigail, your *vatter* is waiting for you in the barn," *Mamm* stated without lifting her sad eyes, as Abby entered the house to deposit her lunch pail. Abigail gulped hard and nodded silently to her mother.

With haste Abigail changed into her chorin' dress and flew out the door. She figured just maybe her punishment might be less severe if she got to the barn quickly. Her hands trembled as she stepped through the creaking door of the old barn. Her eyes widened when she spotted her father sitting on a log holding a leather strap in his rough calloused hands. The fury in his eyes caused Abigail to quake with fear.

"I ordered you to be home for chores as soon as school got out! The other *kinner* arrived five minutes ago. You're late!" Her father rose from the log and stumbled over to where Abigail stood, glaring down at her with his stern dark eyes. She could plainly see that he'd returned home intoxicated – again. "You know what to do," he mumbled.

Without a word, Abby squeezed her eyelids shut and gripped the handle of the barn door with all her might, silently pleading to God for mercy. *Crack!* One, two, three, four, five... the blows from the leather strap lashed against her backside over and over again until Abigail became breathless and lost count. She reeled from the pain as tears flowed from her innocent blue eyes. She tried to focus on Jesus and the suffering he'd gone through before he went to the cross, surely his pain was worse than this. *I can get through this,* she told herself. Finally, the beating was over – for now.

"Now get your work done!" her father howled, as he stomped out the door and ambled into the field.

She wearily picked herself off the floor and dusted the pieces of hay from the front of her brown cape dress. Every movement reminded her of the thrashing she'd just received. With shaking hands and an aching back she quickly took the pitchfork from its hook on the wall and began to muck out the horses' stalls. *Dear Gott, please help me. Take me away from here, away from him...*

"Tell me, Abby. How long have we been friends for?" Daniel asked before taking the last bite of his turkey sandwich.

"Since my first day of school. Six years ago." She smiled, remembering how she'd gotten a strand of her unruly hair stuck in the swing chain and he patiently helped her remove it – without pulling out all her hair.

"So, why won't you tell me what's wrong? You've looked downhearted all day and I want to know why," he insisted.

"I told you, Dan. I don't want to talk about it." She sniffled in an attempt to conceal the tears that threatened to fall from her lashes.

Daniel placed his arm around her back and she let out a suppressed groan. His eyes widened with shock. "Abby, are you hurt?" her friend asked with compassion in his eyes.

Sucking in a deep breath, she abruptly stood up from the steps and started toward the schoolhouse door. Daniel quickly followed after her. "Please let me help you, Abigail."

"I'll be fine, Dan. Thank you for your concern. We have school now," she declared as the school bell banged out its mournful tune.

"All right, if you insist. Then I'll see you at meeting on Sunday?"

"*Jah.* I should be there." While school provided an escape from the turmoil at home, Sundays were Abigail's favorite day of the week. With the men and the women sitting separately during the meeting, she would have as little contact with her father as possible. She felt safe across the room in the presence of other people.

As Susanna Hostettler rang the bell for her scholars to return from their lunch break, she couldn't help but overhear the conversation between Abigail Lapp and Daniel Miller. She had once suspected trouble at the Lapp home and had prayed for their family on occasion. But the way Abigail behaved today sent eerie chills up her spine. Something wasn't right. Susie decided it would be best to have a conversation with her father about the matter.

When school let out, she heard the familiar sound of Jonathan Fisher's buggy approaching. It hadn't been too long since *they'd* attended the one-room schoolhouse where Susanna now taught.

Susie smiled at the pleasant childhood memories. Oh, how Jonathan used to get on her nerves! But things were different now. Somehow Jonathan had outgrown his foolishness – well, *most* of it anyway. Just last week, he asked for her hand in marriage and she happily accepted. They would be husband and wife before the year ended and she was thrilled by the prospect of building a life with her betrothed.

"Ready to go?" Jonathan called from the front door of the schoolhouse.

"*Jah*, just about." Her eyes meandered upward as she gathered the students' papers from her desk. She again realized how irresistible Jonathan's piercing blue eyes were as he held her gaze. "What?" She smiled, wondering why he didn't move his eyes away.

"Nothin'." He grinned. "Just thinking about how I can't wait to take you home on our wedding night." His eyes sparkled.

Susie's cheeks flushed profusely and she gasped. "Jonathan Fisher! What would your *dat* say if he heard you talking like that?"

"Well, I think he'd probably take *my* side on this one," he teased. "I'm sure he probably felt the same way before he and *Mamm* married."

"I think you best be keeping your thoughts and feelings to yourself. We still have another month, you know," she reminded him.

"Oh, I know. I've been counting the days; thirty-six to be exact." He moved toward the front of the room and slipped his arms around her. He bent his head down to steal a kiss.

She cleared her throat, removed his arms from her waist, and quickly stepped away. "Don't start this again. You know I won't kiss you until we're married, so you'll just have to wait."

"Maybe...but I can still have fun trying." One side of his mouth tipped up, indicative of the mischievous boy she'd always known as a girl.

"I'm ready to go now." She walked passed him toward the buggy and he caught her apron straps from the back. Exasperated, she turned her head around and eyed him in frustration. "Should I have Joshua pick me up from now until the wedding?"

Jonathan frowned. "You mean you'd rather ride with your *bruder* than me?"

"If that's what it takes for you to control yourself, then yes."

"Okay, you win." He let go of her apron straps and gestured toward the buggy. Susie took the lead and Jonathan followed close behind.

"My lady," he said as he gallantly offered a hand to help her into the buggy.

"And I'll thank you for being a gentleman." Susanna giggled at their use of *Englischer* words as she took his hand and allowed his unnecessary assistance into the carriage.

CHAPTER 2
Rage

"Wrath is cruel, and anger is outrageous..."
Proverbs 27:4a

$\mathcal{B}$ ishop Judah Hostettler's eyes held a twinkle as he stood up to read the announcements at the close of the Sunday-Go-To-Meeting. He smiled at Gideon Fisher, his long-time friend and confidant, as he announced their *kinner's* upcoming wedding. This was something that both fathers had looked forward to for years now, unbeknownst to Jonathan and Susie.

After the announcement was made Jonathan leaped up and hollered, "Woo-hoo!" before he trotted out the door to see his beloved Susanna. The congregation, along with the bishop, couldn't help but burst into laughter at Jonathan's unorthodox behavior. Judah was certain sure those two would have an interesting marriage and he looked forward to the *kinskinner* they would no doubt produce.

As excited as the bishop was about the announcement though, he could not keep his mind off of what Susanna had told him regarding the Lapp family. Tomorrow he would have to make a trip out to the Lapp place and confront Reuben Lapp – the idea of which he did not relish. He asked his wife Lydia to speak with Reuben's wife, Maggie, after the service today. Hopefully he could gain some insight into the goings on at the Lapp residence.

"Hey, Abby, I was hoping to get a chance to talk to you today," her friend Daniel said as she sat down to eat. He placed one of his long legs over the bench and straddled it next to her.

Abigail nervously glanced over at her father who was talking to some of the other men. He wouldn't take kindly to her talking to a *buwe*, friend or otherwise. She was relieved to see that he had his back turned to her. "*Jah?*"

"How are you feeling? I've been concerned."

"*Denki* for your concern, but I'm fine," she assured him.

"You're sure? Because if there's anything you need to talk about..." His voice trailed off and he placed a caring hand on her forearm, eyes beckoning her to share her burden.

Abigail really wished she could talk to someone, but she was too ashamed. "Well –"

"Abigail!" her father called as he crossed over the grass. "Let's go. Now!"

Abigail looked down and noticed Daniel's hand still on her arm and quickly jumped up. "I-I have to go," she said in an unsteady voice.

Daniel watched as Abby practically ran to her father's buggy. *Something must be wrong,* he thought, wondering what he should do about the dreadful feeling that had been nagging his conscience.

Judah Hostettler drove up to the hitching post near the Lapps' barn. He took a deep breath and prayed for wisdom as he strode out to the field where Reuben was working. Reuben glowered at the bishop as he approached. "What are you here for?" he grunted.

"I'm here to talk to you about some family matters." Judah glanced around, noticing two of the Lapp boys working in the field nearby.

"Make it quick. I've got work to do."

"I was hoping we could sit on the porch and discuss this," Judah urged the stubborn man, wanting to avoid the possibility of Reuben's sons hearing them.

"I ain't got time for no tea party. Now say what you came here for and be on your way."

Judah could see that Reuben was going to be difficult and most certainly would not listen to him alone, so he decided to leave and return later with reinforcements. "I'll leave you to your work and come back at a more convenient time, then. Have a *gut* day." Sensing urgency, the bishop quickly headed over to the other ministers' homes to bring them back for support.

After noticing that the bishop had gone, Reuben quickly hitched the horse up to his rig and rode toward town. About an hour later, he stomped up to the house and into the kitchen where his wife stood preparing dough for bread. "Woman, what did you tell the bishop?" he demanded angrily.

Maggie's frail hands began trembling. "Nothing...I haven't talked to the bishop."

He took a step closer, fury evident in his insistent tone. "Don't lie to me, woman! I saw you talking to the bishop's wife at Meetin' yesterday. He was here and I want to know what you said."

Maggie smelled the foul odor of alcohol emanating from his breath and realized this was one argument she would not win. "Sh-she asked how we were doing. I said everything was fine."

"You're lyin' to me!" he yelled in a fit of rage and flung the back of his hand across her face. She lost her balance and stumbled backwards, hitting the back of her head on the edge of the table before collapsing onto the hardwood floor. Her frail body lay still.

"That'll teach ya not to lie," he mumbled before stumbling down the back steps in the direction of his buggy.

Judah's buggy rumbled up to the Lapps' home once again. He looked out toward the field, but didn't see any sign of Reuben. "I'll go talk to the boys," he said to the two ministers that were with him.

"If you're lookin' for *Dat*, he ain't out here," David Lapp informed the bishop.

"Any idea where he went?" Judah enquired.

"Last I saw him, he was headed toward the house." He shrugged.

"*Denki, Sohn*," Judah told the young man.

He quickly turned and headed toward the back door of the house. The other two ministers stood behind him as he knocked. Lack of an answer required Judah to knock again. He called out, "Reuben, Maggie, is anyone home?"

Still no answer.

Strange. Someone should be home at this time of day, he worried. Concern compelling him onward, he opened the door and gingerly stepped into the house.

"Dear *Gott*, no!"

The other two ministers rushed into the house when they heard Judah yell. Judah knelt next to Maggie Lapp, who lay on the floor with a pool of blood under her head.

J. E. B. Spredemann

"She's gone," Judah's voice shook as he looked up at the other ministers, tears pricking his eyes.

CHAPTER 3
Tragedy

"To him that is afflicted, pity should be shewed from his friend..." Job 6:14a

Abigail froze in place. Three police cars, an ambulance, a white four-door sedan, along with several buggies, dotted the landscape surrounding her home. Her mouth hung open like the flap on their family buggy. She turned around to see her younger brother, Zachariah, running to catch up to her, his lunch pail swinging on his arm. She felt Zack put his chubby hand in hers and squeeze it.

"What are all them folks here for?" he asked, squinting up at her. He shoved his glasses farther onto the bridge of his nose.

Abigail herself was confused, and she ambled toward the house with a calmness that she didn't feel. Something was wrong. Something was dreadfully wrong.

As she and Zack neared the farmhouse, a lady wearing a white pantsuit hurried toward them. "Hello, I'm Penny Morris and I'm here with Social Services. Are you two of the Lapp children?" She held a clipboard, her right hand poised to write.

Abigail's gaze moved toward the house where Bishop Hostettler had just exited. Her blue eyes pleaded helplessly. "Excuse me," Judah interrupted. "I will to speak to the children first." The bishop gently pulled them aside and the social worker meandered back to her vehicle.

"Wh-what happened?" Abigail shifted worriedly, observing the bishop's grief-stricken face.

"Your..." Bishop Hostettler fought to control the quiver in his voice. "Your *mamm* is *dot*."

Abby felt her knees weaken and she immediately began to swoon. The bishop reached out and caught her arm to steady her. "Come, you must sit down." The bishop led her to a lawn chair.

Zack searched her eyes, clearly confused.

The bishop quickly explained. "I came by to see your *vatter* earlier today. He didn't seem to want to talk with me. I sensed the conversation would be difficult so I thought it best to come back with some of the other leaders from our district." He took a deep breath and continued. "He was no longer in the field when I returned and the boys said they thought he'd gone to the house. When I got here I found no trace of your *daed*, but your *mamm*...she was on the floor, pale and no longer breathing."

"What's wrong?" Zack asked, as though he had heard nothing.

"What's *wrong*?" Abigail wasn't sure if she heard right. Her voice rose with emotion and anger. "You're asking what's wrong? Didn't you hear the bishop? *Mamm's* dead. *Mamm's* dead and *Dat* killed her!"

Abigail shot up from her seat and bolted. She had to get away, to be by herself. She needed to think. Her brother began crying, but Abigail didn't hear him. She ran. Vaguely hearing the bishop call her name, she picked up her pace even more. She darted past the house and barn. Past the field where her two older brothers continued to work as though nothing had happened and life was fine and dandy. How could they work at a time like this?

Her vision blurred. She raced down the lane, past the trotting horse that pulled a family buggy, past the neighbors' houses and past their fields. She rounded the corner, and ran over the covered bridge, not caring that her tears were now soaking her dress. She hurried down the small hill that was next to the pond, and she didn't stop.

She wouldn't stop until she reached her secret thinking place: a beautiful spot completely surrounded by willow trees. Daniel had shown it to her years ago. It was *their* hideout. No one else knew where it was. The private sanctuary had been a refuge for her many times. She'd often pretended, under the canopy of willow trees, that it was her special home, a safe place to go when everything else in life seemed dangerous.

Abby sat down, attempting to control her tears so she could find some semblance of rationale. What would they do now that *Mamm* was dead? Sobbing and shaking, Abigail hugged her crossed legs. "It'll be okay. It's gonna be okay," she rocked back and forth whispering the words to herself. If she repeated it enough times, perhaps she might actually believe it.

"You realize we'll have to take Mr. Lapp into the station for questioning," the solemn officer told the bishop matter-of-factly.

"*Jah*, I realize that," Judah replied, knowing that their questioning would confirm what he already knew. Reuben Lapp had killed his wife.

"Have any idea where he might be?" the man in the black uniform asked.

"*Nee*. No. I 'spect he'll be back, though. Probably doesn't realize his *fraa*...his wife is gone." Judah swallowed a lump in his throat.

"The children will be placed in foster care if there are no relatives available to care for them."

"They have older siblings...Andrew and Sadie are of age. I will speak with them," Judah informed the officer.

"Are they here now?" the officer asked as Judah watched a buggy pull up. Judah noticed Reuben's son and strode toward the carriage as the officer looked on.

Andrew Lapp jumped down from the buggy. "Bishop, what's going on? I was told there was an emergency." He looked over Judah's shoulder and saw two emergency medical technicians carrying a gurney covered by a white sheet. A petite body obviously lay under the draped sheet. "Judah? What's happened? Who is that?" he asked in a panicked voice.

"It's your *mamm, sohn.*"

The bishop could see the confusion conveyed in Andrew's eyes. Andrew sprinted toward the covered body. He said something to the two men holding the stretcher, then quickly lifted the sheet and saw his mother's bruised, pale face.

"*Nee. Gott, nee! Nee...*" Andrew fell to his knees and sobbed into his palms.

Judah placed a comforting hand on Andrew's shoulder as he wept bitterly. "*He* did this, didn't he? I should have stopped him. This is my fault. I should have stood up for *Mamm.*"

"'Tis not your fault, *sohn.* You must forgive," the bishop urged.

They watched in consternation as the police officers taped off the house with a yellow plastic "Crime Scene: Do Not Cross" message written on it. As another buggy rumbled up the road, Andrew immediately identified it as his father's. Reuben dismounted from the buggy, bewilderment written on his face.

Outraged, Andrew quickly made his way to his father near the barn and threw a punch at his face. His father stumbled back and Andrew hit him in the face a second time. The third blow to the stomach knocked the wind out of him. Andrew released all the years of pent-up anger and fear.

"I hate you! Do you hear me? I hate you!" Andrew said.

The bishop turned at the commotion and rushed over to Andrew and Reuben, forcing Andrew back.

"That's enough, *sohn*. You must stop. This is not our way." He took Andrew's arm and led him to a stump of wood where he could calm down and signaled one of the other ministers over to console him.

"I know you are feeling upset now, but anger does not help. It only hurts. It will never heal the pain in here." Bishop Hostettler placed a hand on Andrew's chest. "You must ask *Der Herr* to help you, Andrew. He alone can heal." Judah couldn't tell whether his words had any effect, but he prayed they would.

The bishop stood up. "I will talk to your *vatter*."

Judah approached Reuben cautiously. "We must talk."

"What's going on here, Bishop?" Reuben asked, looking dazed, wiping the blood that ran from his busted lip.

"You've killed your *fraa*," he stated as calmly as he could swallowing the lump in his throat. "Maggie is dead."

"Wh...what? How can that be? I only hit her. I...I didn't mean...oh, no." As the reality of the situation dawned on him, his eyes filled with tears. "That's why my boy..."

"*Jah*...Andrew is pretty upset." The bishop rubbed his beard, and then looked up. "Listen, Reuben, the police are going to take you away. You will go to jail. You will lose your *kinner*, too. I spoke with the social worker and she said that the *kinner* can either go with a relative, or you can sign custody over to someone else. I'd like you to give guardianship of your *kinner* over to me. I will see that they get good, loving homes among our people. Will you let me do that?" Judah asked, his heart aching on behalf of Reuben's children.

Reuben thought for a moment, and then hung his head. "*Jah,* I think that would be best. I'm sorry. I'm so sorry."

Judah walked with Reuben over to the social worker and they were joined by two officers.

Daniel sat quietly in the buggy, next to his brother, eager for his old stallion to pick up his pace. When he heard the news of Abigail's mother dying, he instinctively knew she needed him. He was her friend, and friends stood by each other, especially when times were tough. Eventually, they reached the Lapps' farmhouse. Daniel handed the reins to his brother and hopped out of the buggy before Old Tom even had the chance to slow down.

"Anxious to see your *aldi*?" his brother Joseph teased. Daniel shrugged off the comment and marched toward Bishop Hostettler. *How could anyone be teasing at a time like this?* Daniel focused his thoughts on Abby, urgency compelling him forward.

He glanced around, noticing many familiar carriages, and realized most of the community had come to offer assistance. Studying the crowd, he quickly located Bishop Hostettler. "Excuse me, Bishop. Have you seen Abigail Lapp?"

The bishop turned from the officers and looked his way. "She ran off when she learned the news of her *mamm's* passing."

It didn't take long for Daniel to figure out where she would've gone. *Our hideout; that's the only place where she could be alone.* He started off in that direction, sending a "Thank you" over his shoulder to the bishop.

He reached their special spot several minutes later and found Abigail. Her eyes were red from crying and she was lying on the ground asleep. Daniel debated as to whether or not he should awaken her. He decided to let her rest a bit longer. After just a few moments, Abigail began to stir.

"Abigail." He nudged her gently. "It's just me, Daniel."

Abigail aroused slowly. "Dan?"

"Yep, that's my name." Without thinking, he reached out and caressed her long, tangled blond hair which had fallen loose from its tight bun as she slept. "You okay?"

"You wanna know the truth?" Abby's voice shook, sounding like she might burst into tears the next second.

"The whole truth."

She took Daniel's hand as though that would make her stronger. He squeezed both of her hands in his, offering the encouragement she needed. Her voice trembled as she spoke the truth. "I'm scared, Daniel. My *vatter* hurts us. He goes out and drinks lots of alcohol, then he comes back all crazy and mad. And then he...he beats us."

Tears sprung from Abigail's blue eyes. Leaning on Dan's shoulder, she let the tears flow. In between sobs she managed to say, "That's...what...I could never...tell you."

No wonder she'd always seemed so insecure. Daniel had received a few spankings in his life for disobedience, but never a harsh beating. Their people advocated proper discipline when needed, but did not sanction violence – especially in the home.

He allowed her to cry for as long as she needed. He stroked her hair and whispered, "It's okay, go ahead and cry. We'll figure out what to do."

Abby lifted her tear-stained face to his. Daniel took a blue paisley handkerchief out of his pocket and handed it to her. After she wiped her eyes, she noticed something. "*Ach,* I got your shirt all wet. I am a *dummkopp.*"

Dan put his finger under her chin and lifted her gaze to meet his. "No, Abigail Lapp, you are not a *dummkopp,* don't ever think that. You are a *gut* friend, the best friend I've ever known."

His words brought fresh tears to her eyes, but she quickly blinked them away. "You are my *gut* friend, too."

"Do you think we should go back now? They will worry about us, no?"

"I...I'm not ready to go back just yet." Abigail's distraught expression conveyed a message beyond her words: she was frightened. And who could blame her?

"Ya wanna walk by the pond?" Daniel determined to make her feel better. He stood up and stretched out his hand to her. "The sun is going down quickly," he commented.

"*Jah*," she answered simply, taking his out-stretched hand. "*Denki*, Daniel. I've never been able to talk about these things. I was never close to my *brieder* or *schweschdern*."

"Abby, you know you can talk to me about anything." He turned and looked into her eyes. "Anything."

Abigail nodded her gratitude.

Daniel parted the willow branches that enclosed the hide-out, and they walked through. They walked along the bank in silence until they heard a twig snap behind them. Whirling around, they laughed to see that they'd been startled by a squirrel scurrying up a tree.

Their hands parted when Dan bent down to retrieve a small skipping stone. His arm suddenly flew back and then forward as he sent the rock sailing over the pond, bouncing seven times over the calm water. "Did you see that? That's the farthest I have ever gotten a rock to skip."

"Let me try," Abby said as she fell to her knees and excitedly searched for smooth stones.

Daniel handed one to her. "Here's one."

"*Denki*." Abigail swung her arm back released the rock when her arm came forward. It was quite obvious to Daniel it wouldn't go very far. It skipped three times before plunging into the cold spring water. Abby flashed him a smile. "I have a new record!"

Daniel laughed. "Three is your record?"

"*Jah.*"

"I can show you how to throw it, if you'd like." Not waiting for an answer, he explained. "Ya see, you gotta have the right angle. Hold it between your fingers like this…" Daniel continued give her a short lesson and by the time they were done, the moon was up. Abby tried one more time and the rock jumped five times.

Daniel praised Abby and her cheeks reddened. He was certain she'd never received much acknowledgement for anything, and he resolved to encourage her more often.

Turning away from him, she abruptly changed the subject. "We should get back now," she replied softly.

Daniel looked up at the now-darkened sky and nodded in agreement. "*Jah*, you're right. Let's go."

They were about half way to the Lapp home when they heard a voice call, "Abigail!"

A different voice yelled, "Daniel!"

"*Ach*, they're looking for us," Dan said.

Abigail slyly smiled at Daniel. "Race ya." She began running, leaving Daniel in the dust.

It wasn't long before Daniel was past Abigail. He slowed his pace when he reached the outskirts of the Lapp farm. Abby came up behind him, breathing hard.

As they entered the property, they both looked up to see Abigail's father in handcuffs. Two officers escorted him to the back seat of a black and white vehicle with red and blue lights on top. Abigail looked to Daniel with tear-filled eyes.

Daniel placed an arm around her shoulder. "Shh...God will work everything out. You'll see."

CHAPTER 4
The Meeting

"When my father and mother forsake me, then the Lord will take me up." Psalm 27:10

"Thank you, Brethren, for coming today," Deacon Yoder said as he greeted the male members of their church district. "Bishop Hostettler has asked us to come here today for a very important matter: Reuben Lapp's *kinner*. We realize that each one of us has their own family, but we also acknowledge that our brother is in need of help. We do not know how long Rueben will be in jail, but it will probably be quite a while. The *Englisch* courts will decide his fate.

"We only want *Gott's will* for these *kinner*. They will not all go to the same home, but we'd like to at least keep them in pairs. If you think *Der Herr* will have you take these *kinner* into your home, please speak up. But keep in mind that *Gott* will require you to raise them as one of your own with the love and care that each human needs."

Gideon Fisher was the first to speak up. "Most of my children have married. Esther and I are willing to take a couple of them. Since we have young *kinskinner*, maybe the two youngest siblings can live with us."

"That would be Zachariah and Abigail," the bishop spoke up. "I think that would be a *gut* fit."

"Mary loves *kinner* and we've always wanted more boys," Peter Esh stated. "We could take David and Caleb."

"Very well," Judah said. "Andrew is on his own now, so there's Sadie and Deborah left. Neither one of the girls is in school, so they'd be able to help out at home. Philip, you've had experience raising a *dochder*. Would you be willing to take the two girls?"

"I was just about to volunteer. Naomi and I would be happy to have the girls," Philip King agreed with a smile.

"Then I guess it's all settled." Brother Yoder spoke again, "Let us end in prayer."

"*Jah*. I'm going to need all the prayer I can get," Philip muttered under his breath.

"So, how do like living with the Fishers?" Daniel asked Abigail during recess.

"They're nice, but I miss my *mamm*," Abby answered, swinging next to Dan.

"Just your *mamm*?" Daniel raised his eyebrows.

"I don't miss *Dat*, if that's what you're asking. As for my brothers and sisters...our family was never very close. You're more like a brother to me than them."

Daniel chuckled.

"Why was that funny?" Abby wondered aloud.

"Joseph."

"Huh? I don't get it." She frowned.

Daniel blew out a breath. "Well...my brother Joseph calls you my *aldi*."

"Your *aldi*?" She looked at him in surprise.

"Well, I keep tellin' him that we're just friends. I guess he thinks that girls can't be *just* friends."

"If you want, I can tell him that we're friends," Abigail offered.

"Nah, let him think what he wants. It doesn't really matter, does it?" He smiled, and then hopped off the swing to allow one of the other scholars a turn.

"Guess not." She shrugged and followed Daniel to a nearby picnic table.

"*Gut*. Well, I hope things go well for you and Zack at the Fishers'. Susanna and Jonathan will be gettin' hitched soon, *jah*?"

"*Jah*. Will you go to the wedding?" she asked.

"I'm not sure yet. Jonathan did come over the other day. He spoke to my *daed*, but I'm not sure if he just invited *Mamm* and *Daed* or if the *kinner* are invited too."

"I've never been to one, but my *schweschder* has and she said they're lots of fun. I wonder if Susie will keep teaching or if we'll get a new teacher. I guess they'll have to hire a substitute for a while. I hope she's nice like Susie is."

"*Jah*, me too. But at least you'll still get to see her a lot. Won't she and Jonathan be living in the *dawdi haus*?"

"*Jah*. And Jonathan works at the shop with his *daed*."

"Abby, do you think maybe *Gott* put you with the Fishers so you can have another *dat* and *mamm*?" he voiced.

"I don't think I want another *dat*," she stated glumly.

"You know, Abby, not all fathers are like Reuben Lapp."

"I'd rather not talk about it. It's time to go inside now, *jah*?" She changed the subject.

"*Jah*." Even though Daniel wanted to press the subject, he decided to give Abigail some time to sort through her thoughts. She had to know that all fathers weren't like hers – especially their Heavenly Father. *Gott, does she think you're like her dat?* Dan silently prayed, discouraged at the thought.

He had to talk to her more, he decided. "Hey, Abby, may I walk you home today?"

"I...uh, don't think so. I mean, I don't know how Gideon would feel. I don't want to get in trouble." She worried.

"But Abigail –" Daniel tried to reason, but Susie rang the bell, calling the students in from recess. Dan and Abby returned to their seats as did the other scholars.

As soon as school let out, Daniel watched Abigail and Zachariah quickly leave, no doubt heading for home. Did Abigail worry about arriving late? Did she think punishment would be waiting for them if they did? Dan shook his head and said another prayer for his friend.

CHAPTER 5
Sadie

"For the lips of a strange woman drop as a honey comb, and her mouth is smoother than oil."
Proverbs 5:3

*P*hilip King walked into his house after closing up the herb shop. The small health food store had been busy today and he was thankful once again that he had his adopted daughter, Danika, there to help out. Today she had brought along Philip's first granddaughter, Sarah Anne, who was still an infant. Philip took such pleasure in holding his small *grossdochder*, even though he still had little ones of his own.

"How was your day?" he asked while placing a gentle kiss on his wife's head through her prayer kapp.

"Still adjusting, but okay," Naomi replied. "I haven't seen Sadie since breakfast."

A look of concern showed on Philip's face. "But it's after five now. I thought she said she had to go into town for a few things."

"That's what she said." Naomi sighed. "Are Danika and Eli joining us for dinner?"

"We sure are!" Danika smiled with her response. "Eli should be here anytime."

"I think I hear his buggy now," Philip said as he grabbed his hat and strode out the back door.

He walked to the hitching post and was surprised to see Sadie in the buggy next to Eli. Eli stepped down from the buggy and Philip gave him a questioning look. Eli darted his eyes Sadie's direction, signaling he didn't want to talk while she was there.

"Sadie, go ahead inside and help Naomi with dinner," Philip said.

Sadie gave Philip a pouty look, and then reluctantly did as she was told. When she was safely inside, Philip spoke to his son-in-law. "What was Sadie doing riding in your buggy, Eli?"

"She showed up at the buggy shop today asking if we could use a secretary. She said she was looking for work. Since Nathan and I are behind on our paperwork, we decided to hire her part-time," Eli answered nonchalantly. "We were both coming to the same place and she asked for a ride."

"Have you talked to Danika about this?" Philip asked.

"No, but I planned on doing that tonight."

"Do you think it's a wise idea to be driving another woman around in your buggy when you're married to someone else? My daughter." Philip fought to keep the edge out of his voice.

"I didn't want to be rude. What would you have done?" Eli defended himself.

"I would have told her no, especially since it's Sadie. Didn't she used to want you as her beau?" Philip quizzed.

"I had forgotten about that," Eli said sheepishly.

"Well, I'm certain *Danika* has not." Philip raised his eyebrows. "*Kumm*, Eli. I'm sure the ladies have dinner ready about now."

"I think I'm really going to like working in the buggy shop," Sadie stated with a wide smile, throwing a glance at Eli.

Immediately, Danika and Naomi lifted their heads. Danika gave Eli a questioning look.

Eli cleared his throat. "Yeah, um, Sadie came by the shop today looking for a job. We needed a secretary." He looked to Danika and caught her disapproving glare.

"I thought you'd be helping me around the house." Naomi glanced at Sadie.

"Well, I'm sure I can still help out some. It's only part-time. You already have Katie and Deborah here to help you with the house and the little ones. Besides, how am I going to find myself a *mann* if I'm hanging around the house all day?" Sadie answered.

A knot formed in Danika's stomach when she saw Sadie give her husband a flirtatious wink. "We need to go now," Danika stated and abruptly rose from the table.

"But Eli hasn't even had dessert yet," Sadie whined.

"Eli, will you please get Sarah Anne from the crib?" Danika ignored Sadie and glanced at her husband who was presently clearing his plate from the table.

"*Jah*, sure." He strode toward the nursery in the other room to retrieve his infant daughter.

"*Denki* for dinner, *Mamm*," Dani told Naomi while wrapping her in a farewell embrace. "Sorry we can't stay longer. Eli and I need to talk," she whispered.

"I understand." Naomi gave her a sympathetic look.

"Bye, *Dat*." Danika hugged Philip, and then headed out the door behind her husband.

"You're awfully quiet tonight," Eli told his wife while they sat in their living room. "You haven't said a word since we left your *dat*'s house. That's not like you."

Danika kept silent.

"Is this about Nathan and me hiring Sadie?" he pried.

"I don't understand, Eli. Why would you hire Sadie?" Danika couldn't help but feel betrayed.

"Because we needed a secretary and she was available," he answered practically.

"She still wants you, you know. I can tell by the way she looks at you," Dani stated glumly.

"Danika, are you jealous of Sadie Lapp?" Eli teased.

"I don't trust her, Eli," Danika said with a worried expression.

Eli moved to his wife, wrapped his arms around her waist, and pulled her close. "Trust *me*, then. You know I've never been interested in anyone but you and I never will be. I married *you*, Danika Yoder. I love you." The sweet words rolled off his tongue as he placed a soft kiss on her lips. "Let's not think about Sadie right now, *Liewi*. Let's think about us."

CHAPTER 6
Friends

"A friend loveth at all times..." Proverbs 17:17a

"Scholars, I wanted to let you know that there will be no school next Tuesday. I hope that you will all join Jonathan and me for our special day." Susanna smiled as her class cheered.

"What will happen after you get married, teacher? Who will teach us?" PJ King asked.

"You'll have a substitute teacher for a while, and then I should be back until..." Susie's cheeks blushed. "Well, we'll just see how it goes. None of us knows the future for sure, *jah*?"

"What she means to say is she'll teach us until she has a *boppli*. Ain't so, Teacher?"

Poor Susanna attempted to cool her hot cheeks with a stack of papers from her desk. "We don't need to be discussing those kinds of things in school, Micah," she said, sending her young brother a pointed look.

Abigail looked over at Daniel, who smiled back at her. She thought about all of the fun they'd have at the wedding, just four days away. Until then, she would be busy helping to clean and prepare for the big day.

"You're dismissed to go home now," Susie told her scholars. "Hopefully, I'll see you all on Tuesday." The students all retrieved their lunch boxes. The boys found their hats and took them off the pegs on the back wall and the girls placed their prayer kapps on their heads. Each made their way down the steps and started toward home.

"Wait up, Abby!" Daniel hollered, as she and Zack walked the path to the Fishers' homestead.

Abigail stopped and turned around when she heard Dan's voice.

"Whew!" Daniel panted as he tried to catch his breath. "Why are you in such a hurry to get home?"

"I...I just don't want to be late," Abby said nervously.

"May I walk with you then?" he asked.

"Well..." She hesitated.

"Come on, Abby. Can't I even walk a friend home?"

"*Jah*, I guess so."

"*Gut*! I was hoping to talk to Gideon and Jonathan about learning woodworking." Daniel smiled.

"Really?" Abigail's brow raised in surprised.

"*Jah*, it seems like that'd be a fun trade to learn. I could make beautiful things that are useful and sell them too. And if they let me help out, I'll get to see you all the time." He beamed.

"Oh. I guess that might be sort of nice," she answered as they walked along in silence the rest of the way.

As they neared the house, Abigail picked up the pace and hurried inside. Daniel made his way toward the barn to speak with Gideon.

"Daniel Miller. Hello. What brings you by today?" Gideon greeted the young man.

"I'm hoping you'll teach me how to work with wood. I spoke with *Dat* and he said it would be fine if I came by to speak with you about it. Would you and Jonathan mind?"

"We'd be glad to have you, *sohn*." Gideon smiled, and then looked toward his son. "Isn't that right, Jonathan?"

"*Jah*, we can always use another pair of hands around here. Grab that sand paper there and start smoothing out this table top." Jonathan took his own piece of sand paper and gently buffed the course wood. "See, like this."

"All right, I think I can handle that." Daniel smiled as he ran the coarse paper over the wood, then felt the smooth results when he finished the small area. "I think I'm really going to enjoy this."

"You may change your mind tomorrow morning when your muscles are sore from sanding all afternoon." Jonathan chuckled. "But just wait till that table's all finished. Take a look at this piece." Jonathan waved him over to the wall where a finished coffee table sat covered by an old quilt.

Daniel's eyes swept over the beautiful table while he traced the intricate design with his index finger. "This is a work of art! I didn't realize you do all this."

"*Jah*. If we're going to do it, we might as well do it right." Jonathan attempted to conceal the pride behind his voice. He leaned over and whispered to Daniel, holding up a finger to his lips. "This is my wedding gift for Susie."

"She'll love it," Daniel whispered back with a smile. Then and there he determined to do his best so that one day he might make an equally impressive gift for his bride, whoever she might be.

"Abigail, will you help me take these drinks out to the men?" Esther asked.

"*Jah*, sure," Abigail agreed as she lifted two glasses of iced tea from the kitchen counter then followed Esther out to the wood shop.

"I hope you men are hungry because Abigail and I made you a snack," Esther said as she entered through the shop door.

"A workin' man can always eat," Gideon winked at his wife, then slipped her a quick kiss.

Abigail noticed and looked away.

"Daniel, I hope you'll stay for dinner this evening. Abigail and I are making plenty," Esther offered.

Daniel looked at Abigail and she smiled back at him. "I'd love to stay for dinner. I told *Dat* that I wasn't sure what time I'd be home."

"Susie will be here, too," Jonathan added with a smile his face had trouble containing.

"*Denki* for inviting me to dinner," Daniel called back before he stepped out onto the back porch behind Abigail, then closed the door.

"I'm glad you stayed for dinner, Dan," Abby said smiling.

"*Jah*, me too. It was a lot of fun. You've got yourself a *gut* family here, Abby."

"I've never had this much fun in my life. We never played games and had family time like the Fishers do."

"Really?" Daniel asked with surprise. "I'm sorry for all that you've had to go through, Abby."

"Thanks, Daniel, for caring and being my friend."

"Will you sit across from me at the wedding supper...I mean, if Jonathan and Susie don't mind?"

"*Jah*, I'd like that." Abby smiled.

"Guess I'll see ya on Tuesday, then. *Guten nacht*." Daniel placed his hat on his head and waved to Abigail as he disappeared down the lane.

CHAPTER 7
The Big Day

"Let thy fountain be blessed: and rejoice with the wife of your youth." Proverbs 5:18

"I can't believe Susanna and Jonathan are married now! I'm so happy for our teacher." Abigail exclaimed as she sat across from Daniel at the wedding feast.

"I thought for sure Bishop Hostettler was going to pass out when Jonathan took Susie in his arms and passionately kissed her in front of everybody!" Daniel laughed. "I heard they do things like that at *Englisch* weddings, but it's the first I've ever heard of during an Amish wedding. Leave it to Jonathan Fisher to pull something like that. I wonder if he'll have to make a confession." He shook his head in disbelief, then glanced at the happy couple.

Jonathan and Susanna Fisher chatted happily as they sat at the *Eck* with their attendants. Maryanna Hostettler, Susanna's identical twin sister, and Matthew Riehl, along with Annie Yoder and Joshua Hostettler, all seemed to be having a great time.

"Susie, did you know Jonathan was going to kiss you in front of everyone like that?" Annie whispered in her best friend's ear.

"*Nee!* You know Jonathan has a mind of his own." Susie blushed. "I told him that I wouldn't kiss him until we were married, but I didn't expect it *that* soon after *Dat* pronounced us man and wife!"

"Are you two keepin' secrets again?" Jonathan winked at Susie. "What are we going to do with them, Joshua?"

Joshua glanced up from his plate of roasted duck and creamed celery. "My guess is they're talkin' about the kiss; seems like this whole place is abuzz about that. You sure do know how to stir up controversy, Jonathan Fisher." He slapped his friend on the back.

"Here comes your father-in-law now...and he doesn't look too happy," Matthew spoke up.

"Yeah, Dad looks like he may want to speak with you," Maryanna piped in.

Bishop Hostettler approached the bridal table. "*Sohn,* may I have a word with you? In private."

"Sure," Jonathan said with an unabashed smile, then hopped up to join the bishop outside. "*Ich liebe dich,*" he whispered in Susie's ear, then gave her a small peck on the cheek.

Joshua caught his sleeve and laughed. "Hey, I suspected *Daed* might have you make a confession." Jonathan turned to him and wiggled his eyebrows, not the least bit fearful.

Once outside, Judah glanced around to make sure no one was near. He put an arm around his new son-in-law, then whispered, "Can you keep a secret, *sohn*?"

"*Jah.*" Jonathan's amused smile brightened even more.

"I've never told anyone this before, but I thought you'd like to know. I did the same thing to my Lydia at our wedding ceremony. Nobody in *this* church district knows about it, because Lydia and I moved here from Indiana shortly after we were wed."

"Really?" Jonathan asked in disbelief.

"*Jah.* Lydia was madder than a hornet's nest at first. You should have seen her face...much like Susanna's was today." He chuckled. "But she got over it soon enough. Seems like Susie might be over it already." The bishop smiled at his son-in-law. "Well, looks like you better get back inside before you stir up more trouble."

"Bishop –"

"You may call me *Dat, sohn.*"

"All right, *Dat. Denki* for sharing that with me." Jonathan smiled.

"I knew from that first day when you kissed my Susanna at the pond, that we were one and the same. Glad you're part of the family, Jonathan." Judah gave his new son a hug.

"*Jah*, me too," Jonathan said. He couldn't help the tears of joy in his eyes. Who would have thought his dream of marrying Susanna Hostettler would actually come true!

Sadie Lapp gazed at Jonathan and Susie from where she sat and enviously thought, *Jonathan and Susie are barely seventeen and they're already married! I'm twenty and I don't even have a beau.*

As she sat stewing, she began mentally rattling off the names of all the young married couples around her age. *Jonathan and Susie, Joanna and what's-his-name, Chloe and Levi...Eli and... Eli and...Danika.* She forced Danika's name with Eli's in her thoughts, but they rebelled. *No! The nerve of that...that Englischer coming in to our Amish community to steal Eli away from me. Too bad she survived that horse accident a few years ago. Eli was* **mine!** *Why didn't I fight harder for him before they were married? No matter. I bet I could still have him, even if they are married already. Danika thinks she's won, but she's sorely mistaken. I'll fight for Eli...and I intend to win.*

With that decision made, Sadie studied Eli and smiled. She began scheming about how she would strike – but of course she already knew the answer to that. The wheels were already set in motion.

Jonathan hopped down from the buggy, thrilled with the notion of bringing his new bride home for the first time. He raced around to Susanna's side of the buggy and scooped her up into his arms, placing several kisses on her lips. Darkness shrouded the trail to the *dawdi haus* where they would be spending their first night together as husband and wife. Jonathan placed a hand on the door handle and turned the knob but it wouldn't budge.

"What on earth?" he muttered to himself. "Sorry Susie, but I'm going to have to put you down. This door doesn't seem to want to open." Jonathan gently released his bride, then continued to figure out what was wrong with the door. He knew it wasn't locked, so that couldn't be the problem. *It's odd that the handle won't even turn,* Jonathan thought.

An idea popped into Jonathan's head. "Wait here, Susie. I need to get some tools from the shop." He sprinted to the woodworking shop, stumbling over a large rock in the process. "Ouch!" he yelled. *I don't remember a rock being there.*

"*Ach*, Jonathan. Are you okay?" Susie called.

"*Jah,* I'm all right, Susie. Just fell down. Don't worry, *Lieb,*" he reassured his wife. "This is not turning out like I planned," he mumbled to himself.

Quickly grabbing the needed tools, he hurried back to the obstinate door...and his patient wife. Oh, her smile was all it took to wash away all of the mounting frustration. With a renewed sense of determination, he finally decided it would be best to remove the entire door handle. Before opening the door again, he scooped up his bride. Once the door was open, he stepped over the threshold.

Whoosh! White cream poured down on them from above.

"Aah!" Susie screamed. "*Ach!* Jonathan, we're all wet."

Jonathan licked his lips, tasting the soft white fluffy substance. "Mm. Coconut creme pie, my favorite." He set Susie down.

Susie looked up and strained to see where the pie filling came from. She spied a bucket above the door with its contents still dripping. Susanna turned to face her husband. "Jonathan Fisher! Did you plan this?"

Jonathan's head jerked up and he put up his hands in protest. "No, no! I didn't do anything, honest! Why do you think I would do something like this?"

Susie put her hands on her hips and glared at him, although he probably couldn't see her. "I *know* you. You pull stuff like this all the time."

"Well I'm not guilty this time. I know exactly who did this. Just wait, Susie. Let me find the lantern. Don't move."

Jonathan carefully felt his way over to the small kitchen and searched for the lamp. "I know the lantern was here earlier today, but I can't find it anywhere." He checked under the sink where the extra lantern was kept. "The other one is gone too! *Ach*, Susie, I'm sorry. I need to go over to *Daed's* and borrow one of his. I'll be right back." Jonathan hurried out the door.

Returning a couple of moments later with lantern in hand, Jonathan suggested they change their soiled clothes.

"Oh no!" Susie cried as she opened up drawer after drawer searching for something to wear. "All of our clothes are gone. Are you certain *you* didn't plan this?"

Jonathan shook his head adamantly. "I'm going to get them for this!"

"Who?" Susie asked.

"Joshua and Matthew, that's who!" Jonathan's temper began rising, but Susanna let out a laugh. "What are you laughing about?" he smiled.

"They're finally paying you back for all the years of pranks you pulled on them."

"Well, I guess there's not much we can do about it right now. Let's forget about it and go to bed, *jah*?" He pulled his wife close and brushed her lips with his.

"*Jah.*" Susie's cheeks blushed.

Jonathan pulled back the quilts and blankets and Susie gasped. "Feathers! Thousands of feathers...in our bed!"

"I'm so going to pay them back for this!" he declared. He took a handful and threw them in the air.

Susanna laughed as the feathers clung to Jonathan's hair and face.

"What are you laughing at now?"

"You look like a chicken." She giggled.

Jonathan took a handful a feathers, sprinkled them on Susie, and laughed. "You're the chicken. I'm the rooster!"

"Come." Susie took the blanket and covered the feathers. "We'll just sleep on top, *jah*?"

"*Jah.*" Jonathan peered down at his sweet wife and lovingly took her into his arms.

Susanna removed her prayer *kapp* and, one by one, removed the pins from her bun. Her long brown hair flowed around her shoulders and down her back. As they sat on the bed, it made a rippling noise and gently gave way.

"What on earth?" Jonathan pushed both of his hands into the bed sending small swelling waves to the edges.

"Maryanna. This is Maryanna's bed," Susie asserted. "It's called a waterbed!"

"So the girls were in on all this, too! I expected this out of Josh and Matt, but not Annie and Maryanna."

"All right, Jonathan. We need to put our heads together and think of something really good to get them back. It's time for revenge!" Susanna said with a determined look on her face.

"That's my wife, Mrs. Jonathan Fisher!" Jonathan smiled. "You know, we're going to make a great team."

"*Jah*, we do." Susie kissed her husband's lips and turned out the light.

CHAPTER 8
Struggles

"For if ye forgive men their trespasses, your heavenly Father will also forgive you."
Matthew 6:14

After her ice skates where securely tied, Daniel reached out his hands and pulled Abigail to her feet from the frozen pond bank. With the huge ice rink deserted at this time of day, Daniel knew this would be a perfect time for him and Abigail to talk.

He was very much looking forward to Christmas this year. Not just because they would be celebrating the Saviour's birth, but because Daniel had been making something special for Abigail in the wood shop. He knew that this would probably be the happiest Christmas she'd ever had, even though he was sure she'd be missing her mother.

"Whatcha thinkin' about?" Dan asked curiously.

J. E. B. Spredemann

"Oh, just thinkin' about my *mamm*," she said quietly as she skated slowly next to Daniel.

"I bet you miss her a lot, huh?" He turned around, facing her while he skated backwards.

"*Jah*. But sometimes I think she's probably better off. I mean, hopefully she's in Heaven now."

"Did your *mamm* ever trust Jesus as her Saviour?"

"What do mean, Dan?"

"You know, did she ever place her faith in Jesus Christ? Did she repent and trust in Jesus alone for salvation? God promises us eternal life when be believe in him. Jesus shed his blood so we could live with him forever." Daniel tried to explain the best he could.

"Well, when I was younger, *Mamm* used to talk about Jesus more. I guess *Dat* didn't like her talkin' about it, though. I hope she was saved."

"*Jah*, me too."

Changing the subject, Abigail stated, "I think my brothers and sisters and I are better off now that *Dat's* not around. At least we're safe."

"I'm just glad to see you smiling more. You seem much happier now."

"*Jah*, I am. I used to think that maybe all dads were like mine, but Gideon is a very kind man. God blessed me by letting me live with the Fishers."

Daniel picked up speed and she attempted to skate faster. "Hey, wait for me!"

180

"I'm not going anywhere, just wanted to spread my wings a little." He chuckled.

"While you've lived here your whole life, you've had the opportunity to skate all the time. I, on the other hand, am fairly new at this so give me a break."

"Here, take my hand and we'll skate together then." He circled her twice then held out his hand.

"Okay, but not too fast." Abby grasped his hand and her heart leaped as they sped along at a speed she was unfamiliar with. She let out a nervous laugh. "I guess this is sort of fun."

"Give me your other hand and I'll show you how to spin." Abigail opened her mouth to protest, then he added, "I promise I'll go slowly."

Abby gave him both of her gloved hands and they slowly spun around facing each other. Although the air was frigid against her cold cheeks, she was having a wonderful time. She couldn't remember a time when she'd been so carefree. Abigail suddenly became chilled when a shiver shot up her spine and then went through her entire body.

Daniel must have noticed. "Let's go inside now, *jah*? I'm sure *Mamm* has some hot cocoa ready for us," he suggested as he led her to the edge of the pond nearest the house.

"Okay, but I should probably get back before too long."

"No problem. We'll just warm up a bit, then I'll drive you home in the sleigh."

"That sounds like fun. Thanks for inviting me over today, Dan. I've had a *wunderbaar* time."

As they glided along in the sleigh back to the Fishers' house, Daniel had a niggling thought. "Have you heard anything about your *daed* lately?" he wondered.

"No. Why do you ask?" Abigail really didn't care to think about her abusive father.

"Just wondering, you know Christmas is coming up soon."

"And?" Abby wondered what he was getting at.

"Have you written to him or anything?"

"What? After all he put us through...you...you want me to write to him? He killed *Mamm,*" Abigail said indignantly. Her hands began shaking.

"Abby, don't hold on to hatred and bitterness. You need to forgive your father," he said softly.

"I can't believe *you're* saying this, Daniel! I thought you were my friend. Of all people, I thought you understood." She shook her head disappointedly and looked away. A tear slipped down her cheek.

"Friends speak the truth, even when it's difficult," he spoke gently. "Everyone deserves love."

"No, not him! I hope I never see or hear from him again." she huffed.

"You don't mean that, Abigail," Dan said in disbelief.

"Yes, I do. He didn't let *Mamm* live. Why should he get to?" She began sobbing.

"Whoa!" Daniel pulled tightly on the reigns to stop the horse. He moved closer to his friend and slipped his arm around her. "Shh...it's okay, Abby. Just let it all out."

Daniel's heart sank. He had never realized how good his life had been until learning of Abigail's distress. He gently patted her shoulder and allowed her to cry in his arms. He realized it would be a while before Abigail worked through her pain and anger. "I'm sorry, Abigail. Nobody should have to go through what you and your siblings went through. I truly am sorry."

When Abigail got control of her emotions, she was finally able to stop the flow of tears. "I didn't mean to yell at you like that, Dan. It's just, every time I think about him I get so angry. I know I shouldn't. I know I need to forgive him. I just don't know how."

"Give it to God, Abby. He's the only one who can take all of that pain and anger away. He can take your bitterness and replace it with love," Daniel encouraged.

"But how? I can't see how I can ever love him."

"You can't, Abigail." He looked her in the eyes. "You can't. But God can...God does."

Abigail bowed her head right then and there and prayed aloud. She asked God for the courage to face her fears. She asked God to remove this burden from her. She thanked him for Daniel and for her families...both of them. Finally, she asked God to give her a grateful heart so that she could see the blessings all around her. When she finished her prayer, she gazed up at Daniel through tear-filled eyes.

Dan squeezed her hand and smiled. "Let's get you home now. We wouldn't want the Fishers to worry about you."

CHAPTER 9
Deception

"For where envying and strife is, there is confusion and every evil work." James 3:16

" Sadie, when Eli comes in this morning will you let him know that I'll be out for most of the day? They notified me last night that our big shipment came in, so I'll be heading into Lancaster to pick it up." Nathan Hostettler said before donning his black felt hat to head out the door of the buggy shop.

"Sure thing, Nathan. I'll tell him," Sadie answered.

As the door swung shut, Sadie took in a deep breath and smiled cunningly. *Finally, Eli and I will be alone!* Sadie stood up from her desk and hurried over to the small propane camp stove that they kept in the shop. *A pot of fresh coffee should go perfect with the sticky buns I brought today.*

The bell on the front door jingled when Eli stepped into shop. "Sorry I'm a bit late, Nathan," he called out while removing his hat and placing it on a wall peg near the door.

Sadie walked in from the other room. "Oh, Nathan said he was making a trip into Lancaster today. He said some big shipment came in or something."

"Great! We've been waiting on that for a while." Eli yawned wide and covered his mouth.

"A bit tired today?" Sadie asked.

"*Jah*. Little Sarah Anne didn't feel too hot last night, so I was up with her. She seems to be doing better today though," Eli replied.

"That's good to hear. I just put on a fresh pot of coffee. Would you like me to pour you a cup?" Sadie asked sweetly.

"Sure, that'd be perfect."

"How about some sticky buns? I can't possible eat this whole tray by myself. I didn't know Nathan wouldn't be here." Sadie knew Eli wouldn't be able to resist his favorite sweet.

Eli's head popped up. "You brought sticky buns? Yeah, I'd love some. *Denki,* Sadie."

Sadie poured two cups of coffee and put some sticky buns on a plate, then took a seat behind her desk. Eli took a seat on the chair opposite of her desk to enjoy the snack. "So, what orders do we have for today?" Eli asked after taking a swig of his steaming coffee.

"We have the order for the Zooks, I think they wanted an open buggy. Yesterday Jonathan Fisher just put in an order for a family buggy."

"Really?" Eli raised his eyebrows in surprise. "I didn't think they'd need one just yet."

"Oh, well they don't. He said there was no hurry or anything. I think he's just a little excited," Sadie added.

Eli chuckled. "Yeah, that sounds like Jonathan." Eli finished off one of the sticky buns, then looked around the small office. "You know, I gotta hand it to you, Sadie. You've been doin' a real good job puttin' this place in order."

"*Denki.*" Sadie blushed. She wasn't used to compliments – especially from the object of her affection. "*Jah,* it was a bit of a mess when I first got here."

A smile played on Eli's lips. "I'm afraid bookkeeping and filing aren't exactly mine and Nathan's specialties."

"Well, that's what I'm here for." Sadie smiled back, holding his gaze for a moment.

Eli cleared his throat, then pushed back on his chair. "I best be gettin' to work now. *Denki,* again, for the sticky buns and coffee."

"What do you think? Does it look okay?" Daniel showed Jonathan the letter box he'd been working on for Abigail.

Jonathan picked up the box and rubbed his hand over the surface. "Nice and smooth, and you did a *gut* job with the engraving. It turned out nice."

"I wanted to add a butterfly or two next to her name. And, of course, I still need to stain it."

"I think she'll love it. Are you sure you two are just friends?" Jonathan gave Daniel a sly smile.

"Yes. *Gut* friends," Dan asserted.

"Whatever you say, Dan. I know I wouldn't be making something like this for a girl if she was *just* my friend." Jonathan crossed his arms and raised his eyebrows.

"You're starting to sound like my brother, Joseph. Now, what's wrong with having a friend that's a girl?"

"It's not really common for Plain Folk." Jonathan's eyebrows rose. "You don't think she'll get the wrong idea? I mean, the two of you ice skating together, coming over for dinner, making her this nice Christmas gift. It just seems like you might be leading her on a little...if you truly don't have any romantic feelings for her."

"Look, the last thing I want is for Abby to get hurt. She's already been hurt enough. Do you think that maybe I shouldn't give this to her?" Daniel's heart sank at the thought.

"Well, if it is as you say, and the two of you are *just* friends, then I don't see any harm in it. But if I were you, I'd be a little more cautious," Jonathan suggested.

"Hostettler Buggy Shop," Sadie answered the noisy telephone. "Um...*jah*, I think so. Will you hold for a minute?"

Sadie placed the telephone receiver down on her desk, then went to fetch Eli. She peered through the door of the shop in back and signaled to Eli. Eli nodded and removed the welding helmet he was wearing and turned off the torch. He came into the front office and picked up the phone. "May I help you?"

Sadie could only hear Eli's end of the conversation. "Yes. We make commercial buggies, too." Eli grabbed a catalog from under the counter while he stretched out the telephone cord. "Burgundy? Yes, we can upholster the seats in plush burgundy. Just stop by the shop and you can look through the catalog and see what you'd like." Another pause. "We require fifty percent down when you place your order, then the remainder is due when it is picked up." Eli smiled. "Yes, sir. Have a good day." He handed the phone to Sadie.

"Sounded like a good order," Sadie commented.

"*Jah*, he wants two commercial buggies by March. I guess he rents them out for *Englischer* weddings and such. He said he'd stop by tomorrow to place his order."

"Uh...Eli, I had a question about something before you go back to work."

"What's that?"

"This ledger here. For some reason the numbers aren't coming out right." She peered down at the book in front of her on the desk.

Eli walked around the desk and leaned over her shoulder, looking at the numbers in the book. The faint scent of floral perfume assaulted his senses as he tried to concentrate on the numbers before him. "Well, let's see. I think that these numbers here are supposed to be in that column."

J. E. B. Spredemann

Sadie looked up at Eli with her big blue eyes. "You mean these?"

"*Jah*, aren't those the sales we made from the previous week?"

Sadie moved back slightly, causing her shoulder to brush his arm. "*Jah*."

Eli placed one hand on the desk and Sadie was tempted to cover it with hers, but she didn't. "I think you have your weeks mixed up."

"*Jah*, it seems like I have everything mixed up lately," she said pitifully. She put her face into her hands and began sobbing.

Eli sensed her distress and his heart pained. The Lapp family had been through so much. "Would you like to talk about it?"

He always has been so kind, Sadie thought to herself. "It's just, since *Mamm* died..." She began sniveling and was unable to speak.

Eli placed a comforting hand on her shoulder, waiting for her to continue.

"I don't really feel like I belong anywhere. I no longer have a family," she cried.

"What about the Kings? They offered to take you in. I'm sure they care about you," he offered, squeezing her shoulder a bit.

"No, they don't care. They just feel sorry for us, is all. I don't even have any friends."

"Sure you do." Eli racked his brain trying to think of one of her friends, but his mind turned up blank. *Does Sadie truly have no friends?* The thought saddened him.

"Yeah, like who?" she asked sarcastically.

What should I say? "Like me," he squeaked out.

"I mean someone that I can talk to."

Eli shrugged. "You can talk to me. I've heard I'm a good listener."

"Do you really mean that, Eli?" She gazed up into his eyes with her tear-filled ones.

"*Jah*, I do." He smiled sympathetically. Before he realized it, Sadie had stood up and placed her arms around him. He allowed her for just a moment, knowing she truly needed it.

Ding-Ding. The front door flew open. Eli looked up to see Nathan gaping in disbelief.

Nathan glared at Eli as the two of them unloaded the supplies and brought them into the back shop. "So, what was that all about?"

Eli took a deep breath, then blew it out hard. How was he going to explain? "I...I was just comforting Sadie."

"*Jah*, sure," he said sarcastically.

"What? Do you think–" Eli answered defensively.

Nathan interrupted him. "All I know is that you'd better be glad that it was *me* that walked in that door and not Danika. *Your wife*," he curtly reminded his partner.

"Nathan, you know that I would never do anything to hurt Danika."

"I'm quite sure that she would have been hurt if she had walked in on you and Sadie a few minutes ago. What were you thinking, Eli? *Anyone* could have walked in." Nathan's voice carried an edge to it.

"Don't you feel sorry for Sadie?"

"No. Listen, Eli. I think Sadie might be trying to come between you and Danika."

"That's ridiculous! Why would she come after me? I'm married and I have a *boppli*. And Sadie's pretty enough. I'm sure there're many men who would be willing to court her."

Nathan raised his eyebrows, unconvinced. "Uh-huh."

Eli wiped the sweat off his brow with the back of his hand and sighed in frustration. "You know, Nathan, maybe it's better if we *don't* have this conversation. Let's just work."

CHAPTER 10
Christmas

"For unto you is born this day in the city of David a Saviour, which is Christ the Lord." Luke 2:11

"I can't believe Christmas is finally here!" Abigail exclaimed excitedly, as she put another batch of cookies in the oven.

"I've always loved this time of year. Too bad Susie's not feeling very well this morning. I was hoping we could all bake cookies together," Esther Fisher replied.

Baking cookies reminded her of time spent with *Mamm* when she was younger. Life hadn't been frightening in the beginning, Abigail realized. It wasn't until after Zack was born and *Dat* lost his job, that he'd begun drinking. If only life could have stayed as it was when she was younger.

"Are Grace, Isaac, and their families coming for dinner tonight?" Abby asked, choosing to dwell on the positive.

"*Jah*, they'll be here." Esther held up a finger. "That reminds me, I need to have Gideon and Jonathan bring another table in for all those *grosskinner*."

"Do you mind if I give Dan some cookies to take home with him? I think he said he'd be heading home in a bit," Abigail said.

"Oh yes, that's perfectly fine. He's a nice boy, that Daniel."

"*Jah*, he's a *gut* friend." When she heard the men coming in for lunch, Abby rushed upstairs to fetch the scarf and hat that she'd knitted for Daniel.

"As soon as you're done washing up, we can have some soup and sandwiches," Esther called out to the men.

"Abby, can you join me outside for a bit before I leave?" Daniel asked as he slipped into his winter coat.

"Sure, let me grab something real quick." Abigail retrieved the wrapped gift from the table in the living room, then ran back to the small mud room to put her shawl on. "Esther, I'm going outside with Dan for a little bit," she hollered before she opened the back door and stepped onto the porch.

"I wanted to show you something out in the shop," he said as he led the way into the wood shop inside the barn. He held the door open and she stepped in, letting the door swing closed behind her. Daniel grabbed the matches and quickly lit a lantern. They waited in silence a minute before their eyes adjusted to the dim light. "I made this for you," he said proudly, as he held out a rectangular package. "Merry Christmas."

Abigail held out the package that she brought for him and smiled as they exchanged gifts. "And I made this for you."

"You open yours first," he insisted.

"Okay." She nervously unwrapped the package. Her eyes widened in amazement as she held the wooden box up to the light. She gasped, "*Ach*, you made this, Dan? Look at the butterflies. It's so pretty! I love it." She reached out and gave her friend a quick hug.

"I'm glad you like it, Abby. I thought maybe you could keep your letters in there or something." He smiled, delighted by her response.

"Oh, I didn't tell you. My *dat* sent me and Zack a Christmas card," she informed him.

"That's nice. Did he write anything in it?"

"*Jah*. He said he's been thinkin' about us and he misses us."

"Do you miss him at all?"

"Sorry to say that I don't." She decided to change the subject. "Okay, your turn now." She pointed to his gift.

Daniel tore open the plain craft wrapping paper to reveal a black scarf and matching hat. He quickly took off his black felt hat and replaced it with the warm beanie and wrapped the scarf around his neck. "This is perfect, Abby. *Denki*." He smiled and placed a small kiss on her cheek.

Knock...knock...knock. "I wonder who would be calling right now," Esther said as she rose up from dinner table to answer the door.

"Maybe it's the *Englischers'* Santa Claus." Jonathan laughed and Grace's husband Adam gave him a playful slap on the back.

Esther let out a shriek. "Joanna! It's Joanna and Caleb! And they have a *boppli*!"

The entire family stood up from the table and rushed to greet them. "*Ach*! This is such a *wunderbaar* surprise." Gideon smiled, as he embraced his youngest daughter in a hug. "I thought you two were still down in Central America."

"We came back to the States so Joanna could have the baby. We figured we would stay until after the New Year. I hope we're not imposing," he said apologetically.

"Nonsense!" Esther exclaimed. "My son and *dochder* are always welcome here."

"I don't know about you all, but I'm still hungry," Jonathan said unashamedly. "Let's finish eating."

"Same old Jonathan." Joanna laughed. "Hey, is that a beard you're trying to grow?"

"Yep, sure is! Susie and I finally got hitched last month!" Jonathan exclaimed with a smile as big as Texas.

Joanna smiled her congratulations and gave her new sister-in-law a hug. Joanna eyed Susanna's pale face and immediately sensed she wasn't feeling too well.

"Take that *boppli* out of that contraption and let me hold her." Esther pointed to the car seat that Caleb held in his hand.

He bent down and unfastened the five-point harness and gently lifted the tiny pink-clad bundle out.

Esther held out her arms to receive the babe. "*Ach*, she's just the most precious little thing!" The tiny infant squirmed in her arms as she stretched, then settled back down into a comfortable sleeping position. Her perfectly pink little lips made a gentle sucking motion as she seemingly dreamt about nursing.

"I'll get out some extra place settings for Caleb and Joanna." Abigail removed the plates from the cabinet and brought them to the table with the silverware.

"How old is the *boppli*?" Grace asked curiously.

"Essie is almost three months now," Caleb answered.

"Essie?" Isaac asked.

"*Jah*. We named her Esther after *Mamm*. And Esther from the Bible, of course." Joanna informed them.

"Did you hear that, Gideon? They named her after me." Esther beamed.

Jonathan leaned toward Caleb and covered one side of his mouth so his mother wouldn't see. "I don't think she heard the part about Esther from the Bible." He laughed.

"Let's settle down and eat before all this delicious food gets cold," Gideon suggested, then bowed his head to pray.

"So, how do you like living here?" Joanna asked as Susanna showed her the *dawdi haus* where she and Jonathan were now living. Pleasant memories of visiting her grandparents as a child flooded her mind as she took in the familiar surroundings. Both her *grossdawdi* and *mammi* passed away when Joanna was fourteen.

"*Ach*, it's been *wunderbaar*. Well, I mean after we recovered from all the pranks our friends pulled on our wedding night." Susie laughed as she reminisced about Jonathan climbing up the Poplar trees to retrieve their clothes and having to replace the door handle that the guys had Super Glued shut.

"You looked a little pale during dinner. Are you feeling okay?" Joanna asked her sister-in-law.

"*Jah*, I've just had a touch of the stomach flu lately. It strange, though. Sometimes I feel just fine. Like it comes and goes."

A knowing smile formed on Joanna's lips. "How long have you and Jonathan been married now?"

"Almost a month and a half. Why do you ask?"

"Have you had your cycle this month?" Joanna asked excitedly.

"Oh wow...I've been so sick I didn't really notice. No, I guess I haven't." Susie gasped. "You don't think I could be in the family way?"

Joanna nodded her head and smiled. "Yes, Susie. I think you're pregnant! What a wonderful Christmas surprise this will be for Jonathan."

After confirming their suspicions with a test, Susanna and Joanna joined the rest of the family in the living room of the main house. Everybody happily sat around the fireplace talking or playing games.

Joanna spoke up. "Susie would like to give Jonathan his gift first."

Everybody looked to Susanna who was beaming. "We're going to have a baby!"

"*Ein boppli*!?" In one motion, Jonathan jumped up from the floor, not caring that he accidentally tipped over the game of chess he and Isaac had been playing. He ran to Susie, kissed her full on the mouth in front of everyone, and picked her up and spun her around. "I'm a *daed*! I'm a *daed*!" he shouted excitedly. "Woo-hoo!" he yelled as he ran out the back door.

"Where is he going?" Susie asked dizzily and out of breath.

"My guess would be to announce to the world that he's a *vatter*." Gideon chuckled.

They all looked at one another and laughed, then offered Susie their heartfelt congratulations.

"Just when I thought this day couldn't get any better!" Esther exclaimed with a heart full of joy. "We have so much to be thankful for."

"Yes, we do," Abigail agreed.

CHAPTER 11
Concern

"He that refuseth instruction despiseth his own soul: but he that heareth reproof getteth understanding." Proverbs 15:32

Zack and Abigail rode happily along in the back seat of Caleb and Joanna's rental car with baby Essie between them. Joanna offered to take them to visit their brothers and sisters since she and Caleb had been planning to visit the Eshes and the Kings while they were in Paradise. It had been over a year since Joanna had last seen her friends Chloe and Danika, and she was looking forward to spending time with them.

Second Christmas, as they called it, or the day after Christmas, was usually spent visiting family and friends. Esther and Abigail had baked several dozen cookies that Abby brought along to share with their loved ones. Although Abigail and her siblings weren't too close, she was excited to be able to see them again. Since their mother's death and their father's incarceration, they had only seen each other at Sunday-Go-To-Meetings and other church functions.

Chloe and her husband Levi Hostettler were present at the Esh residence to enjoy the enormous feast that Mary Esh, Chloe's mother, had made for Second Christmas.

"Levi and I have an announcement to make," Chloe stated as she looked at baby Essie nestled in her arms. "We just found out we'll be havin' a *boppli,* too!"

"*Ach!* You'll probably be havin' your baby around the same time Jonathan and Susie will be having theirs!" Joanna smiled in wonderment, and hurried to give her friend a hug.

"Jonathan and Susie are expecting, too? That's wonderful-*gut* news, Joanna," Mary Esh replied.

"Paradise will be growing by leaps and bounds with all these *kinner.* The *Gut* Lord has blessed us for sure and for certain." Levi beamed. "I'm happy for my sister and brother-in-law, but God help Susanna if their *kinner* are anything like their *dat!*" The room burst into laughter.

"*Jah,*" Joanna added. "I don't know if Paradise will be able to handle two Jonathan Fishers!"

Abigail and Zack enjoyed time with their two older brothers, Caleb and David, playing in the snow. They had a snowman-building contest to see who could build the best one in the shortest amount of time. After that, they spent the day sledding with the Esh children on one of the freshly snow-covered hills near the Esh farm.

Most of their time at the Kings' house was spent indoors. Danika, Eli, and little Sarah Anne were visiting Philip and Naomi as well. Abigail, Zack, and their sister Deborah played games, while their sister Sadie hovered around Joanna, Caleb, Danika, and of course, Eli. More than once Abigail noticed her oldest sister flirting with Danika's husband Eli and thought, *I need to pray for my sister.*

Nathan Hostettler approached his father after the Sunday-Go-To-Meeting. "*Dat,* may I talk to you about something?"

Judah Hostettler stroked his beard. "Sure, *sohn. Was iss letz?*"

Nathan raked his hand through his dark hair, trying to find the right words to say. Finally, he began, "I think I may have a problem. Eli and I hired Sadie Lapp to be our secretary." He paused.

"Yes, I'd heard."

"When I came back from picking up an order in Lancaster a couple of weeks ago, I walked in on them...in an embrace. When I confronted Eli about it, he shrugged it off as though it were no big deal. He assured me that he was only comforting her and that he didn't want to talk about it. He's apparently unaware of Sadie's wiles. Eli doesn't realize that she's been flirting with him. He's such a *dummkopp* that he doesn't see what Sadie's trying to do."

"Eli isn't a *dummkopp*, Nathan. He's just naive. Many young men tend to be gullible when it comes to things such as this. Eli's always had a tender heart, and it probably was innocent in his eyes. Nevertheless, I'll have a talk with him and Sadie about it."

"*Gut,* I knew you would help. I've been thinking that maybe I should fire Sadie. What do you think?"

Judah nodded. "Give her one more chance. But if she keeps this up, firing her would probably be the best idea."

"*Denki, Dat.*"

Danika looked out the window when she heard the clip-clop of a horse and buggy pull up next to the house. As Bishop Hostettler dismounted the buggy, she wondered what this visit could be about. After washing the last of the dinner dishes, she was about to go answer the door when she noticed Eli walk from the barn to meet the bishop.

I hope there aren't any problems. Danika pondered what would require a visit from the bishop.

"*Wie Gehts*, Eli?" Judah held out his hand.

"Everything is well here. How are you and your family, Bishop?" Eli asked considerately.

"We are doing very well. I'm sure you've heard we have two more *grosskinner* on the way," the bishop stated enthusiastically.

"Yes, congratulations," Eli offered. "Is there another reason you've come out today? Would you like to come in and enjoy a cup of coffee with my wife and me?"

"I'll pass on the coffee, *denki*. But there is something I'd like to speak with you about, Eli. Nathan has brought it to my attention that Sadie Lapp has been a little overly forward where you're concerned and he's worried that things might get out of hand."

Eli sighed. "I wish he hadn't mentioned that. I already explained to Nathan that I was just being a friend to Sadie. The Lapps have been through so much."

"I understand that you have a caring spirit, and that's commendable. But there are some that might take advantage of that."

"I really don't think that Sadie's out to steal me away from Danika, Judah. She knows I'm happily married and that we have a baby."

"Just be careful, Eli. I wouldn't want anything to come between you and your wife." The bishop sighed. *He really is naive.* "Nathan says that if Sadie won't leave you alone, then he will fire her."

"I hardly think that will be necessary. Sadie is a good worker," Eli protested.

"I intend to speak with Sadie about this issue as well, so hopefully she will back off," Judah said. "Good evening, Eli."

"Good evening, Bishop."

Eli mulled over his conversation with the bishop in the barn. He still couldn't comprehend why everyone was making such a big deal over Sadie. He knew that her face lit up whenever he was around and she enjoyed his companionship. But that was Sadie's personality. She'd always been that way. It was who she was. What was the big deal?

After tending to the horses, Eli made his way into the house. He was greeted with a kiss from his wife.

"What did Bishop Hostettler come by for?" Danika wondered aloud. She grasped another dish from the drying rack and began wiping the extra moisture with a hand towel.

"He's worried about Sadie working at the buggy shop."

"Why would he worry about that?"

Eli placed his hat on the rack near the door. "Nathan said he was concerned because he thinks that Sadie's after me."

Danika's eyebrows shot up. "I know she's always liked you, but why would *he* think that?"

Eli gulped and his palms became sweaty determining how to best explain the situation. "Well, one time Sadie was upset. She was distraught over her mother's passing. She was crying and I was just trying to be a friend because I felt bad for her. Before I knew it, she had her arms around me."

"She *what*?" Danika dropped the pan that she had been drying and it hit the floor with a bang. Her hands began trembling and Eli rushed over to her and placed his arms around her. She quickly thrust his arms away stepped back from his embrace. "How...how could you let her do that, Eli? Did you hug her back?" Danika envisioned Eli in Sadie's arms and tears sprang to her eyes.

"Of course not!" Eli answered defensively.

"I...I'm going to bed now." Danika suddenly felt nauseated as tears trickled down her cheeks.

"Danika, please don't do this to me," Eli pleaded.

"Don't do this to *you*?" Danika asked indignantly. "Good night, Eli."

With a defeated sigh, Eli silently prayed to God. *Dear Lord, please help me and Danika get through this time of testing. And please don't let her be mad at me for long. Amen.*

"*What*?" Sadie protested the bishop's accusations. "Nathan said he would fire me? What does Eli have to say about that?"

Judah scratched his beard. "Sadie, it doesn't really matter what Eli's opinion is. Nathan owns the buggy shop."

"Yes, but Eli should have some say in it."

"Do I need to remind you that Eli is a married man?" the bishop chided.

"I think Eli's a big boy and he can make his own decisions," Sadie boldly proclaimed. "He should be able to decide who his friends are."

I don't like where this conversation is going one bit, Judah mused. "Sadie, please don't make this any harder than it needs to be. Just stay away from Eli and you'll be able to keep your job."

CHAPTER 12
Danger

"For the lips of a strange woman drop as a honeycomb, and her mouth is smoother than oil."
Proverbs 5:3

*E*li rolled over and hit the floor with a thud. His stiff neck and cramped legs reminded him that he had, once again, spent the night on the couch.

Alone.

Rubbing his eyes, he placed one hand on the sofa to hoist himself up. *What time is it?* he wondered. There was no light coming in from outside, so he figured it had to be early morning. As he fumbled around in the darkness, his big toe caught the corner of the coffee table. It was all he could do to hold in a yelp. Finally, he made his way into the kitchen where he located a box of matches and a lantern. Four o'clock.

"That's good enough for me," he mumbled quietly to himself, as he pulled on his broadfall trousers. He fastened the front of his long-sleeve shirt, slipped his suspenders over his shoulders, and then took a loaf of bread from the counter and cut himself a couple of slices.

Danika and Sarah Anne would probably still be asleep or at least in their room, until Eli left for the day. It had been two days since Bishop Hostettler stopped by and Eli had received the silent treatment from his wife ever since. Eli was beside himself where his wife was concerned. They had always talked things out when something was bothering one of them. Somehow, Eli had to find a way to get Danika to open up and talk to him, but for now he was letting her have her way. Silence. Complete silence.

And it was driving him crazy.

"Eli, when you're in town don't forget to pick up that paint," Nathan reminded him before he headed out the back door of the buggy shop.

"I got it," Eli hollered back before striding over to his buggy.

Nathan met him outside and Eli raised his eyebrows in question. "Did Sadie say anything to you about leaving?"

"No, what do you mean?" Eli replied.

"I found this on her desk." Nathan thrust a small piece of yellow paper in Eli's direction. The note read: *Finished my bookkeeping. Had some errands to run. Be back before closing time. Sadie.*

"First I heard of it. You don't need me to stick around until she returns, do you? Can you handle the phone on your own?" Eli asked.

"Nah, you go ahead. Try to be back at a decent hour, though," Nathan replied.

As Eli quietly drove his enclosed buggy down the road, he had time to reflect on the last few days. He'd never seen Danika so upset with him before. As he passed by the last few farmhouses on the outskirts of Paradise, he let out a deep sigh.

"What was that for?" a female voice spoke from behind him.

Eli practically jumped out of his seat. "Sadie? What are you doing in here?"

"Thought I'd hitch a ride into Lancaster. You don't mind, do you?" she answered nonchalantly.

"Well, I...I – you shouldn't sneak up on people like that! You could have given me a heart attack!"

Sadie giggled, diffusing the tension in the buggy. "You did look frightened."

"Yeah, I guess I was pretty surprised." Eli moved his neck from side to side trying to work out the kinks.

"What's wrong? Do you have a stiff neck?" She wondered.

"*Jah.* I haven't been sleeping too well lately," he complained.

"Oh? Why not?"

"I've been sleeping on the couch. Danika and I kinda had a fight," he admitted.

Sadie pushed out her bottom lip. "Oh, that's too bad," she lied.

Eli cocked his head to the side again and Sadie placed her hands on the back of his shoulders. Eli flinched.

"Relax," Sadie coaxed in a smooth quiet voice. "Earlier in my *Rumspringa* I took some massage classes. Now breathe in deeply from your nose and exhale through your mouth a few times. You're way too tense."

Eli would have protested, but her warm hands rubbing against his neck and shoulders felt so good. He felt himself relax completely as her fingers gently but firmly worked out the knots in his neck. All the tension of the last couple of days were forgotten under the ministrations of Sadie's skilled hands.

"Normally, the client would lie down on a massage table with their shirt off. It's much easier to rub the massage oil into the skin when there's no barrier," she commented casually. "The warm massage oil is very soothing."

"I can imagine." Eli gulped, somewhat surprised by her frankness. "You really know what you're doing, don't you? Does Philip know that you give massages?"

"No. Why do you ask?"

"I think Philip might let you have a massage business in his herb shop. He has that little storage room inside the shop that would be perfect for it. It goes right along with natural healing. I mean, if you enjoy it and that's what interests you," Eli suggested.

"Hmm..." she said thoughtfully. "Maybe I will talk to him about it. Thanks, Eli."

"No problem, Sadie. *Denki* for the massage, I actually do feel a lot better now."

Sadie finally removed her hands, realizing they were nearing town. "So, if I open up a massage parlor, will you be one of my clients?" Sadie smiled slyly.

"We'll have to see about that, but I definitely enjoyed that massage." Eli smiled as he pulled into the hardware store parking lot and up to the hitching post. "I have a few things to get, so I'll probably be about thirty minutes."

"Okay, I'll meet you back here in thirty then," Sadie agreed when he helped her down from the buggy.

Annie Yoder couldn't believe her eyes when she saw Sadie Lapp getting into her brother, Eli's, buggy. "What do think she was doing in his buggy?" she asked her beau as her brother's carriage disappeared out of sight.

Joshua Hostettler raised his brow. "I don't know, but if *we* were married I know I wouldn't want you riding with another man."

"Do you think I should talk to my brother about it?" Annie asked wide-eyed.

"Maybe I should mention it to *Daed*. Perhaps he could talk to Eli about it," Joshua suggested. "I'd hate to see anything happen to Danika and Eli."

"*Jah*, me too," Annie agreed.

"*Denki* for the doughnuts, Sadie. They were *gut*," Eli comment-ed as they traveled back home from Lancaster.

"Well, if you're still hungry I brought my lunch along. I made two chicken salad sandwiches and I'd be happy to share one with you," Sadie offered.

Eli's stomach rumbled and he remembered that he hadn't brought a lunch today. Danika usually had his lunch ready and waiting for him when he left for work, but ever since their dis-agreement he'd had to prepare his own lunch. "I think I might take you up on that offer. I was in such a hurry to get out the door this morning that I forgot to make my lunch."

"*You* forgot to make your lunch? I thought that was some-thing a *fraa* should prepare. Doesn't your wife make you lunch?" Sadie gave Eli a sidelong glance.

"Well, she used to. Remember I told you we were having a disagreement?" He sighed.

"What about? I mean, if you don't mind me asking," Sadie pried.

"I'd really rather not talk about it, but thanks for offering."

"Remember we're friends. If you ever need to talk, Eli, I'd be glad to listen." She placed her hand over his.

"*Denki*, Sadie. I'll remember that." He squeezed her hand then let it go and gripped the reigns. *Sadie really is a kind per-son.* "You'll make someone a *gut fraa* someday."

"Do you really think so, Eli?" Sadie's eyes brightened.

"*Jah.* Why not? You're kind, thoughtful, *schmaert*, and you're *schee*," he said.

Sadie blushed. "Do you really think I'm pretty, Eli?"

"Of course. I wouldn't have said it if I didn't mean it."

"I'm just not pretty enough for you." She frowned.

Eli looked at her with concern. "Sadie, you know that I'm married to Danika already. And that I love her."

"And if you weren't? If you weren't already married to Danika, would you consider marrying me?"

"But I *am* married," he reminded her.

"It's too bad that she survived," Sadie mumbled.

"What did you say?" Eli asked wide-eyed, suddenly alarmed at her words. *Did I hear her correctly?* He quietly asked himself.

"I said it's too bad she survived that horse accident. If she hadn't, then *we* could be married now," she stated smugly.

Eli became indignant as a thousand thoughts filled his mind all at once. "Sadie! I can't believe you would say such a thing. And about my wife?! How could you even think that? I was wrong about you, Sadie. *Ach*, I was so wrong."

He lifted his hat and raked his hand through his hair, suddenly feeling ill. Pulling hard on the reins, he brought the buggy to the side of the road.

"*Geh raus*," he attempted to say in a calm voice through his clenched teeth.

"Wh...what do you mean?" Sadie's shocked expression befuddled Eli.

"Get out of my buggy now!" he said sharply. "I'm going home...to my wife!"

With tears in her eyes, Sadie quickly got out of the buggy. "I'm a friend to you and this is how you repay me?"

Eli shook his head. "You're no friend of mine." He clicked his tongue to signal the horse. "And by the way, you're fired!" he hollered back. "How could I have been so stupid?" Eli muttered to himself.

CHAPTER 13
A Father

"A father to the fatherless, and a judge of the widows, is God in his holy habitation." Psalm 68:5

As the days flew by, Abigail observed Gideon and realized that he was nothing like her father. She also recognized the fear that failed to creep up at the sight of him, the way it had when her father returned home every evening. In fact, she looked forward to dinner time now, something that never happened in the past.

One night Gideon called to her, beckoning her outside. "Abigail, come. Let's talk for a little bit."

"Uh...all right," Abigail replied and followed him out the door. She immediately began trembling and second-guessing herself. *Is he like Dat after all?* The fretful thought inundated her mind. She racked her brain in search of a reason why Gideon would call her outside alone. As far as she knew, she hadn't done anything wrong lately. But sometimes her *dat* would whip her when she couldn't remember any wrongdoing.

Gideon patted the chair next to him, inviting her to sit on the small back porch. "I just wanted to say I'm sorry for how your *vatter* treated you, and that if there's anything you would like to talk about, I'm right here. You know, our earthly fathers are supposed to be a picture of the Heavenly Father and I'm afraid even the best *daed* falls short of that responsibility. I'm sorry to say that your father was a very poor example to you and your brothers and sisters. Even so, it is not our place to pass judgment and we must offer forgiveness."

At Gideon's kind words, all of her fear and doubt washed away. Abigail burst into tears at his gentleness – something her dad had never shown before.

Gideon's brow creased in alarm. "Are you all right? I didn't mean to make you cry."

Abigail peered at him through her tears. "You're so kind. You're not like *Dat* at all. He never cared whether I cried or not."

Gideon pulled her into his arms. "Shh, it's okay. Go ahead and cry all you need to." Abigail wept in his arms releasing her anxiety, anger, and hate for her dad. She then cried tears of joy and thanked her Heavenly Father for loving her even when her earthly father did not. She also thanked God for Gideon and Esther and for their kindness to her and her brother, as well, and asked God's forgiveness for hating her dad and asked Him to help her forgive her father.

As she finished wiping her eyes on her apron, Esther came outside and announced, "Supper's ready." Then noticing Abigail, she asked concernedly, "Is everything okay?"

Gideon began to say something but Abigail answered, "*Jah*, everything's just perfect now."

Smiling, Esther nodded and disappeared back into the house.

"You got my shirt all wet." Gideon teased, letting her know he wasn't upset. "It's all right, it'll dry. Besides, I needed a bath today anyways, *dochder*." He looked towards the house. "Now, let's go on inside and eat supper. I'm starving."

Abigail happily followed Gideon back into the house.

As Officer Love drove his patrol car down the two-lane highway on the outskirts of Lancaster, he was surprised to see a young Amish woman walking alone. *That's strange,* he thought. While it was pretty common to see the Amish driving down this stretch of road in a buggy, it was quite unusual to see someone walking. *I wonder if something's wrong.*

Officer Love determined to find out if there was a problem. He slowly pulled his vehicle off the road about twenty feet ahead of where the young woman walked in an effort not to stir up dust. The officer exited his vehicle and purposefully approached her. "Excuse me, Ma'am. Are you in need of assistance?" He moved his sunglasses to his head and peered down at her with concern in his hazel eyes.

"No, I'm fine," the young woman said as she wiped a tear from her eye with the sleeve of her blue cape dress.

"Do you mind if I ask you what you're doing out here in the middle of nowhere?"

"My ride...uh...dropped me off."

Not wanting to pry, the officer asked, "May I give you a ride somewhere? It's a little chilly out today. My patrol car's nice and warm."

"Well, I don't know," she answered hesitantly.

"Do you live around here?"

"In Paradise, *jah*."

He whistled. "It's a long way to Paradise by foot. Please let me give you a lift." He wouldn't feel right about leaving a woman all alone along this remote stretch of highway. "Come, please." He motioned with his hand.

She reluctantly followed him to his vehicle and he opened the front passenger side door for her. "I...I don't want to go home. Not right now anyway."

"Okay." Officer Love thought for a moment. *I'd love to get to know this beautiful young woman better.* "Do you drink coffee?"

"*Jah*," she answered with an inquisitive look.

"There's a nice little cafe in Lancaster. I'll be off duty in ten minutes. How about if we go enjoy a cup of Joe, and then I can give you a lift back to Paradise. Sound fair?" he asked, hoping she'd agree.

She nodded.

"Great. But before we go, I need to know your name." He smiled then teased, "I don't ride with strangers."

"You haven't told me your name," she protested with a smile.

"That's right. Forgive me for being rude." He stuck out his hand. "My name is Brandon."

"Sadie." She shook his hand and bit her upper lip to keep from smiling too much.

"Okay, Sadie, tell me about yourself," he stated as they traveled toward Lancaster.

"Why?" she asked cautiously.

"Why? Because I want to get to know you better. You're not very trusting of police officers, are you?"

She shook her head.

"Okay, I'll tell you about me first. My name is Brandon, which you already know. I'm twenty-seven years old. I've been in full-time law enforcement for two years now. I live and work in Lancaster. Now, your turn." He flashed a smile.

"I'm twenty years old. I've lived in Paradise my whole life. I did work at a buggy shop part-time doing paperwork, but I just got fired," she said with a bit of regret.

"You got fired? I didn't know the Amish fire people. What did you do to get fired?" he asked curiously.

She took a deep breath. "I'd rather not say."

"Nothing against the law, I hope."

"*Nee,*" she answered wide-eyed. "I wouldn't do something like that."

"Okay, let's change the subject. Um...are you married?" He raised his eyebrows. *Please say no.*

"No." She shook her head.

"Boyfriend?" *Please say no.*

"No, you?"

"No, I don't have a boyfriend." He laughed, shaking his head.

"*Ach,* I didn't mean that!" She blushed, embarrassed by his answer.

"I know, I was just teasing you." He winked. "No, I'm not married and I don't have a girlfriend." *Yet.* He held up his left hand showing the absence of a ring.

He pulled up to a small, but nice cafe. "Wait there, I'll get the door for you." He hurried around to the passenger side to open it for her.

"I know how to open a car door," she informed him.

"I know. I was just trying to be a gentleman." He smiled then led the way inside.

The hostess showed them to a booth and they were seated in a small corner of the cafe. "Your waitress should be here in a couple of minutes." She placed two menus on the table, then walked away.

"You're welcome to get something to eat if you're hungry," he offered.

"No, thanks. I've already eaten lunch. I'll just take coffee."

"So, do you have a last name, Sadie?" He raised his eyebrows.

"*Jah*, do you?" She mirrored his eyebrow movement.

This girl likes to play games, he smiled to himself. "Yes. My last name is Love," he raised his eyebrows twice in quick succession and winked one eye.

Sadie smiled skeptically and rolled her eyes. "Love? Yeah, right. I've never heard that as a last name before."

"You don't believe me? It's not just a come-on, it really is my name." He laughed.

Just then, a middle-aged waitress approached their table. "Hello, Officer Love. What can I get for you today?"

Brandon looked at Sadie and smiled. "We'll both have coffee. Thank you, Bridgette."

The waitress left the table and headed for the coffee maker.

"See, I told you. Now do you believe me?"

"*Jah*," she said. The waitress returned with two steaming mugs, the dark liquid filling Sadie's senses.

"Now, what did you say your last name was?" Brandon probed.

"I didn't."

"You aren't going to tell me?" He gasped, feigning offense.

"It's Lapp," she stated dolefully, awaiting his reaction.

"Hmm...Lapp. Why does that name sound familiar to me?" He racked his brain for a moment, the memory slowly invading his mind. "Hey, wasn't there a...are you related to Reuben Lapp?" he asked wide-eyed.

"Unfortunately," she answered regrettably, staring at the table.

"I'm sorry. I guess that means you were related to Margaret Lapp, too."

"She was my *mamm*." She heaved as a tear escaped her eye.

Brandon put a hand over hers and lifted her chin to look her in the eye. "I really am sorry, Sadie. Listen, if there's anything I can do for you, please let me know."

They were both silent for a moment as they sipped their coffee. Brandon spoke again, "Did...did your father ever hit you?" He balled his hands into fists under the table at the thought, *I can't stand pathetic jerks that intimidate innocent women and children.* "If you don't feel comfortable answering, you don't have to."

"*Jah*, he hit all of us. I'd rather not talk about it though."

"That's fair. So, who do you live with now...or are you on your own?" he wondered aloud.

"I live with the King family. They own the health food store."

"Oh yeah, I know where that's at. I've stopped by there once or twice to pick something up for my mother." He thought for a moment. "If I stop by there again someday, will I see you?"

"Well, I don't work in the shop. At least, I don't yet. Things are a little up in the air for me right now. My sister and I live in the large house next to the herb shop with the Kings."

"Are you planning on working in the shop?" He seemed confused.

"I haven't talked to Philip yet, but I had taken some massage courses a while back. I was kinda thinkin' that maybe I could possibly have a massage parlor in one of the back rooms."

Officer Love raised his eyebrows. "Sounds like a good idea. I'd love to be your first customer," he said a little too eagerly.

"Oh, would you now?" She crossed her arms and raised her eyebrows. "I guess I'll have to talk to Philip right away then." She smiled.

It was near evening when Officer Love's patrol vehicle pulled into the driveway on the Kings' property. Philip rushed out the back door and quickly walked to the patrol car. Anxiety filled his features. Brandon stepped out of the car and opened the door for Sadie as Philip neared.

"Is everything all right, Officer?" Philip asked, glancing worriedly toward Sadie.

"Yes, everything is fine, Mr. King. I'm just dropping Sadie off." Brandon looked at Sadie and smiled.

"Thank you for bringing her home to us. We were beginning to worry."

"No need, she was in good hands. Back home safe and sound. Hope you have a good evening, Mr. King," Brandon said.

He shook Philip's hand in dismissal and Philip started toward the house. When Sadie didn't follow, he turned around.

Brandon cleared his throat. "Um...she'll be in in just a minute. I wanted to speak with her about something first."

Philip nodded, then strode up the back steps.

Brandon turned to Sadie and momentarily gazed into her blue eyes. "So, you'll join me for dinner on Saturday night?"

She nodded. "If that's what you'd like."

"Oh yes, very much so. I'll pick you up at five then," he confirmed. Brandon hopped back into his patrol car with a wave of his hand.

Sadie watched the vehicle until it was out of sight, then headed toward the house. *This wasn't such a bad day after all,* she mused.

CHAPTER 14
The Visit

"There is no fear in love; but perfect love casteth out fear: because fear hath torment. He that feareth is not made perfect in love." 1 John 4:18

Abigail and her dad silently looked at each other through the plexi-glass window for a moment. Reuben Lapp awkwardly moved closer to the intercom between them then spoke first to Abigail. "How have you been?"

"Good," she spoke into the round silver device.

"Abigail, I'm sorry. I hope you can understand how sorry I am for treating you and your siblings the way I did back at the house. It was terribly wrong of me."

"And *Mamm* too," Abigail added softly.

"Yes, and *Mamm* too," he lamented, swiping a tear from under his eyelash. "She told me I needed to quit drinking, but I was too proud to admit she was right. I was too blind to see how I was ruining our family. I should've listened to her. I wish so much that I had listened. I'm so sorry, Abigail. I hope someday you can find it in your heart to forgive me."

Convinced by the tears in her father's eyes, Abigail realized he was indeed remorseful. "*Dat*, I already have."

"Do you really mean that, Abigail?" A glimmer of hope showed in her father's eyes.

"*Jah*, I do. I forgive you...and I love you, *Dat*." She wished there was no barrier between them so she could take his hand. "And I know that if *Mamm* were still here, she'd forgive you too."

"Oh, Abigail, thank you. You don't know how much this means to me." Relief and gratitude flooded Reuben's face. "You are like your mother in many ways."

Abigail nodded and glanced up at the clock on the wall. "I have to go now. I'll come see you again soon."

"*Denki*." Reuben smiled as his eyes followed Abigail out of the room.

"*Gude mariye*, little *schweschder*," Eli greeted Annie as he entered the buggy shop. "I'm glad you've come to work for us."

"*Jah*, me too. I enjoy doing paper work," Annie stated.

"Well, I'd better get to work. Had some errands to run this morning so I'm getting a late start." With that, Eli sauntered into the back portion of the buggy shop to join Nathan.

Annie Yoder sat at the large oak office desk, organizing the papers and filing them alphabetically according to the customers' last names. When her stomach grumbled, reminding her of the time, she giggled.

Like clockwork, Maryanna opened the front door, jingling the bell that constantly annoyed Annie. "Hey, Annie, time for lunch."

"Coming," Annie replied.

Although Maryanna was still an *Englischer,* she was one of her best friends. Since her friend Susanna had married and was now in the family way, the two of them didn't have as much time together as they had before. But Annie didn't mind too much. She realized that was the way life worked. Nevertheless, she was thankful that she and Maryanna, Susie's twin sister, retained their close bond.

She stood up and walked out of the shop with Maryanna. The girls made their way over to a grassy spot a short way off from the driveway. Annie seated herself on the picnic blanket that Maryanna laid out neatly under a poplar tree.

She looked up when she heard a buggy rumble toward the shop. Matthew Riehl and Joshua Hostettler jumped down from the buggy, tethered the horse, and then walked briskly over to the girls. Joshua caught Annie's gaze with a smile and held it, stealing her breath away.

As if knowing that Annie was at a loss of words, Maryanna spoke up. "While you two are making goo-goo eyes at each other, Matthew and I are going to eat."

Matthew planted himself on the ground next to Maryanna, while Joshua sat across from him next to Annie. During the silent prayer, Annie heard a buggy rolling down the lane. She sneaked a look and quickly identified it as Jonathan's.

Matthew cleared his throat after the silent prayer and they all looked up to see Jonathan and Susanna walking toward them. Susie, now visibly pregnant, had a sneaky look in her eye reminding Annie of the pranks they'd pulled on Susie and Jonathan's wedding night.

"Enjoying your picnic?" Susie asked casually.

"*Jah*," Joshua answered around the food in his mouth.

"Joshua, I thought you'd have better manners around your *aldi*. *Mamm* taught you better than that," Susanna chided.

"Yes, little *schweschder*," Josh said sheepishly, then apologized to Annie.

"So, Annie, I wouldn't think that *you* had anything to do with the pranks on our wedding night?" Susie crossed her arms and raised her eyebrows.

Annie pressed her hand to her heart and gasped, feigning innocence. "*Me*? I'm shocked that you would even think that I had anything to do with that foolishness."

Maryanna choked, trying to hold back a laugh. Susie then turned on her. "And I suppose that *you* didn't have anything to do with the waterbed."

Maryanna looked directly at Susie, attempting to keep a straight face. "You didn't like the wedding gift I gave you? I thought the waterbed would be perfect for you guys."

"Oh yeah, it's a lot of fun!" Jonathan blurted out, waggling his eyebrows at his friends. Susie poked him in the ribs, her cheeks pink as the sunset.

Joshua quickly stuffed the rest of his sandwich in his mouth so he couldn't laugh.

"By the way, thanks for the coconut cream pie! I loved every bit of it." Jonathan's eyes sparkled, sending his wife a knowing glance. "Who made it?"

Annie almost lifted her hand then thought better of it when she realized she was walking into a trap. "Wouldn't you like to know?"

Changing the subject, Maryanna spoke up. "How much longer till the baby comes? I can't wait to meet my little niece or nephew." She eyed her twin's rounded belly.

Jonathan's and Susie's faces lit up at the mention of their *boppli* and they exchanged a loving glance. "About three more months."

"You don't look like you could go another three months, you're pretty big already," Annie said wide-eyed.

"I feel huge," Susie answered, rubbing her back to relieve the pain.

Jonathan came to her rescue right away and began massaging her lower back. "Your belly may be big, but you're still as *schee* as ever," her husband uttered, placing a kiss on her cheek. "*Kumm, Liewe.* Let's go check on our buggy now and see if Eli and your *bruder* have it ready yet. We'll be needing it soon enough."

Jonathan glanced at each of their companions. "We'll see y'all later." Jonathan and Susie both waved goodbye and started toward the buggy shop.

"They're so lucky," Annie commented, as she watched her friends walk away hand in hand.

Joshua moved closer to Annie and placed an arm around her. "They're not the only lucky ones."

"Danika, *Lieb*. You have no idea how happy I am that you're not upset with me anymore." Eli took his wife's hand and kissed it gently. "I really missed you."

"You know I can't stay upset with you for very long." Danika smiled at Eli. "I'm just glad that Sadie's *finally* found a man of her own. Although, I can't say I blame her for falling for you. What did *Dat* say the guy's name is?"

"I think it was Officer Love. Yeah, Brandon Love," Eli recalled.

"Love? Hey, I wonder if he's related to Mike Love!" Danika smiled.

"Mike Love? Who's that?" Eli furrowed his eyebrows and frowned.

"You know, Mike Love from the Beach Boys. Oh, never mind!" Danika laughed.

"Something else from your *Englischer* days, huh?" Eli cocked his head.

"*Jah.* You have no idea how hard it is to get something out of your head...especially when it's something you *love*d."

"All I know is that I *love* you. And I wouldn't want to do anything to get you out of my head." Eli pulled his wife into an embrace and gently brushed her lips with his.

CHAPTER 15
The Surprise

"Lo, children are an heritage of the Lord: and the fruit of the womb is his reward." Psalms 127:3

Daniel walked alongside Abigail by the shore of Miller's pond. "There's a young people's gathering coming up this Sunday here at my *daed's* place. A *gut* place to have a gathering, don't you think?"

"*Jah,* it is," Abigail agreed. "It's so beautiful here. It's the perfect place for a get-together. I'll come for sure and for certain."

"May I meet you at the Fishers' and walk you to the gathering then?"

"*Jah,* Daniel, I would like that."

"*Gut.*" They were silent for a minute before Daniel spoke up again and asked, "How are you doing? I mean, with your *vatter* and all?"

"I'm doing *gut*. I visited him about a month ago and I told him that I love him and that I've forgiven him, too. It made him so happy, and he thanked me for forgiving him. I got a letter from him today. He sends his love and continually apologizes." Abigail's eyes clouded for a minute, but then quickly brightened.

"That's good that you're on speaking terms with your father and that you've forgiven him." Daniel nodded approvingly. "What about your brothers and sisters? Do you know if any of them are speaking with your father?"

"Well, I know Zack is. I'm not too sure about the others. I know that Andrew and Sadie will have a difficult time for sure and for certain. They're carrying around years of bitterness. I hope that they can forgive him, though. I know I felt a lot better after I did." She glanced at Daniel. "Of course, I had some help with advice from a *gut* friend," she teased.

"Really, who is this friend?" he asked playing along with her.

"It was a very nice Amish boy," she informed him, clasping her hands in front of her.

"Anyone I know?" he raised his eyebrows.

"*Nee*, probably not." She shook her head and giggled.

"All right, then. I won't ask." Following Dan's reply came the smile that continued to endear him to her heart.

Slowly, Sadie walked toward the small dwelling place where Eli and Danika lived and knocked on the door.

Danika answered it and silently gasped in surprise. "Sadie," was all she could muster in a voice she hoped sounded polite.

"I need to talk to you and Eli, if that's all right. I hope I didn't come at a bad time," Sadie said meekly. Danika detected a tinge of nervousness in her voice.

Surprised by the change in Sadie's attitude, Danika was slightly taken aback. "Oh no, not at all. Please come in." Danika led Sadie to the small living room where Eli gently played with Sarah Anne who was making an effort to walk without losing her balance.

"Careful, Sarah. You don't want to get yourself hurt," Sadie heard him warn the young toddler.

"Eli," Danika said softly. "We have company."

Eli turned to face Danika and Sadie. His silent penetrating gaze made Sadie feel even more nervous. Her cheeks flamed in embarrassment at her previous behavior and she glanced down at the floor. She took a deep breath, then looked up at both of them.

"I've just come to apologize," she said, to their astonishment. Never in their lives had they seen Sadie apologize for something she'd done wrong, unless an adult compelled her to do so. But here she was apologizing on her own, and apparently she spoke from her heart.

Sadie continued, "It was wrong of me to try to steal your husband away from you, Danika. And it was wrong of me to try to take you away from your wife, Eli. I see now that God meant for you two to be together right from the start. I guess I've sort of always known that, but I wanted you anyway, Eli. It was wrong and I'm truly sorry."

"I forgive you," Eli and Danika chanted in unison.

Danika perked up. "So, are the rumors true, Sadie? Do you have an *Englischer* boyfriend now?"

Sadie's face lit up after a look of relief flitted over her features. "Yes, it's true. He's a wonderful man..." and she proceeded to tell them about Officer Love.

After chatting with Eli and Danika for some time, Sadie finally glanced at the metal-framed clock on the wall and declared, "It's almost four o'clock. I better get home so I can help Naomi fix supper."

As she strode toward the door, Danika asked, "Hey Sadie, will you ask Brandon if he's related to Mike Love?"

Sadie looked bewildered. "What? Who's Mike Love?"

"Just ask him, please." Danika didn't explain.

"Okay, I will." Sadie opened the door and headed back to the Kings' residence.

When she left, Eli approached his wife. "Are you sure there's nothing going on between you and this Mike Love guy?"

Danika's mouth draped open until she realized her husband was teasing. "Why, Eli Yoder!" She picked up a pillow from the sofa to throw at him, but he intercepted it and drew her into his arms instead.

Sadie wondered why Philip wore a peculiar look on his face during dinner, but thought it best not ask. She felt like she'd already gotten herself into enough trouble lately and didn't want to rock the boat.

Glad that Philip and Naomi hadn't put a stop to her dating an *Englischer,* Sadie was thankful that they'd given her freedom. Boy was she glad Officer Love had come along when he had! If not, she's not sure where she'd be now. He seemed to have helped her weather one of the greatest storms in her life.

"Sadie, I'd like to have a word with you," Philip requested, jolting her from her inward musings. "Let's go into the shop."

Entering the herb shop, Sadie wondered what was so pressing as to bring her out here to speak. Philip lit some of the lights in the shop and motioned for Sadie to take a seat on one of the stools across from the juice counter. "I just wanted you to know, Sadie, that Naomi and I are really proud of you."

Is Philip ferhoodled*?* Sadie's eyes grew large. "What?"

"Eli and Danika told us how you went and apologized to them and I know that wasn't easy for you," Philip stated.

"*Jah,* well. I guess God's been teaching me some things lately – even though I am still in my *Rumspringa.*"

"You know, Sadie. What I find interesting is that a lot of people think that *Rumspringa* is just about running around and having a good time and pushing the limits. And for some, I suppose that's true. But the way I see it, *Rumspringa* is about finding what really matters in life. It's about making decisions, learning from your mistakes, and moving on with the wisdom you've gained," Philip proffered.

"Wow, I guess I've never really thought of it like that before."

"I want to show you something." Philip motioned her over to one of the storage rooms. "Eli told me that you've taken massage classes and that you were interested in having a massage business, is that true?"

"*Jah*," she answered hesitantly, then followed Philip to the back corner of the store. Her eyes grew wide in wonderment when she peered into the small room. There sat a massage chair, candles, various essential oils, and a massage table. The room had been decorated simply with a few live plants, giving the room a comfortable relaxing feel. Sadie peered at the room in astonishment. "I-I don't know what to say."

"We all worked together to prepare it for you. Do you like it?"

"Even Danika and Eli?" At Philip's nod, Sadie's eyes filled with tears. "Oh yes! I love it. It's *wunderbaar*. I don't know how to thank you." Her smiled brightened the room even more.

"You can start by giving me a massage," he teased.

"Uh...Jonathan." Susie endeavored to retain her calm demeanor. "Will you go get your *mamm* and call Chloe and Danika?"

Jonathan studied his wife, who sat on the small loveseat, holding her back. His brow creased. "Wha-why? Is something wrong, Susie?" A worried expression crossed his face when he glanced at the mid-section of her dress and noticed it was wet. "Did you...are you?"

"Jonathan, my bag of waters broke. Now *please* go get your *mamm.*" Susanna took a deep breath and waited for the contraction to pass. Jonathan glanced at her nervously then bolted out the door.

"*Daed! Daed!* Call Chloe and tell her the baby's coming! Call Danika and tell her to bring her herb bag," Jonathan hollered to his father in the barn, then bolted to the house to fetch his mother per his wife's request. "*Mamm!* The baby! The baby's coming!!" Jonathan shouted, panting heavily. "It's Susie, she's having the baby! Oh *Gott*, help us."

"*Ach,* calm down, Jonathan," Esther chided. "Susie and the baby will be fine. Abigail and I will be right over."

Jonathan ran back to the *dawdi haus* to be with his wife. He kneeled in front of Susanna and took her hand. "Are you okay, Susie? What do you want me to do? May I make you a cup of tea? Should I put your feet up? Do you want me to carry you to our bed? Can I –"

"Jonathan!" Susanna interrupted. "I need you to take a deep breath and calm down. You are going to drive me crazy."

Esther and Abigail burst through the door and Susanna sent her mother-in-law a pleading look. "Jonathan, I think it might be best if you just wait in the other house or go outside," his mother suggested.

Susie started panting and gave out a moan. "Oh, I hope Chloe's here soon. I don't think I've got much time!"

"Susie!" Jonathan studied his wife worriedly and clutched her hand tightly.

"Ugh!" Susie groaned again.

Jonathan's face began to blanch.

"Jonathan, go outside now! We have everything under control. Why don't you drive over to the Hostettlers' and let them know Susie is in labor. I'm sure her *mamm* and *daed* will want to know," Esther recommended in order to save her daughter-in-law from further stress.

"Uh...okay. Susie, don't worry, *Schatzi*. I'll be right back!" Jonathan kissed his wife, then charged out the door.

"Don't bother," Esther muttered under her breath. "*Ach*, that boy."

Turning to Susie, she said, "Now, relax Susanna. Chloe will be here soon and she's delivered many *bopplin* here in Paradise lately. Just try to rest and breathe through the contractions like she showed you," Esther suggested.

"Is there anything I can do to help?" Abigail offered.

"*Jah.* Go put some water on to boil, get some clean towels, and bring Susie some water to drink."

Shortly thereafter, Chloe came through the door followed by Danika. "How is she coming along?" Chloe asked Esther.

"She's doing fine. Her contractions are just a few minutes apart and her water broke a while ago."

"It looks like she'll be holding the little one in her arms real soon then." Chloe took Esther off to the side and whispered, "She's gone into labor earlier than we expected. She's not due for at least another month. The baby may be premature and, if that's the case, we may need to make a trip to the hospital. I don't want to alarm Susie, though."

"Are you certain she's early? She seems so big," Esther whispered back.

"Well, we couldn't be certain of her due date because she chose not have an ultrasound. It does appear to be early, though," Chloe stated.

"Chloe, Susie's ready to push," Danika hollered.

Chloe quickly turned back to Susanna, whose face was red. "Okay, Susie. Just breathe like I showed you and when you feel like you need to push, go ahead and do so."

Susie huffed in short quick breaths a few times then felt the sudden urge to bear down and push.

"I see it. I can see the baby's head!" Chloe informed Susanna with a smile. "Won't be long now. You're doing great, Susanna."

Susie was too winded to smile back and felt a sudden need to push again.

"That's good, Susie. The head is out. One more push!" Chloe held the baby's slippery head and caught the rest of the infant when it slipped from the womb. "It's a boy! You have a baby boy, Susie."

Danika cut the baby's umbilical cord and whisked the small infant from Chloe's arms to clean it up.

"Ugh!" Susie moaned. Chloe's head perked up when she saw another head crown in the birth canal. Chloe gasped.

"There are *zwei bopplin*. Susie, you have twins!" Chloe announced as she caught baby number two.

A short time later, the babies were cleaned and swaddled in their new blankets. Susanna was lovingly gazing into their eyes when Jonathan walked in to see them.

Jonathan's eyes held wonder and his mouth draped open at the sight of Susanna with two bundles in her arms. "We… we have two *bopplin*?" Tears of joy formed in his eyes when Susanna handed a baby to Jonathan.

Susie thought Jonathan's suspenders might snap as he proudly held one of his tiny sons. His smile was priceless.

"What should we name them?" Jonathan asked as he joyfully peered down at the bundle in his arms.

Susanna's eyes sparkled. "I was thinking we could name one of them Jonathan after their *dat*, and we could name the other one Judah after my *dat*," she replied.

Jonathan bent down and kissed Susie's lips. "That sounds perfect! Abigail, will you tell the others they may come in now?" Jonathan called to Abby.

In a short time, in walked Esther, Gideon, Lydia, and Judah. Judah glanced at the babe in Jonathan's arms, not noticing the one held by Susanna. He peeked into the blanket Jonathan held. "Well, what'd you have?"

Abigail took the liberty to speak up. "Twins. They have twin boys!"

Gideon and Judah looked at each other with wide eyes and exclaimed simultaneously, "Oh no! Double trouble!" The entire room burst into laughter as they offered their congratulations and continued to celebrate the joyous occasion.

Abigail quietly whispered her own prayer of thanksgiving – not only for the two new lives that had just entered the world – but also for the new life God had blessed her with.

The End

A SPECIAL THANK YOU

The authors would like to thank the Billings family.

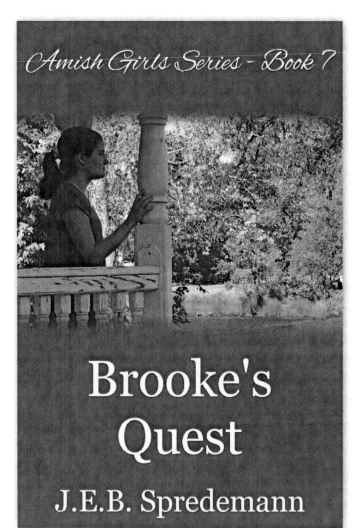

Brooke's Quest

J.E.B. Spredemann

Brooke's Quest

J.E.B. Spredemann

Amish Girls Series - Book 7

For Our Cousins

*May you seek and find the Saviour on
your quest for true love*

CHARACTERS IN
BROOKE'S QUEST

The Spencer family

Brooke – protagonist, only daughter of the Spencer
family
Ethan – Brooke's brother
George – Brooke's father
Lila – Brooke's Mother

The Weaver family

Seth – protagonist, oldest son
Leah – oldest daughter
Noah – Seth's father
Lavina– Seth's Mother

The Fisher family

Gideon – father
Esther – mother
Jonathan & Susie – youngest son & wife, protagonist of
Susanna's Surprise
JJ (Johnny & Judah) Jonathan & Susie's twins
Abigail Lapp – foster daughter, protagonist of Abigail's
Triumph
Zack Lapp – foster son

The King Family

Philip – father, herbalist
Naomi – mother
Katie – daughter
The Yoder Family
Jacob – deacon, father
Annie – daughter, Joshua Hostettler's betrothed,
protagonist of Annie's Decision

The Hostettler Family

Judah – father, bishop of Paradise
Levi & Chloe (Esh) – son & wife, protagonist of Chloe's
Revelation
Joshua – son, Annie Yoder's betrothed
Maryanna – Englisch daughter, Susanna Fisher's twin

Others

Daniel Miller – Abigail's best friend
Matthew Riehl – Maryanna's beau

CHAPTER 1
Summer Vacation

"To everything there is a season, and a time to every purpose under the heaven..." Ecclesiastes 3:1

Brooke Spencer impatiently brushed her damp chestnut-brown hair back into a high ponytail. She glanced at her wrist where the white elastic band that she used to secure her locks had indented her skin. The weather up north seemed a bit milder than what she was used to in summertime, but the heat was still sweltering. Although the vehicle had air conditioning, Dad insisted they roll the windows down and enjoy the fresh air.

"Better get used to it if we're going to be staying at an Amish bed-and-breakfast," he'd said, reminding them that the Plain people didn't use modern conveniences such as air conditioners.

"Mom, are we in Pennsylvania yet?" her Georgian accent hinted exasperation. It seemed as though they had been driving for hours, when in all actuality they'd just stopped thirty minutes ago. She was glad Lancaster County would be the first stop on their trip.

"Yes, honey, we crossed the Pennsylvanian border over ten minutes ago. And you've already asked that twice," Lila Spencer assured.

"Oh." Brooke sighed, as she stared out the window of their Dodge Charger. She had been anticipating their cross-country road trip for years, and now that it was finally here she was tired of all the driving. Brooke couldn't wait to arrive in Paradise. She'd read many Amish novels before, but never in her fifteen years, had she seen the Amish in person. Perhaps she would meet some handsome Amish boy that would sweep her off her feet. Brooke smiled, imagining it. *That would be so romantic.* She then shook herself back to reality and sighed. *Yeah right, like that would ever happen.* Mom had said boys like that only existed in books...and, of course, in her imagination. Nevertheless, she knew she'd have the time of her life on this vacation.

Seth Weaver reorganized the eighteen-ounce glass jars of strawberry jelly for the fourth time. He was already regretting telling *Mamm* that he would stay and manage the road-side stand for the day. Leah had said it was fun and that there was plenty of time for contemplation. He'd smiled when she said that. Leah was more of a quiet, thoughtful person and they had always been close. But Leah was certainly right about that, there was plenty of time to think. Too much time. Seth thought he might go mad just sitting and doing nothing.

He had already thought back to the last Singing when his friends David Lapp and Paul Hostettler had encouraged him to ask a *maedel* if he could drive her home in his buggy. However, Paul and David didn't understand that Seth wasn't ready to court anyone. He was still young and there would be plenty of time to settle down in the future. Besides, there was no one in his district, or any district for that matter, that he was interested in. When he met the right *maedel*, he would know.

Truthfully, he'd rather be working in *Daed's* shop right now building gazebos. At least there he'd be using his hands and doing something constructive. He enjoyed the feel of the redwood after it had been sanded smooth. Every gazebo they built had a piece of their heart and soul in it. And each gazebo took many hours of labor to craft. Their customers knew they were getting a top-quality work of art when they contracted with Gazebos, Etc. Fine craftsmanship, pure and simple. Seth smiled at the thought of satisfaction of a job well done.

Unfortunately, *Daed* was working in the shop alone today. Seth hated leaving him short-handed, but *Mamm* needed Leah to stay and help with last-minute preparations before their guests arrived. So here Seth was attempting to keep his mind occupied as customers, mostly *Englisch* tourists, stopped at the roadside stand to purchase authentic Amish-made treats and gawk at an Amish person. Seth chuckled to himself when he remembered a comment he'd heard earlier in the day from an *Englisch* woman, no doubt a tourist. She'd said, "Oh look, it's a real Amish boy!" He'd had to duck behind a shelf to hide from the onslaught of pictures the woman attempted to capture and reminded her of the sign posted right under her nose that read 'No photos, please'.

Seth plopped back down into his chair, shielding himself from the hot sun under the wooden canopy *Daed* had constructed some years back. Another car rolled up, but this one caught his eye. Although he had never owned a vehicle, he decided that if he ever did it would be a Dodge. He enjoyed the gentle roar of the motor and admired the sleek design of the frame. The back door opened, revealing a girl about his sister Leah's age. She was clad in denim capri pants and a thin fuchsia t-shirt that revealed a white tank top underneath. Dark sunglasses shielded her eyes from the bright sun. The girl walked up and stood under the canopy, then turned to face the car. She appeared to be communicating with someone inside the vehicle. She turned to face Seth and pushed her sunglasses on top of her head.

Seth's mouth dropped open. This was certainly the most gorgeous girl he'd ever seen. Her chestnut hair accentuated her beautiful hazel eyes. The fruity floral scent of her perfume drifted up to his nostrils. He stood there speechless for a few seconds then finally found his voice. "May I help you?" he squeaked out awkwardly. Oh, he felt like such a *dummkopp*! Who would've ever thought he'd become flustered talking to a girl, and an *Englisch* one at that. He certainly had no desire to become an *Englischer*.

"Yeah, um...uh...I was wondering if maybe you could show me...I mean if you knew where the Amish bed-and-breakfast is?" she stammered in her sweet Southern accent, obviously just as embarrassed as he was.

"There are a few of them around here. Which one were you looking for?" Seth answered calmly, hoping these were the guests they'd be lodging.

"I think it's owned by the Weavers?"

"Yes!" he said a little too enthusiastically and his cheeks reddened. "I mean yes, I know where it is. You're almost there, actually. Just keep heading up this road here about half a mile and make a right onto the first lane you see. The driveway is on the right and there's a large gazebo in the yard. You can't miss it."

"Okay, um...thank you," she said glancing around at the jellies, seemingly stalling for time. "Do you –"

"Brooke, did you get the directions?" a male voice called from the car.

She turned to look at the car then back at Seth. "Well, I guess I better go...uh, bye." She smiled then hesitantly walked back to the car.

Seth watched as the Dodge drove down the road and into the lane that led to his house. "So, it's Brooke, huh?" he whispered to himself with a lopsided grin. Maybe this day wouldn't be so dull after all.

Brooke walked back to the car, moving her sunglasses back over her eyes, and closed the door. She glanced back one more time toward the stand. *Oh my goodness, he was so cute!* She tried so hard not to gawk while the handsome blond Amish guy stood in front of her, but it was difficult. His deep blue eyes reflected off his royal blue shirt and the straw hat and suspenders were just like those she'd seen when researching the Amish online prior to their trip. She hoped that somehow she'd be able to see him again. Hopefully, he worked out there every day. She decided that maybe she'd have to take a walk after getting settled in at the bed 'n breakfast.

CHAPTER 2
Settling In

"This is the day which the Lord hath made; we will rejoice and be glad in it." Psalm 118:24

Jonathan Fisher, Daniel Miller, and Gideon Fisher closed up the woodworking shop for lunch and headed toward the house. As they stomped up the porch stairs, one-and-a-half-year-old twins Jonathan and Judah squealed with delight. The towheaded twin boys loved the time spent with their father. The back door flew open and the boys ran to Jonathan and flung their chubby little arms around each leg.

"*Dat!*" they both exclaimed simultaneously. The very first word the boys learned was *dat* and it was no doubt their favorite.

Jonathan scooped both boys up in each of his strong arms and planted a kiss on both blond heads. "How's JJ today?" he asked using the nickname that referred to both Johnny and Judah.

The boys chattered excitedly in a language that seemingly only they could understand, enjoying every second of attention from their father.

"I'm going to give you to *Dawdi,* so I can say hello to your *mamm,*" he informed the boys, handing them to Gideon. Esther Fisher, their grandmother, relieved Gideon of one of the twins.

Jonathan walked toward his wife, Susanna, wrapped his arms around her, and planted a lingering kiss on her lips.

"*Ach,* Jonathan. Not in front of everyone," Susie chided breathlessly, playfully pushing him away.

"Well, it ain't like they can't tell we're in *lieb.* Besides, I should be able to kiss *mei fraa* in my own home." He smiled and patted her expanding belly, causing Susanna's cheeks to flush. "Maybe this time we'll have a *maedel.* I'd love to have a sweet little Susie running around. And hopefully, she'll look just like her beautiful *mamm.*"

Susie knew that God's will was best, but she hoped for a girl as well. She had her hands full with the twins and she was quickly realizing that they would probably turn out to be just as mischievous as their father. Fortunately, there was an upside to that. While Jonathan may have his moments of mayhem, he also had a kind and caring spirit that Susanna loved and hoped would be passed on to their children.

"How's my little *schweschder* doing?" Jonathan walked to the sink, where Abigail Lapp washed her hands, and tweaked her cheek. Then he walked to Zack and tousled his hair. Although Abigail and Zachariah Lapp were not Jonathan's biological siblings, he'd felt a kinship with them since his father and mother took them in after their mother had died. Their father, Reuben Lapp, was still in prison awaiting trial for murder.

"*Gut*," Abigail answered, then glanced at Daniel Miller and smiled. Abigail and Daniel had been good friends for many years and he was a monument of strength for her when she was grieving the loss of her parents. It seemed their friendship grew daily and just the sight of him brought comfort to her heart.

The entire clan now sat around the large table in the Fisher home and Gideon bowed his head for silent prayer. Everyone followed suit except for little Jonathan and Judah who looked on with smiles, not comprehending. The table was spread with fresh bread just baked this morning, butter, jam, cut up fresh vegetables, homemade applesauce, and chow chow.

"Hey *Mamm*, can I get some peanut butter here?" Jonathan asked.

"*Ach*." Susie gasped. "I can't believe I forgot to put that on the table. I'll get it, Esther." Susanna rose from the table with Judah on her hip and opened the refrigerator to retrieve the peanut butter. She quickly grabbed it from the shelf in the door, but not before Judah reached out and caught hold of a jar of pickles. The jar fell off the shelf and crashed to the ground, sending shattered glass, pickles, and pickle juice sprawling across the kitchen floor.

"*Nee!*" Susie scolded the little boy and he broke into a wail.

Jonathan walked over to Susie and took the little guy, who calmed down immediately. Esther and Abigail quickly rose from their seats and helped clean up the mess. They all finally returned to the table and began eating.

Jonathan plunged a spoon into the jar of peanut butter and stuck it in his mouth. "Mmm...mmm!" Judah reached for the spoon in Jonathan's mouth, but he quickly distracted the little one with a piece of bread.

Daniel spoke up after finishing a sandwich. "Did you say that Lavina Weaver wanted us to make her another bookshelf?" he asked Jonathan.

"*Jah*, she really likes the one we built for her. She especially liked the engraving you did." Jonathan smiled at Daniel.

"Really? She said that?" Daniel asked, then glanced at Abby and she smiled back.

"*Jah*. I think you may have a knack for engraving. Do you think you can make another one with the same design?" he said.

"I think so. I'd probably need to go back to the Weavers' and make a sketch. That was the first time I used that design and I didn't have in mind to use it again, but if that's what she wants..." Daniel's voice trailed off.

"*Gut*," Gideon spoke up. "You can go there after lunch, then. We don't want to keep our customers waiting too long."

"Sure." Daniel turned to Esther. "Do you mind if Abby comes along? I'm sure she'd like to say hello to Leah." He looked to Abigail for approval and she smiled back.

"*Jah*, I can spare her. Just be back in time to help with supper," Esther agreed.

Daniel stood up from the table and looked at Abigail. "Ready to go?"

"*Nee*, I need to help with the dishes," she protested, taking her dishes to the sink.

"I'll take care of the dishes. You two run along now." Esther smiled.

"*Denki*, Esther." Abigail gave her foster mother a kiss on the cheek then happily followed Daniel out the door.

"I wonder when those two will get hitched," Jonathan thought aloud. Everyone else looked up in surprise, as though he was off his rocker. "What? It's plain to see that they like each other." He grinned.

"*Nee*, they're just friends," Esther said, shaking her head. "Besides, they're still young."

Jonathan laughed. "That's what they *say*. I can tell by the way they share glances that they're sweet on each other. Kinda like the way I look at my Susie." He affectionately winked at his wife, causing her to blush once again.

"Just let them be, Jonathan. If it's God's will, He'll work it all out. We don't need to go interfering in the Lord's business," Gideon said.

"Well, I think it's time JJ went down for their nap," Susie interjected then picked up the two little munchkins. She brought them to Jonathan and he gave them each a good hug and planted a kiss on the top of their blond heads. "Tell *Dat 'gut nacht'*." Susanna carried the twins to the adjoining door in the kitchen that led to the small *dawdi haus* and disappeared.

"Best be gettin' back to work now." Gideon stood up and walked over to his wife and placed a kiss on her cheek. Jonathan then followed his father out the door to the woodworking shop.

Lavina Weaver glanced up at the clock again. She wasn't sure what time her guests would be arriving today, but she suspected it would be soon. For some reason, she always felt just a little bit nervous when new guests came to stay at her bed-and-breakfast. She wanted to be a blessing to each guest and a reflection of the love of Jesus. She silently sent up another prayer. *Lord, please send people here who need to hear of Your love for them. Help me to be Your hands and feet and let them see You in me. And please help the* kinner *to behave and be good examples as well. Amen.*

She looked around at the spacious living room where her guests usually congregated when they weren't out sightseeing. She was glad her husband had agreed to order a bookshelf from the Fishers. Jonathan Fisher and Daniel Miller had delivered it just yesterday and she already had it half-way filled with books. Their guests often appreciated having reading material available since there were no televisions or radios. They often commented on the quiet relaxing atmosphere.

A gentle rumble caught her attention and she quickly glanced out at the driveway. *They must be here!* "Leah, our guests are here. Please help me greet them." Lavina opened the front door of the large house and stepped out onto the sweeping wraparound porch, another favorite of the guests. She and Leah hurried down the steps.

"*Wie ghets*! Welcome to our home. Would you like any help with your luggage?" Lavina kindly offered.

A gentleman in his early to mid-forties replied, "No, I think we've pretty much got it."

"Well then, come on inside and we'll get you settled in. My name is Lavina, and this is my oldest daughter, Leah."

"Hello, I'm George and this is my wife, Lila, my son, Ethan, and my daughter, Brooke." He gestured to his family and they each reached out their hands and exchanged handshakes with Lavina and Leah.

Lavina led the way up the steps to the porch as her guests glanced around. They walked into the house and Lavina showed them where their rooms were located. "After you've gotten settled, please join us in the kitchen for some iced tea. I hope you'll make yourselves at home here."

"That sounds wonderful. We've been traveling for hours and we could use a little r-and-r," Lila said before disappearing into one of the bedrooms.

As Brooke set her empty suitcase next to the bedroom door, she glanced around the room. Her temporary living quarters housed two twin beds with a small wooden nightstand in between. A plain black Bible sat atop the small handmade dresser. A small desk sat in the corner with a wooden chair, and a large bureau stood against one of the walls. There was no closet, just a row of pegs on the wall that she assumed was for hanging clothes or towels on. The walls were bare, with the exception of a scenic calendar that hung on the wall. With her clothing all packed into the drawers, she headed toward her parents' room.

As she made her way down the hall, she smiled and thought of Leah. She hoped she could get acquainted with the nice Amish girl. It would be nice to have an Amish friend around her own age, and perhaps they could become pen pals. *I wonder if she knows that cute Amish guy.* "Dad, may I go downstairs to see Leah?" she asked as she entered her parents' room.

"Sure. Just remember that the Amish work hard, so try to stay out of their way," came the exhausted reply from her father.

Brooke quickly slipped into her fuchsia flip-flops and headed out the door. Upon walking down the stairs, she heard female voices in the kitchen prattling along in what she thought was probably Pennsylvania German. She hesitantly greeted, "Hello."

"*Ach*, hello." Lavina nodded at her cheerfully. "Would you like some tea?" She brought out a clear glass pitcher and bright yellow plastic cups.

"Yes, please." Brooke smiled, remembering her manners. "That would be great." She settled into a chair, and sipped some of the iced tea Lavina had given her. "So, Leah," she broke the silence, glancing at the pretty, timid girl in the seat next to her. She looked strangely akin to the Amish boy she'd seen at that stand. They both shared the same heart-shaped face, blonde hair, high cheek bones, and both were reasonably tall. But one thing they didn't share was eye color. The Amish boy had deep blue eyes, while Leah, on the other hand, possessed almost haunting blue-gray eyes. *I wonder if they're related.* She'd heard that a lot of the Amish were related in one way or another. "How old are you?"

"Fourteen," Leah answered, quietly. "And you?"

"I'm fifteen. I can't wait until I'm sixteen, though." Brooke sighed. "Ever since Ethan got his driver's license he's been bragging about how fun it is to drive." She became sheepish all of a sudden when she suddenly realized that she was in an Amish home where driving a car was out of the question. She quickly gulped down the last of her iced tea. "Thanks, Mrs. Wea –"

"Lavina," the proprietress interjected with a smile. "Just call me Lavina."

"Okay." Brooke shrugged her shoulders. "Thank you for the tea, Lavina. It was delicious."

"*Gern geschen,* Brooke. You're welcome."

"Hey, Leah, can you come with me to the roadside stand?" Brooke desperately hoped she wasn't blushing. "I want to buy something." She'd feel a little silly trekking to the stand alone, but would if she had no other choice. What if she didn't get another chance to see the Amish guy?

"I'd like to, but *Mamm* needs my help with dinner," she said apologetically. "Perhaps we can go tomorrow."

Just then, they heard a knock at the back door. "Oh, someone must be here. I wasn't expecting anyone, were you?" Lavina asked her daughter.

"*Nee,*" Leah answered then headed toward the door. "I'll get it."

Leah opened the door to reveal Daniel and Abigail. "*Ach, hiya* Abigail. I didn't expect you." She wrapped her friend in a hug and said hello to Daniel.

"I needed to make sketch of the design on the bookcase so I can make a matching one for your *mamm,*" Daniel explained, peering over her shoulder. "I hope we're not interrupting."

"*Nee.*" Lavina came into the kitchen to greet them. "This is a great time. Our guests are resting now; except for Brooke, here." Lavina smiled and waved her hand toward her guest.

Daniel held out his hand. "Hello, I'm Daniel Miller."

Brooke took his hand. "Brooke Spencer."

Abby stepped forward. "I'm Abigail Lapp." Abigail smiled at Brooke then noticed her and Daniel appraising each other. She didn't have a clue as to why, but a hint of jealousy suddenly crept up. *Why do I care if an* Englischer *is interested in Daniel? Because he's my friend, of course. Yes, that must be why,* she told herself. She decided it would be best if they got out there as quickly as possible. It wouldn't do to lose her best friend to the world. She was thankful when Lavina diverted Daniel's attention elsewhere.

"The bookshelf is over here, Daniel." Lavina motioned and Daniel followed her into the large sitting area with pencil and sketch pad in hand. He set to work while Abby chatted with the Leah and her *Englisch* guest.

About ten minutes later, Abigail and Daniel left the Weavers' in his buggy, heading in the direction of the Fisher residence. Daniel seemed to be preoccupied with the scenery while Abigail had other things on her mind.

"I've been thinkin' about becomin' a baby-catcher," Abby said out of the blue.

"I think you would be a *gut* midwife," Daniel said. "I've seen you with Jonathan's *kinner*. You'll make a *gut mamm,* too."

Abby said nothing in response to that. Had he been implying something? Of course not. He was her best friend and that was all. She looked curiously at Daniel now. He had grown quite a bit taller in the last couple of years and was obviously journeying into manhood. Abigail noticed the faint whiskers that poked out from his chin and the deepening of his voice. His arms and chest suddenly seemed larger and more defined and she attributed their expansion to his long hours in the woodworking shop. She hoped their friendship would not end when he decided to start courting.

"Do you think she's *schee*?" Abby asked, as though Daniel could read her mind.

"Who?" Daniel averted his attention, peering at Abigail.

"The *Englischer*," she stated glumly.

"Brooke? Yeah, she's pretty." Daniel shrugged inconsequentially. His eyes discreetly swept over Abigail. *But not as pretty as you,* he mused.

"I saw you and her looking at each other," Abby stated, attempting to keep the accusation out of her voice.

Now Daniel eyed Abigail with curiosity. *Is she jealous?* He pretended not to notice, but a slow smile crept up the sides of his mouth. "Well, it would be rude not to look at someone when you're introduced." He quickly changed the subject. "Hey, you're old enough to attend Singings now. Will you go on Sunday?"

"*Jah*, with the girls," Abigail said.

Daniel took a deep breath, deciding to bare his heart a little. "I hope you won't ride home with any *buwe*."

"Why not?" she asked.

"Well, it ain't really fair. We're the same age, but I can't go for two more years." Daniel reached over and squeezed her hand. "And besides, I was hopin' to get a chance to court you."

She looked at him in wide-eyed wonder and smiled. "*Ach*, really?" Her cheeks burned.

"*Jah*." He glanced at Abby, giving her a brief smile then quickly looked away.

Lavina asked, "Brooke, do you think your family will be joining us for dinner?"

"I can ask before I go. I'm pretty sure they won't want to go out anywhere, though. Mom and Dad seemed pretty tired." Brooke walked to her parents' room and returned shortly with an affirmative answer.

"What time should I be back for supper?" she asked, glancing at the clock on the wall.

"We'll eat at five," Lavina answered.

"All right then, I'll be sure to be back by five," she called back before bounding out the front door.

CHAPTER 3
An Unexpected Encounter

"Surely the serpent will bite without enchantment..."
Ecclesiastes 10:11

As Brooke walked along the road, she quickly realized that the small roadside stand was further than she'd thought. *I should have worn my tennis shoes*, she chided herself. She wiped the perspiration off her brow, and then picked up her pace when she spotted the stand just up ahead. *I wonder how long that cute guy stays out here for*, she mused to herself.

When she approached the stand, she noticed that most of the items were gone. The handsome young Amish man glanced up as he loaded the few last items into a garden cart. Those gorgeous blue eyes peered at her from beneath his straw hat and he graced her with a smile.

"Oh, I guess I'm too late," she said.

"No, that's alright. I was just getting ready to go home, but if there's something you need I can check if I have any left," he offered.

"That's okay. I was just wanting to look around a bit. I can come back tomorrow. I don't want to be a bother." She turned to go.

"Brooke, wait!" he bellowed, and she spun around.

"How did you know my name?" she wondered aloud, the side of her mouth turning up a bit.

"Oh, well...uh. When you were here earlier I heard someone call you from the car," he explained sheepishly.

And he remembered my name? I'm impressed. "And you are?" She raised her eyebrows.

"Oh, sorry. I must have forgotten my manners. I'm Seth. Seth *Weaver*." He grinned offering her his hand.

Her cheeks flushed a bit as they shook hands a little longer than necessary. "Weaver? As in the owners of the bed-and-breakfast?"

"*Jah*," he admitted bashfully. "I'm on my way back home if you'd like to walk back with me," he offered as he wiped down the empty shelves with a rag. He turned the wooden sign over, indicating that the stand was closed for the day.

"Sure, that'd be great," she agreed.

Seth turned, walking to a hidden path behind the stand. He carted the rest of the goods behind him. Brooke fell into step next to him. The path was wide enough for two people, but required them to nearly walk shoulder to shoulder. "This way is a little shorter than the way you came, and much cooler, too. Sometimes it helps to know your way around."

Slowing down, Brooke glanced up at the huge trees that towered over them as they entered a heavily-wooded area along the path. She gasped in amazement at the new-found treasure and breathed in deeply of the heady pine scent. "This place is beautiful. If I lived here, I reckon I'd walk through this area every day. It's so cool. What is it, like ten degrees cooler or somethin'?"

"Not sure exactly. I like it, too, though. It's a very peaceful place to come when you need to think or pray." He glanced toward Brooke walking on his right and took in her beauty. *She's awful pretty. Too bad she's not Amish,* he thought dejectedly.

Brooke looked to her left to steal a glance at Seth. *He's looking at me, too.* Seth's eyes caught hers and she was certain something passed between them. *Maybe I* will *have a handsome Amish boy sweep me off my feet.* She smiled up at him and he grinned back.

Seth cleared his throat then peeled his eyes off her. Trying to come up with intelligent conversation, he asked, "How long will your family be –" He stopped abruptly and put his arm out in front of her.

"Don't move!" he whispered urgently.

"What is it?" She stopped and followed the direction of Seth's eyes. "Aah!" she screamed at the top of her lungs as she caught sight of what he was looking at. It was a snake! An extremely scary-looking one at that, just a foot away from her. After hearing a distinct rattling sound, she jumped back in fright. The snake leaped forward and struck her ankle before slithering off in the other direction. She cried out in pain.

Seth immediately dropped the cart handle and scooped her up into his arms. She would have been ecstatic about it given different circumstances, she decided. He took off in a brisk jog, tucking her close to his chest.

"I'm gonna die! I'm gonna die!" She began to panic.

Seth tried to soothe her. "No, you'll be just fine. I'm going to take you to Philip King. He's the herbalist and he'll know what to do," he said as he effortlessly carried her out of the woods in his strong arms. *I hope I get there in time before the poison spreads.* He silently prayed, *God, please help Brooke. Let her be okay. Work this out for Your good somehow.* He jogged faster, thankful that the herb shop wasn't too far from the Weavers' bed-and-breakfast.

As Brooke felt the poison traveling up her leg she began to panic. "God, please don't let me die. I'm not ready to die!" she pleaded softly.

Seth burst through the door of the herb shop with Brooke in his arms. "Philip! Philip! She's been bit by a snake." The calmness Brooke had seen earlier in Seth disappeared and she wondered if he believed her life to be in serious danger.

A forty-something-year-old man with a dark brown beard swiftly came to their attention. "Set her on Sadie's massage table and I'll get the Plantain." Seth did as Philip ordered and soon Philip returned with some fresh leaves in his hand. He quickly pulverized them in a mortar and placed the green poultice over where the snake had bitten her. He took out a brown dropper bottle and placed several drops of the liquid into a cup of hot tea and advised Brooke to drink it down quickly. "Just keep the poultice on your ankle and it will draw out the poison."

Philip turned to Seth. "What kind of snake was it?"

"A Timber Rattler," he said knowledgeably.

"Hmm...Timber Rattlesnakes seldom strike unless they feel threatened," Philip said.

"Well, I sorta freaked out. I guess it felt threatened by me," Brooke explained.

"In case this ever happens again, I'd like to show you both what Plantain looks like before you leave. That way, you can treat the bite yourself right away. The sooner a venomous bite is treated, the better the chances of survival. Snake bites are not to be messed with so I'm glad you brought her here quickly. There's a rule of thumb that nearly always rings true. When you get bitten by a venomous creature or accidentally encounter a poisonous plant, stop and look around you. Within eye-shot, the herbal remedy for the ailment should be growing somewhere nearby. I've personally never seen it fail," Philip shared.

"Wow, that's amazing!" Brooke declared.

"*Jah*, it is. Please show us this plant and I'll look for it when I go back to get the garden cart," Seth said.

"Oh, I forgot we left it there," Brooke said absentmindedly. "Sorry."

"Don't worry, no one will bother it. Well, that is, if a raccoon doesn't happen upon it," Seth said as he looked down at Brooke's leg. "It looks like that red streak is gone now."

"*Jah*," Philip spoke. "The poison is nearly gone. I'll put a fresh poultice on then you two can be on your way."

"*Denki*, Philip. I really appreciate your help," Seth said.

"Yeah, thanks. I'm glad I'm not dead," Brooke said, then glanced down at her watch. "Oh no, your mother said dinner would be ready at five. It's twenty till."

"That's alright, I think we can make it back on time," Seth assured her.

"You may take my buggy if you'd like. She shouldn't be walking on that leg just yet," Philip advised.

"*Nee*, we'll be fine. But thanks for the offer," Seth answered, and then turned to Brooke. "You ready to go?"

"Yes, but how –" She was rendered silent when Seth scooped her back up into his strong arms again. He turned and pushed the door open by leaning into it with his back, sending a goodbye to the herbalist before exiting. Brooke looked up at him and couldn't keep her cheeks from blushing. She was hoping to be swept off her feet, but goodness, she didn't expect it to happen literally!

"Just hold onto that bottle of tincture Philip gave you and I'll get us home as quickly as possible." He smiled down at her in his arms and he felt her head relax against his chest.

"Thank you, Seth. You couldn't imagine how frightened I was," Brooke admitted.

"I didn't do anything. *Der Herr*...uh, The Lord was looking out for you."

"I thought for sure I was going to die. I'm not ready yet," Brooke shared.

Seth studied her with concern. "What do you mean?"

"I'm not sure whether I'm going to Heaven or Hell," she explained.

"Oh, I see," he said thoughtfully.

"How about you? Do you know if you're going to Heaven?"

"*Jah,* I do."

"How do you know? I mean, how can you know for sure?" she spoke her thoughts.

Seth looked at her intensely. "Brooke, do you believe in God?"

"Yes. I mean, we don't go to church or anything. But I do believe there is a God."

"Have you ever read the Bible?" he asked curiously.

"No, I haven't," she stated matter-of-factly.

"Okay, I'll try to explain it in the most concise way I can think of. The Bible is God's words for mankind. Kind of like a letter that God wrote for His creation." He continued. "About six thousand years ago, God created mankind. God made man to worship Him, but God wants our worship or our love voluntarily. Man chose to sin, thereby choosing his own way instead of God's. The Bible says that the wages of sin is death. Sin must be paid for."

"Okay, I think I understand." Brooke listened.

"God knew that our sin would keep us out of Heaven, so He sent His son Jesus Christ to die on the cross to pay the penalty for our sin. We celebrate His coming at Christmas time." He checked to make sure she understood, and she nodded. "He's the only one who could've paid for our sins, because He was the only one who was sinless. You see, I couldn't have paid for your sins because I'm a sinner and vice-versa."

"But Jesus was sinless?"

"That's correct. God offers us forgiveness of sin and eternal life in Heaven as a free gift. There is nothing we can do to earn it. When we reject God's free gift, then we have to pay for our own sins, which means we'd have to go to Hell," he explained.

"So, how do I accept His gift?" she wondered.

"The Bible says, "That if thou shalt confess with thy mouth the Lord Jesus, and shalt believe in thine heart that God hath raised him from the dead, thou shalt be saved. For with the heart man believeth unto righteousness; and with the mouth confession is made unto salvation.""

"Believeth unto righteousness?"

"Yes. When you accept Jesus as your Savior, you receive the righteousness of Christ. So when you stand before God, He will see you sinless; because Christ paid for your sins. Do you understand?"

"Yes, so confess with my mouth and believe in my heart. I guess that would mean I need to pray to God and mean it with all my heart," she reiterated.

"Yep. That's what I did," Seth said.

They remained silent the remainder of the way home and Seth perceived that Brooke was probably praying. He sent up a quick prayer as well, thanking God for the opportunity to share His love with this amazing girl. He also asked God to show him His will concerning Brooke.

When Seth opened the door to his home with Brooke in his arms, they were met with curious stares. Both Brooke's and Seth's families sat around the long table. Brooke's father noticed the patch on her ankle and eyed his daughter with concern. "Is something wrong?"

"No, not anymore," Brooke said as Seth set her down near the table. She caught the disapproving look Seth's father had given him and hoped she hadn't caused him too much grief.

"She got bit by a Timber Rattler," Seth explained.

Brooke's mother gasped. "Oh, no!"

"I took her to Philip King immediately and he gave her some herbs. They drew the poison out right away, but Philip said she shouldn't walk on her ankle just yet."

"*Ach, Sohn.* You should have borrowed Philip's buggy to come home," his mother chided.

"*Nee.* I didn't mind carrying her." Seth glanced Brooke's way with a knowing smile. She returned his gaze and smiled back. Yep, something was definitely happening between them.

"But she's fine now?" Lila asked, still concerned.

"*Jah.* Philip gave her some herbs to continue taking and said it should be fine to walk on by morning," Seth said.

"How do you feel, honey? Do you think you should be seen by a doctor?" George asked his daughter.

"No. I feel fine, Dad," Brooke answered.

"Philip King is one of the finest doctors there is. He would have told Brooke if he thought it was necessary to see a physician, but you do what feels right for you," Lavina assured him. "We can give you the phone number of a physician if you'd like."

"I would like to have her checked out, just to be on the safe side. We can take her to a clinic after dinner," her father stated.

"Dad, I really don't think that's necessary," Brooke protested, but her father was insistent and she knew not to argue.

"Shall we continue our meal now?" Seth's father, Noah, suggested and everyone contently ate the delicious meal prepared by Lavina and Leah.

CHAPTER 4
New Friends

"A man that hath friends must shew himself friendly..." Proverbs 18:24

"Let's hurry, Brooke. I want you to meet my friends – Ruthie, Katie, and you remember Abby," Leah encouraged excitedly. Lately, she'd been busy helping her *mamm* with the bed-and-breakfast, and since she was done with school, she mostly only saw her friends at Singings and Sunday-Go-to-Meetings. This visit was a treat for Leah, so she wanted to spend as much time with her friends as possible. She'd wanted Brooke to meet her friends, but now she worried that they might tell her that she shouldn't be friends with an *Englischer*.

It doesn't matter, Leah decided as they neared the Kings' property. *Brooke is only staying for a little while.*

"How old is Seth?" Brooke's voice brought Leah out of her musings.

"He's sixteen." Leah looked to Brooke questioningly. "Why do you ask?"

Brooke's cheeks reddened. "I...um...uh...I was just wondering."

It was obvious to Leah that Seth was sweet on Brooke. Did Brooke fancy her brother, too? Leah smiled; she knew how that felt. She'd had a secret crush on Adam Glick for almost a year now and wondered if he'd ever notice her. She was disappointed when, time after time, he'd asked different girls home from the Singings. Just last Sunday, Adam asked her if he could take her home in his buggy and she'd said yes. They had a wonderful time and Adam even asked her to ride home with him again this week. She hoped this was the beginning of something special, since no girl that she knew of had been asked to go riding with him more than once.

"So, do you like him?" Leah knew it wasn't her business, but asked anyway.

"Yeah, he's really nice." She paused, wondering whether she should ask what she was thinking or not. "Does he have a girlfriend?"

"Seth? *Nee*." Leah shook her head. "I don't think he wants an *aldi* right now. He hasn't asked anyone home from a Singing yet."

"Oh." Brooke blew out the air she'd been holding in. "I'm sure many a girl has been disappointed."

"Perhaps. But..." Leah said tentatively, "It seems to me that he might be sweet on you." She looked to Brooke for her reaction.

Brooke's eyes widened. "Do you think so?"

"Well, I saw the way he looked at you when he carried you into the house." Leah laughed out loud. "He sure did get a talkin' to from *Dat*...and *Mamm*."

"Oh, no. I hope he didn't get into trouble because of me." Brooke worried.

"I'm sure Seth considered the consequences beforehand. He must've thought you were worth it." Leah smiled, but then frowned.

"What's wrong, Leah?" Brooke eyed her new friend curiously. "Do you not like me?"

"*Ach, nee.* I'm sorry. Of course I like you. It's just that...oh, I don't know if I should say anything or not. Seth *is* still in his *rumspringa*." She blew out a long breath.

"What do you mean?" Confusion shown on Brooke's pretty face.

"He's allowed to court *Englisch* girls right now, but it could never turn into something serious. I mean, if you and my brother were to fall in love than there would be a lot of problems for both of you," Leah stated glumly.

"I don't understand. Why?"

"Amish can only marry Amish. You're not Amish," Leah stated matter-of-factly.

"Oh, I see." Brooke tried not to let the disappointment show on her face.

"I'd just hate to see Seth get his heart broken, that's all." Leah wiped her sweaty hands on her apron. She lifted her eyes and spotted her friends near Miller's pond. "*Ach*, there they are."

Brooke glanced up to see Leah's three friends, all dressed like her, sitting on a small boating dock. Wispy willow trees graced the bank on one side of the pond. A small island with a few willow trees sat several hundred yards out in the middle of the water. She wondered how deep the small body of water was, thinking it would be fun to swim out to the island.

"Do you swim here?" Brooke asked.

"*Jah*, especially in summer. We could come and swim one day," Leah offered. "I'm sure Daniel's folks won't mind."

"Daniel?"

"Daniel Miller. The one you met the other day with Abigail. His family owns the lake and that house over yonder." Leah pointed to a large white farmhouse, partially hidden from view by trees. "Some people think that Daniel and Abby are sweet on each other."

"Are they?"

"They've been *gut* friends for a long time. I don't know. I don't think so." Leah smiled, and then grasped Brooke's hand, pulling her along. "*Kumm*, I can't wait for you to meet my friends."

Brooke followed Leah around the lake to where the small dock was located. They walked out onto the wooden planks and Leah's friends stood up. A jovial strawberry-blonde-haired girl smiled broadly and reached out her freckled hand. "I'm Ruthie Esh! You must be staying at Lavina's bed-and-breakfast," she said cheerfully.

"Hello, Ruthie. Nice to meet you. I'm Brooke." She shook the friendly girl's hand.

"I'm Abigail Lapp...or Abby. We met at Leah's yesterday," the pretty blonde girl said.

"And I'm Katie King," a cute brunette said. By the volume of her hair, Brooke figured Katie probably had curls; a perfect accent to the small dimple on her cheek. Shirley Temple came to mind and Brooke had to smile to herself.

Brooke thought for a moment, the last name rang a bell. "Are you related to Philip King?"

"*Jah*, he's my *dat*," Katie said, and then her eyes grew wide. "You were bit by a snake, right?"

"Yes. I was so scared. If Seth hadn't carried me to your father, I could have died," Brooke stated in her twangy Georgia accent, and her cheeks flushed a bit at the mention of Seth's name.

"*Jah, Dat* told me about that." Katie's smile quickly faded.

"I heard he carried you back home, too!" Ruthie piped up in a sing-song voice. "That's so romantic."

Abigail sensed Brooke's uneasiness and quickly spoke up, changing the subject. "Did you hear that Joshua Hostettler and Annie Yoder will probably be getting married this fall?"

"*Ach*, I didn't hear that," Leah said. "They haven't been published yet."

"No, but I overheard Annie and Susie talking about planting celery the other day. They both seemed to be excited." Abigail smiled.

"I wonder if some of the bishop's family will be coming over from out of state. It's sure to be a large wedding. Maybe there'll be some cute *buwe* coming!" Ruthie said enthusiastically.

"*Jah;* and maybe you'll get paired up with one." Katie smiled. "Abigail, are you and Daniel going to be there?"

"I don't know; it's still a ways away. He's been working a lot lately with Jonathan, though. They've been really busy." She turned to Leah. "Leah, did you like the bookcase they made for your *mamm*?"

"*Jah*, 'twas beautiful!" Leah praised.

"Daniel designed the carving. I think he did a *gut* job," Abigail said proudly.

"Hey, Abby, have you heard whether Jonathan is planning any pranks for their wedding or not?" Ruthie asked.

Brooke looked at the girls in confusion and they quickly explained to her how friends Jonathan Fisher, Matthew Riehl, and Joshua Hostettler often played pranks on others and on each other. Brooke laughed when she pictured an Amish man climbing up a tree to retrieve clothing. Clearly, the people in

Leah's community knew how to mix fun into their busy work-loads.

"I'm sure he's got somethin' planned or he's cookin' some-thin' up, but I don't know what it is. You know Jonathan," Abigail answered, bringing Brooke out of her musings. "He's certainly the mastermind of the three. And after what Matthew and Joshua did at Jonathan and Susie's wedding, I just can't see him letting Joshua get off scot-free."

Brooke impatiently paced back and forth on the large wrap-around porch, holding a cell phone to her ear. "Listen, Kyle. I called to talk to Kelly, so please put her back on the phone."

Seth strode up the steps and took a seat on the porch swing at the opposite end of the porch, trying not to eavesdrop. It seemed like whoever was on the other end of the telephone was really getting on Brooke's nerves.

"Don't call me 'babe'! I told you that I didn't want to see you anymore." Frustration showed in her face and she tried to stay calm. "Please give the phone back to Kelly. I didn't call to talk to you; I wanted to talk to her!"

"May I?" Brooke felt chills run up her spine when she heard Seth whisper in her other ear, and held out his hand for the phone. She gave him a bewildered look, then relinquished the phone.

"Hello, who's this?" Seth's deep voice spoke into the phone.

"I'm Seth." Pause. "Yes, I am," he stated calmly and Brooke looked at him curiously. He smiled back. "Oh, *hiya*, Kelly. Here's Brooke." Seth handed the phone back to her and she stared at him in amazement.

Seth walked over to the other end of the porch and sat back down on the swing to give Brooke privacy. Brooke perched on the porch railing around the corner and continued the conversation with her friend. Seth stared out at the gazebo trying to occupy his mind with other things. Several minutes later, she returned to the swing and sat down next to Seth.

"What did you say to get Kyle to give the phone over to Kelly?" She raised her eyebrows in curiosity.

Seth cleared his throat. "He asked me if I was your new boyfriend and I said yes."

Brooke's cheeks flushed furiously and she sat there speechless.

"Well, I *am* a boy. And we are friends, right?"

"Yes, that's true. But I don't think he meant –"

"That's okay," he interjected. "Let him think what he wants."

CHAPTER 5
Covered Bridges

"...But be thou an example of the believers, in word, in conversation, in charity, in spirit, in faith, in purity." 1 Timothy 4:12

George Spencer stepped into the large shop where Noah and Seth were busy working. He was taken aback at the sound of power tools. He thought the Amish weren't allowed to use electricity. He glanced around and then noticed a gasoline-powered generator providing power to the tools. *I guess there's ways around everything,* he chuckled to himself.

"Hello, George," Noah Weaver greeted. "Feel free to take a look around the shop. Do you have any questions?"

He ran his hand over a sanded piece of railing. "Wow! You do an amazing job. The craftsmanship on this is remarkable." He noticed an octagon shaped deck, and whistled. "Nothin' like those kits they sell."

"That's our most popular design," Noah stated matter-of-factly.

"What size is this?" He'd mentally figured about twelve feet.

"That'll be a twelve-foot octagon gazebo when it's completed. Also the most popular size," Noah said. "You're welcome to take a look at our catalog, if you'd like."

"Do you ever do out-of-state jobs?" George eyed him curiously as he perused the colorful images in the catalog.

Seth quietly listened to the conversation as he hand-sanded a spindle.

"*Jah*, but there are some extra charges involved. It can get expensive. There's mileage and also accommodations."

"What if accommodations are provided?" he asked curiously and Seth's eyebrows went up.

"Well, then I reckon it would be a mite cheaper," Noah said.

"I'd like to surprise my wife with one for our anniversary. Do you think you'd be able to come down to Georgia in October? I have a travel trailer that you and your son could stay in while you're there," George offered. "How long will it take you to build?"

"About a week," Noah answered. "And, *jah*, Seth and I could do the job if you'd like."

"Great! I'd like to put a down payment on it right now, if that's all right," George said enthusiastically. "Lila will love it. She's been admiring that gazebo out front ever since we arrived. I can't wait to see the look on her face when she sees her very own."

"Just fill out this paperwork so we know what you want. Seth can handle all the details for you," Noah stated confidently as Seth waved George over to a large desk in the corner of the shop.

"Did you enjoy your time in Lancaster yesterday?" Lavina asked her guests as they congregated around the breakfast table once again.

"Oh yeah. We bought some nice souvenirs and ate at a restaurant, but the food wasn't as good as yours," Lila commented.

Lavina's cheeks flushed at the compliment, and she tried to quell the pride that attempted to rear its ugly head. "*Denki.* What are your plans for today?"

"I thought it would be fun to do some sightseeing around here. I'd like to see the covered bridges I've been reading about," Lila said. "Do you ever escort guests in your horse and buggy? We could pay you extra."

"No extra payment is needed. To be hospitable to someone else is a blessing from *Der Herr.* I'll see if Seth can get away," Lavina said and Brooke's eyebrows rose at the mention of Seth's name.

"I'd like to go, too, Mom." Brooke piped up.

"But I thought you said you wanted to stay around here, honey." Lila countered.

"I...uh...changed my mind." Brooke glanced at Leah, who gave her a knowing look and smiled.

Seth bounded into the kitchen through the back door. "Did I hear my name?"

"*Jah, Sohn.* Mrs. Spencer and her daughter were just saying they'd like to take a buggy ride to see the covered bridges. Do you think your *daed* can spare you today?"

Seth briefly locked eyes with Brooke and smiled. "Sure, *Mamm.* I would love to take Brooke on a buggy ride...er...I mean...uh, and her *mamm* too. We've pretty much finished up the last job so *Daed* shouldn't have a problem letting me go."

"Great!" Lila smiled. "When should we be ready to go?"

"How does thirty minutes sound?" Seth asked.

"That sounds great!" Brooke answered and Seth winked at her before stepping outside.

Brooke walked down the hallway to her mother's room and knocked on the door. "Mom, Seth is downstairs already. Are you ready to go?"

A muffled voice came from inside the room that Brooke couldn't decipher. She slowly opened the door and peered inside. Her mother lay on the bed with the back of her hand on her forehead. "I'm sorry, honey. I've just come down with a splitting headache. You go ahead and go without me."

"Are you sure, Mom?" Concern creaked in her voice.

"Yes. And if you see your father on the way out, please tell him I'm resting." She groaned.

"Okay, Mom. I'm sorry you don't feel well. I'll pray that you get better soon." Brooke grimaced as she closed the door. She was looking forward to the time she would spend with her mother and Seth and she wasn't sure whether the plans would be canceled now or not. For some reason, both options frightened her. Because either way, she and Seth would have the whole day to spend together. She quietly reminded herself about what Leah had said earlier, and decided she would try her best to guard her heart.

"I'm sorry that your *mamm* isn't feeling well," Seth offered as he maneuvered the horse and buggy down the lane out to the main road.

"Yeah, me too," Brooke said disappointedly. "I hope she feels better soon."

"It's funny how God works sometimes," he thought aloud.

"What do you mean?" Brooke cocked her head.

"Well, I was thinking that we weren't going to get to spend much time together. Now, here we are with a whole day to ourselves."

"I guess I never really thought about it as a provision from the Lord." Brooke thought for a moment. "Did I tell you that

I've been reading my Bible lately? Well, I guess it's not really *my* Bible, but the one in the room."

"*Nee.*" Seth was glad that she was eager to learn about God. "What did you read?"

"Well, there's something that I'm confused about. You know how in Second Corinthians it talks about not being unequally yoked with unbelievers?"

"*Jah.* I've read that."

"Leah said that Amish only marry Amish. Is that right?" She listened for his response.

"That's right. Unless they become *Englisch* or an *Englischer* becomes Amish."

"Why? I mean, you don't have to be an Amish person to be saved. And just because someone is Amish doesn't make them a believer," she mused aloud.

"You're right," Seth answered. "I guess the Amish mostly intermarry to preserve our heritage and to protect us from becoming too worldly."

"Do you think I'm worldly?" she asked curiously.

Seth blew out a breath. *Should I be honest?* He chose to remain silent and looked away.

"I'll take that as a yes," she concluded glumly.

"Well, the Amish practice humility and modesty. Things that the Bible teaches."

"Do you think I'm immodest?" She appeared slightly shocked at the possibility.

"Honestly? Yes," he said regrettably, hoping he hadn't offended her.

"Why? How?" she said with a bewildered look on her face.

"You wear pants and your shirt is...uh...form fitting." He sighed, not comfortable with where this conversation was headed.

"Everyone wears pants," she defended herself.

"*Nee*. Not the Amish women."

"I see. But what's wrong with it?" She didn't understand.

"Pants and some shirts define every curve on a woman's body. I guess women don't realize that how they dress can be really tempting to a man. It causes us to sin sometimes," he admitted. "I would never allow my wife dress that way."

"Oh, wow. I had no idea that that's what men think." She glanced down at her fitted blouse and tight denim Capri pants and blushed. "I'm sorry. I just...I've never heard anything like that before."

"Look, Brooke. I hope I didn't offend you, but I'm not gonna lie." Seth sighed. "How about if we change the subject? I'm not really all that comfortable talking about this kind of stuff."

"I'm sorry. I never should have brought it up, but I'm glad I did. Next time I get dressed, I'll think twice about what I wear. I think I'll need to do some shopping though." She smiled at the thought of purchasing new, modest clothes.

"I'm glad that you're willing to change and I commend you for it. Most people, even believers, would just shrug some things off and ignore them. Even if the Bible speaks against it."

Seth realized that Brooke really was sincere about doing the right thing and it warmed his heart.

The horse trotted up to a covered bridge and Seth pulled hard on the reins, bringing the large animal to a halt. "This is Miller's Bridge. It's the closest one in these parts. We like it because most *Englischers* don't know about it, so it's still pretty private."

Brooke looked up and all around, taking in the large wooden structure. "How old is it?" She wondered aloud as she noticed the wooden planks under the buggy.

"I reckon it's over a hundred years old."

"It's very pretty. I like the sound of the rushing water underneath," she commented, and glanced at Seth.

"*Jah.* Perfect for a kissing bridge." He smiled.

"Huh? A kissing bridge?" Brooke raised her eyebrows.

"That's what we call 'em sometimes 'cuz boys often bring their *aldis* here." Seth stared at her intently and slowly moved closer. When she held his gaze and didn't move away, he leaned down toward her and closed his eyes, gently placing his lips on hers. A few seconds later, she pulled away.

"Seth, do you really think we should be –" Brooke was abruptly cut off when Seth's lips met hers again. He was hard to resist, but she kept hearing Leah's warning ringing in her head. She pulled away again.

"What's wrong, Brooke?" he asked gently, as he looked deeply into her hazel eyes.

"It's just...I'm not comfortable with this." she tried to explain.

He gave her a concerned look. "But I thought we –"

"No, it's not that. I really like you a lot, Seth."

"Well, then, what's the problem? I don't intend on taking advantage of you, if that's what you're thinking." He frowned.

"That's not it. I know you wouldn't try to do that," she said naively. "It's Leah."

"My sister?" He gave her a puzzled look.

"Yeah. She said that a relationship between us could never work because you're Amish and I'm *Englisch*."

"*Ach, mei schweschder* should mind her own business," he grumbled.

"Not to mention we live like six hundred miles away from each other." She shook her head. "It just seems impossible, that's all."

"But with God, all things are possible." He didn't know why, but for some reason the verse just popped into his mind. "That's what the Bible says."

"So, do you really think a relationship could work?" She hoped it was so. *Would Seth leave his Amish roots or would I have to become Amish? I'm not sure if I could.*

"I supposed it's happened before. I'm willing to give it a try if you are." He smiled. "If it's God's will for us to be together, then He'll make a way."

"It would be hard, but I think I'm willing to take the risk." She smiled back at him.

"Brooke?" He gazed into her eyes again and she lifted her eyebrows in question. "Will you be my *aldi*...my girlfriend?"

"I'd love to." She smiled and he pulled her into an embrace. He leaned down to kiss her, but before their lips met, she quickly turned away, confused as a thought entered her mind. "Seth, do you think God would want us to be doing this? Kissing."

"Well –" He paused, not knowing what to say. *Lord, is it wrong for me to kiss Brooke? If it is, please let me know, because it sure does feel right.* The answer came clearly and quickly. *'Intreat the younger women as sisters, with all purity.'* He definitely wouldn't be this close to his sister; but Brooke wasn't his sister. Oh, it was so hard to resist temptation as she sat right next to him! He knew that this beautiful girl beside him was right, though. *How did she get so wise?* He wondered. "I guess you're right." He sighed disappointedly and scooted back, putting more distance between them.

Attempting to lighten the mood and turn his thoughts elsewhere, Seth changed the subject. "So what else in the Bible have you been reading?"

Brooke visibly brightened at his mention of the Bible. "Well, I first started reading Genesis and it got me confused on some things."

"Such as?"

"Well, it said God made the world – which if He's God, I can see how He would have made it – but at school they teach us that billions of years ago the Big Bang formed the earth from an infinitesimal region and then man evolved over millions of years from primates that evolved from a single-cell organism which came from some kind of pre-biotic soup," Brooke rambled with a bewildered look on her face.

"Huh? Wait a minute, what did you just say?" Seth's face mirrored her confusion. Brooke started to say the same thing and Seth interrupted her. "No, never mind about that. It's just that I've never heard of such absurd things before. They actually teach that stuff in public schools? And people *believe* it?" He wasn't sure whether he wanted to laugh or cry.

"Well, now that you put it that way, it does sound kind of silly," Brooke admitted truthfully.

"Now, you were saying?" Seth prompted.

"Anyways, then it talks about Noah building the ark and stuffing it with a bunch of animals inside, including dinosaurs, right?" Brooke questioned further.

"Right. Please continue."

"Well, how did all the dinosaurs fit? Dinosaurs are huge. It'd be impossible to fit them on the ark along with all the other animals too," she stated logically.

Seth raised his eyebrows. "Are you doubting God's Word?"

"To be truthful, yes." She rubbed her nose reflectively. "I believe God's Word is true, but I have a hard time believing some things, especially considering that I go to public school and it's all I've ever heard of up until now. I mean, you have to look at the facts. Now, about my question."

"Who said the dinosaurs were big?" he asked.

Brooke looked shocked. "Dinosaurs *are* big."

"No, I mean, who said they were full-grown? How do you know the animals weren't babies?" he challenged.

A light dawned on Brooke and she nodded. "Ah, I see now. Noah must have been a total genius to figure it all out."

"*Gott* told Noah what He wanted to be done and he obeyed. He wasn't a genius, but he was definitely wise. This Big Bang theory – has it been proven as a fact? " he challenged.

"Well, no." Brooke thought on it for a moment. "But it's what most scientists believe. And scientists are really smart."

For some reason, believing that man came from soup didn't sound all that intelligent to Seth. "Perhaps, but are they smarter than God?"

And there it was, the heart of the matter.

CHAPTER 6
Love in the Air

"Many waters cannot quench love, neither can the floods drown it..." Song of Solomon 8:7

Leah hummed quietly to herself as she placed another loaf of bread dough into the oven. Since finishing up school, she'd come to love the time spent in the kitchen learning from *Mamm* how to become a *gut Amish fraa*. Would Adam Glick become her *mann?* Heat coursed through her body at the thought. Time seemed to fly when she tended to her daily chores and she looked forward to the day when she'd be able to run her own household. She glanced up at the clock once again and noticed the time. She sighed.

Her brother Seth and Brooke Spencer had been gone for hours now and it worried her. It wasn't that she didn't like Brooke or anything, she just had a nagging concern for her brother. Would he leave the community and their people for a worldly *Englisch* life? As brother and sister, they had always been close and she wasn't ready to lose that bond. And because Seth was still in his *rumspringa* and not a baptized member of the community, he wouldn't be shunned if he left. The more time he spent with Brooke, Leah knew the greater the pull to the outside world would be for her brother. She shuddered at the thought of him leaving their family. *Lord, please don't take Seth away from us. I love my brother and I do want your will, but perhaps you can direct his way to an Amish girl?* Leah knew she shouldn't be telling God what to do, but the Bible did say to make your requests known to God. Was it selfish to want her brother close by?

She turned as she heard a clatter on the back steps. She opened the door to her friend Ruthie Esh and she came bounding merrily through the door. "Hello, Leah!" she exclaimed as she wrapped her friend in an embrace. "Who is that handsome *Englischer* sitting on your front porch?" she ask unabashedly.

"Shh...his *mamm's* just in the other room," Leah whispered. "That's Brooke's brother, Ethan."

"*Ach*, can you introduce me to him?" Ruthie pleaded.

"Well, I don't know –"

"Oh, sorry to bother you, Leah. But my mom asked me to –" Ethan stopped dead in his tracks when he locked eyes with Ruthie and a smile played on his lips.

Oh great! Now Ruthie's gonna go Englisch, *too.* Leah rolled her eyes. "What did you need, Ethan?"

Ethan just stood there, mesmerized. He obviously didn't hear a word Leah said. "Hi," he said as he continued to stare at Ruthie.

"Hi." She smiled back, holding his gaze. To Leah's surprise, it was the first time she had ever seen her friend at a loss for words.

Leah sighed and threw up her hands in exasperation, then walked out of the room. "There must be love bugs in the air or something. I hope I don't get bit," she muttered to herself, then joined Lila Spencer in the sitting room. "I hope you're feeling better now," she sympathized as she wondered what Ethan had originally come into the kitchen for.

"Yes, I am. Thank you. The nap was just what I needed." She glanced toward the kitchen. "I sent Ethan into the kitchen to get some iced peppermint tea. I thought he'd be back by now."

"He must have gotten sidetracked. I'd be happy to get some for you." Leah arose from the rocking chair and strode back into the kitchen. She noticed that Ruthie and Ethan had gone out to the back porch and she breathed a sigh of relief. That last thing she wanted to see was two love birds making goo-goo eyes at each other. She'd seen enough of that with Brooke and Seth. Leah quickly removed two glasses from the cupboard and pulled the pitcher of peppermint tea out of the refrigerator, pouring a glass for herself as well, and rejoined Lila in the sitting room.

"Whoa!" Seth called out to Dandy as he neared the hitching post. He smiled at Brooke, then quickly jumped down to tether the golden-hued mare. He walked to Brooke's side of the buggy, reached for her hand, and gently helped her down. Seth glanced about the yard to be sure no one else was around, then pulled her into an embrace.

"Huh...hmm!" they heard someone on the back porch clearing their throat loudly, and they both immediately jumped back. "Looks like someone had a good time today." Brooke heard her brother Ethan chuckle from the back porch.

"Ethan, don't do that! You scared me half to death," Brooke exclaimed. As she and Seth ascended the back stairs, she noticed her brother's hand intertwined with Ruthie's, one of Leah's Amish friends. She whispered something in Seth's ear and he stepped into the house without her. Brooke turned to her brother. "Ethan, may I talk to you for a minute please?"

"Ah..." He sighed, then turned to Ruthie. "I'll be back in just a minute. Don't go anywhere," He winked before joining his sister and they walked around the porch to the front.

Brooke gave him a stern look. "Ethan, what were you doing?"

"Talking to a pretty girl." He shrugged.

"What about Jessica? Your girlfriend?" she pointedly reminded her brother.

Ethan gave out a long sigh. He and Jessica had been dating for almost a year, but he knew she'd been seeing other guys behind his back. Although he knew this, he'd still been faithful to her – until now. "I'll call her. Later." He looked at his sister and sighed again. "So, what's with you and Seth? You know what, never mind, we can talk about it later. We don't have all that much time and I want to spend as much time with Ruthie as I can."

Brooke raised her eyebrows as she got a wonderful idea. "Hey! Maybe we can talk Mom and Dad into moving here," she suggested hopefully.

"Don't hold your breath, Brooke. We might be able to talk them into staying longer, though." Ethan stood up from the porch swing and kissed his younger sister on the forehead and waved before rounding the corner.

"Good." Now satisfied, Brooke flounced inside, letting the screen door slam behind her.

"Ruthie, would you like to go out with me? On a date," Ethan asked hopefully, sitting on the swing next to her.

Ruthie thought for a moment, wondering if she'd be able to get away. "When?"

"Whenever you're available. My schedule's pretty much open while we're here." He smiled in anticipation.

"Where do you want to go?" She smiled back.

"Well, since I'm not very familiar with the area, I thought maybe you could suggest something." He rubbed his sweaty palms on his jeans.

Ruthie's eyes lit up like a flash of lightning in the dead of night. *"Ach, jah –"*

"I love it when you do that." He lifted her fingers to his lips and gently kissed her fingertips.

Ruthie's cheeks flushed and a shiver of delight coursed through her body. "Do what?"

"When your big beautiful green eyes light up and you speak with that cute little German accent." He grinned.

"I like your accent too." She tried to mimic him in her best Southern accent.

Ethan chortled. "Oh, yeah?" He gazed into her eyes and moved a little closer. "And how about my eyes?"

"Uh...huh." His lips nearly touched hers, but she abruptly backed away.

"What's the matter?" He sat back, raising his eyebrows. "Did I do something wrong?"

"I'm savin' my kisses for the man I marry," she declared, smiling sweetly.

"So, you haven't kissed *anyone* yet?" He thought the concept peculiar and yet a little exciting at the same time.

She shook her head.

"Oh, well, that's good to know."

"How about you?" she inquired.

"Me?" He gulped. *What will she think if I tell her the truth?* "Uh...yeah, I've kissed before," he admitted sheepishly.

"Oh." She stared at the ground now, sounding disappointed. Ethan figured he just blew his chance with her and looked away, frustrated with himself. Ruthie placed a gentle hand atop his, and he turned back. "But I guess we all make mistakes. Nobody's perfect, *jah?*"

"*Jah*," he mimicked her again and smiled back, taking a deep breath. He was definitely convinced now that Ruthie was indeed the sweetest girl he'd ever met. *And I thought that 'love at first sight' was only something that happened in the movies.*

The screen door slammed shut and Ethan walked into the kitchen. He quickly spotted Seth at the table munching on some chocolate chip cookies while he heard the ladies talking in the other room. "Oh, good. I was hoping to talk to you alone, Seth."

Seth raised an eyebrow. "About what?"

"Well." He sighed. "I really like Ruthie."

Seth chuckled. "*Jah*, I could tell."

"This is going to sound totally crazy because I just met her. But I was wondering...how could someone like me...I mean, who's not Amish...marry an Amish girl?" He fumbled over his words. "I guess what I'm trying to ask is how I can become Amish."

Seth's jaw dropped. "You want to marry Ruthie?" he asked in puzzlement.

"Well, I'm not positive. But *if* I did..."

"Becoming Amish is a big thing. And you can't just do it because you want to get married," Seth informed him.

"I can't?" Seth read the puzzled look on Ethan's face.

"*Nee*. I can tell you don't know very much about us...the Plain people." Seth held in a laugh.

"My sister's the one who's done all the research on that." Ethan sighed. "I guess I'll have to take a trip to the library. Too bad I left my laptop at home."

CHAPTER 7
Jonathan

"...Rejoice with the wife of thy youth."
Proverbs 5:18b

Jonathan Fisher stepped through the back door and into the mudroom near the kitchen. He took off his straw hat and threw it like a Frisbee, hoping to catch the hat rack on the wall. It missed its mark and fell to the floor. He stepped over and picked it up again and took four paces backward. Jonathan flung the hat again with the same result. Over and over again, he attempted the same feat and failed miserably. He decided to try one more time. The second his hat left his hand, the back door opened. His father, Gideon, was smacked squarely in the face.

From behind him, he heard a gasp and spun around on his heels. "Jonathan Fisher, what are you doing?" his wife asked.

Gideon piped in, eying his son curiously, "I was just about to ask the same thing."

Jonathan's cheeks reddened, feeling like a child caught with his hand in the cookie jar. He walked over and retrieved his hat from the floor. "Ah, nothin', I guess." He placed the hat on the rack properly and apologized to his father. Jonathan walked over to the stove and lifted a lid on one of the pots, dipping his finger into what looked like a batch of chocolate pudding. "*Donner-wetter!*" he yelled as he quickly pulled his finger away from the simmering liquid.

"*Ach*, Jonathan. What did you do now?" Susie walked over and examined his pink fingertip. She pulled him over to the sink and placed his finger under cold running water. "Is that better?"

"*Jah, denki, Lieb.*" He leaned over and kissed his wife on the cheek.

"*Gut*, now go and rescue your mother. She's been watching the *kinner* for me while I've been sewing. Supper should be ready in about ten minutes." Jonathan promptly left the room to do his wife's bidding. Susanna turned to her father-in-law, shaking her head. "Sometimes I feel like I have three *bopplin* instead of two!"

Gideon chuckled, then placed a reassuring hand on her shoulder. "I know what you mean, *dochder*. I know exactly what you mean."

After the evening meal, Jonathan and Susanna retreated to the *dawdi haus* with the twins. Johnny and Judah happily went into the tub of water their *daed* had run for their bath. Susie heard her husband playing with the boys as she gathered the towels from the linen closet. When she stepped into the bathroom and beheld her two sons, she burst into laughter. Jonathan had a cone shaped hat of bubbles on his head, while the twins sported long white bubble beards.

"How do you like our new look, *Mamm*?" Jonathan smiled at his wife.

Susie looked at the twins and spoke in a soft tone, "You two boys look very handsome in your beards, but I'm afraid it will be a few more years before you can wear them permanently. As for your *dat*," she scooped some of the bubbles from Jonathan's head and placed them between her hands, "this kind of hat will never do." She playfully took the bubbles and rubbed them on his face, punctuating his nose with the white foam.

Jonathan took a large scoop of bubbles from the tub and rubbed them on Susie's face, "I think your *mamm* needs a beard, too." Susie gasped and both of the boys giggled merrily, splashing bubbles everywhere.

Susie decided that she'd better leave quickly before it turned into an all-out bubble war, but then she suddenly stopped when she felt a glob of bubbles running down the back of her neck.

"Jonathan Fisher!" *Now, it's time for revenge!* She made her way back to the bathtub with purposeful steps.

Jonathan must have noticed the impish grin on her face and the mischievous glint in her soft brown eyes. "Uh-oh, better watch out, boys."

Susie began scooping up bubbles into her hands, aware of the eyes on her. Placing a large ball of bubbles into her right hand, she positioned, aimed, and fired. *Smack.* Right in the middle of Jonathan's forehead! Susie laughed triumphantly at the sight of bubbles running down Jonathan's face. The twins joined in with a squeal of giggles.

"Su-sie," Jonathan warned, swatting bubbles away from his eyes. He quickly threw a handful of bubbles at Susie, then reached down for more, launching them in his wife's direction. Relentlessly, he continued pelting her with bubbles, while, as often as she could, she fired them back. Jonathan was on the verge of surrender when a ball of bubbles flew into his mouth, choking out his words. The twins splashed excitedly while watching the entertainment, enthralled by the merriment taking place between the grown-ups.

Jonathan sputtered and rose to his feet, charging his wife. "Aah!" Susie shrieked and frantically scrambled to the door. But Jonathan caught her by her apron and spun her around to face him. He began to tickle her protruding stomach and sides. Susie laughed, trying to twist and turn her way out of his grip, flailing her arms. "Stop," she breathed out hoarsely, nearly keeling over with laughter. But Jonathan showed her no mercy.

When he stopped to wipe his brow, Susie recognized her opportunity and she began her playful assault. Jonathan roared, laughing so hard he thought his sides would burst. Their twins, now sitting in cold water, observed the scene wide-eyed.

Jonathan quickly regained control and continued wiggling his fingers on his wife's sides and belly, causing her to chortle uncontrollably. "I give up," Susie's exhausted voice surrendered and he finally stopped. Two small gasps erupted from the bathtub as she took a step back, tripped over a stray towel, and lost her balance. Jonathan quickly extended his arm, catching Susie inches from the floor.

"That was close," he said, while pulling his wife up cautiously. "We'd better be more careful."

Susie's heart beat wildly in her rib-cage as she stood up, resting her head on her husband's shoulder. Johnny and Judah looked at them, confusion and anxiety etched on their similar features. "Don't worry, *Mamm*'s all right," her soothing voice assured. Her heart finally returned to its normal pace when Jonathan pulled her into a loving embrace. She gazed into his gorgeous blue eyes finding all the tenderness, contentment, and love that so often brought her comfort. The familiar look in Jonathan's eye indicated what was coming next. Silently, he inched his face toward hers and Susie filled in the gap between them, beginning with the lips.

Suddenly, the door swung open and revealed Jonathan's mother, Esther. "*Was in der welt*?!" She gasped. "So, this is what all the commotion was about." Esther shook her head disapprovingly.

Susie immediately straitened, blushing furiously. "We were...uh...giving the twins a bath," she attempted to explain, wishing she had a fan. The bathroom had suddenly grown very warm.

"I think you mean giving the room a bath." Esther's eyes surveyed the area critically and clucked her tongue. "And yourselves, too."

"Give us a break, *Mamm*. Susie and I were just having a little fun," Jonathan said.

"Looks like you've been having more than a little fun. Perhaps there're better places to have fun where your *kinner* aren't sitting in cold bathwater. Hmm?" his mother chided. "Now, I'll just rescue these two sweet *kinner* and leave you two to clean up this mess."

For the first time, Susie studied the room and realized how amiss it was. The walls had globs of soap bubbles trailing downward toward the slippery floor. The toilet paper had been knocked off its perch and now trailed a wet soapy white path across the linoleum. Susie glanced at Jonathan, and then did a double take. His shirt and pants had water stains with a few bubbles remaining, and his beard looked as if it had been dumped into a bucket of soapy water. She then looked at herself and found that she was just as messy as Jonathan, if not more so. Soap was on everything, themselves included.

As soon as Esther stepped out of the room with boys in arms and closed the door, Jonathan and Susanna scanned each other's appearance and exploded with laughter.

CHAPTER 8
Becoming Amish

"Delight thyself also in the Lord; and he shall give thee the desires of thine heart." Proverbs 37:4

"Okay. So let me get this straight." Ethan cocked his head sideways. "When an Amish man gets married, he has to grow his beard, but no mustache?"

"*Jah*, that's correct." Seth smiled as he took another sip of his morning coffee.

"So every guy that I see walking around with a beard is married?" Ethan clarified as Seth nodded. "How about the women?"

"No beards," Seth answered, chuckling.

"Funny, Seth. I meant, how do you know an Amish woman is married?"

"I know. Sorry, couldn't help it." Seth chuckled. "That's easy. She usually has *kinner* all around her or she's in the family way."

Ethan shot him another confused look. "Family way?"

"Expecting a *boppli*." Seth stood up from the bench in the gazebo and looked out toward the forest.

"*Boppli*? I'm guessing that means a baby, right?" He raised an eyebrow.

"*Jah*. Hey, you're already starting to learn some *Deitsch*. That'll help you out a lot if you ever decide to join the Amish," Seth encouraged.

"Wait...don't tell me I have to learn a second language to become Amish. Do I?" Seth got a kick out of Ethan's worried expression and chuckled.

"You don't have to learn it overnight, but yes, if you want to become Amish you'll have to learn Pennsylvania *Deitsch*. And German would be helpful too. *Deitsch* is the primary language in an Amish home. The *kinner* don't learn English until they start school. The German Bible is used during the preaching services."

"Man, too bad it can't be Spanish. I've already taken a year of it in school. *Los Alamanes estan locos*." He laughed.

"Hey, what did you just say?"

"I said the Germans are crazy." Ethan smiled.

Seth chuckled. "Like I said, becoming Amish is no simple task."

"Sheesh! I guess I better think long and hard about this. No cars, no electricity, lots of hard work, a beard, a new language or two, lots of babies. I'll admit, the last part sounds like fun."

Ethan chuckled. "Especially with Ruthie. I think she'd make a great mom."

Seth shot Ethan a pointed stare. "Just remember that the *bopplin* come *after* you get married," he warned.

"Yeah, I know that." Ethan's tone sounded slightly perturbed.

"Sorry. It's just that I've heard lots of stories about *Englischers*. I wouldn't want anything like that to happen to Ruthie. She's awful young still. 'Twould be a shame."

"I admit that I haven't been perfect. I would be extra careful with Ruthie. I know the Amish have high standards. Besides, I won't get a kiss from her until we're married. She's already informed me of that." Ethan smiled to himself, then rubbed his chin. "You and Brooke looked more than a little cozy the other day. I expect that *you'll* behave yourself around my sister."

"*Jah*, for sure and for certain. I care for Brooke," Seth assured.

"So, you said there's a fifties' joint somewhere around here?" Ethan asked, changing the subject.

"Fifties' joint? Do you mean the restaurant I told you about?" Seth wore an uncertain expression.

"Yes. Sorry. The restaurant. Do you know if they ever have sock hops...er...uh...dancing?" Ethan asked.

"I think I saw a sign about something special going on for the *Englischer* holiday coming up." Seth tried to recall what he'd read. "*Jah*. I remember now. It had some old cars on the sign."

"A car show? Oh Seth, we've got to go! Maybe we can double date. What do you say?" Ethan asked excitedly.

"Do you think Brooke would enjoy that?" Seth pondered aloud.

"Enjoy it? She would love it. We grew up around that kind of stuff. My dad even has an old car. It's an Edsel. If ya ever come down to Georgia, I'll take you for a spin in it," Ethan offered.

"All right then. I have to drive into town later today. I can check the sign and find out when it is," Seth said, stretching his arms wide and yawning.

"Awesome! I know Ruthie will have so much fun. We all will." Ethan's smiled was contagious and Seth found himself becoming excited as well. "Do you think her parents would mind if I show up at her house and ask her?"

"You'd better not. Her folks might not be too keen on the idea of their daughter being courted by an *Englischer*. Why don't you write her a letter and have Leah deliver it," Seth suggested.

"Do you think that would be the best way?" Ethan asked.

"*Jah*. The Amish usually court in secret. Most of the time our folks don't know who we're courtin' until we're nigh unto marriage." Seth explained, "And we usually court at night. Mostly after Sunday Singings."

"Wow. So you're *supposed* to sneak around at night with your girlfriend behind your parents' backs?" he asked in astonishment. "The Amish sure do things differently."

"That's our way. But I think my folks know that I'm sweet on your sister," Seth admitted.

"Do they care if she's not Amish?" Ethan gave him sideways glance.

"*Jah*, but they wouldn't forbid me to see her. It's up to me to choose who my mate will be. They will not interfere, though they may give me advice," Seth stated. A nagging thought clouded his mind at that moment, and for the first time he doubted his relationship with Brooke. *Would I be willing to leave the Amish if Brooke doesn't want to leave the* Englisch *world?* Somehow, he didn't think he could...or that he would want to. He would need to commit his thoughts and concerns to prayer. Surely the Lord God Heavenly Father knew what was best for both of them.

With that, Seth bid farewell to Ethan and headed to the barn to begin work for the day.

CHAPTER 9
Independence Day

"...Ye have been called unto liberty..."
Galatians 5:13a

Katie King dipped her fingertips into cool water from the cup on her bureau and smoothed back a stray curl that had escaped her bun. Glancing into the mirror, she straightened her prayer *kapp*, took one last look at her Plain attire, and then made sure her toothbrush hadn't missed any fragments of the snack she'd eaten earlier. Her reflection smiled back at her.

Descending the stairs from her room that overlooked the herb shop, she hummed one of her favorite songs. Her mother Naomi stood in the kitchen mixing up a pitcher of fresh lemonade. "Looks good, *Mamm.*" Katie smiled.

"Are you sure you wouldn't like a glass before your big date?" Naomi raised an eyebrow.

Katie's cheeks blushed furiously and she laughed. "Just that word makes me nervous. And no, *denki*."

"Well, you'd better get going then. I just saw a certain gray pickup pull up to the parking lot of the herb shop. Better catch your man before your *Dat* does. He may just scare him off." Naomi chuckled. Ever since Katie became of courting age, Philip had become quite overprotective of her.

Katie looked out the window then gasped. "*Ach*, you're right! Oh no, he's talking to *Dat* right now. I better go rescue him." She placed a kiss on her mother's cheek and flew out the door.

"It's too bad Leah didn't want to come along," Brooke said from the back seat of her parents' Dodge Charger. "I'm sure she would have had fun."

"*Jah*, but I think she felt a little awkward." Ruthie glanced at Ethan who was behind the wheel. "Going with two couples, ya know." To that, Ethan smiled and grasped her hand, staking his claim.

"She's not too keen on *Englisch* goings-on," Seth added. *I'm beginning to find out that I'm not either*, he thought ruefully. But he still wanted to spend some time with this pretty *Englisch* girl sitting next to him. *If Brooke's not the girl for me, Lord, then who is?* He halfheartedly sent up the silent prayer.

Brooke's smile brightened up the car and Seth remembered once again why he was so attracted to her. "This is going to be so much fun! Aren't you excited, Seth?" She turned to him for an answer.

What should he say? He didn't want to lie, but he also didn't want to hurt Brooke's feelings or dampen her spirit. He squeezed her hand and hoped the smile he sent her way would suffice. Fortunately, it did. A thought suddenly popped into his mind, *I think I'm ready to join the church.*

"I'm curious about the dancing. I've never been to anything like this before. Do *Englischers* really dance in their socks?" Ruthie turned to Ethan again.

He threw a smile her way and winked. "Hopefully not just *Englischers.*"

"Oh, I don't know, Ethan. It sounds like a lot of fun but I've never danced before. I wouldn't want to step on your feet," she said. "Or step on my own."

"That's all part of learning to dance," he answered nonchalantly. "Feel free to step on my feet or trip over me anytime." To that comment, everyone chuckled.

A few minutes later, they pulled around the corner near the fifties diner. Cars lined the streets on both sides and people of all ages walked toward where the shiny classics were displayed in the diner parking lot for all to see. Ruthie noticed a few Plain folk around her own age, but most were *Englischers.* Several of the girls and women wore long, bright solid-colored skirts with a white dog near the bottom and silly looking black and white shoes. Most of them also wore high pony tails with scarves in their hair.

"Is that a special costume?" Ruthie wondered aloud and figured that probably many a person had asked the same thing about the clothes she wore.

"Oh, yes. Those ladies are wearing poodle skirts. They were popular in the fifties," Brooke informed her brother's date, then uttered from the back seat. "Wow! I hope we can find a place to park."

"Don't worry, we'll find a place. We may have to walk a couple of blocks, though. I hope y'all don't mind," Ethan said. Nobody complained. "Here we are. Let's go check out those cars!" His eyes sparkled as he offered Ruthie a hand and pulled her out of the car.

"How long have you worked at the ice cream shop, Katie?" Jason Fleming asked while she strode next to him perusing the array of fancy old cars.

"Just a few months. I really like it, though." She smiled.

"Yeah, I bet you meet all kinds of strange people. Look at me." He wiggled his eyebrows.

Katie laughed. "I wouldn't say you're strange. Everyone needs friends, no? How long will you be in Paradise?"

"Well, pretty much the whole summer. We're visiting my grandparents so I hope I'm not bored to death. I mean no disrespect to my grandparents or anything, but there's just not all that much to do at their place. I'm glad I met you. I hope you don't mind me coming into the ice cream shop as often as I do," he said.

"I must say, there aren't too many customers that come in *every* day." She giggled. "But, no, I don't mind at all. It's nice having company. Sometimes business can get a little slow. My boss doesn't mind if I chat with the customers as long as all my work is done and there are no other customers that need waiting on." The conversation stilled a bit as they strolled between row after row of vehicles.

"I think we've seen most of the cars. What do you think of them?" Jason asked.

Katie surveyed the gleaming vehicles again. "They're *schee*. I mean, pretty. Much different than a buggy, I must say. Very fancy."

"I wouldn't mind owning a classic car myself," he divulged. "Like this one!" Jason's gaze caressed the smooth lines of a blue 1968 Chevrolet Camaro with silver racing stripes.

"*Ach*, I know that car. Jonathan Fisher drove it in his *rum-springa*." Katie reminisced. "He used to keep it parked in the lot of *Dat*'s herb shop."

"I'd say that your friend Jonathan Fisher was a lucky man to have owned a fine piece of machinery such as this." He finally peeled his eyes from the vehicle, considering the needs of his female companion. "Would ya like to go inside now and get something to eat?"

"*Jah*, that sounds *gut*," Katie agreed and followed her date into the packed-out restaurant. Surprisingly, the line to be seated wasn't very long. Even so, Katie figured it would be a good time to sneak over to the ladies' room. "I'll be right back, Jason. I just need to use the restroom real quick."

As Katie made her way to the bathroom, she had to squeeze through a couple of groups of people. "Oh, excuse me. I'm sorry," she said after accidentally bumping into someone. She looked up and found Seth Weaver directly in front her, his blue eyes sparkling. She gasped. "Seth?"

"Katie King," Seth stated, noticing for the first time her beautiful large caramel brown eyes. "What brings you here?"

Katie regained her composure. Boy, was she glad he couldn't read her thoughts! He was ever so handsome. She'd secretly had a crush on Seth Weaver for a year now and was disappointed not to see him at the last hymn sing. She knew via his sister Leah that he'd been with the *Englisch* girl at the time. "Uh, I'm here with Jason Fleming. He's the *Englischer* standing in line over there. The one with the blue baseball cap on."

Seth looked over and eyed the lucky young man clad in blue jeans and a blue and white raglan shirt. *I wonder if she thinks I'm as good looking as he is.* His stomach turned a bit. *Why am I getting jealous?* He gulped. "Oh." Oh, but he felt like such a *dummkopp*! He couldn't find any words to say. "I...I'm here with the *Englischers* who are visiting our bed-and-breakfast," he said clumsily.

Katie flashed her best dimpled smile, seemingly unaffected. *Hmm...I wonder why he didn't say he was with his* aldi. "Brooke, right?"

Seth nodded in affirmation, but his thoughts were not with Brooke right now. He so wanted to reach out and caress the lone curl that escaped her bun and trailed down her neck. *What am I thinking? I must be* ferhoodled!

Katie noticed the line in front of her dwindling. "Well, I better go. Jason will be expecting me soon."

"Of course. It was *gut* seeing you, Katie," Seth said before striding toward a table on the far side of the restaurant. Thankfully, Brooke didn't see that exchange. If she had, she probably would have seen his neck turning red. She would have noticed the longing in his eyes for another girl – one that wasn't his. And most likely, she would have noticed the glare he received from Katie's date as well.

No matter what they did that evening, Seth could not get his mind off the cute Amish girl with the caramel eyes. Not the shiny cars. Not the fast dancing. Not the colorful sparkling fireworks that lit up the sky that night. And as *schee* as she was, not even the *Englischer* Brooke Spencer.

Katie King. She was Plain, unlike Brooke. He was sure she was the prettiest thing he'd ever laid eyes on. Why had he never noticed her before? Perhaps they'd never been in such close proximity to one another. And what of the *Englischer* she was with? Was he her beau? Sure seemed like it by the way he stared Seth up and down in challenge. But when Katie and her *Englisch* date came to their table to say hello, Seth couldn't help but notice that Brooke and Jason seemed to take a keen interest in each other. And it was a *gut* thing too, because he had a hard time keeping his eyes off Katie. He felt himself being drawn to her beautiful eyes and adorable dimpled smile. It turned out Jason and Brooke even attended the same high school back in Georgia. Now, wasn't that a coincidence? Was God's hand at work here? Only time would tell.

CHAPTER 10
The Departure

"Rejoice evermore." 1 Thessalonians 5:16

"Lavina, Leah, thank you so much for your hospitality. We will be sure to recommend your bed-and-breakfast to all of our friends. George and I had such a wonderful relaxing time here. I know everything else on this summer vacation will pale in comparison. The children enjoyed themselves as well," Lila Spencer said as she rolled her red suitcase into the main sitting room.

"I'll take that," Seth offered. "Would you like me to put it into the trunk for you?"

"Oh, yes. Thank you, Seth. You've been a good friend to Ethan and Brooke while they were here. I appreciate you making them feel at home here," Lila said.

Seth's cheeks flushed at the statement. He had overstepped the boundaries of friendship with Brooke, he was certain. Now he was feeling regretful for his overly intimate behavior with the *Englisch* girl. He nodded, quickly grabbed the suitcase, and disappeared down the front porch steps.

"Brooke, Ethan, are you two ready to go? Your dad is already waiting out by the car," Lila called.

"Coming, Mom. I just need to say goodbye to Seth and Leah, then I'll be out," Brooke stated. "Ethan is on the back porch talking to someone. I'll let him know you're ready to go."

Brooke said her goodbyes to Leah, then met Seth on the front porch and gave him a hug. "I'm going to miss you, Seth. You'll never know how much this trip meant to me. Thank you for introducing me to the Saviour and for giving me the Bible. I'll never forget you."

Seth nodded and realized the long embrace spoke more of friendship than anything else. Had she distanced herself emotionally as well? "Anytime you have any questions about the Bible or need someone to scare off old boyfriends, just let me know." He chuckled.

"Kyle was *not* my boyfriend, but thanks anyway." She laughed, then turned serious. "Listen Seth, I gave Leah a letter for you..." Her voice drifted off. "Thanks for everything, I mean it." She gave him a quick peck on the cheek, brushed a lone tear from her eye, and then hurried toward the car without looking back.

"Ruthie, don't you think for a second that I'm walking out of your life. I will write you often and I'll come see you when my parents let me," Ethan said as he delicately brought her fingers to his lips. "I'm gonna miss you somethin' fierce, sweetheart."

"I'll miss you, too." Ruthie smiled at her beau.

"I hope you won't go riding home from Singings with any boys while I'm gone." He slapped his hand on his pant leg in frustration. "Ugh, I wish I was already through with high school. Maybe then I wouldn't even need to go back home. If my parents would let me, I'd find a place to rent here and get a job. At least I'd be close to you then."

"I'll wait for you, Ethan," Ruthie assured him. "Finish school and honor your folks. It's only another year, *jah*? It will go by fast if we keep busy."

"I'm already missing you and I'm not even gone yet." He sighed. "Ruthie, may I take a picture of you with my phone? I know it goes against your beliefs, but it would help me to have your picture nearby so I can look at your pretty face every day."

Ruthie blushed. She looked around and didn't see anyone. "I guess it would be all right."

"Great!" Ruthie didn't think his smile could get any bigger. He quickly tore his phone from his pocket and snapped a picture of her. He sat back down and took one of the two of them together. He showed it to Ruthie and she couldn't help but think they made a wonderful-*gut* couple. "You don't know how happy this makes me."

"Ethan, Mom said we need to get going now," Brooke called from around the side porch.

"Okay, Brooke. Please tell her I'll be right there," Ethan called to his sister then stood up and faced Ruthie. "Well, I guess this is goodbye for now." He pulled her into a fierce hug, then kissed her gently on the top of her head. "I love you, Ruthie. Don't you forget it." A tear formed in Ruthie's eye and Ethan brushed it away with his thumb, her cheeks cradled in his hands. "Shh...don't cry, Precious."

"I'm trying not to." Ruthie sucked in a breath and willed her tears to stop. "I love you, too, Ethan."

Ethan released Ruthie from his embrace, then dashed to the car, not wanting her to see the tears that threatened to escape his own eyes.

Seth sat on his bed cross-legged, unfolding the letter that Brooke had written to him. Leah had given it to him shortly after the Spencers left. Curious at what it might say, he began to read.

Dear Seth,

Thank you for making my stay at your bed-and-breakfast enjoyable. I had a lot of fun. I'll never forget you or all of the wonderful things you taught me. I'm so glad to have met you and I will be indebted to you for the rest of my life. I can't help

336

to think that if we hadn't met, I'd still be on my way to Hell! Please pray for me. I want to tell as many people as possible about God's love. Ethan has already started asking me all kinds of questions.

This next part is kind of hard for me to write and I don't really know how to say it. I've gotten the feeling that you might feel the same way and I hope I'm right. I think it would be best if we just remained friends. I hope that's all right with you. I've heard that long-distance relationships don't usually work out, and I don't want to make you wait for me. Another thing is that I don't think I could ever become Amish and I would never want you to give up the ways of your people. I'm sorry if you are hurt by this. I wanted to tell you in person, but I just couldn't do it. I hope you can forgive me. To be honest with you, my heart is breaking as I write this, but I believe it will be best for us in the long run.

Whew! I'm glad that part is over. I've been dreading writing it. Anyway, I just want you to know that I'll always consider you a good friend. I plan to keep in touch with Leah, so we'll still know what's going on in each other's lives. Thank you again for everything. You'll always hold a special place in my heart.

Sincerely,

Brooke

Seth stood up and wandered toward the window. He looked down at the driveway where Brooke and her family had recently traveled and sighed. His time with Brooke had been bittersweet and he knew he would not be forgetting her too soon. God always worked all things for good of those that love Him and Seth would have to trust that.

He heard Leah's voice from the bottom of the stairs. A minute later, she appeared in his doorway. "Seth, didn't you hear me calling you?" Leah asked impatiently.

"Just now, *jah*," Seth admitted.

"Well, do you want to go or not? If you don't hurry, I'm leaving without you." She huffed.

"Leaving? Where to?"

"*Ach*, Seth. Your head must be in the clouds. Remember, there's a young folks' gathering tonight at the Hostettlers'?"

Seth's eyes lit up. "I forgot all about it. Just give me a couple of minutes and I'll be down," he said excitedly, then kissed his sister on the cheek. "That's the best news I've heard all day."

Leah stared at him in bemusement and shrugged her shoulders. "Don't be long, then."

"Hey, Leah." Seth stopped her in her tracks. "Do you think Katie King will be there?"

"Katie? *Jah*, probably. Why do you ask?" She eyed him curiously.

"Uh...just wondering." He shrugged indifferently but his neck darkened.

Leah finally understood. "Wait a minute. Do you...? But I thought –"

"Never mind, Leah." Seth smiled and closed his door, locking her out.

He heard her mumble through the door. "I will never understand boys for as long as I live." She threw up her hands and trotted down the stairs. *Now Seth is sweet on Katie?*

CHAPTER 11
The Gathering

"Not forsaking the assembling of ourselves together..." Hebrews 10:25a

Maryanna Hostettler slung the softball back in her hand, eyed home plate, and then thrust the ball forward. "Strike one!" the umpire called from behind the catcher.

"Let's go, Maryanna! Strike him out," Annie Yoder called from second base.

"Hey, now. That just wouldn't be right," Joshua said, while practicing to bat next. "She can't strike out her beau."

"Wanna bet?" Maryanna hollered, releasing the ball again.

"Strike two!" the umpire belted out.

Matthew Riehl began to get visibly nervous as he gripped the bat. *Lord, please let me hit this next ball so I don't look like a wimp in front of my friends. Especially my* aldi. The ball flew his way and he hit a pop fly out into left field. Abigail Lapp ran forward and held her mitt just under where the ball descended from the sky and caught it. All at once, the girls' team cheered and the boys groaned.

"Last one, Maryanna!" Annie called.

"Come on, Annie! Give me a break," Joshua hollered to his betrothed.

"What's wrong, Joshy? Can't take the heat?" Maryanna taunted her brother, then pitched a strike.

Joshua groaned. "We'll just see about that. Get ready girls, cuz were taking you down!"

"Strike two!" the umpire called out.

"What was that, Josh?" Ruthie asked from first base.

"Hey, I was just gettin' warmed up. I'm ready now. Come on, Maryanna. Give it all ya got!" Josh answered boldly.

Maryanna perfectly threw the ball into strike zone. Joshua barely tipped the ball with his bat and he ran with all his might toward first base. Maryanna adeptly retrieved the ball and hurled it to Ruthie, who caught it a second prior to Joshua sliding into the base.

"You're outta there!" the umpire belted out.

"Oh, come on, Levi!" Joshua protested, throwing off his helmet.

"Brother or not, I have to call it like I see it. Sorry, Josh. Ruthie got you out fair and square," Levi answered, sending a friendly wink toward his sister-in-law.

Joshua returned to the dugout to retrieve his mitt and hat. He glared at Levi from beneath his straw hat as he walked past, then turned his attention back to his teammates. "Okay, boys, let's show 'em who's boss."

"Oh, please do, Joshy," Maryanna teased her older brother. "I can't wait." She flashed him an impish grin as she stepped up to bat.

Joshua twisted the ball in his hands then released it toward Maryanna. Knowing the ball wasn't worth hitting, Maryanna stepped back and so did Seth, the catcher, and let it fly... right into Levi's leg.

"Oof!" Levi fell back from his squatting position and landed on his backside. "*Ach*, Josh, I got a wife and *kinner* at home to care for and I need that leg. You don't have to take your anger out on me. Ball one."

Joshua turned bright red as the girls' side rumbled with laughter. He waited until Levi regained his bearings before pitching again, this time softly. Too softly. Maryanna's head bobbed as her eyes trailed the bouncing ball. "I came here to play softball, not golf."

Levi couldn't help but chuckle. "Ball two."

"Levi, who's side are you on anyway? If I didn't know any better, I'd say you're going for the *girls*." Joshua huffed.

"He knows a winning team when he sees one. Nobody wants to root for the losers," Maryanna jeered.

"All right, that does it!" Joshua retaliated by thrusting the ball forward with all his might.

"Strike one!" Levi called out.

Maryanna nodded her head in approval. "Hey, Josh. It looks like the anger angle works well for you. Maybe I won't have to give you pitching lessons after all."

Joshua hurled the ball forward again until it connected with Maryanna's bat. He watched as the ball went sailing past the outfielders. Maryanna dropped the bat and ran around all three bases before sliding into home base.

"Home run!" Levi declared.

"I should've walked her," Joshua mumbled under his breath.

After the girls won 10-9, the young people gathered in and around the Hostettlers' barn for snacks and drinks. Groups of girls sat on quilts under shade trees while the boys stood around the corral near the horses. The girls congratulated one another for their victory. The boys, on the other hand, consoled each other, vowing to win next time.

Katie King stood up from the quilt where she sat with Leah, Abigail, and Ruthie. "I'm gonna go get more lemonade. Would anybody else like some?" she offered.

"Sure, thanks." Ruthie handed over her cup.

"*Nee, denki.*" Leah and Abby replied.

"Be right back," Katie promised before meandering into the barn. She happily walked over to the drink table and deftly poured lemonade into two cups. A small sip from her cup told her the wonderful drink was made from fresh-squeezed lemons.

"*Hiya*, Katie," A male voice called from beside her.

"Oh, hello, Seth. I didn't even see you walk up," Katie said. "Would you like a cup?"

"Sure," he smiled, lightly brushing her fingers while taking the drink. "*Denki.*"

Katie's cheeks blushed slightly and she nodded.

"Some game, huh? You girls did real well," he complimented.

"*Jah, denki.* I think Maryanna had a lot to do with that. Her girls' softball team went to the state championships," she noted.

"I heard," he stated, then lowered his voice slightly. "Katie?"

"*Jah,* Seth?" she swallowed hard, sensing he was about to ask her something important.

"Would ya let me take you home tonight?"

Surprised, Katie absentmindedly moved a misplaced curl behind her ear. "Um...*jah*, Seth. I think that would be fine," her cheeks turned rosy.

"*Gut.* So...I'll meet ya by my buggy when you're ready to go." He smiled.

"*Des gut.*" Katie smiled back, then abruptly walked back toward her friends hoping her bright cheeks didn't tell all. *But didn't Seth still have an* Englisch *aldi?*

"Katie, where's the lemonade?" Ruthie asked once she arrived under the large oak tree.

Katie looked down at her empty hands. "*Ach,* I'm such a *dummkopp.* I forgot them in the barn. I'll go –" as she turned around to fetch the drinks, she ran smack dab into Seth. The two cups of lemonade in his hands spilled onto his shirt and her dress. Katie's cheeks flooded with color and she stepped back. "*Ach,* Seth. I'm so sorry."

"*Nee,* it was my fault," he admitted. "How were you supposed to know I was right behind you?"

She glanced at his shirt, then down at her dress. "*Ach,* I look a sight."

"A beautiful sight," he let out, causing her to flush even more. "Let's go refill these cups again." He nodded for her to walk alongside him. She looked back at her friends who gave her knowing smiles, then fell into step next to Seth.

CHAPTER 12
Moving On

"...Go ye into all the world, and preach the gospel to every creature." Mark 16:15

*B*rooke glanced down at the small paper in her hand then back at her cell phone, contemplating whether or not to call Jason Fleming at the next stop. *Would he think I'm too forward?* It was peculiar that they would run into each other at the same time, same place so many miles away from their hometown. She on vacation and he visiting his grand-mother. Could it be fate, or destiny, or as Seth might say, God's will? She couldn't be sure, but it had definitely been an interesting set of circumstances. She would call him.

She eyed the scenery as their car whizzed past and a red-wood gazebo caught her attention. Thoughts of their time spent at the Weaver's Bed-and-Breakfast flooded her mind and she sighed. What were Seth and Leah doing right now? Entertaining more guests? Doing their interminable amount of chores?

Attending a Singin' with their friends? She had to admit the Amish lifestyle did have its merits, but she knew in her heart she would always be *Englisch* Brooke.

And what of her brother Ethan? He sure seemed to be smitten with Leah's friend, Ruthie. Would he eventually become Amish? Brooke didn't think so, but the way he carried on gave her cause to doubt. Sitting in the back seat next to her, he was penning a letter to Ruthie at this very moment. She watched as his mouth curled up in a smile, then noticed him staring out the window as if in some dreamland. When he turned back to his notebook, she abruptly turned away, not wanting him to think she was being nosy.

Before long, summer vacation would be over and all of their adventures would be but a memory. Brooke frowned at the thought. It seemed the older she became, the faster time flew by. She realized all the more that she wanted her life to count for something. Glancing up, she noticed her father pulling the car up to a gas station. Taking in her surroundings, she spotted a small Christian bookstore nearby.

"Mom, do you mind if I stretch my legs a bit? I'd like to go into one of the stores if that's okay," she requested.

"I don't mind as long as Ethan goes with you," her mother answered.

She sent her brother a pleading glance and was happy when he acquiesced without too much of a fight. "Maybe I can find something nice for Ruthie," he shrugged, stepping out of the car.

"You really like her, don't you?" Brooke had never seen her brother in such a state.

"No, I *love* her. She isn't like any other girl I've ever met. Ruthie is so special. I hope I can marry her someday." His eyes sparkled with joy at the thought.

"Wow, you really are serious. Are you thinking of becoming Amish then?" Brooke opened the door to the bookstore and they both entered.

"I'll do whatever it takes, Brooke. I'm not letting her slip through my hands." He then sent her an imploring look. "Please don't say anything to Mom and Dad. I don't want them to freak out. I don't know how they'll feel about me not going to college next year."

"Okay, Ethan. But I hope you know what you're doing." His sister shrugged.

"I've never been more certain of anything in my life." He looked through a rack that held Christian stationary and picked up a set of note cards with a Bible verse on them that read, '*With God, all things are possible.*' "Hey, these are perfect. Don't ya think?" He showed the stationary to Brooke.

"I'm sure Ruthie would be thrilled to get anything from you, but don't you think you should be a little more honest?" Brooke said, thumbing through some Gospel tracts.

"What on earth are you talking about? I haven't lied to her," he answered incredulously.

"These say, '*With God...*' Ethan, you don't have God." She grabbed four different packs of tracts and started toward the counter to purchase the items. Ethan took her arm, giving her a helpless look. "What is it?" She stopped.

"How can I get God?" He stood, confused.

"Go ahead and buy the note cards, Ethan. I'll explain it to you in the car. Mom and Dad are surely growing impatient by now." She handed the cashier the money for her purchases and after Ethan paid for his, they were headed back to the car. Brooke opened up the packages of Gospel tracts and handed one of each to Ethan once they were securely fastened inside the vehicle. "Start by reading these. They'll probably be able to explain it all better than I can."

Ethan thumbed through the miniature comic books. "Hey, these are awesome! May I keep 'em?"

"Sure. Just make certain you read them," she warned.

"Oh, I will!" He eagerly tore open a tract and began reading.

"I can't figure out why I never noticed you before." Seth shook his head, glancing in Katie's direction.

"I haven't been coming to the youth gatherings very long," she reasoned. "But I don't remember seeing you take anyone home before."

He smiled to himself. *So she had noticed me.* "Guess I was never in the market, so to speak. Wait, I don't think that came out right." He attempted to backpedal.

"No, it's fine. I think I know what you mean." She flashed him a smile that formed a small dimple in her cheek, her beautiful caramel eyes sparkling. "So, are you *in the market* now?" she ventured boldly.

He returned the smile and allowed his eyes to sweep over the lovely creature sitting on the seat next to him. "Definitely." He peeled his gaze away from her and cleared his throat, his cheeks flushing at the realization of what he'd just done. "I...I'm sorry." *Quick, think of something to say.* He chided himself.

"So –" they both spoke simultaneously. Katie giggled and Seth joined in, breaking the ice a little.

"You were saying?" he allowed.

"I really didn't have anything important to say, you go ahead." She goaded.

"Nicknames." He smiled. "Did your family give you any nicknames?"

"*Jah.*" She blushed, obviously embarrassed.

"I promise I won't make fun of you," he reassured her. "Okay, I'll go first. Sethosaurus."

"Sethosaurus? Like a dinosaur?"

Seth chuckled, "*Jah.* You see, I used to love dinosaurs. I think I even wanted to *be* one when I was seven."

Katie giggled, causing her dimple to reappear. "Which kind was your favorite?"

"Oh, definitely the Brachiosaurus. I used to imagine riding around on its back. In my mind's eye, I could see for miles. All the way over into Bishop Graber's district, in fact. I was ecstatic when my folks bought me a plastic Brachiosaur for Christmas one year. I still have it, in fact." Katie watched his animated features as he talked about the large creatures, obviously a happy memory for him.

"What are you going to do with it?" she wondered aloud.

"I'm planning on keeping it for my *kinner*. I also have a few books as well," he stated.

"That's good. I'm sure your *kinner* will enjoy them. They'll love hearing your stories too. I think it's good to have an imagination." She smiled.

"Okay, now that I've borne my soul, it's your turn. A nickname," he prodded.

"Honeybee. My *mamm* used to call me Honeybee." She blushed.

"Oh, that's sweet!" He chuckled at his play on words.

"I thought you weren't going to make fun," she protested, jutting out her lip.

"I'm sorry, it was just too perfect. But I do think you're sweet though." He reached over and placed his large hand atop her dainty one.

"I guess you're forgiven," she teased.

"Are you free after the Singin' next week, or do you already have a ride?" he asked. "Unless you already have a beau..."

"No, I don't have a ride yet. And if you're asking about Jason, no he isn't my beau. Just a friend," she asserted.

"Will you think me too forward if I ask to court you?" he chanced, hoping she'd be agreeable.

"*Jah*, I think that would be fine. I'm not quite fifteen, though, so we'll have to take it slow," she warned. "And just to let you know, I want my first kiss to be on my wedding day."

"I like a girl who knows what she wants. The kissing part will be the most difficult to be sure, seeing that I'm already –" Seth lifted his hand to caress her cheek, then stopped abruptly. "*Ach*, I'm sorry. I will do my best to respect your wishes. So, how soon before your folks will let you marry?" he teased.

"*Ach*, Seth! Perhaps I should have said no?" she teased back.

"Oh, no no no no no." He scooted as far away from her as he could. "I'll be good, I promise."

"That's better." She giggled.

CHAPTER 13
Back to School

"Blessed are ye, when men shall hate you, and when they shall separate you from their company, and shall reproach you, and cast out your name as evil, for the Son of man's sake." Luke 6:22

*B*rooke plopped down onto the sofa in her living room and set her backpack on the floor. The first day back at school had been fun, but she'd had a difficult time focusing on her studies. She was happy when her new English teacher encouraged the class to write about their summer vacations in their composition books. She hoped the teacher would read about her conversion to Christianity and that God would use it for His glory. Perhaps her teacher would even get saved.

She had given each of her friends a Gospel tract and encouraged them to take them to heart. She even gave one to Kyle, who mocked her, saying she was some Amish religious freak. She surmised that he was still jealous of Seth. Even so, she decided to be charitable and pray for his salvation. Surely, God could touch his heart. Her other friends were a bit hesitant as well, but did say they would read them. She trusted God would have His way in their lives.

Jason found her at lunch time and invited her to a youth group meeting at his church. She gladly accepted his invitation and was looking forward to Friday night when he'd be picking her up. He also informed her of a Bible study club some of his friends were heading up at school. She realized that even though they didn't share any of the same classes, she and Jason would be seeing a lot of each other.

Brooke decided she would encourage Ethan to attend the meetings as well. She was ecstatic when her older brother received Christ after reading the Gospel tracts she'd given him. He was sure to write to Ruthie right away and tell her all about it. Ruthie, in turn, wrote back to him with the note cards Ethan had sent her, rejoicing as well.

Her parents, on the other hand, were quite a different story. She'd given them tracts also, but was unsure whether they read them or not. "Now, Brooke," her mother had said. "Aren't you just being overly sentimental about your nice Amish friends? Religion is fine for those people, but there's no need to go overboard. Your father and I have always believed in God." But no matter how much Brooke tried to explain that Christianity was not a religion, but a relationship, it seemed she couldn't get anywhere with her parents. She decided she would just have to commit them to the Lord in prayer.

Leah walked into the shop where her father and Seth worked. She was anxious to share Brooke's latest letter with her brother. He had been pleased when Brooke had written some months back that her brother had accepted Christ as his Saviour.

"Ready for a break?" She waved the letter at Seth and he turned off the sander.

"*Jah*, I guess so. Did ya bring me and *Dat* some water?" He wiped the perspiration from his brow.

"*Ach*, no. I'll get some right quick. You go ahead and read the letter." She stepped out of the shop and headed in the direction of the kitchen.

Seth walked to the porch and lounged on the hanging swing his father had made. The gentle breeze felt good as it lifted his sweat drenched hair. It was nice to be out of the shop for a bit. He opened the letter to read Brooke's words.

Dear Leah,

I hope this letter finds you and your family well. I've finally gotten back into the swing of things here at home. School, for the most part, is going well. I'm a little sad to say that I've lost a couple of my friends, though. It seems not everyone is interested in being friends with a Christian. Oh well, I will just continue to pray and leave it in God's hands.

Remember how I told you about the Bible club meetings at school? Well, one of my friends has started coming as well. Her name is Kelly; I think Seth might remember her. Anyway,

I think God might be working on her heart because she's been asking a lot of questions. Will you and Seth please pray for her?

Jason and I have been spending a lot of time together. He has been courting me. And yes, I said courting, not dating. We do it a little bit different than y'all. For purity's sake, we only see each other when there are people around. He's very respectful and I like him a lot. It seems he wants to become a youth leader. I think he'll make a good one. Perhaps he'll even become a pastor one day.

I'm so thankful that fall is here. I don't know about y'all, but the temperature has already dropped dramatically here in Georgia. Before we know it, we'll be celebrating Thanksgiving and Christmas! Well, enough prattling. Please tell Seth and your folks hello for me.

Love,

Brooke Spencer

Seth sighed. *So it seems Brooke has no idea that Daed and I are coming out next week. This will be interesting.* How would she feel about him staying in such close proximity for a whole week? Or maybe he should ask how Katie would feel about it. He still had yet to talk to her about the trip and he hoped that she would be understanding.

"Katie, I need to talk to you about something," Seth said with more urgency in his voice than normal.

Katie looked out at the passing scenery as they rode through a forest trail in his buggy. The pine branches swayed slightly as the gentle wind howled through the towering trees. Since the air had turned cooler, Seth had been bringing along a quilt which she now pulled up around her waist. "*Jah*, Seth?" She hoped nothing was wrong between them.

Seth must have sensed her apprehension because he took her hand. "It's nothing too serious, so you can relax." He chuckled. "I just wanted to let you know that I won't be coming to visit you at the ice cream shop this week."

"Oh." Her countenance fell a bit. "Why?"

He detected disappointment, but ventured on. "You see, *Dat* and I will be traveling out of town. We have a gazebo to build in Georgia." There. He'd said it.

"Georgia?" Her eyebrows shot up. "Isn't that where Brooke is from?"

"*Jah*. As a matter of fact, that's who we'll be building the gazebo for. For her folks, I mean. We'll be staying in a trailer on their property."

"Oh," she simply said, staring out again at the trees.

"Oh? That's it?" Seth gently turned her face to look into her eyes. "You're upset, aren't you?"

"No. I'm not upset, Seth. It is your job, after all. It's not like you can help it." She sighed.

"Then what is it, Katie?" he prodded.

"I guess I'm just worried. Brooke was your *aldi* before me, right?"

"*Jah*."

"Did the two of you...kiss?" She didn't like asking, but she had to know. Perhaps his answer would make her feel more at ease.

Seth gulped. "*Jah*, we did. More than once."

So much for putting her at ease. Now this only magnified her fears. It wasn't as though she was insecure. She just felt like she'd finally found her one true love and she couldn't bear to lose him, especially not to an *Englischer*. She remained silent and couldn't help it when tears formed in the corners of her eyes then spilled down onto the quilt. She felt the buggy wheels come to a stop. Seth gathered her into his arms and pulled her close.

"Shh...I'm sorry, Katie. I didn't mean to hurt you; I just wanted you to know the truth." He kissed the top of her head. "I have no intentions as far as Brooke is concerned. You are the only one for me. Please. Don't cry, Honeybee."

Katie's body shook, and she let out a "hee, hee."

Seth lifted her chin, revealing a smile through her tears. "Are you laughing?"

Katie nodded. "I've never heard anyone call me that before, besides my folks. It just sounded funny to me."

"Well I couldn't think of a better name for a sweet girl like you, my Honeybee. I love you." She smiled and blushed. "Now that's what I like to see." Seth leaned down to kiss her, but she quickly turned away.

"Se-th," she warned.

"Okay, sorry. I had to at least try, though." He shrugged.

"What am I going to do with you?" She threw up her hands, feigning exasperation.

"Oh, I don't know. Love me forever?" he said sweetly, then scooted back to his own side of the buggy.

"I may just do that, Seth Weaver." She smiled broadly, showing both dimples.

CHAPTER 14
The Surprise

"Whatsoever thy hand findeth to do, do it with thy might..." Ecclesiastes 9:10a

O n Monday evening, Brooke thought she heard a faint knocking sound from where she sat on her bed. Her suspicions were confirmed when she heard her dad call out, "Lila, will you get the door, please?" Since they weren't expecting anyone, she was curious to see who had come by. Perhaps it was Jason. She bounced off her bed and started down the hallway. She couldn't believe her ears.

"Mr. Weaver? Seth? What brings you way out here?" Lila Spencer asked in shock.

Noah spoke, "Your husband asked us to come." He didn't explain further. Brooke stepped into the living room and spotted Seth and his father standing near the door. In her own house. She felt just as shocked as her mother looked.

Brooke's mother turned to her father in confusion. "George?"

"Surprise, darling! The Weavers have come to build you a gazebo. I thought it would make a nice anniversary present." George smiled proudly. This would be, no doubt, the best anniversary gift she'd ever receive. "I ordered it when we were in Pennsylvania."

"I...I'm speechless." She walked over and placed an arm around her husband, then looked around the room. "Did I ever tell y'all that I have the best husband who's ever lived?" She stood on tip toes and placed a kiss on his lips. "Thank you, honey."

"That's the reaction I was hoping for." George smiled.

Brooke stepped forward, slightly embarrassed by her parents open display of affection in front of their guests. "May we get y'all something to eat or drink?"

"Oh, yes. Of course. Pardon my manners, I was just so shocked," Lila interjected. "Have y'all eaten dinner yet?"

"*Jah*, Lavina sent us plenty. A drink would be nice, though," Noah said.

"Water, tea, lemonade?" Brooke asked.

"Tea," Seth and his father said simultaneously.

Brooke's mother headed toward the kitchen. "Coming right up. Please make yourselves at home. I'll have to make up the spare bedroom –"

"I've got it all taken care of, honey," George spoke up. "Noah and Seth will be staying out in the travel trailer while they are here. I've already spruced the place up." Brooke's father turned to the Weaver men. "There are several fresh towels, blankets, and such in the trailer. Please let one of us know if there's anything else you'll be needing."

Lila waltzed into the room with tea in hand. "And I insist that you eat your meals with us. Brooke or Ethan will bring out your lunches before they head off to school in the mornings."

"Very well, then. We are tired from all the traveling, so I hope you don't mind if we retire for the evening. We like to get an early start. Would five o'clock be acceptable?" Noah stated.

"It's a little early. Why don't you come in for breakfast at five-thirty and you can start working at six. Our neighbors might not appreciate a bunch of hammering at five in the morning," George suggested. "I'll show y'all to the trailer now, if you're ready."

"*Jah.* I did promise Lavina that I would check in with her to let her know we arrived safely. May I use a telephone?" Noah asked.

"Of course. And don't be shy, ask anytime," Lila said, handing Noah a cell phone.

"*Denki.* I will have Seth return it in a bit." Noah and Seth followed George out the back door.

"Susie, you have a visitor," Jonathan hollered from the door of their *dawdi haus*. He turned back to Annie. "She'll be out in just a minute. She's fixing my lunch right now."

"Okay." Annie shrugged. "I'll just wait here."

She peered into the small room, spotting one of the twins. "Hi there, little guy. Are you Johnny or Judah?"

Susanna appeared from around the corner. "That's Judah. Johnny is eating lunch with his *dat*, which is where you should be little guy." She picked up the toddler and nuzzled his little tummy, then quickly deposited him at the kitchen table with his father.

When she reappeared, she gave Annie a squeeze then beckoned her to step outside for some fresh air. "So, to what do I owe this pleasure? It's not every day that my long, lost friend comes to visit. I miss ya, Annie."

Annie sighed. "I guess having a family to tend to can be overwhelming at times, huh?"

"All right, what's wrong? I know that look. Has my brother done something?" Susie huffed.

"*Nee.* Joshua is great. I guess I'm just a little nervous about the wedding and all. I mean, it's coming up so soon. I just hope I'll make a *gut fraa* for your brother." The worried look in her eyes only intensified.

"Of course you will. I couldn't think of a better person who would be more perfect for Josh," Susie asserted.

"I need to lose weight before the wedding," Annie blurted out.

"Are you *ab im kopp*? You have a perfect body! I'm a little jealous, even. If anyone does not need to lose weight, it's you," Susie insisted.

"No, Susie. You can't see because it's hidden behind my dress. My stomach is too fat," Annie maintained.

"Oh, Annie! What am I going to do with you?"

"Help me," she pleaded.

"In case you haven't noticed, I'm not really in a position to help anyone get into shape." She discreetly pointed to her rounded belly. "I have an idea, though. Why don't you talk to Maryanna? I think she may be able to help you. I saw some exercise stuff at her house one time."

Annie threw her arms around Susanna, nearly knocking the wind out of her. "Oh, thank you, Susie! I knew you would know what to do. I'll be forever indebted to you." Annie wasted no time. She turned on her heel and took off on foot toward Maryanna's house.

Katie turned the sign to 'Closed' and locked the door to the ice cream shop. Her co-worker, Michelle Fuller, an *Englischer*, removed her apron and threw it onto one of the small tables. "I don't know about you, but I'm glad this place closes early on Friday."

Katie glanced up at the clock. *Ten o'clock is early?* She would never understand *Englischers.* "We still have to finish cleaning."

"Yeah, but that won't take but twenty minutes. Hey, are you all right?" She sent Katie a concerned look, noticing her downcast eyes.

"I'm fine," Katie said.

"Have you heard from your boyfriend since he's been out of town?" Michelle asked. Katie had mentioned Seth a few times in their conversations.

"No," she said worriedly. "But his sister said he's been busy."

"I see. I hope that guy isn't cheating on you. Maybe that's why he hasn't called yet." Did she have any idea how much her words mirrored Katie's own concerns?

*Ring...*the phone sounded. "Go ahead and get it. Tell 'em we're closed."

"Hello?" Katie asked, waiting for the voice on the other line.

"Katie? Is that you?" a male voice asked.

"*Jah.* Who is calling?" Katie wore a confused expression.

"Katie, it's me. Seth. I hope no other boys are calling you at work, trying to steal my *aldi,*" he teased.

"*Ach*, Seth. Why are you calling here?" Katie wondered aloud, still absorbing the shock.

"I've tried to get a hold of you every day this week at the herb shop. I don't know how many messages I've left with Sadie. I was beginning to get worried when you never called me back," he said.

"That explains it," she said wryly. "Sadie never gave me any messages."

"You don't know how good it feels to hear your voice. I've missed you so much," Seth said, his voice earnest. "I've dreamt about you every night."

"*Ach*, I've missed you too, Seth. I...I was worried," her voice quavered and she swallowed a sob.

"I'm sorry, Katie. You're not crying, are you? I should be back tomorrow night. May I come by and see you?"

She brushed away a lone tear, not sure whether she was crying for worry or happiness. "*Jah*, Seth. I'll see you tomorrow. Goodbye." Katie placed the receiver back into its cradle. She turned around to see Michelle standing behind her.

"So, I guess he wasn't cheating on you then?"

"No, he's been missing me." Katie smiled to herself, then picked up the broom and started sweeping cheerily.

CHAPTER 15
Exercise

*"For bodily exercise profiteth little: but godliness
is profitable unto all things, having promise of the
life that now is, and of that which is to come."*
1 Timothy 4:8

"I'm not sure about this, Maryanna. What if somebody sees me dressed like this? I'm a baptized church member, I could get into a lot of trouble," Annie protested, glancing down at her black Lycra Capri pants and hot pink halter tank top.

"Annie, I don't know why you're so worried. Your mom said that the kids were going to stay inside, the guys are fishing, and your father is in town with your brother and won't be back for a long time. Besides, you're the one that asked me about exercising. I thought you wanted to lose that tummy fat before the big day arrives? Don't you want to look great for Joshy?" Maryanna reminded.

"*Jah, jah,* you are right. I just wish you could have given me something more Amish to wear." She whimpered.

"You want to work out in a cape dress? I don't think so, Annie. I already told you that's all I have as far as workout clothing goes. I promise if you go into any health club, you'll see others dressed the same. Now let's get started." Maryanna silenced any protests by opening up her laptop and slipping in an exercise DVD. "Now just try your best to keep up. You'll see that country line dancing is a lot of fun."

Annie watched as an *Englisch* woman clad in short cut-off shorts and a flannel shirt started talking. There were several other participants on the DVD as well, and a couple of them were dressed just like her and Maryanna. As the music began playing, Annie and Maryanna followed along with the moves. After the "Grapevine" dance was over, Annie called out to Maryanna, "Hey, this is fun."

"Isn't it? Wait till we do the "Boot Scootin' Boogie", you'll love it," Maryanna said. "Man, if Josh could see you now he'd say you're one hot mama." She giggled.

"Hot mama?" Annie gave her a confused look as she moved back and forth in step with the music.

"Never mind. It's just a term that we *Englischers* use that means you look good," Maryanna explained.

"Oh. I don't think Joshua would be very happy about seeing me like this," Annie said worriedly.

Maryanna laughed. "Annie, you know so little about how men think. Trust me; he would *definitely* like to see you in those clothes. Hasn't your mother ever told you about the birds and the bees?"

"*Ach*, yes. There is a lovely purple martin that comes to perch in our apple tree sometimes. *Mamm* said –"

She was cut off by Maryanna's uncontrollable laughter. When Maryanna finally caught her breath, she tried so hard to keep a straight face, but burst into laughter once again. The fact that Annie just stared at her blankly made matters worse. Maryanna had a time of getting through the exercise video, but she eventually regained her composure.

After about twenty minutes, the girls stopped for a drink of water. Maryanna threw a bottle of water to Annie and they both sat down to take a short break. Annie looked curiously at Maryanna. "So what's going on with you and Matthew? Are you two getting serious?"

"Well, if we could ever get over the fact that he's Amish and I'm not, I think we would be. I think that's the only thing that's keeping us from taking the next step." Maryanna shrugged, wiping sweat from her brow with a small towel.

"So, you've talked about marriage?" Annie asked.

"We go around and around about it. I'm not Amish, nor do I ever intend on becoming Amish. There's just too many restrictions for me. I'm used to being free and doing whatever I want. I wouldn't want to live in fear that if I break a rule, my family and friends will disown me. Yet Matthew's already a baptized member, so if he becomes an *Englischer* to marry me then he'll be shunned and lose his family." Maryanna threw up her hands hopelessly.

"I bet that's hard. Have you talked to the bishop about it?" Annie raised her eyebrows.

"Dad? See, that's the thing. I don't want to put him in a bad position either. And if he makes allowances for his own family, then he'll have to make provision for everyone else as well. Life is just so unfair at times." Maryanna sulked momentarily, then bounced back to her feet. "Well, if you want to get that bod into shape we'd better get off our tushes and get going."

Annie understood her meaning when Maryanna pushed play again and resumed exercising. Annie quickly fell into step, enjoying herself all the while.

Matthew and Joshua headed for the Yoders' barn. Sarah Yoder informed them that the girls had set off in that direction about thirty minutes ago, but hadn't heard from them since. As they approached the door, they heard faint music coming from the inside. Joshua put out his hand to stop Matthew and signaled him to silence.

"What are we doing?" Matthew whispered.

"Don't you want to see what that noise is all about? Let's go around back and peek through the panels." Joshua led the way and Matt followed. When they were out of plain sight, both of the young men closed one eye and waited for their vision to adjust to the darkened barn interior.

"Do you see what I see, Josh?" Matthew's mouth hung open.

"Uh...*jah*." He gulped. "I see."

"They look...what is that word the *Englischers* use? Hot?" Matthew admitted. "What are they doing? And why are they dressed, or should I say undressed, that way?"

"*Jah*, they look hot." Josh had to pick his chin up off the ground. "What should we do? Do you think we should be watching them like this?"

"No, you're right. We shouldn't be watching. Let's go in." Matthew set out for the door only to be abruptly stopped by Joshua.

"Are you *narrisch*? We can't just go in there," Josh asserted.

"Why not?" Matt asked.

"Because. They'll think we've been watching them."

"So? Do you want anyone else stumbling upon them like this?" Matthew reasoned.

"*Nee*, you're right. We must go in, *jah*?" Joshua nodded.

"Uh...*jah*." Matthew gulped.

"Okay, let's do it," Joshua whispered determinedly, grabbing Matthew's hand and pulling him to the barn entrance.

Matthew quickly pulled his hand away. "What are you doing? Why are you holding my hand?" He attempted to keep his frustrated voice down.

Josh's cheeks turned bright pink. "Oh, sorry. Just a little nervous, I guess." Joshua flung the door open and he and Matthew marched inside.

"Joshua, Matthew!" Annie gasped, then sprung in front of the laptop to hide the exercise video, forgetting her own attire.

Maryanna quickly closed the laptop, then threw Annie her dress. "What are you two doing here? You're supposed to be out fishing with Jonathan."

Joshua strolled up to Annie and raised his eyebrows, allowing his eyes to sweep over her. "Maybe we should ask what you're doing. Wow, you look even better up close." Oblivious to Matthew and his sister, Josh inched closer and reached over Annie's shoulder to take hold of the flaxen locks that hung down past her waist in a ponytail. "I must be dreaming," he said as he let Annie's soft hair fall through his fingers.

"Oh, no; this is real." Matthew eyed Maryanna, who stood next to him. "You could never dream up anything this good."

"You're right." Unable to resist, Joshua reached around Annie's small waist and pulled her close. Placing his hand on her bare back, all common sense was thrown out the window. He couldn't get the goofy grin off his face. As he leaned down to kiss his betrothed, the barn door flew open with a crash, this time revealing an irate Deacon Yoder. Josh and Annie immediately broke apart, both trembling. Matthew and Maryanna simply stood dumbfounded.

"What's going on here?" Jacob Yoder demanded. "Joshua Hostettler, will you tell me what your hands were doing wrapped around my daughter's waist?"

Joshua's heart beat a million miles an hour, and at this moment he didn't even know if he had an hour to live. He gulped hard. "I...uh...I..." Words failed him. Oh, but he wanted to run, or cry, or disappear into the ground, or do something to escape the piercing glare of Annie's angry father.

"Annie Elizabeth!" he boomed to his daughter. "You're no longer welcome under my roof. Go home with this man since he can't seem to have the decency to wait for you anyway. *Geh raus, schnell*! I will speak to your father about this matter," he warned Joshua.

Annie hurriedly threw her cape dress over her head after her father stomped out of the barn, her hands were shaking like a leaf in the wind. Tears poured from her eyes as Joshua attempted to comfort her.

Maryanna, now dressed as well, placed a hand on Annie's arm. "Annie, I'm so sorry. This is all my fault."

Annie took a deep breath to quell her sobs. "No, it's my fault. Now, where will we have the wedding? Where am I going to live? Oh, this is all just so upsetting."

"You're coming home with me," Josh insisted. "If this is anyone's fault, it's mine. We'd better go before your father comes back out here and escorts us off his property."

"We'll see you soon, I hope." Matthew called back as he and Maryanna set out in one direction and Joshua and Annie headed in the direction of Bishop Hostettler's house.

CHAPTER 16
Reunion

*"I am crucified with Christ: nevertheless I live;
yet not I, but Christ liveth in me: and the life which
I now live in the flesh I live by the faith of the Son
of God, who loved me, and gave himself for me."
Galatians 2:20*

Jason peeked over his menu at Brooke, who seemed to be in another world. "Penny for your thoughts..."

"Sorry, Jason. Just thinking about the Weavers, that's all," Brooke said, folding her menu and setting it down on the table.

"Uh-oh, not dreaming about old boyfriends, I hope," Jason said, concern creeping into his voice.

"No, not really. I mean I was thinking about Seth, but not in that way. I was just thinking about how much my life has changed since summer vacation. It's almost as if I'm a completely different person." She smiled.

"That's because you are. You've been born again; now Christ lives in you." Jason smiled, longing to take her hand. "I'm glad God has allowed me to get to know you, Brooke. I think you and I make a good team, don't you?"

"Yeah, I do. I'm excited about us teaching the children's class at church. It's going to be a lot of fun."

"It is, you'll see. Just wait until the children are ready to accept Christ and you get to lead them to the Lord. It's wonderful!" Jason encouraged.

"Wow, I never in a million years would have thought my life would turn out this way." Brooke mused.

"That's how God works. He can take two insignificant people like us and do something really great through us. We just have to be willing to let Him use us for His glory."

"That's what I want, Jason. I want to do something really great for God." Brooke smiled.

"You may not realize it, but you already have," Jason asserted.

"I'm so glad you'll be able to stay for Joshua and Annie's wedding." Ruthie smiled at Ethan.

Ethan leaned back on the porch swing and set it to motion with his toe. He'd been staying with the Weavers since he drove Seth and Noah back home from Georgia. "I'm just glad I get to see you before you're snowed in for the winter. Come June,

I'll be moving out here permanently, Lord willing. I hope that Noah will take me on in the gazebo shop."

"That will be *gut*. What do your folks say about it?" Ruthie asked.

"I haven't actually told them yet. I don't plan to tell them until I'm finished with school. I'll be eighteen by then and an adult by law, so it won't really matter." Ethan sighed.

"But you must honor your folks," Ruthie said adamantly.

"I plan to. But if it comes down to them forcing me to go to college, I won't do it. I think the Amish even believe that a grown man has a right to make his own decisions," Ethan countered.

"*Jah*," Ruthie agreed.

"When I go back, I plan to get a job so I can start saving for a place of our own. Do you think someone might rent us their *dawdi haus* for a while? I mean, if we can't afford to buy a place right away?" Ethan asked eagerly.

"Maybe *Dat* and *Mamm* would let us use one of theirs. If not, I'm sure we'll be able to find a place." Ruthie smiled. "Okay, enough of this talk. I'm getting too excited and we still have to wait until I'm seventeen. A lot can happen in two years."

"Perhaps, but my love for you only grows deeper every day." Ethan smiled and rubbed Ruthie's hand. "Do you think I should talk to the bishop already? Is there something that I can do now to prepare for baptism? I'm already taking German in school, so I think that will help a lot as far as understanding the Luther Bible and church meetings go."

"You could. I'm sure Bishop Hostettler will be helpful, he's a *gut* bishop. Have you met him yet?" Ruthie wondered.

"No, I haven't. I did meet Jonathan Fisher, though. Didn't you say he was the bishop's son-in-law?"

"*Jah*, his wife Susanna is the bishop's daughter. And Joshua Hostettler, the bishop's son, is the one who's getting married to Annie Yoder, the deacon's daughter. And my older sister Chloe is married to Levi Hostettler, one of the bishop's older sons. So, in a way, after we get married you'll be related to the bishop too." Ruthie glanced over at Ethan who wore a bewildered look.

"I can tell already that I'm gonna have a hard time keeping everybody straight around here. With everybody having so many children, how do you not confuse everyone? We don't want our children to marry someone they're related to; that could cause some problems." Ethan ran his hand through his hair.

"You worry too much, Ethan." Ruthie giggled. "Here we're not even married yet and you're worrying about who our *kinner* are going to marry!"

"Yeah, I guess it is kind of silly." Ethan chuckled. "Let's just take one day at a time and we'll let tomorrow take care of itself, *jah*?"

"*Jah*," Ruthie agreed.

Joshua climbed up into the haymow to join Annie. He handed her a couple of quilts and a plate of food. "I'm sorry you have to stay up here right now, but I think it's best until I get a chance to talk to *Dat* about everything. Your father came by earlier, but thankfully *Dat* wasn't here. He won't be back home till tonight, so your *dat* probably won't be back till tomorrow."

Annie sighed. "Did he say anything to your *mamm*?"

"*Nee*," Joshua said. "I told *Mamm* that I'd be out late tonight, so I can stay out here with you for a while."

Annie nodded appreciatively and began to eat. She took a few bites of the food that tasted quite bland to her dull taste buds. She pushed the plate to Josh, who held out his hand in protest. "I can't eat any more," she asserted.

"But you've only taken a couple of bites. I hope you're still not trying to get rid of belly fat that doesn't exist." He chuckled a bit. "Annie, your body is perfect. Trust me."

"*Ach*, Josh. How can you laugh at a time like this? We're both in big trouble. And I'm so scared..." Annie put her face into her hands and began bawling again.

Joshua pulled her into his strong arms, attempting to console his betrothed. "Shh...it'll be okay, *Liewi*."

Night had fallen and the evening air of autumn began turning chilly. Josh leaned back on a mound of hay and pulled the blanket up over them. He held Annie in his arms until he could feel her breath steady to a quiet calm. Eyelids heavy, Joshua succumbed to the irresistible pull of sleep as well.

"Oh, it's so good to be back." Seth grinned at his beloved from behind his sundae and reached for her hand. "I've missed you, Honeybee."

Katie giggled at that silly old nickname. She used to think it was bothersome, but it sounded wonderful-*gut* when it came from Seth's lips. Everything did, in fact. Seth had just returned from Georgia the other day, and Katie had been delighted when he'd arrived unexpectedly at the ice cream shop. Since early-morning business was slow, Michelle didn't mind her taking a break in order to talk with Seth.

How good it was to see Seth again! She'd missed him so. Once Katie had gotten over the initial shock of seeing him, she'd almost kissed him – she was *that* pleased. Now she was perfectly content with just staring at his handsome face, basking in the joy of knowing that she was his *aldi*, his sweetheart. She hoped that someday she'd become more than just his girl. She hoped to someday become his bride. Katie's heart instantly warmed at the thought.

"Katie," Seth's gentle voice jolted Katie out of her musings and back to present day.

She refocused her attention on the young man in front of her, hoping that he hadn't asked her a question. "Yes, Seth?"

"Well, did you?" Seth voiced her fears. It was indeed a question.

"I'm sorry, Seth. I was daydreaming. I didn't hear what you said." Katie gulped.

"About me, I hope." Seth grinned mischievously.

"May-be." Katie dragged out the word, not wanting to let on that he was the only one she'd dream about.

Seth smiled.

Katie redirected the conversation. "So, what was it you were asking me?"

"I was askin' you if ya missed me."

"Oh." Katie thought back. She had worried and fretted over Seth being gone. She'd even cried at the possibility of Seth falling in love with Brooke again and becoming *Englisch*. Ruthie was the only one of her friends who understood her since Ruthie herself worried about Ethan, Brooke's brother. *Jah*, she had definitely missed Seth, more than she could say. "Of course. I missed you a lot."

That was all he needed to hear. Seth leaned across the table, as though to kiss Katie.

"Uh, Katie," a familiar female voice called. Seth immediately straightened and Katie looked up to see Michelle behind Seth, staring on with an amused smirk. "People are rollin' in now, so we need to hop to it." Michelle started for the serving counter, talking over her shoulder. "Banana splits don't make themselves."

Katie gave Seth an apologetic look and rose from the table. She hated to see him go. Seth stood up as well.

"I guess I'd better go," he said.

"I guess so." Katie wished he could stay all day. "Goodbye, Seth."

Seth couldn't, or perhaps didn't want to, stop himself. He quickly bent down to kiss Katie and she narrowly dodged him by a quick turn of her head. He consequently kissed Katie's cheek instead. Katie glared up at him, hands on hips, and shaking her head.

"It's not my fault you're so hard to resist," Seth defended himself.

Katie looked away and rolled her eyes. *Some things never change.* A smile threatened to emerge but she quickly suppressed it. Seth didn't need any more encouragement.

CHAPTER 17
Confession

"For the wrath of man worketh not the righteousness of God." James 1:20

"I know what I saw with my own two eyes, Judah!" Jacob Yoder's voice boomed through the early morning air. "Just get your boy, he'll tell ya."

"Please keep your voice down." Bishop Hostettler wiped his eyes and yawned, still not fully cognizant after being rudely awakened at three-thirty in the morning. "I'm certain you're mistaken, Jacob. Joshua wouldn't do anything to dishonor your daughter. Couldn't this have waited an hour or two? My family is still sleeping."

"Just bring your boy down here," Deacon Yoder grumbled.

Seeing he wasn't about to give up, Judah relented. "Very well, I'll get him." A minute later he returned downstairs, alone.

"Well?" Jacob asked, peering over Judah's shoulder. "Where's the boy?"

"He's not there. It doesn't look like his bed's been slept in." Judah sighed.

"I knew it! He's with my Annie, I tell ya. When I get a hold of that boy of yours, I'll –"

Judah interrupted. "You'll not lay a hand on my boy. Now you must calm down before you give yourself another heart attack, Jacob. And let me remind you that you are the deacon in this district, and I'll expect you to exercise some self-control," the bishop reprimanded and ran his hand through his beard. "Why don't you just go back home and when Joshua shows up, he and I will come talk to you."

"I will do no such thing! I'm not leaving this place until I see my daughter. I intend on searching every inch of this property. They've gotta be around here somewhere." Jacob turned on his heel, Judah following close behind.

"I'm going with you, then. Let's check the *dawdi haus* first," Judah insisted. *Dear Lord, please don't let them be in there.*

Joshua woke suddenly, taking in his surroundings. After his eyes adjusted, he realized he was in the haymow. Annie lay sleeping soundly in his arms and he gently placed a kiss on top of her head. He remembered the events of the prior day and decided he should get up so he could speak with his father first thing. He had no desire to awaken Annie though, knowing she was emotionally exhausted and needed rest. Instead, he pulled the extra blanket up over both of them and drifted back to sleep.

"Joshua!" a voice called out and he and Annie both sat straight up. He looked up into the eyes of two angry men – his father and Annie's.

"Do you mind telling me what's going on here, *Sohn*?" his father attempted to ask calmly.

Deacon Yoder began speaking. "I told you –"

"I'm talking to my son, Jacob. Please let him speak." Joshua noticed his father's irritation with the irrational man.

Joshua began to speak softly, squeezing Annie's hand under the quilt, hoping to comfort her. "Matthew and I went looking for Annie and Maryanna. We found them in Deacon Yoder's barn. They were exercising, wearing...uh...*Englischer* clothes."

"Tell 'em the rest," Jacob demanded, and once again Judah held up a hand to silence the man.

Joshua gulped. "I...uh...took Annie in my arms to kiss her when her father walked in. He told her she was no longer welcome in his house. He told me to take her home, so I did." Josh sent Annie a sweet reassuring smile.

"Is this true?" Judah turned to Jacob and he nodded. "Very well, then. I will have Lydia fix up the *dawdi haus* and Annie can stay there until they marry."

"She will do no such thing!" Deacon Yoder protested.

"You said she's not welcome under your roof. Everyone is welcome in our home," Judah said to Jacob, then turned to Annie and Joshua. "Come, I'm sure Lydia has breakfast ready by now. You may move into the *dawdi haus* after breakfast, Annie." He turned to the deacon. "Jacob, you may stay for breakfast if you'd like. I'll send Joshua over with Annie later to retrieve her things."

Jacob Yoder grimaced, then shook his head disapprovingly at Annie and Joshua. "I'm going home." He huffed and stomped off.

CHAPTER 18
Forgiven

"So then he that giveth her in marriage doeth well..." 1 Corinthians 7:38a

Ruthie padded up to the end of the Esh driveway where Ethan waited near his vehicle. "Ready to go?" he asked.

"*Jah*. This will be your first Amish wedding!" Ruthie's eyes sparkled as she slid into the vehicle.

"I'm kind of surprised it starts this early," Ethan commented.

"You do realize that Amish weddings last all day, *jah*?" Ruthie said.

"All day? You mean like four hours or something, right?" He raised his eyebrows.

Ruthie laughed. "No. The festivities usually go on well into the night. It's a lot of fun; you'll see. After the four-hour service, everyone will eat and talk with the bride and groom. In the evening, we usually have another small meal and then play games."

"Well, I guess I can get through anything with you by my side." Ethan smiled and took her hand.

"Men and women sit separately during the service, so I'll be across the room," Ruthie informed him.

Ethan sighed in frustration. "I guess I can sit by Seth then. I just hope I can see you; then I can dream of our wedding day." He smiled now.

"*Jah*, me too." Ruthie blushed.

Annie purposefully walked down the stairs as she had all her life, but today was different. Today, she and Joshua Hostettler would become husband and wife. Joshua looked so handsome in his black pants and jacket. His eyes sparkled as he caught sight of his bride descending the stairs. Annie smiled broadly. She knew there was nothing that would make her happier than this moment.

Joshua took her hands in his and gazed into her eyes. "I'm looking forward to spending the rest of my life with you. I love you, Annie Yoder."

Jacob Yoder placed a hand on Joshua's shoulder. "Enough of this, now. The people are beginning to file in. Better take your places." He paused for a moment, a tear forming in the corner of his eye. "Take *gut* care of my *dochder*."

Joshua simply nodded, but smiled inwardly. Jacob Yoder was not a man to be overly affectionate or generous with complements. He realized the simple words were his way of giving Joshua and Annie his blessing, and he thanked God for softening the heart of his future father-in-law.

CHAPTER 19
Wedding Night

"...For whatsoever a man soweth, that shall he also reap." Galatians 6:7b

"Finally!" Joshua said as he closed the door to the *dawdi haus*. "We get to rest. I don't know about you, Annie, but I am exhausted."

"Just be glad we only have to get married once. A wedding is nice, but it does take a lot out of a person," Annie said. "Well, at least my father was bearable today."

Joshua came near to his wife and drew her into his arms. He longingly ran his fingers over her lips, then bent down to claim his first kiss. "I don't want to talk about your father right now," he said as he began removing the hair pins from her *kapp*.

Knock...knock...knock.

Annie straightened. "Did you hear something?"

Joshua groaned. "I hope not. Let's don't answer," he said as he brushed his lips against his wife's once again.

"But it could be important," Annie asserted.

"If we don't answer, they'll go away. Surely they'll understand...it's our wedding night," Joshua pleaded.

"I hear noise outside, we should probably answer."

Joshua sighed and pulled up his suspenders. "You're right."

Annie and Josh both went to the door and looked out into the darkness. "No one's here," Joshua said. "Let's go back inside. I'll put a note on the door that says 'Do not disturb'."

A soft squeal sounded, and they looked down. There stood Johnny and Judah on their doorstep, clad in suspenders. Annie gasped. "Oh look, it's JJ! What are you two doing here? Where's your *mamm* and *dat*?" She looked beside the small boys and noticed a bag full of baby supplies. "Look, Josh, they're so cute!"

"Oh, no. This is *not* happening!" Joshua ran a hand through his hair. "Jonathan Fisher, you get back here and take your *kinner* home!" he called into the night.

Johnny and Judah both burst into wails, obviously frightened by Joshua's tone of voice.

"Now, look what you've done. You've made them cry." Annie knelt down to comfort the blond-haired cuties. "Shh...it's okay."

"Okay? This is not okay!" Joshua protested loudly. "We are getting in the buggy and taking them straight back to their parents. Right now. I'll go hitch up the horse," he mumbled in frustration, striding toward the barn.

Annie took the two boys by the hand and led them into the *dawdi haus*. *"Kumm, bist du hungerich?"* She set the boys at the table and removed some leftover wedding treats from the refrigerator. She handed each boy a cookie and their faces immediately brightened with delight.

A couple of minutes later, Joshua bounded through the door. "All hitched up. Ready, Annie?" He eyed Jonathan's boys munching on their snack.

"Aren't they so adorable? We could just keep them here," Annie suggested.

"Oh no, not on our wedding night." He held up his hands in protest. "Let's go now." He reached down to pick up one of the boys, who protested with another high-pitched cry. He quickly backed up, removing his hands from little Johnny. "You bring them; I'll get the bag."

Annie took JJ by the hand and helped them up into the family buggy. She sat in the back with a boy on each side of her, while Joshua drove the rig toward the Fisher residence. A short while later, they pulled up to the Fishers' *dawdi haus* where Jonathan and Susanna resided. Joshua climbed out of the buggy, then helped Annie and the twins down.

The boys' eyes lit up at the sight of their familiar home. *"Dat!"* the two boys squealed with delightful anticipation.

Joshua calmed his nerves, then knocked on the door.

No answer.

He knocked again, this time harder.

Still, no answer.

"Jonathan Fisher, you get out here and take your boys!" he yelled through the door.

Annie spoke up, "Joshua, keep your voice down! You're going to wake up his folks. And if you keep hollering like that, you're going to make the boys cry again."

Josh clenched his hands into fists. "All right. Annie, I'm trying *really* hard to stay calm. I am so upset right now, I could just –" he stopped, realizing his voice was rising again. He took a deep breath and pounded on the door again.

Annie gently put a hand on his forearm. "Perhaps they're not home. Let's just take the boys back with us."

"Maybe my *mamm* will take them." He shrugged.

"Josh, it's too late to bother your mother. Everyone is surely asleep by now. We could just go home and put the boys to bed," Annie suggested.

Joshua sighed in defeat. "You're right. Let's go home."

"I'm glad Lavina had an extra room available," Susie smiled up at her husband as they lay in the comfortable guest bed.

"*Jah*, me too." Jonathan smiled, smoothing his wife's auburn hair. "I wish we could've been there to see the look on Josh's face."

"What do you thing they're doing right now?" Susanna asked.

"Who? The twins or Josh and Annie?"

"Both."

"I would guess that Josh is probably pulling out his hair right now." He laughed.

"The twins are probably crying for their *dat!*" Susie added.

"Revenge is so sweet!" Jonathan laughed again, then reached over and put out light. "*Gut nacht, Liewi.* We shall sleep *gut* tonight."

"Okay, so let's get them into their pajamas and they can go to sleep," Joshua said matter-of-factly.

"Here." Annie handed Josh some night clothes. "You dress this one and I'll take the other one."

"Oh no!" Joshua held his nose. "I smell something stinky," he complained in a nasal voice. "I think it's this guy."

"Here, I'll take him." Annie laid the boy on the bed to change him, then opened the bag to find a diaper and wipes. The boy quickly rolled over and squiggled down the bed. "No, Johnny or Judah. You must have your diaper changed." She quickly grabbed the little guy and finally managed to get him to cooperate.

Annie turned to Josh. "There, he has a clean diaper now," she said with a voice of triumph. She looked around the room. "Where's Judah – or Johnny – the other one?"

Joshua spun around. "He was just here a minute ago. I'll go find him." He headed to the kitchen first and found nothing. After searching the small living room, he headed toward the bathroom. When he opened the door, he slipped on the wet linoleum and fell on his rump. "Ow!"

Annie came rushing in and found Joshua sitting in a puddle of water. "What happened?" She had to suppress a giggle. She looked down to see one of the twins with his hands in the toilet water.

The little guy looked up in sheer delight. "*Bad!*" he squealed.

"*Ach, nee*. We're not going to have a bath tonight," Annie said, removing the little guy's hand from the toilet and closing the lid. "Let's get you cleaned up."

Joshua looked around worriedly. "Where's the other one?"

"*Ach.*" Annie waved him off with a smile. "He's already in his pajamas. I put him down for bed."

He breathed a sigh of relief. "*Gut.* One down, one to go."

They walked back to the bedroom with the boy in Annie's arms. Annie looked down at the place where she'd laid the other twin. "Oh no, he's gone!"

Josh rolled his eyes. "I'll go find him. Do you think you can handle that one?"

After Annie nodded, Joshua walked back down the hallway, this time checking the bathroom first. "Jonathan...Judah, where are you? It's *Onkel* Joshua," he called out in a friendly voice. He heard a faint giggling and headed toward the kitchen.

As he rounded the corner, his mouth dropped open. There sat Johnny or Judah on the floor, covered from head to toe in flour. An empty canister lay teetering near the edge of the counter, with a flour dusted chair pulled up close. "*Brot!*" The little one smiled.

Joshua sighed. "No, JJ. We're not going to make bread right now. Annie, you've got to come see this!" he called to his wife.

Annie came to the kitchen with the other twin in her arms. She couldn't help bursting into laughter at the sight. "I'm sorry, Josh, but this is hilarious!" She tried to stop, but couldn't. Soon Joshua and the boys joined in and they were all laughing so hard, their insides ached.

"I think I have a new appreciation for Susie and Jonathan," Joshua said when the twins finally conked out from all the excitement...at about three o'clock in the morning.

"You're right. I never knew how exhausting having little ones could be. Maybe we should offer to babysit more," she suggested.

"Well, one thing's for sure. When they come to pick up the *kinner* tomorrow, we're going to get them good," Joshua said.

"What do you mean?" Annie said as she nestled in his arms.

"You'll see."

CHAPTER 20
The Last Word

"And ye shall seek me, and find me, when ye shall search for me with all your heart." Jeremiah 29:13

"*Brot, brot!*" Annie heard the excited squeals before she opened her weary eyes. The bed felt as though it swayed and she abruptly awoke to find the boys jumping on the bed, their faces alight with mischief. Jonathan's *kinner* for sure and for certain.

Annie turned to face the small clock that sat atop the night stand. Four-thirty. She and Joshua had only gone to bed an hour ago. "Okay," she groaned groggily. "I'll make breakfast in just a little bit."

Joshua was not immune to the twins' doings either. He rolled over on his side and gathered Annie into his strong arms; his lips met hers. "I have the most wonderful, beautiful, *hot* wife in the world!"

"Hot, huh? That sounds like something your sister would say. I hope her *Englischer* ways aren't rubbing off on you," Annie teased, gazing into the dark eyes of her handsome *mann.*

"Nah, I just couldn't think of an appropriate Amish word to use." He became distracted when Judah bounced in between them; Johnny followed. "I don't think we'll get anymore sleep till we ship these guys off to their folks. How about if you start on breakfast and I'll get the boys dressed?"

"That sounds *gut,* but are you sure you can handle them by yourself?" Annie raised her eyebrows doubting, climbing out of the bed.

"If I have any trouble, I'll be sure to holler for you," Josh asserted as he buttoned his shirt.

"All right, I'll just be in the kitchen." Annie grinned, planted a wonderful-*gut* kiss on his lips that left him longing for more, and then sailed out the door.

"That's not fair!" Annie heard Joshua holler as she made her way down the hallway with a smile playing on her lips. She quickly dressed in the bathroom, then started for the kitchen.

"Annie, I need your help!" Josh's voice echoed down the hall.

Annie set the basket of eggs down, then headed in the direction of Joshua's voice. When she reached the room, one of the twins was crying with his shirt stuck on his head and the other one sat in the middle of diapers, clothes, wipes, and all the other contents that filled their overnight bag. "No doubt you're Jonathan Fisher's boy," she muttered. "How on earth did you find so much trouble in so little time?

Joshua was unsure whether she was talking to the twins or to him. Another loud scream pierced the room as the poor little guy on the bed squirmed to get out of the shirt. "Please help me get this off of him," Josh pleaded, attempting to get the shirt over the little one's head.

"*Ach*, you forgot to undo the button." Annie quickly unfastened the button then rescued the boy from his entrapment. "I'll help you get them dressed."

"*Denki*," Josh said appreciatively.

"Why don't you help Johnny or Judah – the other one – clean up that mess?" Annie suggested while she diapered and clothed the other twin. "You know, it would have been a little easier if they would have at least left name tags on these two."

Joshua scoffed. "I don't think they had the word 'easy' in mind when they dropped the *kinner* off last night." He picked the last item off the floor, then safely placed the diaper bag onto the dresser out of the boys' reach.

"There, he's dressed!" Annie said triumphantly as she placed the little one on the floor to play with a plastic horse.

"I think this one's going to need some wipes," Joshua said as he placed the other boy on the bed, holding his nose.

"*Ach*, I already put them away. Will you fetch them for me please?" Annie asked.

"Here they are." Josh handed the package to his lovely wife. He gazed into her eyes with pride. "You are going to make a wonderful *mamm.*"

"And you, a wonderful *dat.*" She smiled until she glanced at the floor. "*Ach, nee!*" Little Johnny had removed his shirt and pants, and his diaper was half off.

"How do they do this?" Joshua asked incredulously. He walked over to little Johnny and plopped him onto the bed. "You need to keep your clothes on if you ever expect your aunt to make us breakfast." He told the little guy who stared blankly back at him.

"You redress him and I'll finish this one. After that, they don't leave our sight," Annie ordered.

After successfully dressing both boys, they all paraded into the kitchen. Joshua and the twins sat at the table while Annie prepared the meal.

"I hope you don't mind something simple this morning," Annie said as she set hard-boiled eggs and bread on the table. She quickly brought out some butter and jam as well.

"Let's pray." Josh and Annie bowed their heads in silence. After about thirty seconds, they lifted their heads and began distributing the food. Their attention was turned to the kitchen floor as they heard a smash.

"Oh no!" Annie cried as she spied the basket of raw eggs tipped onto the floor, yolk and egg white all over Judah's pants.

"I'll put pants on the little one and you wipe up the mess," Joshua said, then squeezed Annie's hand reassuringly. "We can do this. Uh...and Annie, let's reconsider this volunteering to babysit thing."

Annie nodded and began cleaning up the mess, making sure to keep a careful eye on Johnny. When she finally finished, she wiped her brow.

Knock, knock.

"They're here!" Josh said excitedly. "All right, here's the plan. We are going to act as if everything went perfectly, okay?"

A mischievous twinkle came into Annie's eye and she nodded.

"I wonder why they haven't opened the door yet," Susanna asked Jonathan with concern.

Jonathan laughed. "They're probably trying to clean up the tornado the boys left."

"I hope they're okay," Susie said.

"Who? The twins or Annie and Josh?"

"Annie and Josh." Susie laughed. "Knock again. Maybe they didn't hear the first time."

Just after Jonathan knocked a second time, Joshua coolly opened the door. "Hello!" He smiled brightly. Annie stood next to him with a luminous smile, her arm around his waist.

"I hope you two enjoyed our boys!" Jonathan said, mischief in his blue eyes.

"Your boys? What do you mean?" Joshua frowned at Jonathan as if he didn't have a clue as to what he was talking about.

"What do you mean, what do I mean?" Jonathan became concerned. "Matt and Maryanna left the boys on your doorstep last night."

"Oh no!" Susie cried. "Where did they go?"

"Calm down, Little *Schweschder*. I'm just pulling your leg. Your boys are right here, safe and sound." Joshua smiled and Jonathan and Susie both visibly relaxed.

Annie retrieved the boys from their confinement in the bedroom and handed them to their parents, along with their overnight bag. "They're clean and ready to go." Annie smiled sweetly.

Already knowing the answer, Jonathan asked, "How were they?"

Annie beamed. "*Ach*, they were *wunderbaar*!"

"They were?" Jonathan and Susie asked in unison, clearly expecting a different answer.

"*Jah*," Josh piped in. "Just like little angels, no problems at all."

Jonathan and Susie stood dumbfounded, looking at each other. But Jonathan was quickly on to their scheme. "I see. That's great! Susanna and I are taking a trip to see my family next week so we'll need a babysitter. I can tell that the two of you will be the perfect candidates!"

Susanna caught on. "*Jah*, you're right, Jonathan. I don't know why I never thought of them before, but they would be perfect. Well, *denki* for watching the *buwe* for us." She gave them each a quick hug, then led the boys to the buggy.

After the door closed, Joshua and Annie stood speechless for a moment. Josh finally found his voice. "Tell me we didn't just get roped into babysitting next week." He raked his hand through his hair.

"I'm afraid so," Annie said. "Hey, wait a minute! They're not going out of town next week, I know that for a fact. Abigail told me they're throwing an anniversary party for Esther and Gideon."

"*Ach,* they got us again!" Josh said, frustrated. "We've got to start planning our next attack." He determined.

"You go ahead and plot, *Lieb.* I'm going back to bed." Annie began removing her hair pins from her *kapp,* and soon her flaxen hair trailed down her back.

Joshua looked after her longingly and cleared his throat. "You know, I think I'll save the plotting for later. I could use some sleep, too."

Seth almost stumbled down the steps in an attempt to reach the kitchen. He'd heard the telephone ringing several times, then it had finally stopped. Where were Leah and *Mamm*? It wasn't normal for at least one of them not to be in the kitchen. He glanced out the kitchen window and noticed the buggy gone. They must have gone into town to do some shopping. The telephone began ringing once more, so Seth stepped into the small pantry-turned-office and answered the phone.

"Weavers' Bed-and-Breakfast. May I help you?"

"Seth? Is that you?" a vaguely familiar female voice asked.

"*Jah*. Katie?" He didn't know why she'd be calling him since they lived so close.

"No, Seth. This is Brooke Spencer."

"*Ach*, I'm sorry. Hello Brooke." Seth recovered. "I hope your family is well."

"Yes, everyone is doing great!" she said enthusiastically. "In fact, I have some exciting news to tell Leah. Is she there?"

"No, apparently I'm the only one home right now," he said. "But I'll tell Leah you called."

"Okay, just have her call me back." She hesitated, and then continued, "Seth, would you want to hear my news?"

"If it's something you want to tell me."

"Jason gave me a Promise Ring! Isn't that great?"

Seth wasn't sure what that meant. "You're getting married?"

Brooke laughed. "Oh no, not yet anyway. A Promise Ring is sort-of a precursor to an engagement ring. Kind of a 'I really want to marry you but it will probably be a while' ring. He thought it was more fitting than an engagement ring because I'm only sixteen."

"That's *gut*," he said, unsure of what she expected his response to be.

"Ethan and Leah tell me you've been seeing a lot of Katie King. I only met her a couple of times, but she seemed nice. Jason said she's really sweet. I guess he used to visit her at the ice cream shop every day when he was back in Lancaster County. It seems he had a pretty big crush on her, but she only thought of him as a friend." Brooke giggled. "Are you two getting serious?"

"We're courting," he said matter-of-factly. "And, *jah*, I care for her."

Brooke waited for him to expound, but he didn't, so she kept the conversation going. "How was the wedding? Were there any pranks?" she asked.

"*Jah*, 'twas *gut*. I guess the happy couple was left with a pair of troublesome bundles of joy on their doorstep. I heard it made for an interesting wedding night." Seth laughed.

"Oh, that's terrible!" Brooke said. "Did they get any rest? Ethan told me how exhausted he was after the whole-day affair."

"*Nee*, I don't think so. The twins' *dat* and *mamm* stayed at our bed-n-breakfast for the night, so at least *they* got a good night's rest," he added, thinking he should be hanging up soon.

"Lucky them," she said, wryly. "Hey Seth, I have wanted to tell you something for a while now." When he remained silent, she ventured on. "I don't know how much you realize this, but meeting you changed my life in so many ways. Since you introduced me to Christ, I began a whole new life.

"When I first came to Paradise, I thought I was searching for someone to sweep me off my feet – which you did quite literally, by the way." She heard Seth chuckle into the phone, but continued on. "I didn't know it at the time, but I was really on a quest for true love. And I'm not talking about Jason, either. There's only one person who can fulfill that quest for true love and his name is Jesus. So, thank you, Seth. Thank you for introducing me to my true love."

The End

Leah's
Legacy

J.E.B. Spredemann

Leah's Legacy

J.E.B. Spredemann

Amish Girls Series - Book 8

For Our Church Family

Thank you for your love and encouragement

CHARACTERS IN
LEAH'S LEGACY

The Weaver Family

Leah – protagonist, oldest daughter
Seth – protagonist of Brooke's Quest, oldest son
Noah – father
Lavina– mother

The Schrock Family

Ben – protagonist
Faith – Ben's older sister

The Lapp Family

Andrew – carpenter, oldest of the Lapp siblings
Sadie – antagonist of Abigail's Triumph, oldest Lapp daughter

The Fisher Family

Jonathan & Susie – youngest son & wife, protagonists of Susanna's Surprise
JJ (Johnny & Judah) – Jonathan & Susie's twins
Abigail Lapp – foster daughter, protagonist of Abigail's Triumph, Andrew's sister, Leah's friend

The King Family

Philip – father, herbalist
Katie – daughter, Seth's aldi, Leah's friend

The Hostettler Family

Judah – father, bishop of Paradise
Maryanna Hostettler – the bishop's daughter
Annie Hostettler – the bishop's daughter-in-law

Others

Officer Brandon Love – Sadie's fiancé
Jackson – Leah's Englisch friend
Tori – Leah's Englisch friend, Jackson's sister
Adam Glick – Leah's former beau
Daniel Miller – Abigail's beau
Joseph Miller – Daniel's older brother
Ruthie Esh – Leah's friend, Chloe's younger sister
Ethan Spencer – Ruthie's beau
Matthew Riehl – Maryanna's betrothed
Ralf – Ben's boss
Chloe – midwife

CHAPTER 1
Settling In

*"This is the day which the LORD hath made; we will
rejoice and be glad in it." Psalm 118:24*

ndrew Lapp grasped a nail from his toolbelt and
hammered it into the frame of the house. The
scorching sun beat hard on his straw hat and he dabbed the
perspiration from his forehead with a handkerchief. A drink
of water was called for right about now. He glanced down from
the ladder, debating whether he wanted to expend the effort
to retrieve his insulated beverage container. Surrendering to
his demanding thirst, he descended the aluminum rungs. After gulping down several ounces of refreshment, he poured the
last of the water over his face and head.

"Andrew Lapp."

Andrew turned at the sound of Bishop Hostettler's voice
and wondered what the bishop's request would be today. Since
he was the only man in his mid-twenties who didn't have a wife

and *kinner* to care for, he was often called upon to help out when somebody in their community needed assistance. He didn't mind so much, but he often wondered how the others viewed him.

After his father, Reuben Lapp, had killed his mother, Andrew let his anger get the best of him. It seemed that since the day he unleashed his wrath on his father, the women his age had been wary of him. And who could blame them? The community probably thought he was just like his abusive alcoholic father, but nothing could be further from the truth. He swore the day his father was hauled off to jail that he would be nothing like him.

"Hello, Bishop." Andrew extended his hand in greeting.

"How is work going these days?" Judah's eyes swept over the large two-story home.

"Well. *Gott* has blessed me with a lot of work. It wonders me sometimes how I'll ever get it all done."

"I might have a solution for you." Judah rubbed his gray beard. "A new family is moving into Katrina and Maryanna's old home. Benjamin Schrock is seventeen and I believe he could use a job to help support the family. I know he's been looking around for work, but I'm not sure if he's had much construction experience. Would you be willing to hire him on?"

"I reckon I could give him a try." Truth was, Andrew had been praying for someone knowledgeable in construction to hire. Perhaps *Der Herr* was answering his prayer, although he didn't feel he had time to train someone.

"*Wunderbaar.* Would you mind stopping by their place after you're finished for the day?" the bishop asked.

"No problem."

As Judah's buggy drove away, Andrew wondered what the new family was like. Knowing the Thompson's place only had a couple of bedrooms, he figured the family couldn't be very large. He hadn't been there since the Beilers moved out several years ago. It seemed that no matter who moved in, they'd quickly outgrow the place and purchase something larger. The house was probably in need of repair, unless the previous owners had made improvements, which he doubted. No doubt he'd be called upon to complete the needed repairs if there were any. He sighed. *All I need is another project to add to my already-demanding work load. I'd better hire Benjamin quickly.*

Leah Weaver pulled the bran muffins out of the oven and quickly set them on the counter to cool. She took the next two pans of banana walnut muffins, shoved them into the oven, and set the timer. She glanced back at the pile of dishes in the sink and her shoulders dropped. *Please help me get these done before* Mamm *returns*, she breathed the silent prayer.

Ding-ding. At the sound of the front bell ringing, Leah threw up her hands. *I get it; this is a test, right?*

Leah hurried to answer the front door, where, no doubt, impatient guests awaited. Why did it seem that the days *Mamm* went to town always turned out to be the most hectic? While she enjoyed working at their family bed-and-breakfast, she did not relish being the sole person in charge of everything. Leah did not enjoy the extra stress. It was times like this she wondered what an *Englisch* life would be like.

Ding-ding.

Leah was about ready to yank that bell off the wall and scream at the waiting guests when she jerked the door open. To her surprise, a handsome young Amish man stood on the door step. She took a deep breath to calm her frazzled nerves. No doubt he'd caught her flustered face.

"*Hiya.* Do you have a couple of rooms available for about a week or so?" The young man twisted his straw hat in hands.

A feminine voice behind him chided, "*Ach,* Benjamin. Introduce yourself first." A pretty blonde Amish woman in her mid-twenties stepped forward, smiled, and held out her hand to Leah. "I apologize for my *bruder.* My name is Faith Schrock and this is my brother, Benjamin. We'll be moving into the Thompson's old place after some repairs are completed, but we need a place to stay in the meantime. The bishop directed us here."

"*Jah,* sure. I'm Leah Weaver. My *mamm* usually runs the place, but she's out on errands right now. We have two rooms available upstairs for one hundred dollars a night each, but I'm sure *Mamm* will give you a discount since you'll be staying here in Paradise. She should be back by suppertime."

"We'll take 'em," Benjamin spoke, swiping his chestnut bangs off his brow. His hairstyle reminded her more of an *Englischer*, than an Amishman. He was most likely still in *Rumspringa*.

"Are you sure you wouldn't like to see them first?" Leah heard the timer buzz in the kitchen. "*Ach*, I need to get that. Do you mind taking a seat in the *schtupp?*"

"No, of course not. Ben, why don't you help Leah?" Faith suggested.

Benjamin cast his sister a disapproving look.

"*Nee*, I'll be fine," Leah insisted. The last thing she needed was a good-looking Amish guy watching her every move when she had a ton of work to get done. She'd be mortified if Benjamin stepped into the kitchen when she still had a mound of dirty dishes in the sink. Leah hastened to the kitchen and removed the banana walnut muffins, then turned off the oven. Fortunately, her baking was finished for the day and she could tackle the dishes as soon as she got her new guests settled.

"The rooms are this way, if you're ready to see them now." Leah led the way to the stairs with her boarders in tow. The sooner her guests were settled, the sooner she could get back to the kitchen. Nevertheless, a break *was* welcome.

"This is a nice place you've got here," Benjamin commented, eyeing the mahogany paneling and chair rail.

"*Jah*, my *dat* and *bruder* have done a lot of work to it. Most guests enjoy the porch and the gazebo out front. My folks turned it into a bed-and-breakfast about eight years ago." Leah opened a door to a large bedroom with a queen-size canopy bed, a small night stand complete with a shaded lamp, a mirrored dresser, and a petite floral chaise lounge. The décor often reminded her of a room she'd once seen in a magazine featuring old Victorian homes.

"Wow, this is beautiful," Faith remarked. Her eyes swept over the elegant décor. "Are you sure it's not more than one hundred dollars a night?"

Leah laughed. "*Jah,* I'm certain sure. You might not want to say that to my *mamm* though, or she'll think twice about giving you the discount." She winked. "This is our suite and, by far, the most extravagant. I'm afraid the other room is much simpler."

"You may have this room, Faith. I don't need anything fancy," Benjamin insisted.

"*Denki,* Ben." Faith smiled in appreciation.

Leah glanced at Benjamin. "Your room is just next door." She opened the door to the other bedroom and Benjamin nodded.

"This is *gut,*" he said, eyeing the familiar simple furnishings typical of any Amish bedroom.

Leah pointed to another door. "Across the hallway in that room over there is where Ethan Spencer stays. He's an *Englischer* who's been renting from us for a few months now. He plans to become Amish and marry Ruthie Esh, whom I'm sure you'll eventually meet. She's a *gut* friend of mine." Leah paused before descending the stairs. "Oh yeah, the bathroom is at the end of the hallway and there's a small linen closet next to it if you need extra blankets or towels. Do you have any questions?"

"*Jah,*" Faith spoke up. "I need to ride out to the house to meet with the carpenter who is supposed to be helping us. Would you mind if Benjamin stays around? It seems like you could use some help and Ben knows his way around a kitchen."

Out of the corner of her eye, Leah saw Benjamin cringe. "It's all right. He doesn't need to help. I can handle everything. And it's fine for him to stay, if you'd like. I'm used to guests being here."

"All right, if you're sure." Faith then turned to her brother. "Ben, please get our things out of the buggy and bring them upstairs. I need to go now. I'm supposed to meet the carpenter at five o'clock."

"Does that mean you won't be having dinner with us? We usually serve at six," Leah said. "It's an extra eight dollars a night each. Some folks eat here, some eat out at restaurants. We just like to know ahead of time so that there's plenty."

"Could you just keep a plate for me and set it in the refrigerator? I'm not quite sure how long it will take."

"No problem." Leah turned and headed back to her mound of unwashed dishes. She sighed, thinking it *would* be really nice to have some help right about now. But there was no way she was going to make Benjamin help her against his will.

Benjamin flung his shoes off and plopped down onto the bed. He closed his eyes and took a deep breath, exhaling slowly. Moving to Pennsylvania had been more trying than he'd imagined. Not physically speaking, but emotionally. It'd been difficult to leave the place where he'd spent the entire seventeen years of his life. All his friends and family were still back in Ohio – where he longed to be.

Why his sister got the notion to uproot them and move to Pennsylvania, he wasn't certain. Although he had a few ideas of his own as to her reasons, he was convinced the main one was leaving the memory of their folks' death behind. Benjamin sorely missed his folks and would give anything to have them still alive and well, but *Der Herr* saw fit to take them home early, for reasons only known to Him. When they'd left in a van headed to New York to see cousins, Benjamin had no idea it'd be the last time he'd see them alive. There were so many things that were left unsaid. If he'd known, he would have made sure his last words to them were "I love you."

That had been a year ago, when Benjamin was sixteen, but it seemed like yesterday. Since Faith was the only sibling who was still at home and had yet to marry, she felt it was her duty to provide for Benjamin. And protect him.

When their home had burned down, losing the house seemed to be the last straw for Faith. She had no desire to rebuild. It was as though her hopes and dreams for their future in Ohio vanished when their parents and home did. Instead of allowing the community to construct a new home for them,

Faith had decided that a fresh start in a new place would be best. So they'd taken the gracious donations of their community and headed east.

Benjamin wondered what God wanted from him. Why had these things happened? He realized that he might never find the answers to those questions, but he was okay with that. Could *Der Herr* have led them to Paradise, Pennsylvania for a reason?

He hoped things would go well for them here. So far, the People seemed pretty nice. They'd met the bishop, one of the ministers, and Philip King, and expected to meet the remainder of the congregation on Sunday at Meeting. And, of course, they'd just met Leah.

Benjamin's face warmed when he thought of her first answering the door. The last thing he expected to see was a pretty girl standing in front of him. He'd nearly gotten tongue-tied. Then he could've died of embarrassment when his sister mentioned his lack of manners. He wasn't a *boppli* anymore.

Sometimes he felt as though Faith thought she was his mother. He needed her to see that he was old enough to take care of himself. That's one of the reasons he'd bought a car. And that was why it was so important that he find work. But, then, if he started working and found a place of his own, who would care for Faith? As the man, he felt responsible for his sister's well-being. He couldn't just leave her alone. No, if Benjamin decided to settle down, his *alt maedel* sister would have to live with him. Not the most appealing thing when you were looking for a girl to court. Not that he was looking. *Nee*, he'd be too busy working to even think about courting a girl.

He didn't know what the other girls in Paradise were like, but Leah was pretty 'hot' as his *Yankee* friends back home would say. He hoped she'd be the first girl he'd court, but he was certain she already had a beau. Sixteen and gorgeous; *nee*, he didn't stand a chance with her.

CHAPTER 2
Andrew

"A man that hath friends must shew himself friendly." Proverbs 18:24

Faith grimaced when she drove up the long path to the small house she'd purchased. There was so much work that needed to be done. The shrubs that lined the path were terribly overgrown and unruly, not to mention the repairs needed on the house. How much would it cost for someone to do all this work?

The monies received from their community in Ohio had been enough for a decent down payment on the little place, but until she or Benjamin started bringing in more, she would not be able to make the repairs necessary to start her business. But how could she make any money if she didn't first make the repairs? No one would want to come to this place in its present condition and purchase candles from her.

The wheels in her head had already begun turning. She would give away a lot of candles at first, but once her potential customers fell in love with the products, they'd be begging for more. At least that's what her Mennonite friend, Angeline Kreider, had said. She said she could probably open a whole store eventually, after she built her customer base. Paradise seemed like the perfect place, too, since she had yet to find a candle shop anywhere in the vicinity.

As she tied the borrowed horse to the hitching post, she noticed all the weeds that grew in the yard. The bishop had said it had been a year since the previous owners had moved out and it was obvious that nobody had kept the place up since then. If Ben didn't need a job, she'd have him out here pulling weeds and setting the place in order.

Lord, please help us get settled in this new place. Help me find a gut friend and please let Ben find a job...and stay out of trouble. It was that last part she was most concerned about. One of the deciding factors in moving had been to help Benjamin make some new friends, hopefully ones who would keep him on the straight and narrow.

She'd just finished her prayer when she heard a noise coming from inside the house. Was the carpenter already inside? She hadn't noticed a buggy anywhere.

"*Hullo?*" she called.

She peered through the dirty window, but saw nothing. *Should I go in or wait for the carpenter?* Faith slipped the key into the lock and gingerly turned the doorknob. Before stepping in, she listened carefully. Perhaps a mouse-catcher had gotten into the house. She glanced around the dusty entry way, but saw no evidence of a cat anywhere.

She left the door open and took a few cautious steps further into the living room. She heard another noise, as though the floor creaked under somebody's foot in another room. Whispers rose into the stale air and she debated whether she should run.

"*Hullo?*" Faith called out again.

She heard an expletive and then a crash as though a window had shattered. Before she could reach the door, three *Englisch* teenage males ran past her, nearly knocking her over. Faith screamed in her frightened state.

As she attempted to still her rapidly beating heart, an Amish man raced toward her from the barn. He ascended the steps in a single leap and quickly stood by her side. She glanced down at his comforting hand on her forearm.

"Are you all right?" he asked, removing his hand.

Faith breathed a sigh of relief. "*Ach, jah.* Just some *Englisch kinner.* They startled me, that's all."

"Sorry I didn't get here sooner. A customer showed up and I couldn't get away."

"I understand," Faith said. "Are you the carpenter the bishop sent?"

"That'd be me." His hazel eyes sparkled beneath his straw hat. Faith noticed it was a different style than what the Amish men wore in her Ohio district. "My name is Andrew Lapp." He held out his hand.

She smiled and shook his hand. "Faith Schrock."

"Will your husband be here soon?" Andrew inquired, mentally taking in the condition of the home.

"Oh, no; I'm not married." Faith's cheeks colored. "It's just me and my *bruder,* Benjamin. He's seventeen."

"And is he here?"

"No. I came alone. I hope that's not a problem."

"No, it's just that I expected...well, never mind." He shook his head. *Bishop Hostettler must've planned this.* "Would you like to discuss your plans?"

She eyed him curiously. "My plans?"

"*Jah*, for the house," he clarified.

"Of course." Was he as nervous as she was? "First of all, I need to know what you charge. I only have a minimal amount of money right now."

"I see. Well, I usually give a discount for folks in our district. You wouldn't need to pay right away. I mean, whenever you can afford it would be fine."

"Oh, thank you. You don't know how much I appreciate that. Benjamin is looking for a job right now, so hopefully he'll find something soon. And once I have the place ready, I hope to bring money in too."

"What kind of business do you have in mind?" He wondered.

"Candles. I make natural soy candles."

"Candles?" He didn't want to burst her bubble, but he doubted selling candles would bring in much money – especially in their Plain community. They didn't usually buy too many fancy things.

Faith frowned. "You don't think candles will sell very well here?"

How could he explain without hurting her feelings? "Did the Amish folks in Ohio buy these candles?"

Faith nodded enthusiastically. "Oh yes. Amish and *Englisch*." She smiled and remembered the candle she had in her purse. "Just a minute." Faith jogged out to the buggy and retrieved the scented candle. She opened up the glass lid and held the jar out to Andrew.

Andrew took the candle and brought it to his nose, although it hadn't been necessary. He could smell it the second she'd removed the lid. He cocked a brow and smiled. "That smells really nice."

"You may have it. If you don't want to burn it yourself you can give it to your *mamm* or *aldi*."

"I don't have an *aldi*." He grimaced and self-consciously rubbed his beardless chin. "Or a *mamm*."

"Oh, I'm sorry. About your *mamm*, I mean."

He chuckled when he noticed her cheeks color. "So you're not sorry that I don't have an *aldi*?" he teased.

She eyed him suspiciously. "Should I be?"

Andrew suddenly cleared his throat. "What did you say you'd like me to do with the house?"

Faith smiled. Back on track. "Okay, I think the first order of business will be the window that those boys just broke. I didn't notice any other broken windows, but it would probably be wise to inspect those as well."

Andrew drew a small notebook and pencil from his pocket and took notes. He grabbed a measuring tape from his toolbelt. "Where was the broken window?"

"I think in the master bedroom. That's where it sounded like the crash came from." Faith glanced around. "How do you suppose those boys got in here?"

"Probably through one of the windows; we need to make sure they all have locks on them."

"Do you think we'll have any problems with break-ins?" she worried. She hadn't thought that they might be moving to someplace unsafe.

"That shouldn't be a problem. After folks realize someone is living here, they'll probably find another abandoned place to occupy. We've never had any trouble, as far as I know."

"Whew, that makes me feel a lot better." She followed Andrew as he went into the master bedroom and measured the window. "How long will it take to make this place habitable?"

"Depends on what habitable is to you." He smiled. "I can put in an order for the window first thing Monday. I'm on a job right now, so I'll only be available during the evenings."

Faith inadvertently noticed his brawny arm as he held the measuring tape up to the window frame. It was obvious that he'd been in construction for some time. Andrew Lapp was indeed a nice-looking man, she admitted. She wondered why he wasn't married yet. Not that she was in the market for a husband.

"What are you thinking?" Andrew had caught her staring off into space.

Faith flustered as she realized she was still staring at his arm. "*Ach*, nothing. Uh...I'm sorry, did you say something?"

He glanced at his arm and sent her a knowing smile. "Yes, I was asking what you'd like me to take a look at next." He slipped his measuring tape back into his toolbelt.

Me. She cleared her throat. "The front door seems to be in need of repair. And, of course this whole place could use a coat of paint. I'd like to set up the front room as a sort of candle gallery, so if you could make some shelves to line the walls, that would be nice."

"How will you keep the candles from melting?"

Faith bit one side of her bottom lip. "I hadn't thought of that."

"I could install a partition so you can close off this room when the cook stove heats up too much," Andrew suggested.

"Oh, could you do that? That would be wonderful!" She beamed.

Andrew sighed in contentment. It felt good to be wanted and appreciated. "I'll check out the plumbing, too, to make sure everything is in working order." He jotted a few more things down on his list then walked toward the kitchen. "Do you mind if I camp out here while I'm working? Since I'll mostly be working at night, it would be easiest if I just stayed here." He opened up the cabinet and peered under the sink.

"*Nee*, that's fine. Ben and I will be staying at the Weavers' Bed-and-Breakfast until this place is ready to move in to. I'll be coming during the day to clean things up as best as I can."

Andrew walked out to the front porch and lifted his hat. He ran his fingers through his dark wavy hair. "All right. So, if I don't catch you here, I know where to find you in case I have any questions."

"That sounds *gut*. *Denki*, Andrew." Faith nodded and made her way back to the buggy.

"No problem." His gorgeous eyes glistened in the fading sun.

Andrew took a deep breath as Truffle galloped toward home. When Bishop Hostettler sent him to appraise the abandoned house, he had no idea a beautiful single woman would be waiting for him. Andrew smiled. It wasn't the first time their bishop had played matchmaker. He had a suspicion that many of the couples in Paradise had begun with a friendly nudge from Judah Hostettler.

He reached over the seat and grasped the candle Faith had given him. He brought it to his nose and breathed in the delightful fragrance. When he'd asked what the scent was called, she'd sheepishly told him it was called 'Love Trance', named after a famous perfume. But it didn't take a wonderfully fragrant candle to put him under a spell. No, one look at Faith Schrock and he was gone.

Did he even stand a chance with her? Hopefully he'd get an opportunity to speak with her before the rumor mill did. That wasn't likely, considering Meeting would be held tomorrow. For the life of him, he couldn't figure out why she wasn't married. Did she have a checkered past too?

CHAPTER 3
Conflict

"For love is strong as death; jealousy is cruel as the grave..." Song of Solomon 8:6b

*L*eah walked out onto the porch after dinner, hoping for a little peace and quiet. It was the first time, other than mealtime, that she'd gotten a break. The cool breeze felt *wunderbaar* on her skin, dissipating some of the sweltering heat.

She gazed at the beautiful landscape before her. A perfect green lawn met her eyes. A redwood gazebo stood at the end of the Weavers' driveway. The blessings in her life were countless. Yet she felt...unhappy; trapped.

The Amish lifestyle held her captive and, like an imprisoned bird, she longed to fly free and test her wings; to experience something different.

Like the *Englisch* world.

Leah turned back to the house and strode to her bedroom. She carefully closed and locked the door and walked to her bed.

Kneeling beside it, she leaned forward and felt the floorboards beneath her bed. *One, two, three...*she counted the boards as her hand slid across them. Pausing on the fifth one, she lifted it and reached her hand into the narrow opening. When she found what she was looking for, she placed the board back, clutching a composition book. She stood and brushed stray dust off her dress.

She plopped onto the chair at her desk and pulled a pen from its drawer. After thinking for a moment, she began to write...

Dear Journal,

I feel like I'm at a crossroads. I am not sure how to explain this feeling, this desire to leave. I want my life to change somehow. Since when have I become discontent with my life? This emotion seems to have suddenly come over me and I'm not sure what to do with it.

I'm all ferhoodled. *I don't understand this restlessness. It makes me want to leave all I've ever known. My family, friends, church...everything. But I could never do that. Would never want to do that. Yet, somehow I do. Ach, it is all so frustrating!*

Leah paused, unsure of what to write. Dwelling on what she did not understand wasn't helping. Perhaps the Weavers' new guests were a better topic.

We received some more boarders today. A young man named Benjamin Schrock and his older sister, Faith. They seem like nice folks. I 'spect their parents are gone, since

there's just the two of them. From what Ben told us at sup-
per, he's gonna work with the carpenter from our district, An-
drew Lapp. He said Faith is planning to open a candle shop.
She makes the natural kind. They sound nice. I wonder what
scents she'll have.

A knock sounded at her door.

After putting her diary in the desk drawer, Leah stood and made her way to the entrance of her room. "Yes?" She poked her head out the door, enquiring of her older brother's intrusion.

"We're gonna play some games. Wanna join us?" Seth peered down at her, raising a questioning brow. "There's a nice young Amish man that asked about you," he teased in a sing-song voice.

"*Ach*, Seth!" Leah flustered. "Did he really?"

"It wasn't a joke. I wouldn't tease you about matters of the heart."

Leah's eyebrows evidenced her doubt. "You'd better not embarrass me in front of him," she warned.

Seth held up his hands in innocence. "Now, would your kind big brother do something like that?"

Leah shot him a pointed look.

"Okay, maybe I would." Seth grinned. "But I won't this time."

"Promise?"

"Yeah, promise. What do you say?"

"*Jah*, sure. I'll be down in a minute." Leah secured the door and returned her journal to its hiding place. She turned the small hand mirror over, which hung from a peg on the wall, to glance at her reflection. After straightening her *kapp*, she took a deep breath.

A moment later, she descended the stairs and entered the living room. Leah pretended not to notice the pleased look on Benjamin's face when he glanced up from the couch. Ethan sat next to him with his *aldi*, Ruthie Esh, at his side.

"Oh, good; I was hoping you'd come, Leah." Ruthie beamed.

"Seth talked me into it," Leah admitted. "I probably won't play for long. I'm so tired..." She yawned, then covered her mouth and giggled.

"I think we could all use some extra sleep tonight. I know I can," Ben said with a slight smile directed at Leah.

"Aw, we were hoping the five of us could go to the ice cream shop in Ethan's car. I know Seth wants to see Katie." Ruthie grinned.

Seth smiled. "Sure do. And a banana split would be nice too."

Ben's countenance glistened. "I love banana splits."

"Let's go another day, *jah*?" Leah hated to put a damper on everyone's plans, but she wasn't really up to it today.

"I'll probably start my new job Monday." Ben rubbed the back of his neck.

Leah detected the disappointment in his voice.

"Wow, you just rolled into town today and you already have a job? Impressive," Ethan interjected.

"Maybe two; Andrew Lapp wants me to start working for him also," Ben said.

Ruthie's eyes pleaded with Leah's. "It looks like we may not get another chance to all go together."

"*Ach*, okay." Leah acquiesced. "But we can't stay out all night."

"Let's go now then, *jah*?" Ruthie shot up from her seat. "We can play games another time."

The group agreed and Leah and Seth told their folks of their plans. After Ben also informed his sister, they were on their way to the ice cream shop. Ruthie rode up front, next to her sweetheart, and Leah was seated in the back between Seth and Benjamin.

Leah's heart warmed as she noticed Ethan reach over and grasp Ruthie's hand, gently intertwining his fingers with hers. What would it be like to find the love of your life – the one you would spend the remainder of your days with?

Leah sighed. Right now, she wasn't sure what she wanted. She knew she'd probably marry and settle down someday, *jah*, but at this moment in her life she felt stuck. Trapped. Confused. Like she was standing on the side of the road just watching the cars go by, waiting for one to stop and ask her to hop in.

Ben glanced over at Leah. She seemed to be deep in thought. He covertly drank in her lovely presence. Her golden blonde hair, which no doubt hung past her waist, was twisted near her temples and secured tightly in a bun at the nape of her neck, covered by her white, heart-shaped prayer *kapp*. The blue dress she wore, partially concealed by a black apron of nearly the same length, did much to bring out her striking cerulean irises. He'd noticed that earlier. His gaze couldn't help but meander to her frame; not too thin and not too plump, just right. A slight smile lifted a side of his mouth. Honeysuckle perfume wafted to his nostrils and he momentarily closed his eyes.

Seth cleared his throat and Ben's head jerked up. Seth's pointed look told Benjamin he'd been caught admiring Leah. And was there a flash of warning in his eyes? He grimaced as he realized he wasn't being as subtle as he'd thought. He needed to remind himself that the Weavers were the owners of the bed-and-breakfast and Faith would not be happy if his actions resulted in them being evicted. Perhaps he should convert Seth into an ally so they could join forces. *Jah*, that was a w*underbaar* idea.

As Ethan maneuvered the vehicle into a small parking lot, Ben smiled at Leah. He wanted to do all he could to make certain she didn't regret coming along. As much as he enjoyed being with a group of young people his own age, he wished it were just him and Leah in *his* car. That way, he'd have a chance to get to know her without others listening in.

Ben opened the door to the vehicle and slid out. He waited for Leah to follow before he closed the door behind her. He glanced at her brother to be sure he was on safe ground, but apparently Seth had his mind on other things. When they walked through the door of the ice cream parlor, Ben realized what – or rather who – had captured Seth's thoughts. His first hint was the pretty brunette behind the counter whose face radiated pleasure the moment she caught Seth's eye.

Benjamin walked to the counter and ordered his banana split, noticing that Leah declined a dessert when Katie asked for her order. Ben made certain to grab two spoons. Ethan and Ruthie took a seat at a nearby table after receiving their orders. The dessert shop was small and the largest table where the others sat only seated four, so Ben took a seat at one of the tables with only two chairs. Hopefully Leah would join him.

Seth bent down and whispered something in Leah's ear and Ben pretended not to notice.

"Do you mind if I sit with ya?" Leah's cheeks darkened a shade.

"'Course not. By all means." Ben gestured to the chair across from him.

Leah looked around, her discomfort evident.

"So, how long have you lived in Paradise?" Ben spooned a bite of the vanilla ice cream mixed with pineapple and savored the creamy sweetness.

"Forever, it seems." Leah seemed to relax a little.

Benjamin handed her a spoon, but she refused. "Oh no, I couldn't."

"Sure you can. Watch." Ben lifted the spoon he'd offered to Leah and dipped into the chocolate side. He boldly brought the ice cream to Leah's lips.

She shook her head in refusal.

"Ah, come on. You *know* you want some." His eyes sparkled.

Leah sighed. "Oh okay. I'll just take one bite."

"No one can take only one bite of a banana split." Ben laughed.

"You're right." She reached across the table, grabbed the plastic dish, and slid it toward her.

Ben's eyes widened as Leah took a huge bite, hot fudge dripping from her chin. "Now there's a girl after my own heart." His grin broadened.

Leah laughed and wiped her mouth with a napkin. She slid the banana split back to Ben's side.

"And here I thought you were all prim and proper," he teased.

Leah crossed her arms, feigning offense.

Other customers filed into the small shop, and began placing orders or taking seats. Seth, Ethan, and Ruthie had moved to an outside table to make room for the new wave of customers. Ben and Leah seemed to be lost in their own little world. Neither of them noticed the *Englisch* girl standing at their table until she spoke.

"Leah? Is that you?"

Leah's gaze moved from Ben to the young woman. "Tori! What are you doing here?"

Tori's eyes lifted. "Ice cream."

"I guess that makes sense." Leah laughed.

"Hey, my brother's here." Tori glanced at Ben, then back to Leah.

Ben noticed Leah's cheeks flush when she looked in the direction Tori was pointing. Was there something going on between Leah and Tori's brother? Ben's jaw clenched.

"And so is Lisa," Tori recovered. "Why don't you come over and say hello?" She motioned toward the corner table.

Leah's pleading eyes met Ben's. He nodded toward the corner, signaling his consent. He wouldn't want her to be rude to her *Englisch* friends just because he was here.

Leah mouthed an excited 'thank you' and followed Tori.

Ben sighed in disappointment as he watched Leah converse merrily with her *Englisch* friends. He grimaced in disgust when Tori's brother made no secret of noticing Leah's figure. When he shot Ben a dirty look, Ben dealt it right back. He wasn't going to stand for anyone disrespecting one of his friends.

"So, who's the farm boy?"

Leah caught the revulsion in Jackson's tone. She'd never heard him speak this way. "That's Ben. He's a guest at the b and b."

"Looks like he's got a thing for you." Jackson frowned.

"We're just friends, Jackson," Leah assured. Why was he acting so jealous? This was not the sweet Jackson she knew.

"You looked way hotter in those jeans you were wearing last weekend, but I guess the dress ain't too bad either."

Leah's cheeks flushed furiously.

"Jackson!" Tori warned.

"Just stating a fact. I'm sure farm boy over there would agree if he'd seen her." Jackson smirked.

"Forgive him, Leah. He had a couple of beers on the way over," Tori said.

"We can get some more after this. What do you say, Leah?" he mumbled, pulling her into his lap.

Leah gasped and struggled to her feet. "Jackson, stop. This isn't appropriate." She glanced up and noticed Ben hastening toward the table.

"Leave the girl alone," Ben demanded.

"Oh yeah? What are you going to do about it, farm boy?" he sneered.

Ben glanced at Leah. "You don't wanna find out."

"Jackson, no," Leah pleaded. She turned to Ben. "Let's just go, *jah*?"

Jackson got to his feet and grasped Leah's upper arm, forcing her close. "Come on, sweetheart. Don't leave. We haven't had any fun yet."

"Take your hands off her," Ben commanded calmly, though his body began to tense.

Leah caught Tori's horrified expression. Her friend offered an apologetic look on her brother's behalf. "Jackson, we're leaving now," Tori said.

"No, we aren't. I wanna see what farm boy's gonna do," Jackson hissed.

Ben reached over and quickly located Jackson's pressure point, causing him to wince. Jackson involuntarily released Leah from his grasp. Ben swiftly clutched Leah's wrist and pulled her behind him. "Go to your brother."

"But, Ben —"

"Now!" Ben turned to Leah to make sure she obeyed.

When he swung back around, Jackson's clenched fist slammed against his face, causing him to stumble. He blocked the next punch, but couldn't intercept the blow to his stomach. Getting out of this without retaliation wasn't going to be a possibility. Benjamin regrettably threw a jab into Jackson's gut, resulting in him losing his balance. He fell back and caught the chair with the back of his head.

"Seth!" Leah cried as she ran out the glass doors. "Ben's fighting!"

Seth and Ethan both swiftly rose from their seats. "You girls stay here."

Leah nodded and nervously bit down on her nails. "What have I done?"

"What did you do?" Ruthie's jaw dropped.

Leah shrugged. "My *Englisch* friends are here. I guess Ben and Jackson didn't take a liking to each other."

Ruthie's eyes bulged. "They're fighting over you? That's so romantic."

"Ruthie!" Leah gasped.

"Well, it is. Just think of it," she said wistfully. "Two men fighting over the woman they love."

"You read too many romance novels." Leah rolled her eyes. "Besides, neither of them loves me."

"Don't be so sure about that." Ruthie motioned toward the door where Seth and Ethan exited the ice cream shop. They each held one of Ben's arms to help him walk upright.

Leah noticed the blood dripping from his mouth and a black eye. "*Ach*, Ben! You look terrible." She shuddered; it was painful just looking at him.

"I feel terrible," Ben said wryly, barely able to open his eye.

"We need to go." Seth nodded toward Ethan's vehicle.

CHAPTER 4
The Aftermath

"He that is slow to wrath is of great understanding: but he that is hasty of spirit exalteth folly."
Proverbs 14:29

Droplets of sunshine trickled through the small opening in the white lace-trimmed curtain, informing Ben that morning was upon him. He shifted slightly and groaned. Every inch of his body ached from his scuffle the night before. He knew he had to get out of bed, but he was not ready to meet his sister. He could only imagine the words that would fly.

Ben lay in bed, contemplating the best way to approach his sister. Of course, one look at his bruised face and she'd know what had happened. There was no hiding it. He sucked in a sharp breath as he heard soft footsteps approach his door. A gentle knock sounded.

"Ben?" Faith's voice was soft, like her. But he was certain she wasn't going to be soft when she saw his face.

"*Jah*, I'm up." He rolled over and stifled a moan.

"Lavina said breakfast will be served in a few minutes. You should be out of bed already."

"Be there in a bit."

"All right. Don't be late."

Ben listened until the sound of his sister's footsteps faded. When he heard the stairs creaking, he painfully hoisted himself out of bed. He stared at the trousers on the nightstand and cringed at the thought of pulling them on.

Finally dressed, Ben looked into the hand mirror in order to survey the damage. He winced. There was no way he'd be able to begin working tomorrow. He'd have to call his boss at the pizza parlor and inform him that he wouldn't be able to come in for a few days. Hopefully he wouldn't lose his job before he'd even started. And what of the carpentry position with Andrew Lapp? *Faith's gonna kill me.*

Benjamin closed his eyes and breathed a silent prayer.

Leah glanced toward the staircase when she heard Ben's sluggish footsteps. She studied the others at the table, already guessing what their reactions would be. *Mamm* gasped when she noticed Benjamin's face. Faith turned to see her brother and her jaw dropped.

"What happened to you, *sohn*?" *Dat* asked.

Ben glanced at Leah. "I...uh...got into a fight last night."

"Benjamin Schrock, I need to have a word with you. Outside." Leah didn't miss the exasperation in Faith's tone. "Please, excuse us."

Dat and *Mamm* both nodded in understanding.

Leah watched as Faith rose from her seat and followed her beaten brother out to the front porch. She noticed a slight smirk on Ethan's and Seth's faces. However, concern adorned the countenances of both of her parents. No one spoke a word. It would be inappropriate to speak of such things in front of a guest. But Leah was certain a hundred questions were swirling in their minds as they sat quietly, attempting to pretend that nothing was wrong.

"Ben!"

Benjamin looked down into his sister's disapproving glare and shrugged.

"You promised! You said you were going to stay on the right side of the law this time." Faith's arms crossed her chest.

Ben remained silent, allowing Faith to vent.

"We've been here one day – *one day* – and you've already managed to make an enemy and get into a fight?" Her voice rose and she began pacing back and forth on the porch. "We have Meeting tomorrow! You know how people are going to perceive you, don't you? As a troublemaker. That was not the first impression I was hoping for. Ben, we need these people."

Ben swallowed when he noticed the tears in her eyes. "I'm sorry."

"You're sorry?"

"What else do you want me to say?" He eased onto the porch swing, feeling every movement.

"It's not about what I want you to say, but how you *should* act. Like a responsible man." She huffed and continued pacing. "What about work? What about the job you were supposed to start tomorrow?"

"I'll call my boss and let him know. He'll understand. He already asked if I wanted to wait a week before starting since we just arrived yesterday. I'll tell him I changed my mind."

"Ben, I was counting on that money. How am I going to pay Andrew Lapp for the work he's doing?"

"I have a few dollars."

Faith sneered. "A few dollars? Do you have any idea how much carpenters make per hour?"

Ben nodded sheepishly.

Faith took a deep breath and looked on her brother with compassion. Her voice softened. "You look awful."

"Trust me; I feel a lot worse than I look." He grimaced.

She sank next to him on the porch swing. She squeezed her eyelids closed and pinched the bridge of her nose. "Oh, Ben; what am I going to do with you?"

"It wasn't my fault, Faith."

"It never is." She rolled her eyes.

"I tried not to fight back."

"But you did." There was no masking the disappointment he'd detected in her voice.

"I had to, Faith."

"No, you didn't. You *always* have a choice. You could have walked away."

Ben sighed. It wouldn't do any good to try to reason with his sister. She would never understand.

Dear Journal,

I really don't know what I want to write right now, but I needed to air my feelings somehow. It's about Benjamin, the guest I wrote about last time. I know I hardly know him, but I feel he's everything I've ever wanted in a man. He's strong and willing to fight for what he believes is right. He is kind and funny. And ever so handsome.

My heart is so full...yet it's also confused. I enjoy my English friends and I want what they have. Freedom! I want to be able to go anywhere and do whatever I want to do. Why does my Amish district have so many rules? I know that we have fewer rules than others, and I am thankful for that. But... it's just...I don't know. My Englisch friends, they can just hop in their cars and drive to the beach. They can go anywhere, do anything.

I feel like it's not fair that I was born Amish. There. I said it.

That's all for now, I guess.

Leah closed her journal and slid it back into its special place. Now, to find Ben. She thought he'd gone to his room, but she wouldn't disturb him. One of the rules of her folks' bed-and-breakfast was to not disturb the guests. So she'd have to wait. Leah walked out to the porch, hoping for some fresh air. She'd need to leave for Meeting before too long.

"Hey."

Leah lifted her gaze at the sound of Ben's voice. She walked over to the gazebo where Ben sat and whimpered internally when she saw his face again. His left eye was bruised and swollen shut. His lips showcased a small cut that looked as though it would swell too. His right cheek was a bluish purple.

Ben lifted one side of his mouth in an attempt to smile. "I look pretty bad, don't I?"

Leah shook her head. "No, Benjamin Schrock. You look *gut.* You look very good." Leah leaned down and pressed her lips to the cheek that wasn't bruised. "Thank you."

Benjamin sat dumbfounded as he watched Leah re-enter the house. *What did she mean by that?* He raised his hand to touch his cheek where she'd just kissed him. *Was that a friendly*

thank you or an 'I'm interested in you' thank you? He couldn't be certain. But he would take his chances anyway. He was determined to take Leah home from the next Singing, which would be tonight. And if she said yes...well, Ben wouldn't think that far in advance. One step at a time.

"What do you mean I can't go to the Singing?" Ben practically yelled the words at his sister.

Faith looked into the hallway behind her, then stepped in and closed the door to Benjamin's room. "I don't think it's a good idea, Ben. Look at you. Besides, how do I know you're going to behave?"

"Behave? You are not *Mamm*, Faith." He huffed.

"No, but you are still underage and I am responsible for you. If I say you are not going to the Singing, then you're not going!"

"Fine. I'm not going to Meeting then, either!"

Faith put her hand on her forehead. Why did her brother have to make everything so difficult? She would concede this once. "Okay. You don't have to go this time. I understand if you're embarrassed because of your face –"

"W-w-w-wait a minute. You think I'm not going because of my face? For your information, I'm proud of how my face looks, whether *you* are or not. And you know what Leah did? She *thanked* me! Imagine that. She actually *respects* me for the fact that I had the courage to stand up for her." Ben wouldn't tell her about the kiss. He was quite certain his sister would *not* see that as a positive thing.

So this is about a girl? "Ben, you know that's not the way of our people." She walked to the foot of Ben's bed and sat down.

"Well, maybe our people are wrong. Maybe I just might not want to be Amish." As Ben spoke the words, he knew they were not true. But Faith had him so rattled right now that he was inclined to say anything.

Faith gasped. "Ben! I sincerely hope you don't mean that. What would *Dat* and *Mamm* say if they heard you talking like this?"

Ben's Adam's apple bobbed when he noticed tears in his sister's eyes. "I don't know."

"They would be disappointed. After all the years of love and care and steering you in the right direction, you just turn your back on everything they valued?" Faith knew that wasn't the half of it. She didn't want to lose Ben to the world. After they'd come so far to begin a new life, she couldn't imagine going at it alone.

Ben shrugged. "Maybe. Look, I don't know exactly what I want. But I do know that I want *you* off my back. I'm never going to become a man if my sister's always bossing me around and telling me what to do. This is my *rumspringa*, Faith. Let me make my own decisions. Even if you don't think they're the right ones. I'm going to make mistakes. I'm going to mess up."

"Ben, you can't afford to mess up anymore," she gently reminded.

"I told you that I would stay on the right side of the law. I aim to keep that promise."

"Good." Faith stood and walked to the door. She turned around before twisting the knob. "Ben, you know you can be arrested for fighting, right?"

"Do you think I go around looking for fights to start?"

Faith shook her head. "Okay, I'll let it slide this time. I know you don't go around looking for trouble." She turned the knob and Ben not-so-eloquently hopped up from the bed. He was obviously in pain.

"So, does this mean that I can go to the Singing?"

Faith almost gave in to his pleading, albeit swollen, puppy dog eyes. "No." She knew she had to remain firm for Ben's sake. Otherwise, he would think he could get away with anything.

"But –"

Faith closed the door to Ben's protests. She decided he would deal with this in his own way. She would not argue with him about it all day long. She had to leave for Meeting soon.

Andrew Lapp should be there. The thought brought a flutter of anticipation to her soul.

CHAPTER 5
Trials

"Be ye angry, and sin not: let not the sun go down
upon your wrath: Neither give place to the devil."
Ephesians 4:26-27

$\mathcal{A}$ndrew Lapp glanced across the yard to where Faith Schrock carried a pitcher of water. He hadn't been able to take his mind off her since they'd met yesterday. Of course, keeping her scented candle on the bureau in his room didn't help. Every time he walked into the room, or the house even, he was reminded of her.

He would need to speak to Faith about her brother's employment since he hadn't seen Benjamin anywhere. He thought it odd that her brother wasn't present at Meeting; not that it was any of his business. It wasn't too often that folks missed Meeting. He could probably count on one hand how many times he'd missed.

When Faith finally came near his table to replace the empty water pitcher with a full one, Andrew decided now would be the best time to get her attention. He cleared his throat. "Faith?"

She glanced up and arched a brow. "Hello, Brother Lapp."

He surveyed the other men at the table and determined it would be best to keep their discussion private. He stood up and walked back toward the Millers' house with her. "I was hoping to talk with Benjamin. I haven't seen him anywhere."

She wiped her brow. "*Jah*, he stayed home today. He's not doing that well."

"I hope he's not sick." His brow lowered in concern.

"Oh, no. He...uh..." She glanced around and noticed they were drawing the attention of others. "Let's walk by the pond, *jah*?"

"Sure, of course."

Faith quickly went into the kitchen to drop off the empty pitcher then promptly returned.

Andrew led the way, leaving the congregation behind them.

Faith sighed. "I'm having some trouble with Ben right now, actually. He got in a fight last night."

"Oh, wow. Is he all right?"

"He is. It's just, he doesn't look too good." Faith frowned. "Sometimes, I just don't know what to do with him."

Andrew sympathized. He wished he could turn her frown upside down. "I could try talking with him. Maybe he needs a man's input about some things. I'm sure it wasn't easy for him to leave his friends in Ohio."

"Would you really do that?"

"Sure. When would you like me to talk to him?"

"Didn't you say you wanted to talk to him about work? Would you like to come over this evening?"

"I can come after Meeting." He raised his hand to touch her forearm, but then thought better of it. "Look, Faith. I have a phone in my barn. I'm not always around to answer it, but I do have an answering machine. If you need to call me about Ben, or for any reason, you're welcome to." He pulled out his wallet and handed her a business card. "My number's on there."

"Thank you, Andrew. This means a lot. I'm truly grateful."

He heard the clip-clop of horses and knew that others were leaving for home already. "Did you bring your buggy or come on foot?"

"I rode with the Weavers. I'd better go now; they might be ready to leave."

"Did you have a chance to eat?"

"*Ach, nee.* That's all right. I had a large breakfast. I can just make a snack when I get back to the Weavers'."

"You should really eat something. I could give you a ride back if the Weavers are ready to leave," he offered. "I'm headed that way anyhow."

Suppertime had proved to be the most antagonizing part of the evening. Seth, Leah, and even Ethan, the *Englischer,* chatted excitedly about the Singing tonight. It wasn't their fault, but Ben's agitation toward his sister grew. He exchanged several unfriendly looks with Faith, but she stood firm in her resolve.

Well, that was just fine. He didn't *need* her permission to go.

Ben waited patiently until all was quiet in the bed-and-breakfast. The others had been gone several hours already. In the house he heard only stillness now, with the exception of the heavy breathing of the occupants inside and an occasional snore from Leah's *dat*. Sleep had finally fallen on everyone inside the quiet home – everyone except Ben. He smirked.

Tonight I'm going to the Singing and no one *is going to stop me. I'm old enough to make my own decisions, without my sister's meddling.* Besides, if he didn't go, Leah might just ride home with someone else. He was determined *not* to let that happen. He'd asked Seth earlier if Leah had gone riding with any other boys in their district. His response was a positive, but it wasn't positive for Ben. No, as he thought of that Adam fellow, who Seth had said still fancied Leah, jealousy shot through his veins like a venomous poison.

Well, he couldn't wait a moment longer. If he didn't leave now, the Singing would be over before he arrived. Ben picked up his boots and slowly tiptoed to the door in his socks. As he twisted the knob and pulled the door open, he released a sigh of relief that it hadn't made any noise. The stairs and kitchen door downstairs would be a little trickier.

Faith rolled over and kicked the heavy blanket off her legs. She couldn't sleep. The trouble she'd been having with Ben was too disturbing. It was hard enough to say no and stand her ground without Ben's dejected looks. She didn't relish the fact that she had to act as his parent. No, she longed for how their relationship was in the past, where she was simply his sister. Trying to be both proved extremely difficult.

She sighed. *Mamm, what would you and Dat have done?* She knew not to expect an answer, but going about this alone was not easy. She thought of Andrew. He'd been kind to offer his support, but she didn't want to be a burden to him. Or feel indebted to him. She would already have enough of that with all the work he'd be performing around the house.

Faith stared into the blackness, praying silently for help. *Click.* The sound was ever so faint. She listened closely and couldn't mistake the slight creak of the mudroom door downstairs. Perhaps the Weaver children were returning home from the Singing. Or perhaps...

Ben!

Faith shot up out of bed and quickly slipped into her robe. She quietly padded to Ben's door, hoping her suspicions were wrong. She turned the knob on Ben's door and clicked on the flashlight in her hand. She shined the blinding rays toward Ben's bed. Empty!

I could scream! Benjamin Schrock, just wait until I get my hands on you. She forced herself to take a deep breath. *Okay, calm down.*

"God, please give me some wisdom here. What should I do?" She breathed the silent prayer of desperation.

Andrew. Call Andrew Lapp.

CHAPTER 6
The Singing

"Likewise, ye younger, submit yourselves unto the elder. Yea, all of you be subject one to another, and be clothed with humility: for God resisteth the proud, and giveth grace to the humble." I Peter 5:5

After pulling up to the Millers' magnificent white barn, Ben turned the ignition off and slipped his keys into his pocket. It was times like this he was thankful to have his car. What would have been twenty-five minutes on foot only took ten with his car. It would have been less if he hadn't had to sprint to Kings' herb shop to fetch his vehicle.

Fortunately, everyone seemed to still be present. He hadn't seen any buggies out on the road. He was certain he'd missed the entire Singing, but that was okay. He was here for the important part. As soon as he ducked into the barn, he noticed Leah standing around with some of her friends who she'd introduced him to earlier. There were others he hadn't met yet, but he realized now might not be the best time to make their acquaintance, given the condition of his face and all.

Ben searched for Seth and quickly located him. He was standing with a group of other young Amish men. Ben confidently walked up to the group. "Hey."

"So you did make it. I didn't know if you'd show." Seth chuckled.

"I told you I would find a way out. I just hope Faith doesn't get wind of my absence."

Seth turned to the friends around him. "Hey y'all, this is Ben. He's staying at the b-and-b. He and his sister just moved to Paradise."

"Daniel Miller," one of the young men stretched out his hand.

"Benjamin Schrock. *Gut* to meet ya." He shook Daniel's hand.

"I'm his brother, Joseph. What's up with your face?"

Ben shrugged. "Fight."

Joseph chuckled. "Figured. Which girl was it?"

Ben said nothing, but Joseph followed his eyes.

"Ah, I see. Leah Weaver." Joseph patted his back. "You might have a little competition. Adam Glick has his eye on her too."

"He's from Bishop Mast's district," Seth added, remembering that he'd forgotten to inform Ben of that detail.

"So I've heard," Ben said to Joseph.

"Did I hear my name?" A young man approached. He was a couple inches taller than Ben and a couple inches broader too. Ben glanced at his muscled forearms and hoped this handsome fellow wasn't who he thought he was.

"Hey, Adam." Joseph chuckled. "Meet your competition. Ben here has his eye on Leah."

Adam's brow raised and Ben thought he noticed a scowl flit briefly across his face. "Leah's already taken."

"We'll see about that," Ben challenged, unwilling to back down easily.

Adam pulled Ben aside. His hand waved in front of his face as though he were swatting a fly. "Ah, go ahead and try her out. She's a lot of fun, if you know what I mean." He smirked and raised his eyebrows twice in quick succession.

Ben's face darkened, but he was certain Adam hadn't noticed. "What do you mean by that?" He swallowed hard.

"I think you know."

Ben should have controlled his temper and walked away, but he wasn't going to let Leah be spoken of with disrespect. He could tolerate it a little more from an *Englischer*, but this Adam fellow wouldn't get away with it. He gave Adam a slight shove.

"You don't know what you're asking for," Adam hissed. "Let's go outside."

Not gawking proved difficult for Leah when Adam walked over to Ben. It seemed as though they were conversing about her, by the way they both glanced in her direction. When she noticed Ben clenching his fists, she suspected trouble. She gasped when Ben pushed Adam.

Leah quickly ran to Maryanna Hostettler, one of the chaperones, and informed her of the situation. They both moved quickly when they noticed the two young men heading for the exit.

"Matthew!" Maryanna immediately called to her betrothed. "There's trouble."

Matthew Riehl quickly summoned another male chaperone and the four of them hurried toward the barn door. They made it outside just in time to see Ben dodge a punch. Matthew quickly stepped in between the two and put his arms out to separate them. "You two need to calm down."

Leah breathed a prayer of thankfulness when she realized that no one had been injured yet. She wasn't sure Ben could take much more after his fight yesterday. Certainly he was still in pain. This fight could have gone very badly for him, had it not been broken up.

Rushing to Ben's side, Leah grasped his hand to pull him away. She glanced up and Adam briefly locked eyes with her. She caught the disappointment in his gaze.

"*Ach*, she's not worth it anyway," Adam uttered under his breath.

Leah felt Ben's hand ball into a fist.

"No, Ben. Come on, let's go," Leah prodded gently.

Benjamin studied Leah and lifted a half-smile. *"Jah,* okay."

Leah felt the tension fade from Ben's grip and she released a relaxing breath as they walked away from the crowd.

Ben strolled hand-in-hand with Leah as they came near the shore of Miller's Pond. The moonlight glistened off the water and they could hear the fading voices of the others near the barn. One by one, the clip-clop of horse hooves and the turning of buggy wheels could be heard as couples traveled home from the Singing.

But Ben wasn't ready to go back yet. No, he'd been aching to spend some time alone with Leah. He realized that he didn't just want her; he needed her. Her presence produced a calming effect on his soul and he desired to be who she needed him to be.

Ben led Leah to a solitary willow tree and they both sat under its flourishing canopy. Until now, they hadn't said much to each other. Ben figured Leah was allowing him time to cool down.

"Look, Leah. I'm sorry I caused a commotion back there." Ben sighed. How was it that he was always finding himself in these situations?

"Ben..." Leah's voice trailed off for a moment.

He waited for her to gather her thoughts. A gentle breeze picked up causing the willow branches to sway and the water to gently lap against the shore. The sound was soothing.

"What did Adam say to you?" Leah's pretty blue eyes twinkled despite the darkness.

"I won't repeat it."

"Okay, so I'm guessing he said something unkind about me. Am I correct?"

Ben nodded. "I was not going to stand for that. I won't let –"

"Ben," Leah interjected. "Sometimes it's best to just ignore folks' foolishness and walk away. Let them say what they will. Let them think what they want. Because all that really matters is what God says and thinks about us."

"But Leah, I care for you."

"If you care for me then let it go. Because it's easier for me to stand against someone's unkind words than it is for me to look into your bruised face knowing that *I* was the one who caused it. So if you truly do care for me, please just let it go." She lifted her hand to caress the less-bruised side of his face, and her countenance flooded with compassion.

Ben scooted closer and cradled her face in his hands. "May I...may I kiss you?" His eyes begged for permission.

Leah opened her mouth to say something, but no words would come. She nodded her consent instead, her heart fluttering in anticipation as he leaned near.

Faith attempted to sit patiently, as she and Andrew traveled toward the Millers' place in his buggy. At any other time, she suspected this might be enjoyable – just the two them in one another's company. But at this moment in time she felt like wringing her younger brother's neck.

No telling what the people of this new community were thinking about them. She'd hoped to make a good first impression, but that seemed nearly impossible with Ben and his antics. She clenched her fists and exhaled in frustration.

"Faith, if it's all right with you, I'd like to be able to speak with Benjamin first." Andrew must've sensed her mounting frustration.

"Okay. *Jah*, I think that would be best." Faith nodded, trying to convince herself.

The buggy rolled to a stop and Faith and Andrew quickly alighted. Before Andrew had a chance to harness the mare, Faith had already set off to find Ben.

Andrew quickly caught up with her. "I'll go ask Matthew Riehl if he's seen Ben."

Faith nodded and followed after him.

"Matthew, this is Faith Schrock. She and her brother are new to Paradise," Andrew introduced. "Faith's looking for her brother Benjamin. Have you seen him?"

Joseph Miller approached and spoke up. "*Jah*, he's seen him. Poor Matt had to break up a fight between him and Adam Glick earlier. He and Leah Weaver set off toward the pond, last I saw."

"Oh no!" Faith covered her eyes.

Matthew and Andrew both scowled at Joseph. "I stopped the fight before it got out of hand. I don't think anyone was injured," Matthew assured.

"Thank you, Matthew." Andrew dipped his head, then gently grasped Faith's elbow. "Let's go find them."

CHAPTER 7
Amazing

"A word fitly spoken is like apples of gold in pictures of silver." Proverbs 26:11

Andrew flicked on the flashlight and shined it where he thought he'd seen two figures under a willow tree. At the sound of a gasp and blinding light shining in their eyes, Ben and Leah's lips unlocked in short order. Benjamin jumped up, shielding the light from his face. A groan escaped his lips as Faith's eyes shot daggers at him. "Faith, what are you doing here?"

"Just what do you think *you* are doing here, young man?" Faith's hands settled on her hips.

Andrew sighed. *So much for letting me speak to Ben first.*

"I would think it was obvious. I went to the Singing and I am taking Leah home." He cast an apologizing glance at Leah, who was no doubt blushing. This is not how he'd envisioned his first date with Leah.

"No, you are *not* taking Leah home! *We* are going home right now, and we're going to have a *long* talk. You came here against my command."

"Against your *command*? I shouldn't have to get your *permission* to go to a Singing! I'm in my *rumspringa*; I'm old enough to make my own decisions. Without your interfering," he added loudly.

"Here we go again." Faith's hands flew up in exasperation.

Andrew cleared his throat. "May I say something?"

"No!" both siblings shouted simultaneously.

"I mean, yes, Andrew. Of course you may," Faith recanted.

"Great," Ben sarcastically muttered under his breath.

"Faith, why don't you and Leah go wait for us by the buggy," Andrew suggested. He waited to continue his speech, until the ladies had walked off. "I had planned to speak with you later, Ben, but now seems like an appropriate time."

Ben sighed. "Okay, I want to get this over with, so go ahead and lecture me."

Andrew studied Ben and perceived that it would take more than mere words to change his attitude. He grasped Benjamin's upper arm and squeezed. He looked Ben in the eye. "You can stop with the disrespectful attitude right now or you'll wish you'd never come here."

Ben didn't flinch, but nodded in assent.

Andrew released his hold. "You need to obey your sister and respect her authority."

"Why?" Ben's arms crossed over his chest. "Just because she's a few years older than I am doesn't mean she knows what's best for me."

"That may be true. But she's the authority God has placed over your life at this time." Andrew continued. "We *all* have people in authority over us. When we reject that authority, we're fair game as far as the devil's concerned."

"What do you mean by that?" Ben's skeptical brow rose.

"Do you know anything about my family?"

Benjamin shook his head.

"My father refused to follow his authority and it wrecked our lives. He sits in jail for murdering my *mamm*."

Ben's jaw dropped. "I've never heard of such a thing."

"You want to come to the prison with me next time I visit my father?" Andrew's brow lifted. "He's very repentant. He's sorry that he'll never be able to see my mother again or ask her forgiveness."

"Wow, that's pretty heavy. I had no idea. I'm sorry to hear that."

"I think I have a solution that might remedy this whole thing." Andrew rubbed his chin.

"And what's that?"

"You want to work with me, right?" At Ben's nod, he continued. "I think it would be best if you gave your sister a little peace. I'm staying at your new place in the evening because it gives me more time to work and it's closer to my other jobs. I want you to come and stay with me."

"But there's no furniture in the house. Where are you sleeping?"

Andrew shrugged. "On the floor in a sleeping bag."

"And Faith has approved of this?"

"She will when I suggest it," Andrew said confidently.

"But Leah –"

"Will be fine without you. Haven't you ever heard that absence makes the heart grow fonder?"

Ben shot Andrew a puzzled look. "So she'll like me *more* if I stay away from her?"

Andrew nodded.

As Faith and Leah walked back to the Millers' barn, Faith contemplated what to say to Leah. She knew that Ben and Leah's love relationship wasn't really her business, but she wasn't certain Leah was the right girl for Ben. She couldn't be a very *gut maedel* if she'd already allowed Ben to kiss her. What kind of girl kisses a boy on their first date? And they hadn't even gone for a buggy ride together!

"I think that it's best that you and Ben not see each other anymore," Faith blurted out.

Leah's eyes widened, but she stayed silent. She bit her trembling lip and nodded.

"He's planning on getting a job and he really doesn't need any extra distractions right now. He was supposed to begin his job tomorrow, but now he has to wait a week at the pizza parlor because of his face." Faith continued on. "I realize it's not entirely your fault, but I don't think Ben would have gotten in that fight if it wasn't for you. And I'm guessing the fight he was nearly in tonight was over you too. Is that correct?"

Leah nodded and a tear slipped down her cheek.

"I think it would be best," Faith repeated, probably more to convince herself.

"What would be best?" Ben's voice echoed from behind them. He glanced at Leah and noticed the tears in her eyes. "Leah, what's wrong?" Ben glanced frantically from Leah to his sister.

Ben walked up to Faith, standing mere inches from her. "Why is she crying? What did you say to her?"

"Ben, I..." Faith sighed. This was not turning out well.

He tightened his fists, becoming visibly irritated. "What did you say to her, Faith?"

Faith helplessly looked to Andrew, who nodded for her to share. His confident gesture gave her self-assurance.

"I asked Leah not to see you anymore." She released a nervous breath.

"You have no right to ask her to do that!" Ben raked his hands through his hair. "Now you're trying to dictate Leah's life too? Stay out of my business and quit trying to ruin my life!" Ben turned to Leah and grasped her hand. They quickly set off toward his car.

Faith's hands flew to her face as she heard Ben slam his car door and peel out of the driveway. "Oh, no! What have I done?"

Andrew stepped near and hesitantly placed a hand on her shoulder. When he noticed the tears streaming down her cheeks, he pulled her to his chest and held her tight. Faith sobbed for a few moments and Andrew patiently allowed her the time she needed.

When Faith eventually pulled away, Andrew wished she hadn't. He didn't realize what was taking place, but he felt as though they'd just shared something special, something precious. An overwhelming desire to become a rock of strength for Faith flooded his being.

He cradled her face and gently brushed her tears away with the pads of his thumbs. He longed to kiss her, but wouldn't until she initiated it. He was quite certain that one of the reasons he'd lost Joanna Fisher as an *aldi* was because he was over-eager to kiss her; which never happened, to his disappointment. Now she'd been married to an *Englischer* for over five years and had a couple of *kinner*. And he was still single. Nope, he wouldn't blow it this time.

Leah glanced over at Ben as they traveled down the road. She winced once again when she noticed his beaten face. Faith's words played in her mind, *Ben wouldn't have gotten in that fight if it wasn't for you.* She hated being the cause of Ben's misfortune and the rift in his and Faith's relationship. Maybe it would be better if she wasn't in his life.

"I'm leaving the Amish," Leah stated.

Ben turned his head and almost ran off the road. He took a sharp turn and brought the car to a halt on the side of the road. "What?? Leah, no!"

"I think you'd be better off without me, Ben. Look at everything that's happened. You've practically ruined your relationship with your sister. You've nearly gotten into two fights in two days. Maybe we're just not right for each other." Leah shrugged.

"Oh, I get it. I'm too much trouble for you?"

"No, Ben. That's not what I'm saying. I've been thinking about it a lot, even before you got here. I feel like I just need to get away." She sighed.

"I can take you wherever you want to go. We...we can get married."

"Ben, listen to yourself. We just met one day ago – one day! We can't get married; we don't even really know each other all that well."

"I'm crazy about you, Leah. We'll get to know each other. We can make it work out."

"Ben, running from your problems isn't going to help. Your sister is the only family you have here. You need her – she needs you. I just feel like I've caused you both so much heartache."

"Leah, look at me." Leah lifted her gaze to his. He took her hands into his own and searched her eyes. "What has happened

J. E. B. Spredemann

between me and my sister is not your fault. If it's anyone's fault, it's mine. I..." Ben sighed. "I'm going to talk to my sister."

"Really?"

Ben nodded. "Andrew showed me that I haven't been acting the way I should. Following my authority and all...I was about to apologize until I found out she was trying to control your life too. She just makes me so mad sometimes."

Leah reached up and soothingly rubbed his arm. She spoke softly, "Ben, there will always be people and situations in our lives that we can't control. But we *can* control ourselves. Could you just try to let things go? Anger is an emotion, but it's also a choice. We can *choose* to not get angry."

"I don't know if I can do that."

Leah lifted his chin and looked into his eyes. "I believe in you, Benjamin Schrock."

"Has anyone ever told you that you're the most amazing person on this planet?" Ben smiled.

"Not since yesterday."

Ben's brow rose in question.

"Well, I read this verse in the Bible yesterday: *But God commendeth His love toward us, in that, while we were yet sinners Christ died for us.* I figure I have to be pretty amazing if God would send His Son to die for me. And guess what? You're pretty amazing, too, because it wasn't just me He died for."

"Wow, Leah. I don't know how you do that to me."

Leah smiled. "Do what?"

"Everything you say is infused with wisdom. I just feel like I can't get enough of you."

"Okay, you're scaring me now. You're not one of those obsessed psychopaths, are you?" She giggled.

"Not since I last checked." Ben chuckled and pulled Leah close. "I'm hopelessly in love with you, Leah Weaver."

CHAPTER 8
Work

*"Pleasant words are as an honeycomb, sweet to the
soul, and health to the bones." Proverbs 16:24*

*D*ear Journal,
 Ach, *what have I gotten myself into? Ben is already
talking about marriage. Marriage!*

*Okay, I admit that excites me some. But it also scares me.
Ben is ever so handsome. Well, he looked a lot better when his
face wasn't all beaten up. I guess I haven't written about that
yet. Ben got in a fight with Jackson the other night. And nearly
another one at the Singing with Adam Glick. Ruthie thinks it's
romantic that boys are fighting over me.*

*Anyway, I do like Ben. A lot. But...I'm afraid that if I get
too attached to him that I'll just end up getting married young
and I won't ever be able to taste the* Englisch *life. I think I need
to distance myself from Ben.*

One good thing is he's going to leave the b-and-b and stay at his house with Andrew Lapp while they fix it up. And Ben should begin working soon so he won't have as much free time.

It wonders me if maybe Ben's sister and Andrew like each other. Oh well, I guess it's none of my business.

Until next time...

Benjamin opened his eyes in confusion. He'd smelled the dust and wood even before he awakened. His cheek felt cold from the hard wooden floor. Sometime in the night he must've rolled off the bed, he figured. Until he realized where he was.

Now fully awake, he looked around and understood his surroundings. This was their house – his and Faith's.

"Oh good, you're up," Andrew's voice echoed from the kitchen area. "I made some coffee already. Come and eat so we can start working. I have a list of things for you to do today."

Ben groaned under his breath. His body still ached, but he would not complain about it to Andrew. Part of being a man was being tough, and he had no intention of acting like a wimp. He quickly grabbed his shirt and buttoned it over the white t-shirt he'd slept in.

"What's the plan?" Ben poured himself a cup of coffee and sat in one of the wooden chairs Andrew had brought.

"I'd like you to work out in the yard today. I brought my mower and pruning shears, so that should keep you busy most of the day. Your sister wants the place to look inviting for her customers and the condition of the outside will be their first impression, so be sure to do a *gut* job."

Ben nodded.

"I think it would look nice if we planted some flowers along the lane. Do you know which kind your sister prefers?"

Ben shrugged. "Probably anything that smells nice."

"I'll pick some up after I'm done working for my *Englisch* customers. Later this week I'd like to go by the Fishers' and pick up some nice shelving for Faith's candle display. I'd like you to go with me so you can meet them and my youngest brother and sister. You may have met my sister at the Singing already."

"No, I didn't meet any *maed*. Just a few of the guys."

Andrew gulped down the remainder of his coffee and rinsed out his mug in the sink. "All right, shall we get started?"

As Faith maneuvered the horse and buggy into the driveway, she immediately noticed Benjamin pruning one of the bushes. She surveyed the yard, amazed that he'd been able to do so much in such a short time. Her heart melted when she saw him wipe the sweat from his brow.

She pictured her baby brother working outside with *Dat* on the farm when he was just a few years old and a tear formed in her eye. She wished she could be the parent that he so desperately needed, but she constantly came up short. There were so many things she didn't know about raising a young man. Inadequate couldn't begin to describe how she felt. She often wondered why God entrusted her with this task. *Please help me guide Benjamin the way* Mamm *and* Dat *would, Lord.*

As soon as she pulled up to the hitching post near the small barn, Ben approached and helped her unhitch the mare.

"I brought you a sandwich." Faith lifted a small insulated cooler from behind the buggy seat.

Ben smiled. "*Gut*, I'm starving. Did ya bring somethin' to drink too?"

Faith shook her head. "No, but there's water in the kitchen. Do you need some?"

Ben nodded and took another bite out of his turkey sandwich. He peeked into the container she carried. "Ya got anything else in there?" He mumbled around a mouth full of food.

Faith handed him an apple and a banana.

"*Denki.*"

"No; thank you, Ben. You've been doing a real *gut* job here."

When her brother's shoulders straightened and his face immediately brightened, Faith realized that that was exactly what he needed to hear. It seemed all of their conversations lately, aside from when he apologized, had been negative. *Ben, don't do this. Ben, don't do that. How could you do that, Ben? Ben, what have you done this time?*

Faith hurried inside, leaving her brother to his tasks. After placing the cleaning supplies on the small table, she sat down and allowed the tears to fall. *God, thank you for showing me how I've been lately. I know I needed to see that. Ben really is a good boy. Please help me to use words that will encourage him and draw him closer to You.*

CHAPTER 9
Temptation

"My son, if sinners entice thee, consent thou not."
Proverbs 1:10

Andrew and Benjamin stepped into Gideon Fisher's open workshop, surprised to be met with silence. They had come to pick up a few shelves that Faith had wanted for the house. Ben scanned the darkened interior of the building.

"Wonder where they went?" Andrew looked toward the empty workbench.

"Well, I suppose they could be having an early dinner. Should we go check the house?" Ben suggested.

"*Jah.* But let's look around the barn first. They'd most likely be out yonder rather than inside."

The two men walked around the shop but didn't see anyone. They wandered toward the barn's entrance on the opposite side of the shop.

Andrew popped his head inside. "Empty."

Benjamin and Andrew both surveyed the yard for any sign of the Fishers. They were nowhere to be seen. They rounded another corner of the barn, the only side they hadn't checked.

Ben smirked and Andrew's eyebrows elevated. A young couple appeared to be too preoccupied with one another to notice – or even hear – their meandering about. Ben wondered if they should interrupt, when Andrew cleared his throat. Loudly.

"Abigail!" Ben noticed obvious frustration in Andrew's tone.

The young woman's hands quickly released their grip on the young man's shoulders. His hands dropped from her waist and they abruptly sprang apart. Their cheeks flamed in embarrassment from being caught.

Ben noticed that the young man was Daniel Miller, one of Seth's friends at the Singing.

"A-Andrew! What are you doing here?" The young woman bit her bottom lip and wouldn't meet his intense gaze.

Andrew shook his head in disapproval, sighed, and then introduced Ben through gritted teeth. "Ben, this is my youngest sister Abigail and her beau, Daniel Miller."

Ben smiled and greeted each of them. He didn't bother mentioning to Andrew that he'd already met Daniel at the Singing. He felt bad intruding on the young couple's privacy, especially when Abigail's blush deepened. He was quickly reminded of Leah.

"Ben and I were looking for Gideon. No one was at the shop." Andrew shifted his feet slightly and crossed his arms over his chest as though waiting for an explanation.

"We're taking a break," Daniel spoke up, saving his sweetheart from further embarrassment. "Gideon went into town for more supplies. We can't do much until he returns. Jonathan wanted to see his *fraa* and *kinner,* so he went inside the *dawdi haus.*"

"I see."

An awkward silence hung between them for several painful seconds.

"Would you like to speak with Jonathan? I'm sure he can help you with whatever it is you need," Daniel offered.

"*Jah.*"

They marched to the *dawdi haus* in silence. Ben found it difficult to conceal his amusement as Andrew glared warningly at Daniel. Abigail hurried into the house ahead of them. They stepped inside, not bothering to knock.

"*Ach,* hello," a young woman greeted them with a wooden spoon in her hand.

Andrew nodded in greeting. "*Guten mayrie,* Susie. I came to pick up some shelves. Is Jonathan around?"

"He's eating with the *kinner.* He should be almost done though." She led them to the dining area. "Jonathan, you have –" She stopped mid-sentence. "Jonathan Fisher!'"

Ben stepped out from behind Andrew to see what the commotion was all about. A young married man, two tow-headed young boys, and a baby girl all sat at the table. The man - Jonathan he presumed - held the *boppli*, who was presently swiping food off his shirt with her fingers and eating it. Judging by the mess on Jonathan, the *kinner*, and the surrounding area, they had just been engaged in an all-out food fight.

"It wasn't my fault," Jonathan spoke up, holding his hands up in surrender. "Judah started it." He pointed at one of the twins just as they turned their fingers on him.

"*Dat!*" the twins confessed simultaneously.

Susanna frowned. "I don't care who started it, Jonathan. You should be more responsible than the twins! *You* are going to clean every bit of this mess and I – I'm going for a walk." She huffed out of the house, having apparently forgotten about their visitors.

Ben looked at Jonathan, whose eyes followed his wife.

Jonathan grinned mischievously, set the baby girl down on the bench, and stood. "Hello, Andrew."

Andrew nodded, smirking slightly. "We came to get some shelves. But I can see you're a bit preoccupied."

"Daniel can help you. As you can see," he smiled wryly and looked around, "I have a bit of a mess to clean up."

"I'm so glad you called me, Leah." Tori glanced at her friend and squeezed her hand. "We are going to have so much fun!"

Leah smiled at her *Englisch* friend, knowing that her words were true. She always enjoyed herself when she spent time with Tori.

"Let's swing by my house so you can change, and I'll do your hair and makeup," Tori said.

"What you have in mind for tonight?" Leah's enthusiasm stirred.

"Well, there's this pool hall that we go to sometimes. It also has a dance floor. There are usually a lot of cute guys there." Tori grinned. "Have you ever played pool?"

Leah shook her head.

"You'll love it. Don't worry; Jackson will show you how to play. He's great at it."

"Is he coming with us?" Leah clasped her hands in her lap.

"Nah, he and his friends will already be there."

Leah thought of Ben. She hadn't seen him the whole week. Faith said he and Andrew had been making great progress at their home and they'd probably be able to move in next week. Faith had asked her to go thrift store shopping next week for furniture and Leah was excited about it. Tomorrow she would see Ben at Meeting but she wouldn't think about that right now.

Nope. Tonight she would embrace the *Englisch* life with her friends.

"Oh wow, Leah! I can't believe how different you look." Tori squealed and turned the swivel chair Leah sat on around to get a better look. "I didn't really know what to do with all your hair, so I just did the French twist thing and curled the ends. I think it looks really cute."

Tori dragged Leah over to a full-length mirror. "Well, what do you think?"

Leah's jaw dropped. She hardly recognized herself under all the makeup Tori had painted on her. And with her hairstyle and dress, she looked to be about eighteen or nineteen. She tugged at the skirt above her knees, attempting to pull it lower. "Uh, *jah*, I sure look different."

"You look hot. I bet every guy there will want to dance with you." Tori snapped her fingers over her head and shook her hips back and forth as though she were dancing to an imaginary tune. "Well? Let's go!"

When Tori pulled into the parking lot, Leah couldn't believe all the cars. Tori finally found a spot to park in when a vehicle vacated one a few doors down from the pool hall. Leah clenched her teeth thinking about walking any distance in the heels Tori had lent her. She'd only been wearing them for twenty minutes and already felt two blisters forming.

"It looks like all the tables are taken. Do you see Jackson anywhere?" Tori scanned the crowded room.

"No. What's in there?" Leah pointed to a door that she'd seen someone exit.

"Oh, that's the dance floor. If you've never been, it'll seem a little loud at first. Let's look for Jackson and play some pool." Tori pulled Leah through the crowd of people, surveying each table for her brother. "He usually likes the corner table."

"Whoa, little sis. Who's that you got?" Jackson's mouth dropped open when Leah turned around. "Leah? This is the best thing I've seen you in yet."

One of Jackson's friends walked over. "Hey Jack, who's your friend?"

Leah felt uncomfortable when she noticed both of the guys staring at certain areas of her body.

"This is Leah. And she's *my* date tonight." Jackson slipped his arm around Leah's waist. "Wanna go dance, baby?"

Leah's eyes pleaded with Tori to rescue her.

"We wanted to play some pool first. Leah's never played." Tori sat on a nearby barstool. "Why don't you two play a game and show her how it's done?"

"Sure thing, babe. Just watch the pros." Jackson winked at Leah.

Leah watched Jackson and his friend play pool for several minutes before she and Tori were invited into the game. She found bending over the table quite difficult in her short dress and opted out of the other games. After she'd danced to a song with Jackson, her feet hated her. It would've been much more comfortable barefoot, she supposed. For the most part, Jackson behaved himself like a gentleman, to her surprise.

"Hey, let's go for some pizza," Jackson suggested.

Leah didn't protest since she knew Ben wouldn't be starting his job at the pizza parlor until Monday.

When they arrived, the dining area looked pretty busy, but it was a Saturday night so it was probably typical. Leah and Tori went and found a spot toward a back corner and Jackson and his friend ordered a couple of pizzas.

Ben rushed through the back door of the pizza parlor's kitchen after making his deliveries. His first day had been busy, but he'd already made thirty dollars in tips. His boss had been shorthanded, so he'd called Ben and asked him to start working today instead of Monday. Since most of his bruises had faded and he and Faith needed the money, he agreed.

"Hey, Ben; I need you to take this order to table number twelve." His boss pointed to a table near the back.

"Sure, Ralf." Ben picked up the two pizza pans with potholders and delivered them to the table. As he passed by another table where two young men were seated, he noticed something – or someone – familiar. It was Jackson, the guy he'd been in a fight with at the ice cream shop. *Oh no, I hope he's not going to stir up trouble.*

Just then, Ben noticed two young women exit the restroom and approach the table.

"Hey look, Leah. Your farm boy is here." Jackson chuckled.

Ben's eyes widened when he noticed one of the young women was indeed Leah. He glanced at her tight dress and tried his best not to gawk, but it proved quite difficult. Ben felt wrath rising in his veins once again and his jaw clenched. *God, please help me not to do anything stupid. You know I need this job.*

Leah frowned, and then offered a half-smile. "Uh...Ben! I...I thought you didn't start until Monday."

Ben stared at her in confusion. Why would an Amish girl dress in such a manner? It totally did not fit the Leah he knew. She was much better than this.

"My boss called me in." He looked back toward the counter. His concern for Leah overruled his frustration with Jackson. "I have a break in a few. Can we talk?"

Leah glanced at Jackson. "Uh...sure." Leah turned to her *Englischer* friends. "I'll be back in a bit."

"I'll be right here waiting for ya, babe." Jackson winked.

Leah followed Ben up to the front counter where he spoke to his boss momentarily.

"Let's go outside," Ben suggested.

Leah nodded silently.

"You want to sit in my car? It's a little bit warmer in there."

"Sure."

Ben opened the car door for her and she slid in. He noticed Leah's hands fidgeting. "Are you here with Jackson?"

"Well, we all came together."

"Leah, that's not what I asked. I think you know what I meant." Ben sighed. "Let me be clearer. Where did you go tonight?"

"To the pool hall with Tori. Jackson and his friend were already there." Leah bit her top lip.

"Did you know he was going to be there when you put this dress on?" Ben's brow lifted.

Leah nodded.

Ben took off the cap he was wearing and raked a hand through his hair. "Do you know how this dress makes you look?"

Leah nodded. "Like an *Englischer.*"

"Not like an *Englischer.* Like a harlot." Ben frowned.

Leah gasped.

Ben knew his words offended her, but he also knew she needed to hear them. Her *Englisch* friends certainly weren't going to tell her the truth. "Leah, I can hardly take my eyes off your body. That dress accentuates every curve you have. To a man, it's very appealing...and tempting. I've already had more than one impure thought in the few minutes I've seen you."

"Well, then maybe you shouldn't be looking if you can't handle it," Leah retorted.

"Oh, boy. Leah, that's how a man's mind works. *All* men, not just mine." He brushed her arm with his fingers. "I thought you were my girl."

"So I have to dress Amish. Is that what you're saying, Ben? Because if you can't accept me for the way I am, then I don't

want to be with you. My real friends accept me for who I am."
A tear slipped down Leah's cheek. "And if you loved me, you
wouldn't call me a harlot!"

Ben watched helplessly as Leah slammed the door to his
car and stormed back into the pizza parlor. He was certain he
would dread the remainder of the evening. He couldn't tolerate
the thought of Leah wearing that dress and leaving with Jackson. Ben whispered a silent prayer for his beloved Leah.

CHAPTER 10
Reconciliation

"Let thine eyes look right on, and let thine eyelids look straight before thee. Ponder the path of thy feet, and let all thy ways be established." Proverbs 4:25-26

*A*ndrew moved the paintbrush over the trim, applying the finishing touches to Faith's candle display room. He admitted Faith's ideas were great, especially the two-tone paint. Andrew was a little surprised when Bishop Hostettler approved of her color choices – a medium-light bluish-green with white trim. Typically only white or a variation of it was allowed, but because this room was to be for Faith's business, Judah approved of it.

Ben had seemed to be in a somber mood for several days now and Andrew desired to help him with whatever was troubling him. He'd been much quieter than usual and wasn't eating much. Other than work and sleep, Ben did little else. Faith

J. E. B. Spredemann

had expressed her concern to Andrew this morning, so he was determined to speak with Ben.

Andrew stepped out onto the small back porch and surveyed the yard. The beautiful place was inviting for customers, he confessed. Ben had done a *gut* job pruning the bushes and planting the flowers he'd purchased. He was a good worker and Andrew recognized his value as an employee the first day Ben worked for him. Perhaps, if things went well between him and Faith, he and Ben could someday forge a family-owned construction business.

"Ben," Andrew called when he spotted him near the barn.

Ben glanced up, but said nothing.

Andrew put his paint brush in a bucket of water. "I'd like to speak with you for a few minutes."

"Sure."

Andrew gestured to an antique bench in the yard; it had been one of Faith's thrift store treasures. He and Ben took a seat and sat in silence for a moment. "What's been bothering you, Ben?"

Ben shrugged.

"Is it Leah?" Andrew figured that was the most logical assumption.

Ben nodded.

"I see." Andrew rubbed his chin. "Are you two not courting anymore?"

Ben shook his head. "She wasn't even at the last Singing."

"Where do you think she was?"

"With her *Englisch* friends."

"And that's a bad thing?"

"Last time I saw Leah, she was smoking." Ben clenched his hands. "What is she doing? Why can't she see that she's ruining her life? I've been praying for her, but it's so hard to wait patiently while Leah's life could be in danger."

"Have you tried talking to her about it?"

"Once. It didn't go well. That's when we stopped seeing each other." Ben sighed. "She won't even talk to me now."

"I see." Andrew pondered a moment. "Have you considered writing her a letter?"

Ben shook his head. "I wouldn't know what to write."

"Why don't you tell her what you just told me? But perhaps be a little more tactful."

Ben chuckled. "*Jah*; I think my lack of tact may have scared her off in the first place."

Andrew lifted a brow. "What did you say?"

Ben grimaced. "I told her she looked like a harlot."

Andrew winced. "*Jah*; that's pretty bad. You might want to send flowers and an apology note too."

"I think I'll do that."

Andrew loaded his tools into the back of his buggy. Faith's home was nearly complete and he hated to think that he wouldn't be seeing her as often as he had over the past few weeks. As soon as Faith arrived, he would discuss what had been on his mind. They'd maintained an easy friendship so far, but Andrew wondered if Faith desired something more. He knew *he* did.

When Faith pulled into the lane, Andrew hastened to help her unhitch the driving horse. He tended to the mare, while she took some of her purchases into the house. As soon as he finished, he picked up the remaining grocery bags from the buggy and carried them to the house.

He stepped inside the house and found Faith examining every inch of work he and Benjamin had accomplished.

Faith's mouth hung open in awe as she ran her hand over the finished trim. "Oh, Andrew! You and Ben did such a *gut* job."

Andrew attempted not to allow his heart to swell with pride. "I hoped you'd like it."

"Like it? This is amazing." She carefully studied the smooth shelves. "*Ach*, these are perfect."

Faith turned around, and Andrew thought her lips might crack from her enormous smile. She seemed to have difficulty containing her excitement. He'd never seen anyone derive that much pleasure from his work and her exuberance lifted his soul.

When their eyes met, her admiration was undeniable. As was his attraction to her. Faith stepped near and slipped her arms around his back. "Thank you."

Andrew's heart beat rapidly at Faith's nearness and the desire to kiss her intensified. She pulled away much too soon for his liking and the moment was gone.

"Will you stay for supper?" Faith asked as she neared the kitchen. She began putting her grocery items away one by one. "Ben's working tonight so it'll just be us."

How could he say no to that? "I'd love to." Andrew lifted his straw hat and raked a hand through his hair. "Uh...I wanted to ask you something."

Faith turned from the counter where she now prepared a salad and arched her brow.

"I have an *Englisch* wedding to attend. It's my sister Sadie's, actually."

"She's marrying the cop, right?"

"How did you know?"

"I met her and Danika Yoder when I visited the Kings' health food store last week. I gave her a candle." Faith smiled.

"Which she loves, by the way. I love mine too. I think your candles are great." He forged on. "Anyway, Sadie's wedding is in a couple of weeks and she insisted that I not attend alone. So, would you like to join me?"

"That sounds like fun." Faith lifted a half-smile. Could she sense his nervousness?

"It does?"

Faith giggled at his response. "I think so. I've never attended an *Englisch* wedding. Have you?"

"*Nee*, I haven't. I'm actually supposed to be *in* the wedding." He sighed. "I guess at *Englisch* weddings the father of the bride usually gives his daughter away. Sadie asked me if I would do it since our father...well, I guess I haven't told you that story yet."

"Ben mentioned that your father is in jail for murdering your mother." Her sympathetic gaze met his.

"And...you knew that and *still* agreed to come with me?"

Faith walked toward Andrew and placed a hand on his forearm. When he lifted his downcast eyes, her breath caught. "Why wouldn't I say yes? You've been the dearest friend I've known since we moved here. You've taken Ben under your wing and are the best influence he's had in a long time. Andrew, I..." Faith's voice trailed off and she tenderly caressed his cheek.

Andrew pulled her close and did not refrain from the gentle press of her lips to his. He closed his eyes as though entranced in a dream. Faith's *wunderbaar* kiss was well worth the wait, he decided. He could have reveled in her embrace all night, but quickly realized that would not have been a *gut* idea. He reluctantly withdrew himself from the pleasurable moment.

"That was better than I'd imagined it would be." He smiled, tracing her lips with his finger.

"*Jah.*" It was all Faith could manage. She glanced at the counter behind her. "I...I'd better tend to supper, *jah*?"

Andrew nodded. "I'll help."

Leah opened the note that Seth had given her earlier and read Ben's words.

Leah,

Please meet me at the gazebo at ten-thirty tonight.

Ben

Leah sighed. She had a mind to stand Ben up, and she might have done that if she wasn't curious about what he had to say. Or didn't miss him desperately. She thought being away from him the last few weeks would be punishment for him. Or perhaps even torture.

But Ben had proven her wrong. He seemed content without her. He'd even taken Lizzy Hostettler home from the last Singing. Leah realized that if she had any intentions toward Ben, she'd better make them known before he gave his heart away to someone else.

She decided to meet him, but she would meet him on her own terms.

CHAPTER 11

Priorities

"Wine is a mocker, strong drink is raging: and whosoever is deceived thereby is not wise."
Proverbs 20:1

*B*en glanced at the chocolates, teddy bear, flowers, and card on the seat next to him. Would it be too much? Would Leah even be there to meet him? And if she did meet him, would he say the right words to her or would he just make matters worse? He took a calming breath and prayed for wisdom.

As Ben pulled into the Weavers' lane, he quickly turned his lights off so as not to bother anyone inside. He glanced at the gazebo. *Empty.* Had he been a fool to hope Leah would forgive him? Perhaps she wasn't the girl he believed her to be. He turned off the motor and sat patiently in his car. When the window of the front door reflected in the moonlight, he knew Leah was on her way outside. *Thank you, Lord.*

Ben opened the door and once again looked at the items in the seat. Thinking about it now, he felt a little foolish. Oh, well. He quickly picked up the items and tucked them under his arm, carrying the bouquet of flowers in his hand.

His hands began to tremble as Leah approached. Seeing the outline of her figure in the moonlight didn't help either. Couldn't she have worn her Amish clothes to meet him instead of the form-fitting jeans and blouse? Although the evening was cool, Ben felt beads of perspiration forming on his upper lip and forehead. This was going to be more difficult than he'd thought.

"Leah," he squeaked out.

"Hi, Ben." She twirled her elbow-length blonde locks between her fingers. Had she cut her hair, her crowning glory? He fought to conceal his disappointment.

Ben quickly handed her the items he'd purchased. "Uh... these are for you."

"All this?" She chuckled and it didn't help his uneasiness.

Ben nodded.

Leah smiled and stepped near to kiss his cheek. "*Denki,* Ben."

"You, uh, want to go for a drive?" He tugged on his collar for more air. He couldn't remember being this nervous since his first Singing back in Ohio.

"Sure. Let me just put these in the house and grab my purse."

In spite of himself, he watched her every movement as she walked toward the house. Her golden hair seemed to catch the stray moonbeams. How was he going to guard himself against temptation tonight? Ben closed his eyes in an attempt to refocus. He must not lose sight of the task at hand. And no amount of gawking at Leah, no matter how incredible she looked, was going to help him accomplish that goal. Now, if he could just remember *that* for the remainder of the evening, he'd be all right.

Leah brought the flowers to her nose and breathed in their delightful fragrance before filling a jar with water for them. It was the first time she'd been given something so beautiful. She wouldn't take them to her room, but instead decided to leave them on the coffee table in the *schtupp* for everyone to enjoy.

Curiosity drew her attention to the card. What had been written inside? She hastily opened the envelope, knowing Ben was patiently waiting outside for her. She pulled out a lovely floral card with no words printed on the front. She glanced down at Ben's handwriting on the inside of the card.

Please forgive me.

Ben

Leah picked up the soft teddy bear and clutched it to her chest. Ben's scent filled her senses and she smiled. She would be sleeping with this teddy bear tonight, she was certain. That way she could have sweet dreams of her and Ben. Maybe.

She hurried outside and slid into the passenger's seat. Ben seemed to have relaxed a little.

"Where are we going?" She pushed the button on the door panel to allow a breeze through the window.

"I thought we could go to my place. You haven't seen it since Andrew and I began fixing everything up."

"I don't know how well we'll be able to see everything in the dark. And it's late; is your sister still up?"

"Oh, uh, *jah*. I guess I wasn't thinking." He scratched his head. "Maybe we could just sit on the porch then."

"Okay." Leah desired to talk to him – really talk to him. "Ben, thank you for the card. I read it when I was inside."

Ben nodded as he pulled the vehicle up to the barn. He opened the door for Leah and reached for her hand. "I could get us something to drink," he offered.

Leah glanced down at her purse. "I brought something for us. Just one, but we can share."

Ben's eyebrows evidenced his curiosity. He politely offered her one of the lawn chairs on the small porch. This house was tiny compared to Leah's folks' place.

Leah pulled an aluminum can out of her purse and popped open the tab before Ben could protest. She put the beverage to her lips and swallowed, then offered Ben a drink.

Ben shook his head.

"You're going to make me drink all of this by myself?" She stuck a pouty lip out, demonstrating her disappointment.

Ben reached for the can and she smiled when he took a drink. "Ugh! I've always hated that stuff." He handed it back to Leah.

"So, what do you think of my outfit?"

"It's…uh…tempting." Ben gulped. "Look, Leah. For me, you don't need to put on *Englisch* clothes. You don't need to drink beer or smoke. I want you to be you. I thought you were beautiful from the first day we met. And I'm not just talking about being attracted to you, which I very much am, by the way. When we sat at the ice cream shop and talked, and when we went to the Singing, I realized that you are the girl for me. I am still in love with you, Leah."

"But you took Lizzy home from the Singing."

"You were there?" Ben's mouth dropped at her nod. *Why hadn't she shown herself?*

"I took Lizzy home because she needed a ride and her brother asked me to." Ben reached over and interlaced his fingers with hers. "Leah, I can't even think of anyone else but you. But if you want to be my *aldi*, then it'll just have to be me; none of this Ben and Jackson, or Ben and Adam. I want you all to myself. I'm not good at sharing when it comes to you."

Leah offered a half-smile. "So, I've noticed."

"What do you think?"

"I think you're a great guy and I don't deserve you. And I don't think your sister likes me either." She grimaced.

"She will, you'll see. I think she just needs to see some of your good qualities." Ben smiled.

Ben and Leah both turned at the sound of the creaking door.

"Ben, Leah, what are you..." Faith's voice trailed off when she noticed the beer in Leah's hand. She crossed her arms over her chest and frowned.

Andrew spoke up, but didn't answer their curious glances. "We need to have a talk."

Ben and Leah nodded.

"Let's go inside," Faith suggested.

After Leah followed Faith inside, Ben raised a brow and whispered to Andrew, "You're here late."

Andrew nodded. "We're not discussing my life right now."

Ben sat on the small couch next to Leah, and Faith and Andrew sat in nearby hickory rockers. Andrew tilted his head and looked to Ben. "Where'd you get the alcohol?"

Ben glanced at Leah. "It doesn't matter."

Andrew cut Ben and Leah a sharp stare. "Yes, it does. For one thing, you're underage and drinking alcohol is against the law."

"My *Englisch* friends," Leah admitted.

Andrew glanced at Faith. "I think Faith agrees with me when I say I don't ever want to see you two drinking again."

"We weren't hurting anybody," Leah protested.

"You were hurting yourselves and possibly your future children and grandchildren. Nobody who drinks alcohol only affects themselves." Andrew scratched his forehead.

"How's that?" Ben's brow lowered.

Andrew met Ben and Leah's eyes. "Do you know of anyone who drinks alcohol?"

Leah shrugged. "My friends."

"What happens to them when they drink?" He glanced at Faith and offered a reassuring half smile.

"Well, when they drink too much they start acting stupid," Leah said. She quickly added, "But they don't always drink a lot. Sometimes they just have a beer or two."

"It always starts with one or two beers; one or two drinks. I don't know of anyone who says to themselves, 'Someday, I want to be an alcoholic,' or 'Someday, I want to wreck my marriage,' or 'Someday, I want to father a child out of wedlock,' or 'Someday, I want to get behind the wheel of a car and kill somebody's *mamm*,' or 'Someday, I want to beat my *kinner* until they can no longer walk,' or 'Someday, I want to kill my *fraa*.' *Nobody* begins that way, with those thoughts. No, they begin with 'I'll just have a beer or two. I won't hurt anyone. What's the big deal?'

"Well, I'll tell you what the big deal is. You can never ever have a drink without it affecting someone. That's how my father started. Every time he returned home drunk, we could guarantee that we were going to get beaten. It's like the alcohol unleashed all his emotions and he could no longer control himself." Andrew released a wry chuckle. "You know, it's interesting that alcohol is often called 'spirits', because that is exactly how my father acted when he was under the influence. It was as though there was another spirit – an evil spirit – inside him that took over."

Faith steadily watched Andrew as he shared his heart-breaking story. When his eyes filled with tears, hers did too. She reached over and clasped his hand for support.

"Most alcoholics begin drinking in their teens," Andrew added.

Leah stared at Ben who appeared to be deep in thought, as was she, contemplating Andrew's sobering words.

"Just think about it. What kind of legacy do you want to leave for your children? What kind of life do you want to have ten years down the road – twenty years down the road? Do you want a life filled with misery and heartache? Because that's exactly the legacy my father left for his children. Every one of us has to fight daily to overcome it."

Tears pricked Leah's eyes when she thought of her friend Abigail and all that she'd gone through. It had taken her years to open up and talk about the abuse she, her siblings, and *mamm* had suffered at the hands of their alcoholic father.

Leah nodded in understanding. She stood up and walked to the door.

"Where are you going?" Ben asked.

"I have to do something." Leah opened the door and stepped onto the porch. She reached down beside the chair she'd been sitting in and picked up the can of beer. Turning the can upside down, she dumped the remainder of the contents onto the lawn. With a satisfied grin, she turned around and walked back into the house.

CHAPTER 12
Welcome

"The heavens declare the glory of God; and the firmament sheweth his handywork." Psalm 19:1

ear Journal,
Life has been great! Ben is so wonderful and he makes me feel beautiful and perfect. He's coming to see me tonight. I can't wait!!!

I broke up with Jackson. He wasn't too happy about it. Furious is probably the best word to describe how he acted. At first, he acted like I hadn't said a word, like I was just teasing him. But when he realized I was serious, he was really upset. He yelled at me, saying how I was a horrible person and calling me names I won't repeat. I'd never seen him so angry. But I just walked away. I can't believe I actually thought he cared about me.

Tori was really shocked. In a way, I still want to be friends with her. But then again, if I stay Amish, that might be a bad idea.

Yes, I'm considering staying Amish. How could I not with Ben? As long as I'm with him, I wouldn't mind being Amish or Englisch.

Leah looked up from her diary when she heard the quiet rumble of an engine. She looked out the window and smiled. *Ben.*

She slid her journal into her desk drawer and put out the candle she'd been using. She quietly opened her door and tip-toed down the stairs, holding her breath and praying for still-ness. Blindly, she wandered through the dim light to the back door. Letting it shut softly behind her, she hurried to the ga-zebo, where Ben sat.

"Hey," she breathed, lowering herself beside him on the bench.

"Hey." Ben slipped his arm around her shoulders and looked down at her feet. "You're barefoot."

Leah scooted closer to him, leaning into his warm torso. "Guess I was so excited to see you I forgot my shoes." She smiled up at him and he returned the grin.

They sat in silence for a few moments, content with being together as they gazed at God's magnificent display of spar-kling stars.

"Aren't they amazing?" Ben spoke up.

"The stars?"

He nodded. "Every single one of them, bright and beautiful, twinkling for all to see as they manifest the wonder of their awesome Creator." He shifted to point at the sky and she moved away so she could see his face. "I've heard someone say that you can find the Gospel written in the stars. Can you imagine it? Like God reached down and wrote the Bible into the night sky." His face shone with a look of uncontainable awe.

"Ben."

"Hmm...?" He dragged his stare away from the brilliance to look at her.

She rested a hand on his shoulder and gazed into his eyes. "I wanna kiss you."

At the invitation, Ben pulled her nearer and she leaned into him, shutting her eyes when their lips met.

Life was definitely perfect.

With a sigh, Faith sank into one of the two sturdy oak rocking-chairs in the small living room. *Finally* she could relax after spending the last several hours unpacking their belongings and cleaning the house. There was still much to be done to spruce things up, but it could wait. She released an exhausted breath; right now what she needed was a break.

With a gentle rocking motion, she was transported to a time not too far in the past, when *Dat* and *Mamm* were still alive. Beloved memories of her folks filled her thoughts. *This chair was once* Mamm's. It was the only piece of furniture they'd rescued from the fire, and the only furniture they'd brought from Ohio. *Mamm* would sit in it, swaying to and fro on cold nights while knitting socks, beanies, mittens and other practical items for her family.

When her parents were alive, she had never known life could be so hard. They hadn't kept their children from hard work but, rather, taught them to enjoy it. They'd reminded their children that the ability to work was a gift from *Der Herr*.

She supposed they had kept them from many of work's pressures and stresses to keep them from being discouraged, or from growing up too quickly. After childhood came adulthood; *that* change was permanent. When it *had* been time to mature, her parents had graciously guided them in that direction.

I had gut *parents, the best I could have ever wanted,* she realized. She silently asked for the millionth time, *why did* Mamm *and* Dat *have to die?* Had they lived, Faith would love to have told them about Andrew. She sighed.

Andrew. What an unexpected blessing he'd been.

Knock, knock.

Faith snapped out of her musings and glanced toward the door. She hastily rose from her rocking-chair and crossed the space to the front entrance. She put her hand on the knob, twisted it, and pulled it ajar.

Three familiar-looking Amish women, near her own age, stood outside; two of them, who Faith guessed to be identical twins, had auburn hair and the other young woman had flaxen-blond hair, her middle displaying signs of a beginning pregnancy. One of the twins held a glass dish in her hands.

"*Guten tag,*" the twin without the pan greeted. "We just wanted to drop by and say hello. By the way, I'm Susanna Fisher, Susie for short." She extended a friendly greeting. "We met at Meeting, but I was unsure whether you'd remembered my name. I'm sure it's difficult to remember everyone's name."

Faith smiled and shook the sociable woman's hand. "Faith Schrock."

"I'm Maryanna Hostettler, her identical twin sister," Susanna's double needlessly inserted, nodding her head in her twin's direction.

"And I'm Annie Hostettler," the flaxen-haired woman put in. "*Gut* to meet you, Faith."

"I made you a casserole." Maryanna proudly lifted the dish toward her.

"What do you mean *I*, Maryanna Hostettler?" Annie's large blue eyes widened.

"All right, *we* made you a casserole," Maryanna amended.

"*Denki.* Please come in." Faith received the casserole from her visitor's outstretched arms. She walked inside and the three young women followed her to the living room. "Just make yourself at home."

While each of her guests found a comfortable seat, Faith strode to the kitchen and set the dish on the counter. She shortly rejoined her company in the living room bringing a pitcher of sweet tea and four glasses with her. She set them down on the small coffee table and offered her guests a glass of refreshment.

"*Denki*," the three said in unison, and then giggled.

"Oh wow! This place looks a lot different from when Mom and I lived here." Maryanna surveyed the two-tone paint and candle shelves.

"Andrew and my brother, Ben, have done a *gut* job of fixing it up, ain't so?" Faith's countenance brightened.

"*Jah*." Susanna glanced around.

"So, you three are all sisters?" Faith's brow raised.

"Sisters-in-*law*," Annie clarified. "I'm married to their older brother, Joshua."

"Yeah, she made off with Joshy," Maryanna teased.

Annie smiled and placed a hand over her abdomen. "He was so happy to find out about the *boppli*."

"I guess our *bopplin* will be born about the same–" Susie's eyes enlarged and she quickly cupped her hand over her mouth.

"*Ach*, you're expecting too, Susie?" Annie asked wide-eyed. "We're so lucky."

Susie put a finger to her lips. "Only we and Jonathan know as of yet, and I hope to keep it that way for now."

"I won't tell." Faith smiled. It would be nice to find herself in a similar circumstance in the not-too-distant future. "Congratulations to both of you."

"Thank you," Annie and Susie answered in unison.

"Man." Maryanna slapped her leg. "Matthew and I better hurry up and get busy; we'll have a lot of catching up to do if you guys keep going at this rate."

Annie cleared her throat. "Just make sure to catch up *after* the wedding."

"When will *Dat* publish it?" Susie questioned.

"Next Meeting," Maryanna confirmed. She turned to Faith and explained. "We didn't marry sooner because I'm still an *Englischer* at heart and we didn't want Matthew to be shunned. He's already baptized in the church, but I was raised *Englisch* for most of my life."

Faith's eyebrows arched to her mid-forehead.

"We'll explain it all to you someday," Susie offered.

Maryanna continued, "We talked to Dad about it – he's the bishop, you know – and he suggested we become members of a faster Amish district. Matthew can still keep the old ways that he's used to, and I can still have my electricity." She grinned.

"Then it works out all the way around." Faith smiled.

"Yeah." Maryanna laughed. "I remember once telling Mom I would *never* marry an Amish guy, but now I wouldn't change it for the world. Matthew is so sweet."

"*Der Herr* has a way of working things out. I never thought I'd be interested in Jonathan, but now I'm glad to have gotten him. And while he is still full of mischief, he's a *gut dat* and a *gut* man, and I love him." Susie sighed contentedly.

Maryanna waved her hand. "You can *have* him."

"Forgive our chattering; we tend to do that when we get together." Susie shifted on the couch. "Do you have any other siblings beside the brother you mentioned?"

Faith nodded. "*Jah*, Ben and I have several siblings out in Ohio."

"You said he helped fix the place up?" Susie inquired.

"*Jah*, he and Andrew Lapp," Faith explained.

Smiling coyly, Maryanna asked, "You like him, don't you?"

"Maryanna!" Susie scolded and Annie frowned at their forward friend. "It's none of our business. You're worse than Jonathan."

"We're courting, actually," Faith divulged. With her face flustered, she desperately wanted a change in topic. Spying the forgotten tea and glasses on the table, she spoke up. "Would any of you ladies care for some tea?"

Also grateful for the shift of conversation, the women immediately accepted. After taking a sip of her tea, Annie commented, "It smells really good in here."

Faith perked up. "I make candles and sell them. Would you like to see some?" Receiving permission, she left the room and shortly returned with a wicker basket of small candles containing various scents. "Feel free to smell them."

Susie brought a creamy-white candle to her nose and took a whiff. "Mm, smells like vanilla."

"Vanilla Bean is a common favorite," Faith informed.

Annie inhaled a coffee-colored one and asked, "Ooh, what's this scent?"

She handed the candle to Faith who sniffed it and promptly answered, "Mochaccino. Yummy, isn't it?"

"Mm-hmm." Annie nodded in affirmation.

"Whoa! This smells like a forest; Matthew would love this one." Maryanna's gaze caught a small dark-green candle.

"That's Pine," Faith verified.

"Appropriately named; this is really strong." Maryanna breathed in the scent again then turned to Faith. "You made all these?"

"*Jah*, it's not hard if you have all the stuff and you know how to make them. Some *Englischers* like to make them at young girls' birthday parties, something fun to do for the *kinner*. Would you like to learn how? We could meet here again sometime and I could teach you," Faith offered.

Her company shared a glance. "If it's not too much trouble—" Annie began.

"*Ach*, it's no trouble at all," she assured. "It would be fun. Would next Thursday afternoon at two suit you?"

Maryanna shrugged. "I'm not doing anything next Thursday. I'll be here."

"I'll write it on my calendar," Annie affirmed.

"And I'm sure I can find someone to babysit the *kinner* for a few hours," Susie asserted.

"*Gut*." Faith beamed. "Thursday it is then."

"Speaking of the *kinner*, I should probably be getting home." Susie sighed. "Who knows *what* they've gotten into since I left."

"Who's watching them?" Annie asked curiously.

Susie sighed again. "Jonathan."

"No *wonder* you're worried," Maryanna stated. "We should probably go then." She turned to Faith. "Thanks for the tea, and the conversation."

"You all are welcome any time." Faith walked them to the door. "By the way, go ahead and take these home with you." From behind her back, she pulled out the three small candles her friends had been eyeing earlier.

"Oh, we couldn't–" Susie protested.

"Of course you can. Just consider it a thank you for the casserole, from a friend."

"Hey, Ben, can you take these deliveries?"

"Sure. Where's the list?"

His coworker gave him a stack of pizza boxes. "Right here." She placed the list on top of the pile of boxes.

"Thanks." Ben walked to his car and placed the pizzas in the passenger seat.

He typed the address into the GPS his boss insisted he use, and started the engine. As he drove to the first place, he thought about Leah. She was like a dream. He smiled, remembering the kiss they'd shared two nights ago.

Ben was glad when he arrived at his first destination, forcing him to think of something else. He grabbed the two pizzas and strode up the walkway to the small white house. He rapped his knuckles against the door frame and waited for someone to answer.

A young teen opened the door and eyed him. She turned behind her. "Mom! Pizza!"

Another woman appeared. "Don't be so rude, Shailee," she admonished her daughter then looked at him. "Hello. Uh, let me get your tip."

She handed him a five dollar bill and took the pizzas.

"Thank you, ma'am." Ben turned and went back to his car, heading to the next place. This person had ordered fifteen pizzas. They must've been having a party.

When he turned into the recipient's driveway, he realized that that's exactly what was happening. Rock music blared loudly as young people wandered around the property. He tried not to notice the immodestly dressed girls and the bottles of alcohol. He was quickly reminded of Andrew's story and now looked at the brown bottles with disdain. It's funny how quickly your opinion of something can change when a healthy dose of reality is infused.

He spotted a man with a bright blue mohawk and recognition sent a chill down his back. One of Jackson's buddies.

Someone he didn't recognize sauntered up to him. "How much, pizza man?"

"It's paid for." He felt like saying, 'except for the tip' but he wouldn't. He knew not to expect much in tips, and had learned to count each one as a blessing.

The man handed him a few dollars and Ben set the boxes down on a nearby table.

An uneasiness came over him and he suddenly felt every instinct telling him to leave. Not bothering to look behind him, Ben swiftly but casually made his way back to his car. He was nearly ten feet from the vehicle when a familiar, sneering voice sounded behind him.

"What's your hurry, farm boy?"

CHAPTER 13
Ben

"Trust in the Lord with all thine heart; and lean not unto thine own understanding. In all thy ways acknowledge him, and he shall direct thy paths."
Proverbs 3:5-6

*F*aith smiled charmingly as Andrew helped her out of his buggy. "*Denki*, Andrew. You're a very *gut* man."

"My pleasure," he replied warmly.

Their date had been *wunderbaar*. Andrew discovered a few new things about Faith. She absolutely loved coconut. The gardenia was her favorite flower. She also had candle scents of both. She loved rain. And reading was one of her favorite pastimes.

Their night had gone so well that he hated for it to end.

He escorted Faith to her house and she paused before entering. "Andrew." She twisted her hands behind her back. "Would you like to come inside and stay a little while? We could have some coffee or tea."

Andrew grinned. Apparently, he wasn't the only one.

Leah glanced at the clock on the wall. Nine o'clock. She smiled. Just thirty more minutes until she saw Ben.

"Leah, it's your turn," her little sister spoke up.

"What?"

"It's your turn. Seth just went so now it's your turn to go."

Leah refocused her attention on their Scrabble game, looking down at her letters. "Let's see..."

Ben's gut twisted as he gradually turned to face Jackson. "I have pizzas to deliver."

"Sounds like an excuse to me." Jackson snorted, obviously intoxicated.

A gorgeous brunette rubbed his shoulders, a cigarette hanging from her lips. She gave Ben a tantalizing wink.

"You stole Leah from me. Ever heard it's wrong to steal?"

Ben remained silent.

Jackson huffed. "Didn't even get a chance to try her out."

Ben tried his best to ignore the powerful urge to punch Jackson. "I have to go." He turned and took about two steps before a strong hand latched onto his arm.

"You aren't going anywhere, farm boy." Jackson spun him around.

Ben was unprepared for the fist that flew into his face. He stumbled back as pain exploded across his jaw. Seeing another blow heading for his middle, he tightened his muscles to lessen the impact. Jackson paused, giving him a chance to fight back. But he wouldn't. For Faith.

Ben dodged and blocked as many blows as he could, refusing to do any more than that.

Jackson grew more impatient by the second. He nodded and two men grabbed Ben's arms and held him still and defenseless. "This is gonna be fun." Jackson smiled, sending another fist into his face.

Dear Gott, *please let this be over soon.*

Leah's eyes returned to the clock. Nine thirty. *Ben should be here any minute!*

"Jackson, he looks pretty bad," Darren observed.

Exhausted after releasing his fury, Jackson panted heavily. He glanced down at Ben and knew his friend was right. Farm boy was crumpled on the ground, unconscious. The blood and bruises across his face made Jackson wince.

A sickening thought pushed panic into Jackson's veins. "Is he – is he dead?" He couldn't have killed him. Couldn't. He would go to jail for manslaughter. *Please be alive.*

"He's breathing. Barely."

"Good." Jackson smiled in relief, his mind scrambling for a way out of his dilemma. "Darren, put him in the car and drive away. Then leave him in the middle of nowhere. I'll follow you and pick you up, all right?"

"Sure. Help me get him in the car."

Faith contently glanced up at Andrew as they conversed. They'd discussed practically anything and everything, it seemed. A short while ago, he'd begun sharing about his past family life and the struggles they'd gone through. He told her of his mixed emotions toward his father and sorrow for his mother. She grieved for him, recognizing the pain in his voice. They had lapsed into a peaceful silence and she was unprepared for his next question.

"What about your folks?"

"My parents? They were great. My father was hard-working and strong. And my *mamm* was kind and gentle. With so many of us *kinner* the house ran smoothly."

"How many siblings do you have?"

"There're eight, including Ben; five older than me and two between Ben and me. We were the only ones left in the house when my folks died," she concluded in a low tone.

"I'm sorry, Faith. I didn't mean to cause you pain."

"No, that's all right." She lifted her tear-brimmed eyes to his. "It's just hard. And raising Ben hasn't been easy either. I keep –" she paused to collect herself and discreetly scanned Andrew's features. She didn't want to make him uncomfortable. His reassuring gaze encouraged her to continue on.

"I keep feeling like I'm a failure; like I should be a better woman, a better sister. I just don't know if I'm doing things right. I have to be strong for Ben, and strong for myself. But inside I'm breaking. I can't –" Her sobs choked off her words and she dropped her head into her hands.

Strong arms enveloped her and she wept into Andrew's warm chest. His large hand rubbed her back consolingly. "You're not a failure," he whispered. His words opened the floodgates and she sobbed even more. To feel that someone cared about her. She'd been craving this masculine comfort that he now exuded. It felt so good.

But was it real? Was he simply comforting her as a friend? Or was he comforting her as a man, as someone who wanted to love and be loved by her?

"You don't have to be strong on your own, Faith. I'll be strong for you."

He said it so softly, that Faith almost thought she'd imagined him saying the words. But the huskiness in his voice told her otherwise.

She sniffled and wiped away her tears. She receded, desiring to see his face but not wanting to be out of his embrace. "I think I'm in love with you," she admitted softly.

He smiled. "I *know* I'm in love with you."

She lifted her face to his. Andrew's eyes widened when he understood her meaning. His mouth met hers a bit hesitantly. The kiss was slow and sweet and tender.

A pounding on the front door shattered the spell and they jumped slightly, breaking their brief contact.

Andrew graced her with an endearing smile before he went to answer the door. Faith's heart beat wildly, her emotions jumbled into a tangled knot. She did her best to refresh her appearance before following her beau.

Leah glanced at the clock. Two minutes after eleven. What was taking Ben so long? Her mind grew frantic with worry. *Did he forget? Did he not want to see her? Was he in an accident? Did he die?*

Her family had gone to sleep nearly two hours ago but sleep was the last thing on her mind. She'd waited quietly, knitting to keep herself from going mad.

Unable to wait any longer, she stood. Still fully dressed, she grabbed her flashlight and crept down the stairs. She scurried outside and started toward Ben's house when a hand clamped over her mouth.

"It's just me," her brother whispered, releasing her.

"Seth! What are you doing?"

"What's it look like? I'm going with you."

Leah raised her hand to protest. "But –"

"Nothing you say is going to make me stay here, so you might as well save your words so you can lecture Ben when we find him." He grinned.

"How did you know I was looking for Ben?"

"You are way too predictable, *schweschder*. Now, where are we going?"

Ignoring the urge to throttle her annoying brother, she pointed. "I was planning on heading to Ben's house. I wish they had a phone. It'd be a lot easier just to call."

Seth nodded in agreement. "Well, they don't. So let's go."

They set off at a jogging pace and didn't stop until they were on the Schrocks' property. Leah spotted a buggy by the barn and wondered whose it might be. Still panting from her run, she knocked on the door sharply.

Andrew Lapp opened it and for a fleeting moment, Leah wondered why he was here so late.

"Is Ben here?" Leah enquired.

A disheveled-looking Faith appeared behind Andrew. "Seth? Leah? What's wrong?"

Leah didn't miss the comforting hand Andrew placed on Faith's back, but she was too distressed to ponder the situation now.

"Is Ben here?" Leah reiterated. "He was supposed to pick me up at nine thirty, but he never came. I'm worried something may have happened to him."

"No, he isn't here. Maybe he had to work late," Faith suggested.

"*Nee*, he would have called to tell me," Leah reasoned.

"We'll help you look. I'm sure we'll find him." Andrew turned to Faith. "Do you need to fetch your purse or a jacket?"

Faith nodded and returned promptly.

Once they were all situated in the buggy, they determined heading for the pizza place where Ben worked would be their best course of action. Leah thought the ride over there seemed to take forever. She closed her eyes and prayed, but trusting God proved difficult when she couldn't see the road up ahead. Upon reaching the restaurant, the group rushed inside.

Faith marched up to an employee. "Is Ben here?"

"No," the female worker said. "He took some deliveries a couple of hours ago, but I never saw him return. This place has been busy, so I haven't really been keeping tabs on everyone's whereabouts. I thought his shift was over."

Leah worriedly glanced at Faith. "May we speak with the manager please? This is an emergency."

The girl's eyes widened and she nodded. She hurried into the back, returning with a stocky man a minute later.

"I'm Ralf, the manager. What's this about?"

"Do you, by any chance, know where Benjamin Schrock is? He should have been home a while ago. I'm his sister."

"Ben? No. Haven't a clue where the kid went. He took off to deliver pizzas 'bout two and a half hours ago. Haven't seen him since. His shift was just about over, so I let it slide. Probably joined a party or something." He shrugged nonchalantly. "But don't get riled. He's a kid. That's what they do. Happens all the time."

Leah shook her head. "Ben's not like that. He's honest and dependable. He wouldn't take this long unless something went wrong."

"Well, I don't know what to tell you, lady. I suggest you wait until he comes back." Ralf shrugged. "It's up to you."

Faith turned to Andrew. "What do you think we should do, Andrew?"

"I think you and Leah should stay here, in case Ben comes back."

"What about you and Seth?" Leah spoke up.

"I'll get a list of the addresses Ben was supposed to deliver pizza to and we'll go look for him."

Faith nodded. "Sounds good."

The men left in search of Ben, while the girls waited for their return. Leah drummed her fingers on the top of a table agitatedly. If only she had her knitting needles. She shifted and glanced at the clock. Only three minutes since Andrew and Seth had left. She shut her eyes tightly against the emotion roiling inside her. *Where are you, Ben?*

The darkness closed in around him tightly. Fighting against it with every fiber in him, Ben was able to open his right eye. His head throbbed as his vision focused. More darkness. Where was he?

A volley of memories rushed to his brain. Pizza...party... Jackson... The remembrance sent a shock of feeling into his numb body. He was suddenly aware of every excruciating bruise, felt every punch and kick. A pounding began in his head, each beat more and more agonizing. He moaned in anguish. *Help me, Lord.*

Doing his best to block out the torrent of pain, Ben attempted to take in his surroundings. The plushness underneath him could be one of several things: a bed, a couch, the seat of a car. The faint pizza scent told him it must be the latter. He couldn't hear anything so he figured he must be alone. Either that or he'd gone deaf. Since it was dark outside, Ben assumed that several hours had passed.

The darkness returned, dragging him back. His eyelids weighted down. He tried his utmost to fight back but he was just too weak. Too weak...

CHAPTER 14
Waiting

"What time I am afraid, I will trust in thee."
Psalm 56:3

Faith's eyes wandered to the digital clock on the wall. Eleven fifty-six. Not even a minute had gone by since she'd last looked at it. She sighed and glanced at Leah. The young woman was turned to the side, clutching her knees and staring into the darkness outside. Her frame trembled slightly.

Faith stood and slid onto the seat next to her. She placed a hand on her shoulder. Leah turned to her, tears trailing down her cheeks. She leaned towards Faith, who welcomed her with open arms. Ben's *aldi* cried in her arms for a little while before she lifted her tear-stained face. "I'm so afraid. He...he could be lost, or hurt, or maybe even dead." Her chin wobbled and more moisture welled in her eyes.

Faith shook her gently. "We can't think like that, Leah. *Gott* will take care of him. I know He will." Faith bowed her head. "Dear *Gott,* You know where we are. You know where Ben is. I pray that You keep him safe, Lord. If he's lost, please guide him home. If he's hurt, please bring him help. Please be with him, Lord. Please..."

Officer Love rode along silently next to his partner in the squad car. He took a swig of his coffee, hoping it'd help sharpen his senses. He couldn't wait to get home to Sadie. He smiled at the thought of his beautiful wife.

"Hey, Brandon, is that a car over there?"

His eyes followed the direction of Officer Douglas' finger. "Yeah. It is. Looks like it belongs to some pizza place. Wonder what it's doing out here in the middle of nowhere. Think it could be a robbery?"

"Maybe."

They pulled up behind the vehicle and stepped out of the squad car. Officer Love cautiously started toward the driver's side, his partner a pace behind him. He knocked on the window. No response. He put his flashlight to the window and shined the beam into the car. Opening the door, his gut twisted.

"This doesn't look good," Brandon mumbled. *Please be alive.* He gingerly felt the teen's neck for a pulse. A faint twitch beat against his fingers. *Thank God.* "We need an ambulance!"

Andrew had given up. They'd searched everywhere and hadn't found a trace of Ben. He was tired, cold, hungry, and needed to use the restroom. "We're going back."

Seth looked up at him and yawned. "I agree."

Andrew changed the horse's direction. They drove towards the pizzeria in silence. He had no idea what he would tell Faith. She would be devastated. Andrew prayed that Ben had found his way back. He dreaded the thought of informing Faith of their fruitless search. He longed to be her hero, the one to have found Ben and brought him back safely.

When they reached the plaza, Andrew tied the horse to the hitching post and headed inside. Seth followed him, shuffling his feet as he went. They entered the restaurant and were promptly met by Faith and Leah.

After glancing at their faces, the hope in the girls' countenances vanished. Faith's shoulders drooped and her expression went from confident to grief-stricken. Leah slumped against her, ready tears pooling into her eyes. They looked devastated, as though someone had sucked the life out of them. Andrew's heart sunk to the ground.

He was preparing to comfort them when two police officers stepped into the pizzeria. One looked strangely familiar...

"Brandon?"

The cops turned. Officer Love smiled. "Hey, Andrew. What are you doing here?"

"We're looking for Benjamin Schrock, Faith's brother. He didn't return from work a few hours ago and –"

"Excuse me," the other policeman interrupted. "But did you say his name was Ben?"

"Benjamin, *jah*. Have you seen him?"

The officer whispered something to Brandon and the two men retreated to converse privately.

Leah stepped forward. "Is there something wrong? Do you know where Ben is?" Her tone edged hysteria. "Is he hurt?"

Officer Love turned back to them. "About twenty minutes ago, while we were on patrol, we spotted a car on the side of the road. A young man was inside of the vehicle, unconscious. His name tag said 'Ben' and the car he was in had a magnet on the side doors advertising this pizzeria. If that was the Ben you're speaking of, you might want to head for the hospital."

"Oh no." Faith's breath caught and Andrew grasped her hand. "How bad is he?"

Brandon's jaw clenched, setting his mouth in a grim line. "I'd start praying."

Leah's eyes draped shut as she leaned against the wall in the waiting room. A wash of weariness swept over her and she slumped to the ground, hugging her knees.

They had arrived at the hospital nearly two hours ago and hadn't received any word regarding Ben. Andrew was holding

Faith as she cried and Seth was slouched in a chair close by. She was unsure of whether he was asleep or praying.

Every muscle in Leah's body screamed for rest but she wanted to be awake when the doctor came. It was an intense battle that she was rapidly losing. She'd just entered dreamland when she felt a hand on her shoulder. Her eyes fluttered open.

Her brother smiled. "The couch is a lot more comfortable."

Seth helped her up and led her to the sofa. She sank into the plush cushions, immediately relaxing. She was asleep within seconds.

Faith pulled away from Andrew and sniffed. He handed her a handkerchief. She smiled her thanks, dabbing at her eyes. "Seems like I'm always crying on you."

The corners of his mouth lifted. "I don't mind."

"Is someone here for Benjamin Schrock?" A woman's voice asked loudly.

Faith quickly rushed to the doctor. "I am his sister, Faith."

The doctor smiled. "Nice to meet you. I'm Doctor Norton."

Faith nodded. "How is Ben?"

"Your brother is in critical condition, Miss Schrock. He has three broken ribs and has lost a good amount of blood. He also appears to have taken some heavy blows to the head. If your brother awakens, it is very possible that he will have brain damage."

Faith felt her emotions return full force. *Not now.* "Uh..." She struggled not to cry. "What...what do you mean *if* he awakens?"

"Miss Schrock, your brother is presently in a comatose state. At this stage, we are unsure of his ability to fight this." The woman placed a hand on Faith's arm. "I hate to be so frank, but it would take a miracle for your brother to survive."

"If my brother is anything, he's a fighter." As Faith said the words, she knew this time she would be urging him to fight for once. *Come on, Ben. Fight for your life.*

CHAPTER 15
A Miracle

"Death and life are in the power of the tongue: and they that love it shall eat the fruit thereof."
Proverbs 18:21

Leah couldn't take her eyes off Ben. She stared at his bruised and swollen face in shock. How could anyone do something like this? And for what? A couple of dollars?

She gently took his hand. The physician said talking to him would help. Though she had no idea how and didn't know what to say, if it'd bring Ben back, she'd do it.

"Hey, Ben. Uh...I'm not really sure what to say. You're the first unconscious person I've ever talked to." She laughed nervously. "I guess that wasn't very funny.

"Please wake up. We all miss you and want you back. Nearly everyone in the community has come to see you and you've only been here for two days. Everybody's praying for you.

"Faith hasn't left the hospital. And since she's staying, so is Andrew. I'm pretty sure he's in love with her. I think she likes him too. He always holds her when she cries. He's been by her side the whole time. He'll make a good husband for her.

"I've been here too. Just sitting and waiting for a chance to talk to you. My *mamm* and *dat* are trying to make me go home with them but I don't want to leave. I can't leave you. I couldn't bear if you woke up or died while I was gone." Her lip trembled at the last thought. "But you're *not* going to die. You're going to stay here with me. Please, Ben. I can't lose you."

Leah sucked in a breath. It wouldn't do Ben any good for her to be a jumbled mess of nerves. She needed to be strong for him. She changed the subject to something brighter.

"I'm really beginning to hate hospitals. They're too sterile, and serious. Nobody laughs in a hospital. But I suppose that's understandable. I'm not about to laugh either."

She blinked back the tears that formed in her eyes and smiled. "There I go getting sad again. Doctor Norton said to be positive and hopeful but it's not very easy. Not with you like this."

"Leah," her mother's voice called from the door. "Come here, please."

She stood and leaned over Ben, placing a kiss on his unresponsive lips. "I love you. Be back as soon as I can," she whispered.

Leah stepped into the hall where Lavina was waiting. "What is it, *Mamm*?"

"They've discovered more about what happened to Ben. There's a police officer waiting to talk to us."

The two women quickly made their way to the waiting room. Seth, Andrew, Faith, Leah's father, and the policeman stood together. Andrew nodded for the officer to speak when they arrived.

"In the car Benjamin was driving, we found a list of addresses for his deliveries. We went to the last address he'd been to and met a young man named Darren Royce."

Leah's mouth grew dry at the familiarity of the name.

"When threatened with jail time and offered leniency, Darren confessed to being involved in Ben's beating. Apparently, Ben had gone to deliver pizzas at a fraternity party. When he arrived, another young man..." the officer paused and glanced down at his notebook, "...Jackson Lane, beat the pulp out of him. He was heavily intoxicated, but had the help of several friends, including Darren. Darren said that when Jackson realized the consequences of what he'd done, he told Darren to drive the car away from town and leave Ben there. We have already taken Jackson and his accomplices into custody."

Faith threw her hands up. "Why would somebody do that to Ben? He's a good kid."

"Thank you, Officer." Andrew shook his hand and the policeman left.

Leah sank into a chair, trembling violently. Faith came up to her and placed an arm around her shoulders. "What's wrong, Leah?"

"Jackson was my *Englisch* boyfriend. We broke up about a week ago. He – he must've done it to get revenge. It's all my fault. Ben might die because of me." Leah sobbed.

"No, Leah. It's not your fault," Faith reassured her, ignoring her own tears. "Jackson is responsible for his own actions. He made the decision to behave like that. You can't blame yourself."

Despite Faith's soothing words, Leah couldn't help but feel that she was somehow accountable.

Andrew sighed as the small clock on the wall struck twelve.

Day five.

He shifted slightly and Faith roused. "What? Is Ben dead? Did he wake up?"

"Shh." Andrew leaned toward her. "Nothing's happened. Go back to sleep."

She slumped tiredly and dropped her head on his shoulder.

He smiled. Faith. Stubborn, wonderful Faith. The woman had refused to take a step out of the hospital until something happened. Which meant Andrew was stuck since he wasn't about to leave her side.

He gently slipped a pillow under her head.

Ben had showed no signs of change. He hadn't necessarily slipped further into the coma but his condition wasn't exactly positive either. He simply hovered between life and death.

Oh, dear Lord, please bring him back.

Leah grasped Ben's hand tightly, wanting to squeeze life back into him. "You listen to me, Benjamin Schrock. I have been talking to you about anything and everything for what seems like forever. I think you know my whole life story. Seeing how today is the seventh day you've been here, and since seven is the number of perfection, I'd say it's the perfect day for you to wake up. I'll make you a deal. I'll talk to you all day long if you promise to wake up today, all right?"

His breathing hitched for a moment then continued a notch faster than before.

She smiled. "It's a deal then!"

Leah talked, and talked, and talked. She spoke of everything she thought of. She told him the story of when she grew her very first plant, and how it died two days after it had emerged from the soil. She recounted childhood memories, both good and bad. She informed him of every misdeed she'd done, whispered every secret she had. She informed him of her secret dream to fly and how she'd tested the law of gravity when she was seven and learned that jumping from the haymow earned you a broken limb instead of wings. She told him about the latest novel she'd read.

She laughed as she recounted tales of Jonathan Fisher's mischievousness. Leah told Ben of how Joanna Fisher ended up marrying an *Englischer*, and how Danika Yoder used to *be* an *Englischer*. She told him about Chloe's blind beau – or so her friend Ruthie had once thought – that ended badly. She talked about Susanna and how she and Jonathan were a perfect couple. By the time she'd finished her rambling, she was certain Ben knew the stories of everyone in Paradise. She repeated nearly every story she knew.

"Once –"

A hand rested on her shoulder. "Leah, visiting hours are over in three minutes."

"Sure, Faith. Just give me a minute."

Ben's sister nodded and walked out of the room.

"You promised, Ben." Tears trailed her cheeks. "You have to wake up today. You can't break your promise. You can't." Leah let her head fall to his side as she wept. She wearily continued on. "Remember the legacy that we talked about? You and me, we're going to get married and have *kinner* and raise them to trust in *Der Herr*. I thought about names for our *bopplin* when they come. What do you think of Elisabeth or Jacob? Elisabeth Schrock. Sounds *gut*, ain't so? But Ben, I can't have 'em by myself. I need you. They're gonna need a real *gut Dat* and I know you'll be perfect."

"Leah?" a somewhat hoarse voice asked.

Her head shot up. "Ben?" She screamed when she saw that his eyes were open. "You're alive! Faith, Andrew! Ben's back!" She leaned forward and brushed his face with kisses. "Oh, thank you, God! Oh, thank you, thank you!"

Ben lifted a half-smile and muttered, "Did I hear you say you were going to marry me?"

EPILOGUE
The Legacy

"Lo, children are an heritage of the Lord..."
Psalm 127:3a

"It's a boy!" Chloe, the midwife, declared when Benjamin entered the room. She quickly handed the tiny bundle to his father.

Ben's face beamed as he studied his precious son in his arms. "Welcome, little Jacob."

"Me want see," two-year-old Elisabeth tugged on her father's pant leg.

Ben crouched down, allowing little Elisabeth to admire her baby brother.

"Me want see, too, *Dat!*" Leah mimicked her daughter.

"All right, Lis. Let's show Mama your new *bruder*." Ben brought the small bundle to Leah and tenderly kissed her cheek.

Elisabeth climbed up into the bed next to her and stroked the *boppli's* head.

Leah admired her husband and two beautiful children and breathed a silent prayer of thanksgiving. She turned to the midwife, who presently packed her belongings into the satchel she'd brought. "*Denki*, Chloe, for helping us today. Seems like little Jacob and your Rachel will be near the same age, ain't so?"

"*Jah*. And Elisabeth is the same age as Matthew and Mary-anna's little Mattie. Seems like they'll all be in school together like we were, although you and Ruthie began about the time Joanna, Danika, and I finished." Chloe released a contented sigh. "*Ach*, such *gut* memories!"

"I know. Time sure does fly quickly, doesn't it?" Leah mused. "And folks change so much."

Chloe laughed. "Can you believe Jonathan Fisher was chosen as minister? Poor Susie will have her hands full for certain sure, with two sets of twins and all the other *kinner*."

"His folks are still there to help, ain't so?" Leah continued at Chloe's nod. "That's what I love about our People, and one of the reasons I chose to stay Amish. There is always help when you need it; you're never alone. We are fortunate to have family and friends who love us and are willing to help out – any time, day or night." Leah adjusted little Jake's position in her arms and drew him to her chest. Ben whisked Elisabeth from the bed and tickled her tummy.

Chloe sighed contently. "And we have a *gut* bishop who has chosen to let *Der Herr* guide our congregation through His Word, shunning the laws of man for God's perfect will. I love our ways and our People, but some folks look at us and think that it is our Plain ways we're trusting in to get to Heaven. When all one actually needs is Jesus."

"That is what Ben and I talked about years ago." Leah smiled at her husband, who was presently bouncing young Elisabeth on his knees, keeping her occupied so *Mamm* could feed the *boppli*. "We wanted to leave a legacy for our children – a strong Christian heritage that would help them weather any storm. That is something only God can do. I hope my children always know that, whether they decide to remain Amish or not, God is always there for them. He's waiting for them with open arms and His love never fails."

After the midwife left, Ben set Elisabeth down and took little Jacob from Leah's arms to relieve him of his excess gas. After a small burp escaped the *boppli's* lips, he handed the infant back to his mother. "That's right, *Lieb. Der Herr* has been *gut* to us. I'll never cease to thank Him for giving me you."

When Ben's lips met hers, Leah remembered how wonderful *gut* God's goodness could be.

The End

A SPECIAL THANK YOU

The authors would like to thank Hannah Spredemann.

The End

*Learning to Love – Saul's Story is a
continuation of Chloe's Revelation*

**Two Novellas in One (for adults) Coming
Spring 2014 at participating online retailers**

Introducing:

Amish Fairly Tales
Cindy's Story

°*Cindy's*°

°*Story*°

An Amish Fairly Tale

Novelette

J.E.B. Spredemann

A fun novelette for adults!

Prologue

Ella stood near her father's grave. *He's really gone.* Tears welled in her eyes and dripped onto the ribbon of her prayer *kapp* as she thought of *Mamm's* funeral several years earlier. She'd been just three then, but she still remembered *Mamm's* beautiful smile and kind words. Although her father had remarried, the gaping hole left by her mother's death had never been filled.

A cold hand on her arm demanded her attention. *"Mother said we need to go now,"* her stepsister Priscilla said in Pennsylvania Dutch.

Ella nodded and brushed her tears away. She followed Priscilla to the family buggy and stared out at the gray sky as she, her stepmother, and two older stepsisters traveled toward home. The clip-clop of the horse's hooves didn't soothe her the way they usually did.

"We are moving tomorrow," Mother Clara declared. "I have no need of this large farm and with no man around, we won't be able to keep up with it. I've already accepted an offer which is more than generous. We will be able to buy something much smaller that will suit our needs."

Nine-year-old Matilda bounced excitedly. "Where will we move, *Mamm*?"

"I thought Indiana might be a nice place. Since it's so cold up north, I plan to join one of the smaller settlements in the south," she answered satisfactorily.

"But I'd have to leave *Dat* and *Mamm*," Ella worried aloud.

Mother Clara squeezed her hand tightly and Ella winced. "We won't have any bad attitudes about this. Do you hear me, Ella? Your parents are dead now. You can stop your nonsense."

Ella nodded silently as moisture gathered in the corners of her eyes.

"*Gut*. Girls, you must begin packing immediately. Ella, you will tend to the animals. You may eat your supper when the chores are completed."

Ella wanted to protest and ask when she would have time to pack up *her* things, but she wouldn't risk more of her stepmother's reproof. She guessed she'd be packing while the rest of the house slept in peace. Just as long as she could take her *Mamm's* special chest with her. Right now, that's all that mattered.

Chapter 1

Ten years later...

"*Donner wetter!* You *ferhoodled* horse – get back here!" Nathaniel called out. He leaped onto Winsome's back and charged after the wild steed. "Go get him, girl."

Nat watched in dismay from atop Winsome as the white stallion jumped their pasture fence and raced down the lane. If he didn't reach him before he reached the main highway...

He wouldn't allow his thoughts to ponder that possibility. Besides, that was several miles away. Surely the horse would be in his secure grasp long before then. He hoped...and prayed.

"Whoa! Whoa!" Nathaniel called out to the new horse. Winsome began to slow down. "No, not you girl!" He squeezed his thighs, urging his horse to continue forward. "I knew I should have kept Bishop in his pen. Stupid dog," he uttered under his breath.

"Prince, you've got to slow down!" he hollered as he watched the frightened horse fade from his view. *God, I need your help. You've got to stop that horse...*

Available NOW at participating online bookstores!

A Christmas of Mercy

(An Amish Girls Holiday)

As Christmas draws near, Katrina Thompson looks forward to the birth of her first grandchild. But when the blessed event digs up the discovery of her buried criminal past, Officer Love feels obligated to report the wrongdoing. The Amish community of Paradise has long since forgiven Katrina for her past mistakes, but will she receive mercy at the hands of the law?

Available Fall 2014

CPSIA information can be obtained
at www.ICGtesting.com
Printed in the USA
LVOW11s0318140817
544909LV00004B/359/P